DEATH OF KINGS

Books by Bernard Cornwell

THE FORT
AGINCOURT

The Saxon Tales

THE LAST KINGDOM
THE PALE HORSEMAN
THE LORDS OF THE NORTH
SWORD SONG
THE BURNING LAND
DEATH OF KINGS

The Sharpe Novels (in chronological order)

SHARPE'S TIGER
Richard Sharpe and the Siege of Seringapatam, 1799

SHARPE'S TRIUMPH
Richard Sharpe and the Battle of Assaye, September 1803

SHARPE'S FORTRESS
Richard Sharpe and the Siege of Gawilghur, December 1803

SHARPE'S TRAFALGAR
Richard Sharpe and the Battle of Trafalgar, 21 October 1805

SHARPE'S PREY
Richard Sharpe and the Expedition to Copenhagen, 1807

SHARPE'S RIFLES
Richard Sharpe and the French Invasion of Galicia, January 1809

SHARPE'S HAVOC
Richard Sharpe and the Campaign in Northern Portugal, Spring 1809

SHARPE'S EAGLE
Richard Sharpe and Talavera Campaign, July 1809

SHARPE'S GOLD
Richard Sharpe and the Destruction of Almeida, August 1810

SHARPE'S ESCAPE
Richard Sharpe and the Bussaco Campaign, 1810

SHARPE'S FURY
Richard Sharpe and the Battle of Barrosa, March 1811

SHARPE'S BATTLE
Richard Sharpe and the Battle of Fuentes de Onoro, May 1811

SHARPE'S COMPANY
Richard Sharpe and the Siege of Badajoz, January to April 1812

SHARPE'S SWORD
Richard Sharpe and the Salamanca Campaign, June and July 1812

SHARPE'S ENEMY
Richard Sharpe and the Defense of Portugal, Christmas 1812

SHARPE'S HONOR
Richard Sharpe and the Vitoria Campaign, February to June 1813

SHARPE'S REGIMENT
Richard Sharpe and the Invasion of France, June to November 1813

SHARPE'S SIEGE
Richard Sharpe and the Winter Campaign, 1814

SHARPE'S REVENGE
Richard Sharpe and the Peace of 1814

SHARPE'S WATERLOO
Richard Sharpe and the Waterloo Campaign, 15 June to 18 June 1815

SHARPE'S DEVIL
Richard Sharpe and the Emperor, 1820–21

The Grail Quest Series

THE ARCHER'S TALE
VAGABOND
HERETIC

The Nathaniel Starbuck Chronicles

REBEL
COPPERHEAD
BATTLE FLAG
THE BLOODY GROUND

The Warlord Chronicles

THE WINTER KING
THE ENEMY OF GOD
EXCALIBUR

The Sailing Thrillers

STORMCHILD
SCOUNDREL
WILDTRACK
CRACKDOWN

Other Novels

STONEHENGE
GALLOWS THIEF
A CROWNING MERCY
THE FALLEN ANGELS
REDCOAT

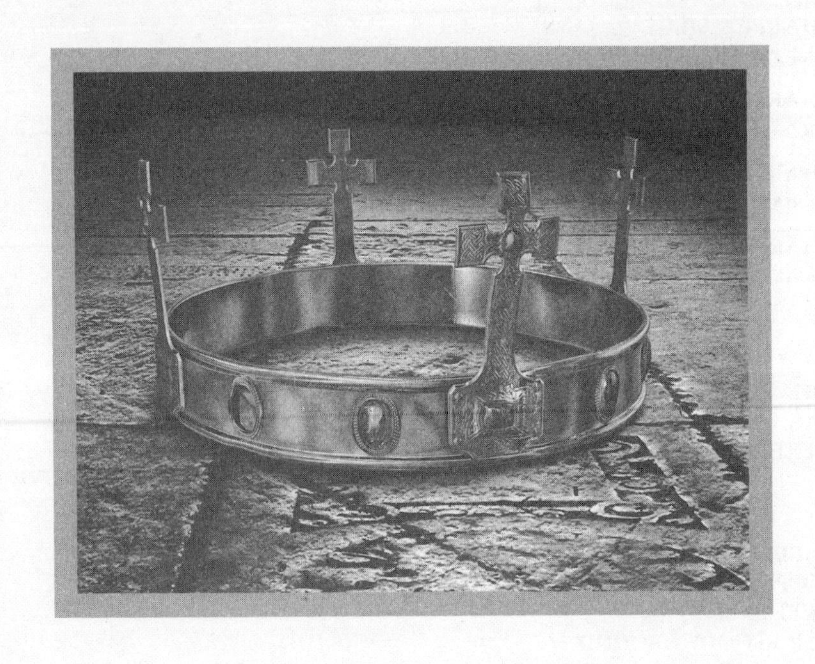

DEATH OF KINGS

A NOVEL

BERNARD CORNWELL

HARPER

An Imprint of HarperCollins*Publishers*

www.harpercollins.com

HarperCollins books may be purchased for educational, business, or sales promotional use. For information, please write: Special Markets Department, HarperCollins Publishers, 10 East 53rd Street, New York, NY 10022.

Published in Great Britain in 2011 by HarperCollins Publishers.

FIRST U.S. EDITION

Designed by William Ruoto

Library of Congress Cataloging-in-Publication Data has been applied for.

ISBN: 978-0-06-196965-2

11 12 13 14 15 ID/RRD 10 9 8 7 6 5 4 3 2 1

Death of Kings is for
Anne LeClaire,
novelist and friend,
who supplied the first line.

Contents

N
Bebbanburg
North Sea
Eoferwic
Irish Sea
Ceaster
Buchestanes
Dee
Snotengaham
Scrobbesburh
MERCIA
EAST ANGLIA
Eleg
Use
Huntandon
Eanulfsbirig
Grantaceaster
Sæfern
Buccingahamm
Bedanford
Natangrafum
Gleawecestre
Fagranforda
Cirrenceastre
Cracgelad
Temes
Beamfleot
Lundene
WESSEX
KENT
Wintanceaster
Wimburnan
0
20
40
60
80 miles

Place-Names

The spelling of place names in Anglo-Saxon England was an uncertain business, with no consistency and no agreement even about the name itself. Thus London was variously rendered as Lundonia, Lundenberg, Lundenne, Lundene, Lundenwic, Lundenceaster, and Lundres. Doubtless some readers will prefer other versions of the names listed below, but I have usually employed whichever spelling is cited in either the *Oxford* or the *Cambridge Dictionary of English Place-Names* for the years nearest to AD 900, but even that solution is not foolproof. Hayling Island, in 956, was written as both Heilincigae and Hæglingaiggæ. Nor have I been consistent myself; I should spell England as Englaland, and have preferred the modern form Northumbria to Norðhymbralond to avoid the suggestion that the boundaries of the ancient kingdom coincide with those of the modern county. So this list, like the spellings themselves, is capricious.

Baddan Byrig	Badbury Rings, Dorset
Beamfleot	Benfleet, Essex
Bebbanburg	Bamburgh, Northumberland
Bedanford	Bedford, Bedfordshire
Blaneford	Blandford Forum, Dorset
Buccingahamm	Buckingham, Bucks
Buchestanes	Buxton, Derbyshire
Ceaster	Chester, Cheshire
Cent	County of Kent
Cippanhamm	Chippenham, Wiltshire
Cirrenceastre	Cirencester, Gloucestershire
Contwaraburg	Canterbury, Kent
Cracgelad	Cricklade, Wiltshire
Cumbraland	Cumberland
Cyninges Tun	Kingston upon Thames, Greater London
Cytringan	Kettering, Northants
Dumnoc	Dunwich, Suffolk
Dunholm	Durham, County Durham

Eanulfsbirig	St. Neot, Cambridgeshire
Eleg	Ely, Cambridgeshire
Eoferwic	York, Yorkshire (called Jorvik by the Danes)
Exanceaster	Exeter, Devon
Fagranforda	Fairford, Gloucestershire
Fearnhamme	Farnham, Surrey
Fifhidan	Fyfield, Wiltshire
Fughelness	Foulness Island, Essex
Gegnesburh	Gainsborough, Lincolnshire
Gleawecestre	Gloucester, Gloucestershire
Grantaceaster	Cambridge, Cambridgeshire
Hothlege, River	Hadleigh Ray, Essex
Hrofeceastre	Rochester, Kent
Humbre, River	River Humber
Huntandon	Huntingdon, Cambridgeshire
Liccelfeld	Lichfield, Staffordshire
Lindisfarena	Lindisfarne (Holy Island), Northumberland
Lundene	London
Medwæg, River	River Medway, Kent
Natangrafum	Notgrove, Gloucestershire
Oxnaforda	Oxford, Oxfordshire
Ratumacos	Rouen, Normandy, France
Rochecestre	Wroxeter, Shropshire
Sæfern	River Severn
Sarisberie	Salisbury, Wiltshire
Sceaftesburi	Shaftesbury, Dorset
Sceobyrig	Shoebury, Essex
Scrobbesburh	Shrewsbury, Shropshire
Snotengaham	Nottingham, Nottinghamshire
Sumorsæte	Somerset
Temes, River	River Thames
Thornsæta	Dorset
Tofeceaster	Towcester, Northamptonshire
Trente, River	River Trent
Turcandene	Turkdean, Gloucestershire
Tweoxnam	Christchurch, Dorset
Westune	Whitchurch, Shropshire
Wiltunscir	Wiltshire
Wimburnan	Wimborne, Dorset
Wintanceaster	Winchester, Hampshire
Wygraceaster	Worcester, Worcestershire

The Royal Family of Wessex

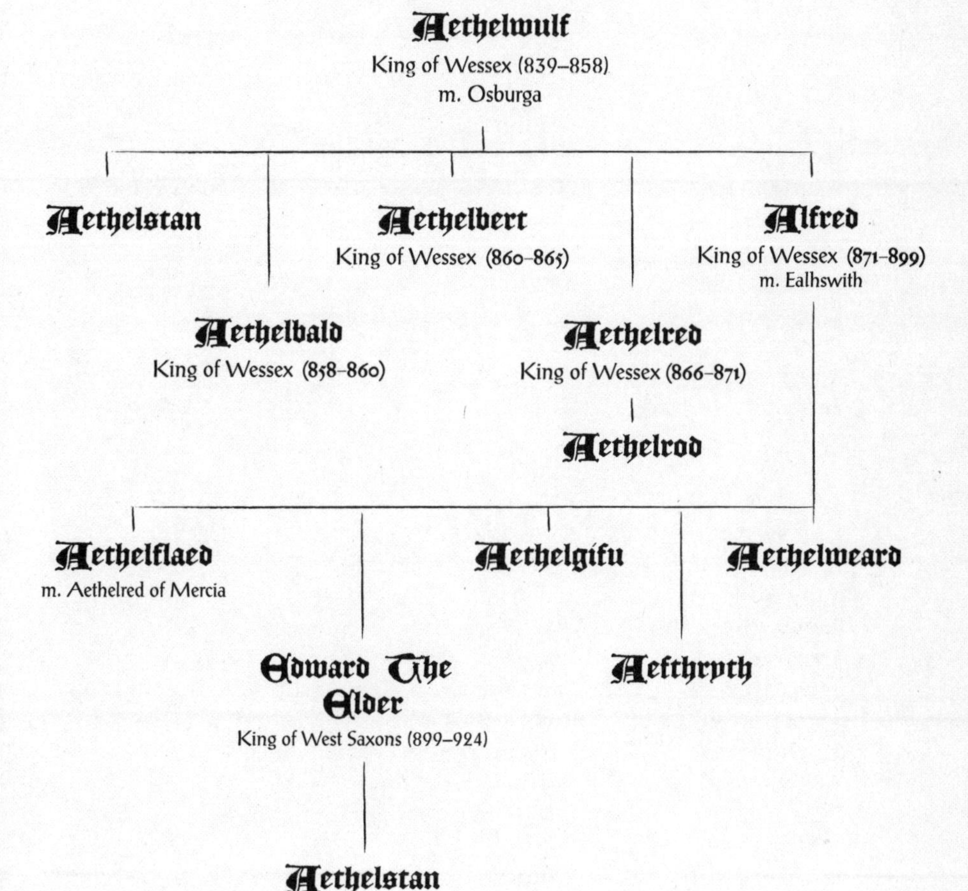

PART ONE

THE SORCERESS

One

"Every day is ordinary," Father Willibald said, "until it isn't." He smiled happily, as though he had just said something he thought I would find significant, then looked disappointed when I said nothing. "Every day," he started again.

"I heard your driveling," I snarled.

"Until it isn't," he finished weakly. I liked Willibald, even if he was a priest. He had been one of my childhood tutors and now I counted him as a friend. He was gentle, earnest, and if the meek ever do inherit the earth then Willibald will be rich beyond measure.

And every day is ordinary until something changes, and that cold Sunday morning had seemed as ordinary as any until the fools tried to kill me. It was so cold. There had been rain during the week, but on that morning the puddles froze and a hard frost whitened the grass. Father Willibald had arrived soon after sunrise and discovered me in the meadow. "We couldn't find your estate last night," he explained his early appearance, shivering, "so we stayed at Saint Rumwold's monastery." He gestured vaguely southward. "It was cold there," he added.

"They're mean bastards, those monks," I said. I was supposed to deliver a weekly cartload of firewood to Saint Rumwold's, but that was a duty I ignored. The monks could cut their own timber. "Who was Rumwold?" I asked Willibald. I knew the answer, but wanted to drag Willibald through the thorns.

"He was a very pious child, lord," he said.

"A child?"

"A baby," he said, sighing as he saw where the conversation was leading, "a mere three days old when he died."

"A three-day-old baby is a saint?"

Willibald flapped his hands. "Miracles happen, lord," he said, "they really do. They say little Rumwold sang God's praises whenever he suckled."

"I feel much the same when I get hold of a tit," I said, "so does that make me a saint?"

Willibald shuddered, then sensibly changed the subject. "I've brought you a message from the ætheling," he said, meaning King Alfred's eldest son, Edward.

"So tell me."

"He's the King of Cent now," Willibald said happily.

"He sent you all this way to tell me that?"

"No, no. I thought perhaps you hadn't heard."

"Of course I heard," I said. Alfred, King of Wessex, had made his eldest son King of Cent, which meant Edward could practice being a king without doing too much damage because Cent, after all, was a part of Wessex. "Has he ruined Cent yet?"

"Of course not," Willibald said, "though . . ." he stopped abruptly.

"Though what?"

"Oh, it's nothing," he said airily and pretended to take an interest in the sheep. "How many black sheep do you have?" he asked.

"I could hold you by the ankles and shake you till the news drops out," I suggested.

"It's just that Edward, well," he hesitated, then decided he had better tell me in case I did shake him by the ankles, "it's just that he wanted to marry a girl in Cent and his father wouldn't agree. But really that isn't important!"

I laughed. So young Edward was not quite the perfect heir after all. "Edward's on the rampage, is he?"

"No, no! Merely a youthful fancy and it's all history now. His father's forgiven him."

I asked nothing more, though I should have paid much more attention to that sliver of gossip. "So what is young Edward's message?" I asked. We were standing in the lower meadow of my estate in Buccingahamm, which lay in eastern Mercia. It was really Æthelflaed's land, but she had granted me the food-rents, and the estate was large enough to support thirty household warriors, most of whom were in church that morning. "And why aren't you at church?" I asked Willibald before he could answer my first question. "It's a feast day, isn't it?"

"Saint Alnoth's Day," he said as though that was a special treat, "but I wanted to find you!" He sounded excited. "I have King Edward's news for you. Every day is ordinary . . ."

"Until it isn't," I said brusquely.

"Yes, lord," he said lamely, then frowned in puzzlement, "but what are you doing?"

"I'm looking at sheep," I said, and that was true. I was looking at two hundred or more sheep that looked back at me and bleated pathetically.

Willibald turned to stare at the flock again. "Fine animals," he said as if he knew what he was talking about.

"Just mutton and wool," I said, "and I'm choosing which ones live and which ones die." It was the killing time of the year, the gray days when our animals are slaughtered. We keep a few alive to breed in the spring, but most have to die because there is not enough fodder to keep whole flocks and herds alive through the winter. "Watch their backs," I told Willibald, "because the frost melts fastest off the fleece of the healthiest beasts. So those are the ones you keep alive." I lifted his woolen hat and ruffled his hair, which was going gray. "No frost on you," I said cheerfully, "otherwise I'd have to slit your throat." I pointed to a ewe with a broken horn. "Keep that one!"

"Got her, lord," the shepherd answered. He was a gnarled little man with a beard that hid half his face. He growled at his two hounds to stay where they were, then plowed into the flock and used his crook to haul out the ewe, then dragged her to the edge of the field and drove her to join the smaller flock at the meadow's farther end. One of his hounds, a ragged and pelt-scarred beast, snapped at the ewe's heels until the shepherd called the dog off. The shepherd did not need my help in selecting which animals should live and which must die. He had culled his flocks since he was a child, but a lord who orders his animals slaughtered owes them the small respect of taking some time with them.

"The day of judgment," Willibald said, pulling his hat over his ears.

"How many's that?" I asked the shepherd.

"Jiggit and mumph, lord," he said.

"Is that enough?"

"It's enough, lord."

"Kill the rest then," I said.

"Jiggit and mumph?" Willibald asked, still shivering.

"Twenty and five," I said. "Yain, tain, tether, mether, mumph. It's how shepherds count. I don't know why. The world is full of mystery. I'm told some folk even believe that a three-day-old baby is a saint."

"God is not mocked, lord," Father Willibald said, attempting to be stern.

"He is by me," I said. "So what does young Edward want?"

"Oh, it's most exciting," Willibald began enthusiastically, then checked because I had raised a hand.

The shepherd's two dogs were growling. Both had flattened themselves and were facing south toward a wood. Sleet had begun to fall. I stared at the trees, but could see nothing threatening among the black winter branches or among the holly bushes. "Wolves?" I asked the shepherd.

"Haven't seen a wolf since the year the old bridge fell, lord," he said.

The hair on the dogs' necks bristled. The shepherd quietened them by clicking his tongue, then gave a short sharp whistle and one of the dogs raced away toward the wood. The other whined, wanting to be let loose, but the shepherd made a low noise and the dog went quiet again.

The running dog curved toward the trees. She was a bitch and knew her business. She leaped an ice-skimmed ditch and vanished among the holly, barked suddenly, then reappeared to jump the ditch again. For a moment she stopped, facing the trees, then began running again just as an arrow flitted from the wood's shadows. The shepherd gave a shrill whistle and the bitch raced back toward us, the arrow falling harmlessly behind her.

"Outlaws," I said.

"Or men looking for deer," the shepherd said.

"My deer," I said. I still gazed at the trees. Why would poachers shoot an arrow at a shepherd's dog? They would have done better to run away. So maybe they were really stupid poachers?

The sleet was coming harder now, blown by a cold east wind. I wore a thick fur cloak, high boots and a fox-fur hat, so did not notice the cold, but Willibald, in priestly black, was shivering despite his woolen cape and hat. "I must get you back to the hall," I said. "At your age you shouldn't be outdoors in winter."

"I wasn't expecting rain," Willibald said. He sounded miserable.

"It'll be snow by midday," the shepherd said.

"You have a hut near here?" I asked him.

He pointed north. "Just beyond the copse," he said. He was pointing at a thick stand of trees through which a path led.

"Does it have a fire?"

"Yes, lord."

"Take us there," I said. I would leave Willibald beside the fire and fetch him a proper cloak and a docile horse to get him back to the hall.

We walked north and the dogs growled again. I turned to look south and suddenly there were men at the wood's edge. A ragged line of men who were staring at us. "You know them?" I asked the shepherd.

"They're not from around here, lord, and eddera-a-dix," he said, meaning there were thirteen of them. "That's unlucky, lord." He made the sign of the cross.

"What . . ." Father Willibald began.

"Quiet," I said. The shepherd's two dogs were snarling now. "Outlaws," I guessed, still looking at the men.

"Saint Alnoth was murdered by outlaws," Willibald said worriedly.

"So not everything outlaws do is bad," I said, "but these ones are idiots."

"Idiots?"

"To attack us," I said. "They'll be hunted down and ripped apart."

"If we are not killed first," Willibald said.

"Just go!" I pushed him toward the northern trees and touched a hand to my sword hilt before following him. I was not wearing Serpent-Breath, my great war sword, but a lesser, lighter blade that I had taken from a Dane I had killed earlier that year in Beamfleot. It was a good sword, but at that moment I wished I had Serpent-Breath strapped around my waist. I glanced back. The thirteen men were crossing the ditch to follow us. Two had bows. The rest seemed to be armed with axes, knives, or spears. Willibald was slow, already panting. "What is it?" he gasped.

"Bandits?" I suggested. "Vagrants? I don't know. Run!" I pushed him into the trees, then slid the sword from its scabbard and turned to face my pursuers, one of whom took an arrow from the bag strapped at his waist. That persuaded me to follow Willibald into the copse. The arrow slid past me and ripped through the undergrowth. I wore no mail, only the thick fur cloak that offered no protection from a hunter's arrow. "Keep going," I shouted at Willibald, then limped up the path. I had been wounded in the right thigh at the battle of Ethandun and though I could walk and could even run slowly, I knew I would not be able to outpace the men who were now within easy bowshot behind me. I hurried up the path as a second arrow was deflected by a branch and tumbled noisily through the trees. Every day is ordinary, I thought, until it gets interesting. My pursuers could not see me among the dark trunks and thick holly bushes, but they assumed I had followed Willibald and so kept to the path while I crouched in the thick undergrowth, concealed by the glossy leaves of a holly bush and by my cloak that I had pulled over my fair hair and face. The pursuers went past my hiding place without a glance. The two archers were in front.

I let them get well ahead, then followed. I had heard them speak as they passed and knew they were Saxons and, by their accents, probably from Mercia. Robbers, I assumed. A Roman road passed through deep woods nearby and masterless men haunted the woods to ambush travelers who, to protect themselves, went in large groups. I had twice led my warriors on hunts for such bandits and thought I had persuaded them to make their living far from my estate, but I could not think who else these men could be. Yet it was not like such vagrants to invade an estate. The hair at the back of my neck still prickled.

I moved cautiously as I approached the edge of the trees, then saw the men beside the shepherd's hut that resembled a heap of grass. He had made the hovel with branches covered by turf, leaving a hole in the center for the smoke of his fire to escape. There was no sign of the shepherd himself, but Willibald had been captured, though so far he was unhurt, protected, perhaps, by his status as a priest. One man held him. The others must have realized I was still in the trees, because they were staring toward the copse that hid me.

Then, suddenly, the shepherd's two dogs appeared from my left and ran howling toward the thirteen men. The dogs ran fast and lithe, circling the group and sometimes leaping toward them and snapping their teeth before sheering away. Only one man had a sword, but he was clumsy with the blade, swinging it at the bitch as she came close and missing her by an arm's length. One of the two bowmen put a string on his cord. He hauled the arrow back, then suddenly fell backward as if struck by an invisible hammer. He sprawled on the turf as his arrow flitted into the sky and fell harmlessly into the trees behind me. The dogs, down on their front paws now, bared their teeth and growled. The fallen archer stirred, but evidently could not stand. The other men looked scared.

The second archer raised his stave, then recoiled, dropping the bow to clap his hands to his face and I saw a spark of blood there, blood bright as the holly berries. The splash of color showed in the winter morning, then it was gone and the man was clutching his face and bending over in pain. The hounds barked, then loped back into the trees. The sleet was falling harder, loud as it struck the bare branches. Two of the men moved toward the shepherd's cottage, but were called back by their leader. He was younger than the others and looked more prosperous, or at least less poor. He had a thin face, darting eyes, and a short fair beard. He wore a scarred leather jerkin, but beneath it I could see a mail coat. So he had either been a warrior or else had stolen the mail. "Lord Uhtred!" he called.

I did not answer. I was hidden well enough, at least for the moment, but knew I would have to move if they searched the copse, but whatever had drawn blood was making them nervous. What was it? It had to be the gods, I thought, or perhaps the Christian saint. Alnoth must hate outlaws if he had been murdered by them, and I did not doubt that these men were outlaws who had been sent to kill me. That was not surprising because in those days I had plenty of enemies. I still have enemies, though now I live behind the strongest palisade in northern England, but in that far-off time, in the winter of 898, there was no England. There was Northumbria and East Anglia, Mercia and Wessex, and the first two were ruled by the Danes, Wessex was Saxon while Mercia was a mess, part Danish and part Saxon. And I was like Mercia because I had been born a Saxon, but raised as a Dane. I still worshipped the Danish gods, but fate had doomed me to be a shield of the Christian Saxons against the ever-present threat of the pagan Danes. So any number of Danes might want me dead, but I could not imagine any Danish enemy hiring Mercian outlaws to ambush me. There were also Saxons who would love to see my corpse put in its long home. My cousin Æthelred, Lord of Mercia, would have paid well to watch my grave filled, but surely he would have sent warriors, not bandits? Yet he seemed the likeliest man. He was married to Æthelflaed, Alfred of Wessex's daughter, but I had planted the cuckold's horns on Æthelred's head and I reckoned he had returned the favor by sending thirteen outlaws.

"Lord Uhtred!" the young man called again, but the only answer was a sudden panicked bleating.

The sheep were streaming down the path through the copse, harried by the two dogs that snapped at their ankles to drive them fast toward the thirteen men and, once the sheep had reached the men, the dogs raced around, still snapping, herding the animals into a tight circle that enclosed the outlaws. I was laughing. I was Uhtred of Bebbanburg, the man who had killed Ubba beside the sea and who had destroyed Haesten's army at Beamfleot, but on this cold Sunday morning it was the shepherd who was proving to be the better warlord. His panicked flock were tightly packed around the outlaws, who could hardly move.

The dogs were howling, the sheep bleating, and the thirteen men despairing.

I stepped out of the wood. "You wanted me?" I called.

The young man's response was to push toward me, but the tightly packed sheep obstructed him. He kicked at them, then hacked down with his sword, but the more he struggled the more scared the sheep became, and all the while the dogs herded them inward. The young man cursed, then snatched at Willibald. "Let us go or we kill him," he said.

"He's a Christian," I said, showing him Thor's hammer that hung about my neck, "so why should I care if you kill him?"

Willibald stared at me aghast, and then turned as one of the men shouted in pain. There had again been a sudden flash of holly-red blood in the sleet, and this time I saw what had caused it. It was neither the gods nor the murdered saint, but the shepherd who had come from the trees and was holding a sling. He took a stone from a pouch, placed it in the leather cup, and whirled the sling again. It made a whirring noise, he let go one cord, and another stone hurtled in to strike a man.

They turned away in pure panic and I gestured at the shepherd to let them go. He whistled to call the dogs off and both men and sheep scattered. The men were running, all but the first archer who was still on the ground, stunned by the stone that had struck his head. The young man, braver than the others, came toward me, perhaps thinking his companions would help him, then realized he was alone. A look of pure fright crossed his face, he turned, and just then the bitch leaped at him, sinking her teeth in his sword arm. He shouted, then tried to shake her off as the dog hurtled in to join his mate. He was still shouting when I hit him across the back of the skull with the flat of my sword-blade. "You can call the dogs off now," I told the shepherd.

The first archer was still alive, but there was a patch of blood-matted hair above his right ear. I kicked him hard in the ribs and he groaned, but he was insensible. I gave his bow and arrow-bag to the shepherd. "What's your name?"

"Egbert, lord."

"You're a rich man now, Egbert," I told him. I wished that were true. I would reward Egbert well for this morning's work, but I was no longer rich. I had spent my money on the men, mail, and weapons that had been needed to defeat Haesten and I was desperately poor that winter.

The other outlaws had vanished, gone back northward. Willibald was shaking. "They were searching for you, lord," he said through chattering teeth. "They've been paid to kill you."

I stooped by the archer. The shepherd's stone had shattered his skull and I could see a ragged, splintered piece of bone among the blood-matted hair. One of the shepherd's dogs came to sniff the wounded man and I patted its thick wiry pelt. "They're good dogs," I told Egbert.

"Wolf-killers, lord," he said, then hefted the sling, "though this is better."

"You're good with it," I said. That was mild, the man was lethal.

"Been practicing these twenty-five years, lord. Nothing like a stone to drive a wolf away."

"They'd been paid to kill me?" I asked Willibald.

"That's what they said. They were paid to kill you."

"Go into the hut," I said, "get warm." I turned on the younger man who was being guarded by the larger dog. "What's your name?"

He hesitated, then spoke grudgingly, "Wærfurth, lord."

"And who paid you to kill me?"

"I don't know, lord."

Nor did he, it seemed. Wærfurth and his men came from near Tofeceaster, a settlement not far to the north, and Wærfurth told me how a man had promised to pay my weight in silver in return for my death. The man had suggested a Sunday morning, knowing that much of my household would be in church, and Wærfurth had recruited a dozen vagrants to do the job. He must have known it was a huge gamble, for I was not without reputation, but the reward was immense. "Was the man a Dane or a Saxon?" I asked.

"A Saxon, lord."

"And you don't know him?"

"No, lord."

I questioned him more, but all he could tell me was that the man was thin and bald, and had lost an eye. The description meant little to me. A one-eyed, bald man? Could be almost anyone. I asked questions till I had wrung Wærfurth dry of unhelpful answers, then hanged both him and the archer.

And Willibald showed me the magic fish.

A delegation waited at my hall. Sixteen men had come from Alfred's capital at Wintanceaster and among them were no less than five priests. Two, like Willibald, came from Wessex, and the other pair were Mercians who had apparently settled in East Anglia. I knew them both, though I had not recognized them at first. They were twins, Ceolnoth and Ceolberht who, some thirty years before, had been hostages with me in Mercia. We had been children captured by the Danes, a fate I had welcomed and the twins had hated. They were close to forty years old now, two identical priests with stocky builds, round faces, and graying beards. "We have watched your progress," one of them said.

"With admiration," the other finished. I had not been able to tell them apart when they were children, and still could not. They finished each other's sentences.

"Reluctant," one said.

"Admiration," his twin said.

"Reluctant?" I asked in an unfriendly tone.

"It is known that Alfred is disappointed,"

"That you eschew the true faith, but . . ."

"We pray for you daily!"

The remaining pair of priests, both West Saxons, were Alfred's men. They had helped compile his code of laws and it appeared they had come to advise me. The remaining eleven men were warriors, five from East Anglia and six from Wessex, who had guarded the priests on their travels.

And they had brought the magic fish.

"King Eohric," Ceolnoth or Ceolberht said.

"Wishes an alliance with Wessex," the other twin finished.

"And with Mercia!"

"The Christian kingdoms, you understand."

"And King Alfred and King Edward," Willibald took up the tale, "have sent a gift for King Eohric."

"Alfred still lives?" I asked.

"Pray God, yes," Willibald said, "though he's sick."

"Very close to death," one of the West Saxon priests intervened.

"He was born close to death," I said, "and ever since I've known him he's been dying. He'll live ten years yet."

"Pray God he does," Willibald said and made the sign of the cross. "But he's fifty years old, and he's failing. He's truly dying."

"Which is why he seeks this alliance," the West Saxon priest went on, "and why the Lord Edward makes this request of you."

"King Edward," Willibald corrected his fellow priest.

"So who's requesting me?" I asked, "Alfred of Wessex or Edward of Cent?"

"Edward," Willibald said.

"Eohric," Ceolnoth and Ceolberht said together.

"Alfred," the West Saxon priest said.

"All of them," Willibald added. "It's important to all of them, lord!"

Edward or Alfred or both wanted me to go to King Eohric of East Anglia. Eohric was a Dane, but he had converted to Christianity, and he had sent the twins to Alfred and proposed that a great alliance should be made between the Christian parts of Britain. "King Eohric suggested that you should negotiate the treaty," Ceolnoth or Ceolberht said.

"With our advice," one of the West Saxon priests put in hastily.

"Why me?" I asked the twins.

Willibald answered for them. "Who knows Mercia and Wessex as well as you?"

"Many men," I answered.

"And where you lead," Willibald said, "those other men will follow."

We were at a table on which were ale, bread, cheese, pottage, and apples. The central hearth was ablaze with a great fire that flickered its light on the smoke-blackened beams. The shepherd had been right and the sleet had turned to snow and some flakes sifted through the smoke-hole in the roof. Outside, beyond the palisade, Wærfurth and the archer were hanging from the bare branch of an elm, their bodies food for the hungry birds. Most of my men were in the hall, listening to our conversation. "It's a strange time of year to be making treaties," I said.

"Alfred has little time left," Willibald said, "and he wishes this alliance, lord. If all the Christians of Britain are united, lord, then young Edward's throne will be protected when he inherits the crown."

That made sense, but why would Eohric want the alliance? Eohric of East Anglia had been perched on the fence between Christians and pagans, Danes and Saxons, for as long as I could remember, yet now he wanted to proclaim his allegiance to the Christian Saxons?

"Because of Cnut Ranulfson," one of the twins explained when I asked the question.

"He's brought men south," the other twin said.

"To Sigurd Thorrson's lands," I said. "I know, I sent that news to Alfred. And Eohric fears Cnut and Sigurd?"

"He does," Ceolnoth or Ceolberht said.

"Cnut and Sigurd won't attack now," I said, "but in the spring, maybe." Cnut and Sigurd were Danes from Northumbria and, like all the Danes, their abiding dream was to capture all the lands where English was spoken. The invaders had tried again and again, and again and again they had failed, yet another attempt was inevitable because the heart of Wessex, which was the great bastion of Saxon Christendom, was failing. Alfred was dying, and his death would surely bring pagan swords and heathen fire to Mercia and to Wessex. "But why would Cnut or Sigurd attack Eohric?" I asked. "They don't want East Anglia, they want Mercia and Wessex."

"They want everything," Ceolnoth or Ceolberht answered.

"And the true faith will be scourged from Britain unless we defend it," the older of the two West Saxon priests said.

"Which is why we beg you to forge the alliance," Willibald said.

"At the Christmas feast," one of the twins added.

"And Alfred sent a gift for Eohric," Willibald went on enthusiastically. "Alfred and Edward! They have been most generous, lord!"

The gift was encased in a box of silver studded with precious stones. The lid of the box showed a figure of Christ with uplifted arms, around which was written "Edward *mec heht Gewyrcan,"* meaning that Edward had ordered the reliquary made, or more likely his father had ordered the gift and then ascribed the generosity to his son. Willibald lifted the lid reverently, revealing an interior lined with red-dyed cloth. A small cushion, the width and breadth of a man's hand, fitted snugly inside, and on the cushion was a fish skeleton. It was the whole fish skeleton, except for the head, just a long white spine with a comb of ribs on either side. "There," Willibald said, breathing the word as if speaking too loud might disturb the bones.

"A dead herring?" I asked incredulously. "That's Alfred's gift?"

The priests all crossed themselves.

"How many more fish bones do you want?" I asked. I looked at Finan, my closest friend and the commander of my household warriors. "We can provide dead fish, can't we?"

"By the barrelful, lord," he said.

"Lord Uhtred!" Willibald, as ever, rose to my taunting. "That fish," he pointed a quivering finger at the bones, "was one of the two fishes our Lord used to feed the five thousand!"

"The other one must have been a damned big fish," I said. "What was it? A whale?"

The older West Saxon priest scowled at me. "I advised King Edward against employing you for this duty," he said. "I told him to send a Christian."

"So use someone else," I retorted. "I'd rather spend Yule in my own hall."

"He wishes you to go," the priest said sharply.

"Alfred also wishes it," Willibald put in, then smiled. "He thinks you'll frighten Eohric."

"Why does he want Eohric frightened?" I asked. "I thought this was an alliance?"

"King Eohric allows his ships to prey on our trade," the priest said, "and must pay reparations before we promise him protection. The king believes you will be persuasive."

"We don't need to leave for at least ten days," I said, looking gloomily at the priests. "Am I supposed to feed you all till then?"

"Yes, lord," Willibald said happily.

Fate is strange. I had rejected Christianity, preferring the gods of the Danes, but I loved Æthelflaed, Alfred's daughter, and she was a Christian and that meant I carried my sword on the side of the cross.

And because of that it seemed I would spend Yule in East Anglia.

Osferth came to Buccingahamm, bringing another twenty of my household warriors. I had summoned them, wanting a large band to accompany me to East Anglia. King Eohric might have suggested the treaty, and he might be amenable to whatever demands Alfred made, but treaties are best negotiated from a position of strength and I was determined to arrive in East Anglia with an impressive escort. Osferth and his men had been watching Ceaster, a Roman camp on Mercia's far northwestern frontier where Haesten had taken refuge after his forces had been destroyed at Beamfleot. Osferth greeted me solemnly, as was his manner. He rarely smiled, and his customary expression suggested disapproval of whatever he saw, but I think he was glad to be reunited with the rest of us. He was Alfred's son, born to a servant girl before Alfred discovered the dubious joys of Christian obedience. Alfred had wanted his bastard son trained as a priest, but Osferth had preferred the way of the warrior. It had been a strange choice, for he did not take great joy from a fight or yearn for the savage moments when anger and a blade make the rest of the world seem dull, yet Osferth brought his father's qualities to a fight. He was serious, thoughtful, and methodical. Where Finan and I could be rashly headstrong, Osferth used cleverness, and that was no bad thing in a warrior.

"Haesten is still licking his wounds," he told me.

"We should have killed him," I grumbled. Haesten had retreated to Ceaster after I had destroyed his fleet and army at Beamfleot.

My instinct had been to follow him there and finish his nonsense once and for all, but Alfred had wanted his household troops back in Wessex and I did not have enough men to besiege the walls of the Roman fort at Ceaster, and so Haesten still lived. We watched him, looking for evidence that he was recruiting more men, but Osferth reckoned Haesten was getting weaker rather than stronger.

"He'll be forced to swallow his pride and swear loyalty to someone else," he suggested.

"To Sigurd or Cnut," I said. Sigurd and Cnut were now the most powerful Danes in Britain, though neither was a king. They had land, wealth, flocks, herds, silver, ships, men, and ambition. "Why would they want East Anglia?" I wondered aloud.

"Why not?" Finan asked. He was my closest companion, the man I trusted most in a fight.

"Because they want Wessex," I said.

"They want all of Britain," Finan said.

"They're waiting," Osferth said.

"For what?"

"Alfred's death," he said. He hardly ever called Alfred "my father," as though he, like the king, was ashamed of his birth.

"Oh there'll be chaos when that happens," Finan said with relish.

"Edward will make a good king," Osferth said reprovingly.

"He'll have to fight for it," I said. "The Danes will test him."

"And will you fight for him?" Osferth asked.

"I like Edward," I said noncommittally. I did like him. I had pitied him as a child because his father placed him under the control of fierce priests whose duty was to make Edward the perfect heir for Alfred's Christian kingdom. When I met him again, just before the fight at Beamfleot, he had struck me as a pompous and intolerant young man, but he had enjoyed the company of warriors and the pomposity vanished. He had fought well at Beamfleot and now, if Willibald's gossip was to be believed, he had learned a little about sin as well.

"His sister would want you to support him," Osferth said pointedly, making Finan laugh. Everyone knew Æthelflaed was my lover, as they knew Æthelflaed's father was also Osferth's father, but most people politely pretended not to know, and Osferth's pointed remark was as close as he dared refer to my relationship with his half-sister. I would much rather have been with Æthelflaed for the Christmas feast, but Osferth told me she had been summoned to Wintanceaster and I knew I was not welcome at Alfred's table. Besides, I now had the duty of delivering the magic fish to Eohric and I was worried that Sigurd and Cnut would raid my lands while I was in East Anglia.

Sigurd and Cnut had sailed south the previous summer, taking their ships to Wessex's southern coast while Haesten's army ravaged Mercia. The two Northumbrian Danes had thought to distract Alfred's army while Haesten ran wild on Wessex's northern border, but Alfred had sent me his troops anyway, Haesten had been stripped of his power, and Sigurd and Cnut had discovered they were powerless to capture any of Alfred's burhs, the fortified towns that were scattered all across the Saxon lands, and so had returned to their ships. I knew they would not rest. They were Danes, which meant they were planning mischief.

So next day, in the melting snow, I took Finan, Osferth, and thirty men north to Ealdorman Beornnoth's land. I liked Beornnoth. He was old, grizzled, lame, and fiery. His lands were at the very edge of Saxon Mercia and everything to the north of him belonged to the Danes, which meant that in the last few years he had been forced to defend his fields and villages against the attacks of Sigurd Thorrson's men. "God Almighty," he greeted me, "don't say you're hoping for the Christmas feast in my hall?"

"I prefer good food," I said.

"And I prefer good-looking guests," he retorted, then shouted for his servants to take our horses. He lived a little north and east of Tofeceaster in a great hall surrounded by barns and stables that were protected by a stout palisade. The space between the hall and his largest barn was now being blood-soaked by the slaughter of cattle. Men were hamstringing the frightened beasts to buckle them to the ground and so keep them still while other men killed them with an ax blow to the forehead. The twitching carcasses were dragged to one side where women and children used long knives to skin and butcher the corpses. Dogs watched or else fought over the scraps of offal thrown their way. The air stank of blood and dung. "It was a good year," Beornnoth told me, "twice as many animals as last year. The Danes left me alone."

"No cattle raids?"

"One or two." He shrugged. Since last I saw him he had lost the use of his legs and needed to be carried everywhere in a chair. "It's old age," he told me. "I'm dying from the ground up. I suppose you want ale?"

We exchanged news in his hall. He bellowed with laughter when I told him of the attempt on my life. "You use sheep to defend yourself these days?" He saw his son enter the hall and shouted at him. "Come and hear how the Lord Uhtred won the battle of the sheep!"

The son was called Beortsig and, like his father, was broad-shouldered and heavy-bearded. He laughed at the tale, but the laughter seemed forced. "You say the rogues came from Tofeceaster?" he asked.

"That's what the bastard said."

"That's our land," Beortsig said.

"Outlaws," Beornnoth said dismissively.

"And fools," Beortsig added.

"A thin, bald, one-eyed man recruited them," I said. "Do you know anyone who looks like that?"

"Sounds like our priest," Beornnoth said, amused. Beortsig said nothing. "So what brings you here?" Beornnoth asked, "other than the need to drain my ale barrels?"

I told him of Alfred's request that I seal a treaty with Eohric, and how Eohric's envoys had explained their king's request because of his fear of Sigurd and Cnut. Beornnoth looked skeptical. "Sigurd and Cnut aren't interested in East Anglia," he said.

"Eohric thinks they are."

"The man's a fool," Beornnoth said, "and always was. Sigurd and Cnut want Mercia and Wessex."

"And once they possess those kingdoms, lord," Osferth spoke softly to our host, "they'll want East Anglia."

"True, I suppose," Beornnoth allowed.

"So why not take East Anglia first?" Osferth suggested, "and add its men to their war-bands?"

"Nothing will happen till Alfred dies," Beornnoth suggested. He made the sign of the cross. "And I pray he still lives."

"Amen," Osferth said.

"So you want to disturb Sigurd's peace?" Beornnoth asked me.

"I want to know what he's doing," I said.

"He's preparing for Yule," Beortsig said dismissively.

"Which means he'll be drunk for the next month," the father added.

"He's left us in peace all year," the son said.

"And I don't want you poking his wasps out of their nest," Beornnoth said. He spoke lightly enough, but his meaning was heavy. If I rode on north then I might provoke Sigurd, then Beornnoth's land would be thudded by Danish hooves and reddened by Danish blades.

"I have to go to East Anglia," I explained, "and Sigurd's not going to like the thought of an alliance between Eohric and Alfred. He might send men south to make his displeasure known."

Beornnoth frowned. "Or he might not."

"Which is what I want to find out," I said.

Beornnoth grunted at that. "You're bored, Lord Uhtred?" he asked. "You want to kill a few Danes?"

"I just want to smell them," I said.

"Smell?"

"Half Britain will already know of this treaty with Eohric," I said, "and who has the most interest in preventing it?"

"Sigurd," Beornnoth admitted after a pause.

I sometimes thought of Britain as a mill. At the base, heavy and dependable was the millstone of Wessex, while at the top, just as heavy, was the grindstone of the Danes, and Mercia was crushed between them. Mercia was where Saxon and Dane fought most often. Alfred had cleverly extended his authority over much of the kingdom's south, but the Danes were lords of its north, and till now the struggle had been fairly evenly divided, which meant both sides sought allies. The Danes had offered enticements to the Welsh kings, but though the Welsh nursed an undying hatred of all Saxons, they feared the wrath of their Christian God more than they feared the Danes, and so most of the Welsh kept an uneasy peace with Wessex. To the east, though, lay the unpredictable kingdom of East

Anglia, which was ruled by Danes, but was ostensibly Christian. East Anglia could tip the scales. If Eohric sent men to fight against Wessex then the Danes would win, but if he allied himself with the Christians then the Danes would face defeat.

Sigurd, I thought, would want to prevent the treaty ever happening, and he had two weeks to do that. Had he sent the thirteen men to kill me? As I sat by Beornnoth's fire, that seemed the best answer. And if he had, then what would he do next?

"You want to smell him, eh?" Beornnoth asked.

"Not provoke him," I promised.

"No deaths? No robbery?"

"I won't start anything," I promised.

"God knows what you'll discover without slaughtering a few of the bastards," Beornnoth said, "but yes. Go and sniff. Beortsig will go with you." He was sending his son and a dozen household warriors to make sure we kept our word. Beornnoth feared we planned to lay waste a few Danish steadings and bring back cattle, silver, and slaves, and his men would be there to prevent that, but in truth I only wanted to smell the land.

I did not trust Sigurd or his ally, Cnut. I liked both of them, but knew they would kill me as casually as we kill our winter cattle. Sigurd was the wealthier of the two men, while Cnut the more dangerous. He was young still, and in his few years he had gained a reputation as a sword-Dane, a man whose blade was to be respected and feared. Such a man attracted others. They came from across the sea, rowing to Britain to follow a leader who promised them wealth. And in the spring, I thought, the Danes would surely come again, or perhaps they would wait till Alfred died, knowing that the death of a king brings uncertainty, and in uncertainty lies opportunity.

Beortsig was thinking the same. "Is Alfred really dying?" he asked me as we rode north.

"So everyone says."

"They've said it before."

"Many times," I agreed.

"You believe it?"

"I haven't seen him for myself," I said, and I knew I would not be welcome in his palace even if I wanted to see him. I had been told Æthelflaed had gone to Wintanceaster for the Christmas feast, but more likely she had been summoned for the death-watch rather than for the dubious delights of her father's table.

"And Edward will inherit?" Beortsig asked.

"That's what Alfred wants."

"And who becomes king in Mercia?" he asked.

"There is no king in Mercia," I said.

"There should be," he said bitterly, "and not a West Saxon either! We're Mercians, not West Saxons." I said nothing in response. There had once been kings in Mercia, but now it was subservient to Wessex. Alfred had managed that. His daughter was married to the most powerful of the Mercian ealdormen, and most Saxons in Mercia seemed content that they were effectively under Alfred's protection, but not all Mercians liked that West Saxon dominance. When Alfred died the powerful Mercians would start eyeing their empty throne, and Beortsig, I supposed, was one such man. "Our forefathers were kings here," he told me.

"My forefathers were kings in Northumbria," I retorted, "but I don't want the throne."

"Mercia should be ruled by a Mercian," he said. He seemed uncomfortable in my company, or perhaps he was uneasy because we rode deep into the lands that Sigurd claimed.

We rode directly north, the low winter sun throwing our shadows far ahead of us. The first steadings we passed were nothing but burned out ruins, then after midday we came to a village. The people had seen us coming, and so I took my horsemen into the nearby woods until we had rousted a couple out of their hiding place. They were Saxons, a slave and his wife, and they said their lord was a Dane. "Is he in his hall?" I asked.

"No, lord." The man was kneeling, shaking, unable to lift his eyes to meet my gaze.

"What's his name?"

"Jarl Jorven, lord."

I looked at Beortsig, who shrugged. "Jorven is one of Sigurd's men," he said, "and not really a jarl. Maybe he leads thirty or forty warriors?"

"Is his wife in the hall?" I asked the kneeling man.

"She's there, lord, and some warriors, but not many. The rest have gone, lord."

"Gone where?"

"I don't know, lord."

I tossed him a silver coin. I could scarcely afford it, but a lord is a lord.

"Yule is coming," Beortsig said dismissively, "and Jorven has probably gone to Cytringan."

"Cytringan?"

"We hear Sigurd and Cnut are celebrating Yule there," he said.

We rode away from the wood, back into a damp pasture. Clouds were hiding the sun now, and I thought it would begin to rain before long. "Tell me about Jorven," I said to Beortsig.

He shrugged. "A Dane, of course. He arrived two summers ago and Sigurd gave him this land."

"Is he kin to Sigurd?"

"I don't know."

"His age?"

Another shrug. "Young."

And why would a man go to a feast without his wife? I almost asked the question aloud, then thought that Beortsig's opinion would be worthless and so I kept silent. Instead I kicked my horse on until I reached a place where I could see Jorven's hall. It was a fine enough building with a steep roof and a bull's skull attached to the high gable. The thatch was new enough to have no moss. A palisade surrounded the hall and I could see two men watching us. "This would be a good time to attack Jorven," I said lightly.

"Thcy'vc lcft us in pcacc," Bcortsig said.

"And you think that will last?"

"I think we should turn back," he said, and then, when I said nothing, he added, "if we want to make home by nightfall."

Instead I headed farther north, ignoring Beortsig's complaints. We left Jorven's hall unmolested and crossed a low ridge to see a wide valley. Small smoke trails showed where villages or steadings stood, and glimmers of dull light betrayed a river. A fine place, I thought, fertile and well watered, exactly the sort of land that the

Danes craved. "You say Jorven has thirty or forty warriors?" I asked Beortsig.

"No more."

"One crew, then," I said. So Jorven and his followers had crossed the sea in a single ship and sworn loyalty to Sigurd, who in return had given him frontier land. If the Saxons attacked, Jorven would likely die, but that was the risk he ran, and the rewards could be much greater if Sigurd decided to attack southward. "When Haesten was here, last summer," I asked Beortsig as I urged my horse forward, "did he give you trouble?"

"He left us alone," he said. "He did his damage farther west."

I nodded. Beortsig's father, I thought, had become tired of fighting the Danes and he was paying tribute to Sigurd. There could be no other reason for the apparent peace that had prevailed on Beornnoth's land, and Haesten, I assumed, had left Beornnoth alone on Sigurd's orders. Haesten would never have dared to offend Sigurd, so doubtless he had avoided the lands of those Saxons who paid for peace. That had left him most of southern Mercia to ravage, and he had burned, raped, and pillaged until I took away most of his strength at Beamfleot. Then, in fear, he had fled to Ceaster.

"Something worries you?" Finan asked me. We were riding down toward the distant river. A thin rain was blowing from our backs. Finan and I had spurred ahead, out of earshot of Beortsig and his men.

"Why would a man go to the Yule feast without his wife?" I asked Finan.

He shrugged. "Maybe she's ugly. Maybe he keeps something younger and prettier for feast days?"

"Maybe," I grunted.

"Or maybe he's been summoned," Finan said.

"And why would Sigurd summon warriors in midwinter?"

"Because he knows about Eohric?"

"That's what's worrying me," I said.

The rain was coming harder, gusting on a sharp wind. The day was closing in, dark and damp and cold. Remnants of snow lay white in frozen ditches. Beortsig tried to insist that we turn back, but I kept riding north, deliberately going close to two large halls.

Whoever guarded those places must have seen us, yet no one rode out to challenge us. Over forty armed men, carrying shields and spears and swords, were riding through their country and they did not bother to discover who we were or what we did? That told me that the halls were lightly guarded. Whoever saw us pass was content to let us go in the hope that we would ignore them.

And then, ahead of us, was the scar on the land. I checked my horse at its edge. The scar ran across our path, gouged into the water meadows on the southern bank of the river, which was being dimpled by raindrops. I turned my horse then, pretending no interest in the trampled ground and deep hoofprints. "We'll go back," I told Beortsig.

The scar had been made by horses. Finan, as he rode into the cold rain, edged his stallion close to mine. "Eighty men," he said.

I nodded. I trusted his judgment. Two crews of men had ridden from west to east and the hooves of their horses had trampled that scar into the waterlogged ground. Two crews were following the river to where? I slowed my horse, letting Beortsig catch us. "Where did you say Sigurd was celebrating Yule?" I asked.

"Cytringan," he said.

"And where's Cytringan?"

He pointed north. "A good day's journey, probably two. He keeps a feasting hall there."

Cytringan lay to the north, but the hoofprints had been going east.

Someone was lying.

Two

I had not realized quite how important the proposed treaty was to Alfred until I returned to Buccingahamm and found sixteen monks eating my food and drinking my ale. The youngest of them were still unshaven striplings, while the oldest, their leader, was a corpulent man of about my own age. He was called Brother John, and was so fat that he had trouble offering me a bow. "He is from Frankia," Willibald said proudly.

"What's he doing here?"

"He is the king's songmaster! He leads the choir."

"A choir?" I asked.

"We sing," Brother John said in a voice that seemed to rumble from somewhere inside his capacious belly. He waved a peremptory hand at his monks and shouted at them, "the *Soli Deo Gloria*. Stand up! Breathe deep! Upon my word! A one! A two!" They began chanting. "Mouths open!" Brother John bellowed at them, "Mouths wide! Mouths wide as little birdies! From the stomach! Let me hear you!"

"Enough!" I shouted before they had finished their first line. I tossed my sheathed sword to Oswi, my servant, then went to warm myself by the hall's central hearth. "Why," I asked Willibald, "must I feed singing monks?"

"It's important we make an impressive display," he answered, casting a dubious eye on my mud-spattered mail. "We represent Wessex, lord, and we must demonstrate the glory of Alfred's court."

Alfred had sent banners with the monks. One showed the dragon of Wessex, while others were embroidered with saints or holy images. "We're taking those rags as well?" I asked.

"Of course," Willibald said.

"I can take a banner showing Thor, perhaps? Or Woden?"

Willibald sighed. "Please lord, no."

"Why can't we have a banner showing one of the women saints?" I asked.

"I'm sure we can," Willibald said, pleased at the suggestion, "if that's what you'd like."

"One of those women who were stripped naked before they were killed," I added, and Father Willibald sighed again.

Sigunn brought me a horn of mulled ale and I gave her a kiss. "All well here?" I asked her.

She looked at the monks and shrugged. I could see Willibald was curious about her, especially when I put an arm around her and drew her close. "She's my woman," I explained.

"But," he began and finished abruptly. He was thinking about Æthelflaed, but did not have the courage to name her.

I smiled at him. "You have a question, father?"

"No, no," he said hurriedly.

I looked at the largest banner, a great gaudy square of cream linen emblazoned with an embroidery of the crucifixion. It was so large that it would need two men to parade it, and even more if the wind was blowing anything above a gentle breeze. "Does Eohric know we're bringing an army?" I asked Willibald.

"He has been told to expect up to one hundred people."

"And does he expect Sigurd and Cnut too?" I inquired acidly, and Willibald just stared at me with a vacant expression. "The Danes know about this treaty," I told him, "and they'll try to prevent it."

"Prevent it? How?"

"How do you think?" I asked.

Willibald looked paler than ever. "King Eohric is sending men to escort us," he said.

"He's sending them here?" I spoke angrily, thinking that I would be expected to feed even more men.

"To Huntandon," Willibald said, "and from there they take us to Eleg."

"Why are we going to East Anglia?" I asked.

"To make the treaty, of course," Willibald said, puzzled by the question.

"So why isn't Eohric sending men to Wessex?" I demanded.

"Eohric did send men, lord! He sent Ceolberht and Ceolnoth. The treaty was King Eohric's suggestion."

"Then why isn't it being sealed and signed in Wessex?" I persisted.

Willibald shrugged. "Does it matter, lord?" he asked with a trace of impatience. "And we're supposed to meet at Huntandon in three days," he went on, "and if the weather turns bad," he let his voice fade away.

I had heard of Huntandon, though I had never been there, and all I knew was that it lay somewhere beyond the vague frontier between Mercia and East Anglia. I gestured to the twins, Ceolberht and Ceolnoth, and they hurried over from the table where they had been sitting with the two priests sent with Willibald from Wessex. "If I were to ride straight to Eleg from here," I asked the twins, "what way would I go?"

They muttered together for a few seconds, then one of them suggested that the quickest route lay through Grantaceaster. "From there," the other one continued, "there's a Roman road straight to the island."

"Island?"

"Eleg is an island," a twin said.

"In a marsh," the other added.

"With a convent!"

"Which was burned by the pagans."

"Though the church is now restored."

"Thanks be to God."

"The holy Æthelreda built the convent."

"And she was married to a Northumbrian," Ceolnoth or Ceolberht said, thinking to please me because I am a Northumbrian. I am the Lord of Bebbanburg, though in those days my vicious uncle lived in that great ocean fortress. He had stolen it from me and I planned to take it back.

"And Huntandon," I asked, "lies on the road to Grantaceaster?"

The twins looked surprised at my ignorance. "Oh no, lord," one of them said, "Huntandon lies farther north."

"So why are we going there?"

"King Eohric, lord," the other twin began, then faltered. It was plain that neither he nor his brother had thought about that question.

"It's as good a route as any," his brother said stoutly.

"Better than Grantaceaster?" I demanded.

"Very nearly as good, lord," one of the twins said.

There are times when a man feels like a wild boar trapped in woodland, hearing the hunters, listening to the hounds baying, feeling the heart beat harder and wondering which way to flee, and not knowing because the sounds come from everywhere and nowhere. None of it was right. None of it. I summoned Sihtric who had once been my servant, but was now a house-warrior. "Find someone," I told him, "anyone, who knows Huntandon. Bring him here. I want him here by tomorrow."

"Where do I look?" Sihtric asked.

"How do I know? Go to the town. Talk to people in taverns."

Sihtric, thin and sharp-faced, looked at me resentfully. "I'm to find someone in a tavern?" he asked, as if the task were impossible.

"A merchant," I shouted at him. "Find me someone who travels! And don't get drunk. Find someone and bring them to me." Sihtric still looked sullen, perhaps because he was unwilling to go back into the cold outside. For a moment he looked like his father, Kjartan the Cruel, who had whelped Sihtric on a Saxon slave, but then, controlling his anger, he turned and walked away. Finan, who had noticed Sihtric's truculence, relaxed. "Find me someone who knows how to get to Huntandon and to Grantaceaster and to Eleg," I called after Sihtric, but he gave me no answer, and walked out of the hall.

I knew Wessex well enough, and I was learning parts of Mercia. I knew the land around Bebbanburg and about Lundene, but much of the rest of Britain was a mystery. I needed someone who knew East Anglia as well as I knew Wessex. "We know all those places, lord," one of the twins said.

I ignored the comment because the twins would never have understood my fears. Ceolberht and Ceolnoth had devoted their lives to the conversion of the Danes, and they saw the proposed treaty with Eohric as proof that their god was winning the struggle against the heathen deities and they would be dubious allies for an idea that was tempting me. "And Eohric," I asked the twins, "is sending men to meet us at Huntandon?"

"An escort, lord, yes. It will probably be led by Jarl Oscytel."

I had heard of Oscytel. He was the commander of Eohric's housecarls and thus the warrior-in-chief of East Anglia. "And how many men will he bring?" I asked.

The twins shrugged. "Maybe a hundred?" one said.

"Or two?" the other said.

"And together we shall all go to Eleg," the first twin said happily.

"Singing joyfully," Brother John put in, "like little birdies."

So I was expected to march to East Anglia carrying half a dozen gaudy banners and accompanied by a pack of singing monks? Sigurd would like that, I thought. It was in his best interest to stop the treaty ever happening, and the best way to do that was to ambush me before I ever reached Huntandon. I was not certain that was what he planned, I was simply guessing. For all I knew, Sigurd really was about to celebrate Yule and had no intention of fighting a swift winter campaign to prevent the treaty between Wessex, Mercia, and East Anglia, but no one survives long by assuming his enemy is sleeping. I gave Sigunn a light slap on the rump. "You'd like to spend Yule in Eleg?" I asked her.

"Christmas," one of the twins could not resist muttering the correction, then blanched at the look I gave him.

"I'd rather have Yule here," Sigunn said.

"We're going to Eleg," I told her, "and you're to wear the gold chains I gave you. It's important we make an impressive display," I added, then looked at Willibald. "Isn't that right, father?"

"You can't take her!" Willibald hissed at me.

"I can't?"

He flapped his hands. He wanted to say that the glory of Alfred's court would be contaminated by the presence of a pagan Danish beauty, but he did not have the courage to say the words aloud. He just stared at Sigunn, who was the widow of one of the Danish warriors we had killed at Beamfleot. She was about seventeen years old, a lithe, slight girl with fair skin, pale blue eyes, and hair like shining gold. She was clothed in finery; a dress of pale yellow linen edged with an intricate blue border of embroidered dragons that writhed about the hem, neckline, and sleeves. Gold hung at her throat and showed at her wrists, symbols that she was privileged, the possession of a lord. She was mine, but for most of her life she had only known the company of Haesten's men, and Haesten was on the other side of Britain, in Ceaster.

And that was why I would take Sigunn toward Eleg.

It was Yule 898, and someone was trying to kill me.

I would kill him instead.

Sihtric had appeared strangely reluctant to obey my orders, but the man he brought me was a good choice. He was a young man, scarce more than twenty, and claimed to be a magician, which meant he was really a rogue who traveled from town to town, selling talismans and charms. He called himself Ludda, though I doubted that was his real name, and he was accompanied by a small, dark girl called Teg, who scowled at me from beneath thick black eyebrows and a bird's nest of tangled hair. She seemed to be muttering under her breath as she looked up at me. "Is she casting spells?" I asked.

"She can, lord," Ludda said.

"Is she?"

"Oh no, lord," Ludda reassured me hurriedly. He, like the girl, was kneeling. He had a misleadingly open face, with wide blue eyes, a generous mouth, and a quick smile. He also had a sack strapped to his back, which proved to contain his charms, most of which were elfstones or shining pebbles, along with a bundle of small leather bags, each of which contained one or two rusty scraps of iron.

"What are those?" I asked, nudging the bags with my foot.

"Ah," he said, and gave a sheepish grin.

"Men who cheat the folk who live on my land are punished," I said.

"Cheat, lord?" He gazed up innocently.

"I drown them," I said, "or else I hang them. You saw the bodies outside?" The corpses of the two men who had tried to kill me still hung from the elm.

"It's hard to miss them, lord," Ludda said.

I picked up one of the small leather bags and opened it, spilling two rusty clench-nails onto my palm. "You tell folk that if they sleep with this bag beneath their pillow and say a prayer then the iron will turn to silver?"

The wide blue eyes became wider. "Now why would I say such a thing, lord?"

"To make yourself rich by selling iron scraps for a hundred times their real value," I said.

"But if they pray hard enough, lord, then Almighty God might hear their prayer, mightn't He? And it would be unchristian of me to deny simple folk the chance of a miracle, lord."

"I should hang you," I said.

"Hang her instead, lord," Ludda said quickly, nodding toward his girl, "she's Welsh."

I had to laugh. The girl scowled, and I gave Ludda a friendly cuff around the ears. I had bought one of those miracle bags years before, believing somehow that prayer would turn rust to gold, and I had bought it from just such a rogue as Ludda. I told him to stand and had the servants bring both him and his girl ale and food. "If I were traveling to Huntandon from here," I asked him, "how would I go?"

He considered the question for a few heartbeats, looking to see if there was some trap in it, then shrugged. "It's not a hard journey, lord. Go east to Bedanford and from there you'll find a good road to a place called Eanulfsbirig. You cross the river there, lord, and keep on north and east to Huntandon."

"What river?"

"The Use, lord." He hesitated. "The pagans have been known to row their ships up the Use, lord, as far as Eanulfsbirig. There's a bridge there. There's another at Huntandon, too, which you cross to get to the settlement."

"So I cross the river twice?"

"Three times, lord. You'll cross at Bedanford too, but that's a ford, of course."

"So I have to cross and recross the river?" I asked.

"You can follow the northern bank if you wish, lord, then you don't have to use the bridges beyond, but it's a much longer journey, and there's no good road on that bank."

"Can the river be forded anywhere else?"

"Not downstream of Bedanford, lord, not easily, not after all this rain. It will have flooded."

I nodded. I was toying with some silver coins, and neither Ludda nor Teg could take their eyes from the money. "Tell me," I said, "if you wanted to cheat the folk of Eleg, how would you travel there?"

"Oh, through Grantaceaster," he said immediately. "It's by far the quickest route and they're mighty gullible folk in Grantaceaster, lord." He grinned.

"And the distance from Eanulfsbirig to Huntandon?"

"A morning's walk, lord. No distance at all."

I tumbled the coins in my palm. "And the bridges?" I asked. "Are they wood or stone?"

"Both wooden, lord," he said. "They used to be stone, but the Roman arches collapsed." He told me about the other settlements in the valley of the Use, and how the valley was still more Saxon than Dane, though the farms there all paid tribute to Danish lords. I let him talk, but I was thinking about the river that would have to be crossed. If Sigurd planned an ambush, I thought, then he would place it at Eanulfsbirig, knowing we must cross the bridge there. He would surely not pick Huntandon because the East Anglian forces would be waiting on the higher ground just north of the river.

Or maybe he planned nothing at all.

Maybe I saw danger where there was none.

"Have you been to Cytringan?" I asked Ludda.

He looked surprised, perhaps because Cytringan was very far from the other places I had asked him about. "Yes, lord," he said.

"What's there?"

"The Jarl Sigurd has a feasting-hall there, lord. He uses it when he hunts in the woods there."

"It has a palisade?"

"No, lord. It's a great hall, but it's empty much of the time."

"I hear Sigurd is spending Yule there."

"That could be, lord."

I nodded, then put the coins back in my pouch and saw the look of disappointment on Ludda's face. "I'll pay you," I promised him, "when we come back."

"We?" he asked nervously.

"You're coming with me, Ludda," I said, "any warrior would be glad of a magician for company, and a magician should be mighty glad of warriors for an escort."

"Yes, lord," he said, trying to sound happy.

We left next morning. The monks were all on foot, which slowed us, but I was in no great hurry. I took almost all my men, leaving only a handful to guard the hall. There were over a hundred of us, but only fifty were warriors, the rest were churchmen and servants, while Sigunn was the only woman. My men wore their finest mail. Twenty of them led us and almost all the rest formed a rearguard, while the monks, priests, and servants walked or rode in the center. Six of my men were out on the flanks, riding ahead as scouts. I expected no trouble between Buccingahamm and Bedanford, and nor did we find any. I had not visited Bedanford before, and discovered a sad, half-deserted town that had shrunk to a frightened village. There had once been a great church north of the river, and King Offa, the tyrant of Mercia, was supposedly buried there, but the Danes had burned the church and dug up the king's grave to seek whatever treasure might have been interred with his corpse. We spent a cold, uncomfortable night in a barn, though I spent part of the darkness with the sentries, who shivered in their fur cloaks. The dawn brought mist across a wet, drab, flat land through which the river twisted in great lazy bends.

We crossed the river in the morning mist. I sent Finan and twenty men across first and he scouted the road ahead and came back to say there was no enemy in sight. "Enemy?" Willibald asked me. "Why would you expect enemies?"

"We're warriors," I told him, "and we always assume there are enemies."

He shook his head. "That's Eohric's land. It's friendly, lord."

The ford was running deep with bitterly cold water and I let the monks cross by using a great raft, which was tethered to the southern bank and was evidently left there for just such a purpose. Once across the river we followed the remnants of a Roman road that ran through wide waterlogged meadows. The mist melted away to leave a sunlit, cold and bright day. I was tense. Sometimes, when a wolf pack is both troublesome and elusive, we lay a trap for the beasts. A few sheep are penned in an open place while wolfhounds are concealed downwind, and then we wait in hope that the wolves will come. If they do, then horsemen and hounds are released and the pack is hunted across the wild land till it is nothing but bloody pelts and ripped meat. But we were now the sheep. We were walking north with banners aloft, proclaiming our presence, and the wolves were watching us. I was sure of it.

I took Finan, Sigunn, Ludda, Sihtric, and four other men and broke away from the road, leaving Osferth with orders to keep going until he reached Eanulfsbirig, but not to cross the river there.

While we scouted. There is an art to scouting land. Normally I would have two pairs of horsemen working either side of the road. One pair, watched by another, would go forward to investigate hills or woodlands, and only when they were certain that no enemy was in sight would they signal their comrades who, in turn, would investigate the next stretch of country, but I had no time for such caution. Instead we rode hard. I had given Ludda a mail coat, a helmet, and a sword, while Sigunn, who rode a horse as well as any man, was in a great cloak of otter fur.

We passed Eanulfsbirig late in the morning. We went well to the west of the small settlement and I paused in dark winter trees to stare at the glint of river, the bridge, and the tiny thatched houses that leaked a small smoke into the clear sky. "No one there," Finan said after a while. I trusted his eyes better than mine. "At least no one to worry about."

"Unless they're in the houses," I suggested.

"They wouldn't take their horses inside," Finan said, "but you want me to find out?" I shook my head. I doubted the Danes were there. Maybe they were nowhere. My suspicion was that they watched Eanulfsbirig, though perhaps from the river's far bank. There were trees beyond the far river meadows and an army could have been hidden in their undergrowth. I assumed that Sigurd would want us to cross the river before he attacked, so that our backs were to the stream, but he would also want to secure the bridge to prevent our escape. Or perhaps, even now, Sigurd was in his hall drinking mead and I was just imagining the danger. "Keep going north," I said, and we pushed the horses across the furrows of a field planted with winter wheat.

"What are you expecting, lord?" Ludda asked me.

"For you to keep your mouth shut if we meet any Danes," I said.

"I think I'd want to do that," he said fervently.

"And pray we haven't passed the bastards," I said. I worried that Osferth might be walking into ambush, yet my instincts told me we still had not found the enemy. If there was an enemy. It seemed to me that the bridge at Eanulfsbirig was the ideal place for Sigurd to ambush us, but as far as I could see there were no men on this side of the Use, and he would surely want them on both banks.

We rode more cautiously now, staying among trees as we probed northward. We were beyond the route that Sigurd would expect me to take and if he did have men waiting to cut off our retreat then I expected to find them, yet the winter countryside was cold and silent and empty. I was beginning to think that my fears were misplaced, that no danger threatened us, and then, quite suddenly, there was something strange.

We had gone perhaps three miles beyond Eanulfsbirig and were among waterlogged fields and small coppiced woods with the river a half-mile to our right. A smear of smoke rose from a copse on the river's far bank and I gave it no thought, assuming it was a cottage hidden among the trees, but Finan saw something more. "Lord?" he said, and I curbed the horse and saw where he pointed. The river here made a great swirling bend to the east and, at the bend's farthest point, beneath the bare branches of willows, were the unmistakable shapes of two ship prows. Beast-heads. I had not seen them until Finan pointed to them, and the Irishman had the sharpest eyes of any man I ever met. "Two ships," he said.

The two ships had no masts, presumably because they had been rowed beneath the bridge at Huntandon. Were they East Anglian? I stared, and could see no men, but the hulls were hidden beneath the thick growth of the river bank. Yet the rearing prows told me two ships were in a place where I had expected none. Behind me Ludda was again saying how Danish raiders had once rowed all the way to Eanulfsbirig. "Be quiet," I told him.

"Yes, lord."

"Maybe they're wintering the ships there?" Finan suggested.

I shook my head. "They'd drag them out of the water for the winter. And why are they showing their beast-heads?" We only put the dragon or wolf heads on our ships when we are in enemy waters, which suggested these two ships were not East Anglian. I twisted in the saddle to look at Ludda. "Remember to keep your mouth closed."

"Yes, lord," he said, though his eyes were bright. Our magician was enjoying being a warrior.

"And the rest of you," I said, "make sure your crosses are hidden." Most of my men were Christians and wore a cross just as I wore a hammer. I watched as they hid their talismans. I left my hammer showing.

We kicked the horses out of the wood and crossed the meadow. We had not gone halfway before one of the prow-mounted beasts moved. The two ships were moored against the farther bank, but one of them now came across the river and three men scrambled up from its bows. They were in mail. I held my hands high to show I was not holding a weapon, and let my tired horse walk slowly toward them. "Who are you?" one of them challenged me. He shouted in Danish, but what puzzled me was the cross he wore over his mail. It was a wooden cross with a small silver figure of Christ pinned to the crossbar. Maybe it was plunder? I could not imagine any of Sigurd's men being Christians, yet the ships were surely Danish. Beyond him I could now see more men, maybe forty altogether, waiting in the two ships.

I stopped to let the man look at me. He saw a lord in expensive war gear with silver trappings on his harness, arm rings glinting in the sun, and a hammer of Thor prominent about my neck. "Who are you, lord?" he asked respectfully.

"I am Haakon Haakonson," I invented the name, "and I serve the Jarl Haesten." That was my story, that I was one of Haesten's men. I had to assume that none of Sigurd's followers would be familiar with Haesten's troops and so would not question me too closely, and if they did then Sigunn, who had once been part of Haesten's company, would provide the answers. That was why I had brought her.

"Ivann Ivarrson," the man named himself. He was reassured that I spoke Danish, but he was still wary. "Your business?" he asked, though still in a respectful voice.

"We seek Jarl Jorven," I said, choosing the name of the man whose homestead we had skirted with Beortsig.

"Jorven?"

"He serves Jarl Sigurd," I said.

"And is with him?" Ivann asked, and did not seem in the least surprised that I sought one of Sigurd's men so far from Sigurd's territory, and that was my first confirmation that Sigurd was indeed nearby. He had left his lands and he was on Eohric's country where he had no business except to prevent the treaty from being signed.

"That's what I was told," I said airily.

"Then he's across the river," Ivann said, then hesitated. "Lord?" His voice was full of caution now. "Might I ask you a question?"

"You can ask," I said grandly.

"You mean Jorven harm, lord?"

I laughed at that. "I do him a service," I said, then twisted in the saddle and pulled the cloak-hood from Sigunn's head. "She ran away from him," I explained, "and Jarl Haesten thinks he would like her back."

Ivann's eyes widened. Sigunn was a beauty, pale and fragile looking, and she had the sense to look frightened as Ivann and his men examined her. "Any man would want her back," Ivann said.

"Jorven will doubtless punish the bitch," I said carelessly, "but maybe he'll let you use her first?" I pulled the hood back, shadowing her face again. "You serve Jarl Sigurd?" I asked Ivann.

"We serve King Eohric," he said.

There is a story in the Christian scriptures, though I forget who the story is about and I am not going to summon one of my wife's priests to tell me because the priest would then see it as his duty to inform me that I am going to hell unless I grovel to his nailed god, but the story was about some man who was traveling somewhere when a great light dazzled him and he suddenly saw everything clearly. That was how I felt at that moment.

Eohric had cause to hate me. I had burned Dumnoc, a town on the East Anglian coast, and though I had had good reasons to turn that fine port into a charred ruin, Eohric would not have forgotten the fire. I had thought he might have excused the insult in his eagerness to make an alliance with Wessex and Mercia, but now I saw his treachery. He wanted me dead. So did Sigurd, though Sigurd's reasons were far more practical. He wanted to lead the Danes south to attack Mercia and Wessex and he knew who would lead the armies that opposed him. Uhtred of Bebbanburg. I am not immodest. I had reputation. Men feared me. If I were dead then the conquest of Mercia and Wessex would be easier.

And I saw, at that moment, in that damp riverside meadow, just how the trap had been set. Eohric, playing the good Christian, had suggested I negotiate Alfred's treaty, and that was to lure me to a place where Sigurd could ambush me. Sigurd, I had no doubt, would do the killing, and that way Eohric would be absolved of blame.

"Lord?" Ivann asked, puzzled by my silence, and I realized I was staring at him.

"Sigurd has invaded Eohric's land?" I asked, pretending to stupidity.

"It's no invasion, lord," Ivann said, and saw me gazing across the river, though there was nothing to see on the farther bank except more fields and trees. "The Jarl Sigurd is hunting, lord," Ivann said, though slyly.

"Is that why you left your dragon-heads on the ships?" I asked. The beasts we place at the prows of our ships are meant to frighten enemy spirits and we usually dismount them when the boats are in friendly waters.

"They're not dragons," Ivann said, "they're Christian lions. King Eohric insists we leave them on the prows."

"What are lions?"

He shrugged. "The king says they're lions, lord," he said, plainly not knowing the answer.

"Well, it's a great day for a hunt," I said. "Why aren't you in the chase?"

"We're here to bring the hunters across the river," he said, "in case the prey crosses."

I pretended to look pleased. "So you can take us across?"

"The horses can swim?"

"They'll have to," I said. It was easier to make horses swim than try to coax them on board a ship. "We'll fetch the others," I said, turning my horse.

"The others?" Ivann was immediately suspicious again.

"Her maids," I said, jerking a thumb at Sigunn, "two of my servants and some packhorses. We left them at a steading." I waved vaguely westward and indicated that my companions should follow me.

"You could leave the girl here!" Ivann suggested hopefully, but I pretended not to hear him and rode back to the trees.

"The bastards," I said to Finan when we were safely hidden again.

"Bastards?"

"Eohric lured us here so Sigurd could slaughter us," I explained. "But Sigurd doesn't know which bank of the river we'll use, so those boats are there to bring his men over if we stay on this side." I was thinking hard. Maybe the ambush was not at Eanulfsbirig at all, but farther east, at Huntandon. Sigurd would let me cross the river and not attack until I was at the next bridge, where Eohric's forces would provide an anvil for his hammer. "You." I pointed at Sihtric, who gave me a surly nod. "Take Ludda," I said, "and find Osferth. Tell him to come here with every warrior he has. The monks and priests are to stop on the road. They're not to take a step farther, understand? And when you come back here, make damned sure those men in the boats don't see you. Now go!"

"What do I tell Father Willibald?" Sihtric asked.

"That he's a damned fool and that I'm saving his worthless life. Now go! Hurry!"

Finan and I had dismounted and I gave Sigunn the reins of the horses. "Take them to the far side of the wood," I said, "and wait." Finan and I lay at the wood's edge. Ivann was clearly worried about us because he stared toward our hiding place for some minutes, and then finally walked back to the moored ship.

"So what are we doing?" Finan asked.

"Destroying those two ships," I said. I would have liked to have done more. I would have liked to ram Serpent-Breath down King Eohric's fat throat, but we were the prey here, and I did not doubt that Sigurd and Eohric had more than enough men to crush us with ease. They would know precisely how many men I had. Doubtless Sigurd had placed scouts near Bedanford, and those men would have told him exactly how many horsemen rode toward his trap. Yet he would not want us to see those scouts. He wanted us to cross the bridge at Eanulfsbirig, and then get behind us so that we would be caught between his forces and King Eohric's men. It would have been a raw slaughter on a winter's day if that had happened. And if, by chance, we had taken the river's northern bank, then Ivann's ships would have ferried Sigurd's men across the Use so that they could get behind us once we had passed. He had made no attempt to hide the ships. Why should he? He would assume I would see nothing threatening in the presence of two East Anglian ships on an East Anglian river. I would have marched into his trap on either bank and news of the slaughter would have reached Wessex in a few days, but Eohric would have sworn that he knew nothing of the massacre. He would blame it all on the pagan Sigurd.

Instead I would hurt Eohric and taunt Sigurd, then spend Yule at Buccingahamm.

My men came in the middle of the afternoon. The sun was already low in the west where it would be dazzling Ivann's men. I spent some moments with Osferth, telling him what he must do and then sending him with six men to rejoin the monks and the priests. I gave him time to reach them, and then, as the sun sank even lower in the winter sky, I sprang my own trap.

I took Finan, Sigunn, and seven men. Sigunn rode, while the rest of us walked, leading our horses. Ivann expected to see a small group, so that is what I showed him. He had taken his ship back across the river, but his oarsmen now rowed the long hull back to our bank. "He had twenty men in the ship," I said to Finan, thinking how many we might have to kill.

"Twenty in each ship, lord," he said, "but there's smoke in that copse," he nodded across the river, "so he could have more just warming themselves."

"They won't cross the river to be killed," I said. The ground was soft underfoot, squelching with each step. There was no wind. Beyond the river a few elms still had pale yellow leaves. Fieldfares flew from the meadow there. "When we start killing," I told Sigunn, "you take our horses' reins and ride back to the wood."

She nodded. I had brought her because Ivann expected to see her and because she was beautiful and that meant he would watch her rather than look toward the trees where my horsemen now waited. I hoped they were hidden, but I dared not look back.

Ivann had clambered up the bank and tethered the ship's bows to a poplar's trunk. The current swept the hull downstream, which meant the men aboard could leap ashore easily enough. There were twenty of them, and we were only eight, and Ivann watched us, and I had told him we were bringing maidservants and he could not see them, but men see what they want to see and he only had eyes for Sigunn. He waited unsuspectingly. I smiled at him. "You serve Eohric?" I called as we drew near.

"I do, lord, as I told you."

"And he would kill Uhtred?" I asked.

The first flicker of doubt crossed his face, but I was still smiling. "You know about . . ." He began a question, but never finished it because I had drawn Serpent-Breath, and that was the signal for the rest of my men to spur their horses from the trees. A line of horsemen, hooves throwing water and clods of earth, horsemen holding spears and axes and shields, death's threat in a winter afternoon, and I swung my blade at Ivann, just wanting to drive him away from the boat's mooring line, and he stumbled to fall between the ship and the bank.

And it was over.

The bank was suddenly milling with horsemen, their breath

smoky in the cold bright light, and Ivann was shouting for mercy while his crew, taken by surprise, made no attempt to draw their weapons. They had been cold, bored and off-guard, and the appearance of my men, helmed and carrying shields, their blades sharp as the frost that still lingered in shadowed places, had terrified them.

The crew of the second ship watched the first surrender, and they had no fight either. They were Eohric's men, Christians mostly, some Saxon and some Dane, and they were not filled with the same ambition as Sigurd's hungry warriors. Those Danish warriors, I knew, were somewhere to the east, waiting for monks and horsemen to cross the river, but these men on the ships had been reluctant participants. Their job had been to wait in case they were needed, and all of them would rather have been in the hall by the fire. When I offered them life in exchange for surrender they were pathetically grateful, and the crew of the far ship shouted that they would not fight. We rowed Ivann's boat across the river, and so captured both vessels without killing a soul. We stripped Eohric's men of their mail, their weapons, and their helmets, and I took that plunder back across the river. We left the shivering men on the far bank, all but for Ivann, who I took prisoner, and we burned the two ships. The crews had lit a fire in the trees, a place to warm themselves, and we used those flames to destroy Eohric's ships. I waited just long enough to see the fire catch properly, to watch the flames eat at the rowers' benches and the smoke begin to thicken in the still air, and then we rode hard south.

The smoke was a signal, an unmistakable indication to Sigurd that his careful ambush had gone wrong. He would soon hear that from Eohric's crews, but by now his scouts would have seen the monks and priests at Eanulfsbirig's bridge. I had told Osferth to keep them on our bank, and to make sure they attracted attention. There was a risk, of course, that Sigurd's Danes would attack the nearly defenseless churchmen, but I thought he would wait until he was certain I was there. And so he did.

We arrived at Eanulfsbirig to find the choir singing. Osferth had ordered them to chant, and they were standing, miserable and singing, beneath their great banners. "Sing louder, you bastards!"

I shouted as we cantered up to the bridge. "Sing like loud little birdies!"

"Lord Uhtred!" Father Willibald came running toward me. "What's happening? What's happening?"

"I decided to start a war, father," I said cheerfully. "It's so much more interesting than peace."

He stared at me aghast. I slid from the saddle and saw that Osferth had obeyed me by piling kindling on the bridge's wooden walkway. "It's thatch," he told me, "and it's damp."

"So long as it burns," I said. The thatch was piled across the bridge, hiding lengths of timber that made a low barricade. Downriver the smoke from the burning ships had thickened to make a great pillar in the sky. The sun was very low now, casting long shadows toward the east where Sigurd must have heard from the two ships' crews that I was close by.

"You started a war?" Willibald caught up with me.

"Shield wall!" I shouted. "Right here!" I would make a shield wall on the bridge itself. It did not matter how many men Sigurd brought now because only a few could face us in the narrow space between the heavy timber parapets.

"We came in peace!" Willibald protested to me. The twins, Ceolberht and Ceolnoth, were making similar protests as Finan arrayed our warriors. The bridge was wide enough for six men to stand abreast, their shields overlapping. I had four ranks of men there now, men with axes and swords and big round shields.

"We came," I turned on Willibald, "because Eohric betrayed you. This was never about peace. This was about making war easier. Ask him," I gestured at Ivann. "Go on, talk to him and leave me in peace! And tell those monks to stop their damned caterwauling."

Then, from the far trees, across the damp fields, the Danes appeared. A host of Danes, maybe two hundred of them, and they came on horses led by Sigurd who rode a great white stallion beneath his banner of a flying raven. He saw we were waiting for him and that to attack us he must send his men across the narrow bridge and so he curbed his horse some fifty paces away, dismounted, and walked toward us. A younger man accompanied him, yet it was Sigurd who drew attention. He was a big man, broad-shouldered and with a scarred face half hidden by his beard that was long enough to be plaited into two thick ropes that he wore twisted around his neck. His helmet reflected the reddening sunlight. He was not bothering to carry a shield or draw a sword, but he was still a Danish lord in his war-splendor. His helmet was touched with gold, a chain of gold was buried among the plaits of his beard, his arms were thick with golden rings, and the throat of his sword's scabbard, like the weapon's hilt, glinted with more gold. The younger man had a chain of silver, and a silver ring surrounding his helmet's crown. He had an insolent face, petulant and hostile.

I stepped over the piled thatch and went to meet the two men. "Lord Uhtred," Sigurd greeted me sarcastically.

"Jarl Sigurd," I answered in the same tone.

"I told them you weren't a fool," he said. The sun was now so low above the southwestern horizon that he was forced to half close his eyes to see me properly. He spat onto the grass. "Ten of your men against eight of mine," he suggested, "right here." He stamped his foot on the wet grass. He wanted to draw my men off the bridge, and he knew I would not accept.

"Let me fight him," the younger man said.

I gave the young man a dismissive glance. "I like my enemies to be old enough to shave before I kill them," I said, then looked back to Sigurd. "You against me," I told him, "right here." I stamped my foot on the road's frost-hardened mud.

He half smiled, showing yellowed teeth. "I would kill you, Uhtred," he said mildly, "and so rid the world of a worthless piece of rat shit, but that pleasure must wait." He pulled up his right sleeve to show a splint on his forearm. The splint was two slivers of wood bound tight with linen bands. I also saw a curious scar on his palm, a pair of slashes that formed a cross. Sigurd was no coward, but nor was he fool enough to fight me while the broken bone of his sword arm was mending.

"You were fighting women again?" I asked, nodding at the strange scar.

He stared at me. I thought my insult had gone deep, but he was evidently thinking.

"Let me fight him!" the young man said again.

"Be quiet," Sigurd growled.

I looked at the youngster. He was perhaps eighteen or nineteen, nearly coming into his full strength, and had all the swagger of a confident young man. His mail was fine, probably Frankish, and his arms thick with the rings Danes like to wear, but I suspected the wealth had been given to him, not earned on a battlefield. "My son," Sigurd introduced him, "Sigurd Sigurdson." I nodded to him, while Sigurd the Younger just stared at me with hostile eyes. He so wanted to prove himself, but his father would have none of it. "My only son," he said.

"It seems he has a death wish," I said, "and if he wants a fight, I'll oblige him."

"It isn't his time," Sigurd said. "I know, because I talked to Ælfadell."

"Ælfadell?"

"She knows the future, Uhtred," he said, and his voice was serious without any trace of mockery. "She tells the future."

I had heard rumors of Ælfadell, rumors as vague as smoke, rumors that drifted across Britain and said a northern sorceress could speak with the gods. Her name, that sounded so like our word for nightmare, made Christians cross themselves.

I shrugged as if I did not care about Ælfadell. "And what does the old woman say?"

Sigurd grimaced. "She says no son of Alfred will ever rule in Britain."

"You believe her?" I asked even though I could see he did because he spoke simply and plainly, as if telling me the price of oxen.

"You would believe her too," he said, "except you won't live to meet her."

"She told you that?"

"If you and I met, she says, then your leader will die."

"My leader?" I pretended to be amused.

"You," Sigurd said grimly.

I spat onto the grass. "I trust Eohric is paying you well for this wasted time."

"He will pay," Sigurd said harshly, then he turned, plucked his son's elbow, and walked away.

I had sounded defiant, but in truth my soul was crawling with fear. Suppose Ælfadell the Enchantress had told the truth? The gods do speak to us, though rarely in plain speech. Was I doomed to die here on this river's bank? Sigurd believed it, and he was gathering his men for an attack, which, if its result had not been foretold, he would never have attempted. No men, however battle-skilled, could hope to break a shield wall that was as strong as the one I had placed between the bridge's sturdy parapets, but men inspired by prophecy will attempt any foolishness in the knowledge that the fates have ordained their victory. I touched Serpent-Breath's hilt, then the hammer of Thor, and went back to the bridge. "Light the fire," I told Osferth.

It was time to burn the bridge and retreat, and Sigurd, if he was wise, would have to let us go. He had lost his chance to ambush us and our position on the bridge was dauntingly formidable, but he had the prophecy of some strange woman ringing in his head and so he began haranguing his men. I heard their shouted responses, heard the blades beating on the shields and watched as Danes dismounted and formed a line. Osferth brought a flaming torch and thrust it deep into the piled thatch, and smoke thickened instantly. The Danes were howling as I elbowed my way into the center of our shield wall.

"He must want you dead very badly, lord," Finan said with some amusement.

"He's a fool," I said. I did not tell Finan that a sorceress had foretold my death. Finan might be a Christian, yet he believed in every ghost and every spirit, he believed that elves scuttled through the undergrowth and wraiths twisted in the night clouds, and if I had told him about Ælfadell the Sorceress he would have felt the same fear that shivered my heart. If Sigurd attacked I must fight because I needed to hold the bridge until the fire caught, and Osferth was right about the thatch. It was reed, not wheat straw, and it was damp, and the fire burned sullenly. It smoked, but there was no fierce heat to bite into the bridge's thick timbers that Osferth had weakened and splintered with war axes.

Sigurd's men were anything but sullen. They were clattering swords and axes against their heavy shields, and jostling for the honor of leading the attack. They would be half blinded by the sun and choked by the smoke, yet they were still eager. Reputation is everything and is the only thing that survives our journey to Valhalla, and the man who cut me down would gain reputation. And so, in the day's dying light, they steeled themselves to attack us.

"Father Willibald!" I shouted.

"Lord?" a nervous voice called from the bank.

"Bring that big banner! Have two of your monks hold it over us!"

"Yes, lord," he said, sounding surprised and pleased, and a pair of monks brought the vast linen banner embroidered with its picture of Christ crucified. I told them to stand close behind my rearmost rank and had two of my men stand there with them. If there had been the slightest wind the great square of linen would have been unmanageable, but now it was blazoned above us, all green and gold and brown and blue, with a dark streak of red where the soldier's spear had broken Christ's body. Willibald thought I was using the magic of his religion to support my men's swords and axes, and I let him think that.

"It will shade their eyes, lord," Finan warned me, meaning that we would lose the advantage of the low sun's blinding dazzle once the Danes advanced within the great shadow cast by the banner.

"Only for a while," I said. "Stand firm!" I called to the two monks holding the stout staffs that supported the great linen square. And just then, perhaps goaded by the flaunted banner, the Danes charged in a howling rush.

And as they came I remembered my very first shield wall. I had been so young, so frightened, standing on a bridge no wider than this one with Tatwine and his Mercians as we were attacked by a group of Welsh cattle thieves. They had rained arrows on us first, then charged, and on that distant bridge I had learned the seethe of battle-joy.

Now, on another bridge, I drew Wasp-Sting. My great sword was called Serpent-Breath, but her little sister was Wasp-Sting, a brief and brutal blade that could be lethal in the tight embrace of the shield wall. When men are close as lovers, when their shields are pressing on each other, when you smell their breath and see the rot in their teeth and the fleas in their beards, and when there is no room to swing a war ax or a long-sword, then Wasp-Sting could stab up from beneath. She was a gut-piercing sword, a horror.

And that was a horror-slaughter on a winter's day. The Danes had seen our piled kindling and assumed there was nothing but reeds smoking damply on the bridge, yet beneath the reeds Osferth had stacked roof timbers and when the leading Danes tried to kick the reeds off the bridge's roadway they kicked those heavy timbers instead and stumbled.

Some had hurled spears first. Those spears thumped into our shields, making them unwieldy, but it hardly mattered. The leading Danes tripped on the hidden timbers and the men behind pushed the falling men forward. I kicked one in the face, feeling my iron-reinforced boot crush bone. Danes were sprawling at our feet while others tried to get past their fallen comrades to reach our line, and we were killing. Two men succeeded in reaching us, despite the smoking barricade, and one of those two fell to Wasp-Sting coming up from beneath his shield rim. He had been swinging an ax that the man behind me caught on his shield and the Dane was still holding the war ax's shaft as I saw his eyes widen, saw the snarl of his mouth turn to agony as I twisted the blade, ripping it upward, and as Cerdic, beside me, chopped his own ax down. The man with the crushed face was holding my ankle and I stabbed at him as the blood spray from Cerdic's ax blinded me. The whimpering man at my feet tried to crawl away, but Finan stabbed his sword into his thigh, then stabbed again. A Dane had hooked his ax over the top rim of my shield and hauled it down to expose my body to a spear-thrust, but the ax rolled off the circular shield and the spear was deflected upward and I slammed Wasp-Sting forward again, felt her bite, twisted her, and Finan was keening his mad Irish song as he added his own blade to the slaughter. "Keep the shields touching!" I shouted at my men.

This is what we practiced every day. If the shield wall breaks then death rules, but if the shield wall holds then it is the enemy who dies, and those first Danes came at us in a wild rush, inspired by a sorceress's prophecy, and their assault had been defeated by the barricade that had tripped them and so made them easy prey for our blades. They had stood no chance of breaking our shield wall, they were too undisciplined, too confused, and now three of them lay dead among the scattered reeds that still burned feebly, while the smoking beams remained as a low obstacle. The survivors of those first attackers did not stay to be killed, but ran back to Sigurd's bank where a second group readied to break us. There may have been twenty of them, big men, spear-Danes, coming to kill, and they were not wild like the first group, but deliberate. These were men who had killed in the shield wall, who knew their business, whose shields overlapped and whose weapons glittered in the dying sun. They would not rush and stumble. They would come slowly and use their long spears to break our wall and so let their swordsmen and axmen into our ranks.

"God, fight for us!" Willibald called as the Danes reached the bridge. The newcomers stepped carefully, not tripping, their eyes watching us. Some called insults, yet I hardly heard them. I was watching them. There was blood on my face and in the links of my mail coat. My shield was heavy with a Danish spear, and Wasp-Sting's blade was reddened. "Slaughter them, O Lord!" Willibald was praying. "Cut down the heathen! Smite them, Lord, in thy great mercy!" The monks had started their chanting again. The Danes pulled dead or dying men backward to make room for their attack. They were close now, very close, but not yet in reach of our blades. I watched their shields touch each other again, saw the spear-blades come up, and heard the word of command.

And I also heard Willibald's shrill voice over the confusion. "Christ is our leader, fight for Christ, we cannot fail."

And I laughed as the Danes came. "Now!" I shouted at the two men standing with the monks. "Now!"

The great banner fell forward. It had taken the women of Alfred's court months of work, months of making tiny stitches with expensively dyed wool, months of dedication and prayer and love and skill, and now the figure of Christ fell forward onto the leading Danes. The vast linen and wool panel fell like a fisherman's net to drape itself over their first rank to blind them, and as it engulfed them I gave the order and we charged.

It is easy to pass a spear-blade if the man holding it cannot see you. I shouted at our second rank to grab the weapons and haul them clear while we killed the spearmen. Cerdic's ax sliced down through linen, wool, iron, bone, and brain. We were screaming, slaughtering, and making a new barricade of Danes. Some slashed at the banner, which shrouded and blinded them. Finan was sawing his sharp blade at the wrists holding spears, the Danes were desperately trying to escape their entanglement, and we were hacking, cutting and lunging, while all around us and between us the smoke of the scattered reeds thickened. I felt heat on one ankle. The fire was at last catching. Sihtric, his teeth bared in a grimace, was chopping a long-hafted ax again and again, driving the blade down into trapped Danes.

I hurled Wasp-Sting back to our bank and snatched up a fallen ax. I have never liked fighting with an ax. The weapon is clumsy. If the first stroke fails then it takes too long to recover and an enemy can use that pause to strike, but this enemy was already beaten. The ripped banner was red with real blood now, soaked with it, and I struck the ax down again and again, beating the wide blade through mail into bone and flesh, and the smoke was choking me, and a Dane was screaming, and my men were shouting, and the sun was a ball of fire in the west and the whole flat wet land was shimmering red.

We pulled back from the horror. I saw Christ's surprisingly cheerful face being consumed by fire as the linen caught the flames. Linen burns easily, and the black stain spread across the layers of cloth. Osferth had brought still more reeds and timbers from the cottage he had pulled down and we threw them onto the small flames and watched as the fire at last found strength. Sigurd's men had taken enough. They too pulled back and stood on the river's far bank and watched as the fire took its grip on the bridge. We dragged four enemy corpses to our side of the bridge and we stripped them of silver chains, arm rings, and enameled belts. Sigurd had mounted his white horse and just stared at me. His sullen son, who had been kept from the fight, spat toward us. Sigurd himself said nothing.

"Ælfadell was wrong," I called, but she had not been wrong. Our leader had died, maybe a second death, and the charred linen showed where he had been and where he had been consumed by fire.

I waited. It was dark before the roadway collapsed into the river, sending a sudden seethe of steam into the flame-lit air. The stone pilings that the Romans had made were scorched and still usable, but it would take hours of work to make a new roadway and, as the charred timbers floated downstream, we left.

That was a cold night.

We walked. I let the monks and priests ride because they were shivering and weary and weak, while the rest of us led the horses. Everyone wanted to rest, but I made them walk through the night, knowing that Sigurd would follow us just as soon as he could put men across the river. We walked under the bright cold stars, walked all the way past Bedanford, and only when I found a wooded hill that could serve as a place to defend did I let them stop. No fires that night. I watched the country, waiting for the Danes, but they did not come.

And next day we were home.

Three

Yule came, Yule went, and storms followed, bellowing from the North Sea to drift snow across the dead land. Father Willibald, the West Saxon priests, the Mercian twins, and the singing monks were forced to stay at Buccingahamm until the weather cleared, then I gave them Cerdic and twenty spearmen to escort them safe home. They took the magic fish with them, and also Ivann, the prisoner. Alfred, if he still lived, would want to hear of Eohric's treachery. I gave a letter for Æthelflaed with Cerdic, and on his return he promised me he had given it to one of her trusted maid-servants, but he brought back no answer. "I wasn't allowed to see the lady," Cerdic told me. "They've got her mewed up tight."

"Mewed up?"

"In the palace, lord. They're all weeping and wailing."

"But Alfred lived when you left?"

"He still lived, lord, but the priests said it was only prayer keeping him alive."

"They would say that."

"And Lord Edward is betrothed."

"Betrothed?"

"I went to the ceremony, lord. He's going to marry the Lady Ælflæd."

"The ealdorman's daughter?"

"Yes, lord. She was the king's choice."

"Poor Edward," I said, remembering Father Willibald's gossip that Alfred's heir had wanted to marry a girl from Cent. Ælflæd was daughter to Æthelhelm, Ealdorman of Sumorsæte, and presumably Alfred had wanted the marriage to tie Edward to the most powerful of Wessex's noble families. I wondered what had happened to the girl from Cent.

Sigurd had gone back to his lands from where, in petulance, he sent raiders into Saxon Mercia to burn, kill, enslave, and steal. It was border war, no different from the perpetual fighting between the Scots and the Northumbrians. None of his raiders touched my estates, but my fields lay south of Beornnoth's wide lands and Sigurd concentrated his anger on Ealdorman Ælfwold, the son of the man who had died fighting beside me at Beamfleot, and he left Beornnoth's territory unscathed, and that I thought was interesting. So in March, when stitchwort was whitening the hedgerows, I took fifteen men north to Beornnoth's hall with a new year's gift of cheese, ale, and salted mutton. I found the old man wrapped in a fur cloak and slumped in his chair. His face was sunken, his eyes watery, and his lower lip trembled uncontrollably. He was dying. Beortsig, his son, watched me sullenly.

"It's time," I said, "to teach Sigurd a lesson."

Beornnoth scowled. "Stop pacing around," he ordered me. "You make me feel old."

"You are old," I said.

He grimaced at that. "I'm like Alfred," he said. "I'm going to meet my god. I'm going to the judgment seat to find out who lives and who burns. They'll let him into heaven, won't they?"

"They'll welcome Alfred," I agreed. "And you?"

"At least it will be warm in hell," he said, then feebly wiped some spittle from his beard. "So you want to fight Sigurd?"

"I want to kill the bastard."

"You had your chance before Christmas," Beortsig said. I ignored him.

"He's waiting," Beornnoth said, "waiting for Alfred to die. He won't attack till Alfred's dead."

"He's attacking now," I said.

Beornnoth shook his head. "Just raiding," he said dismissively, "and he's pulled his fleet ashore at Snotengaham."

"Snotengaham?" I asked, surprised. That was about as far inland as any seagoing ship could travel in Britain.

"That tells you he's not planning anything other than raids."

"It tells me he's not planning seaborne raids," I said. "But what's to stop him marching overland?"

"Perhaps he will," Beornnoth allowed, "when Alfred dies. For now, he's only stealing a few cattle."

"Then I want to steal a few of his cattle," I said.

Beortsig scowled and his father shrugged. "Why prod the devil when he's dozing?" the old man asked.

"Ælfwold doesn't think he's dozing," I said.

Beornnoth laughed. "Ælfwold's young," he said dismissively, "and he's ambitious, he asks for trouble."

You could divide the Saxon lords of Mercia into two camps, those who resented the West Saxon dominance of their land and those who welcomed it. Ælfwold's father had supported Alfred, while Beornnoth harked back to earlier times when Mercia had its own king and, like others of his mind, he had refused to send troops to help me fight Haesten. He had preferred his men to be under Æthelred's command, which meant they had garrisoned Gleawecestre against an attack that had never come. There had been bitterness between the two camps ever since, but Beornnoth was a decent enough man, or perhaps he was so close to death that he did not want to prolong old enmities. He invited us to stay for the night. "Tell me stories," he said. "I like stories. Tell me about Beamfleot." That was a generous invitation, an implicit admission that his men had been in the wrong place the previous summer.

I did not tell the whole story. Instead, in his hall, when the great fire lit the beams red and the ale had made men boisterous, I told how the elder Ælfwold had died. How he had charged with me and how we had scattered the Danish camp, and how we rampaged among the frightened men at the hill's edge, and then how the Danish reinforcements had countercharged and the fighting had become bitter. Men listened intently. Almost every man in the hall had stood in the shield wall, and they knew the fear of that moment. I told how my horse had been killed, and how we made a circle of our shields and fought against the screaming Danes who had so suddenly outnumbered us, and I described a death that Ælfwold would have wanted, telling how he killed his enemies, how he sent the pagan foemen to their graves, and how he defeated man after man until, at last, an ax blow split his helmet and felled him. I did not describe how he had looked at me so reproachfully, or the hatred in his dying words because he believed, falsely, that I had betrayed him. He died beside me, and at that moment I had been ready for death, knowing that the Danes must surely kill us all in that blood-reeking dawn, but then Steapa had come with the West Saxon troops and defeat had turned into sudden, unexpected triumph. Beornnoth's followers hammered the tables in appreciation of the tale. Men like a battle-tale, which is why we employ poets to entertain us at night with tales of warriors and swords and shields and axes.

"A good story," Beornnoth said.

"Ælfwold's death was your fault," a voice spoke from the hall.

For a moment I thought I had misheard, or that the comment was not spoken to me. There was silence as every man wondered the same.

"We should never have fought!" It was Sihtric speaking. He stood to shout at me and I saw he was drunk. "You never scouted the woods!" he snarled. "And how many men died because you didn't scout the woods?" I know I looked too shocked to speak. Sihtric had been my servant, I had saved his life, I had taken him as a boy and made him a man and a warrior, I had given him gold, I had rewarded him as a lord is supposed to reward his followers, and now he was staring at me with pure loathing. Beortsig, of course, was enjoying the moment, his eyes flicking between me and Sihtric. Rypere, who was sitting on the same bench as his friend Sihtric, laid a hand on the standing man's arm, but Sihtric shook it off. "How many men did you kill that day through carelessness?" he shouted at me.

"You're drunk," I said harshly, "and tomorrow you will grovel to me, and perhaps I will forgive you."

"Lord Ælfwold would be alive if you had a scrap of sense," he yelled at me.

Some of my men tried to shout him down, but I shouted louder. "Come here, kneel to me!"

Instead, he spat toward me. The hall was in uproar now.

Beornnoth's men were encouraging Sihtric, while my men were looking horrified. "Give them swords!" someone called.

Sihtric held out his hand. "Give me a blade!" he shouted.

I started toward him, but Beornnoth lunged and caught my sleeve in a feeble grip. "Not in my hall, Lord Uhtred," he said, "not in my hall." I stopped, and Beornnoth struggled to his feet. He had to grip the table's edge with one hand to stay upright, while his other hand pointed shakily toward Sihtric. "Take him away!" he ordered.

"And you stay away from me!" I shouted at him. "And that whore wife of yours!"

Sihtric tried to break away from the men holding him, but they had too tight a grip and he was too drunk. They dragged him from the hall to the jeers of Beornnoth's followers. Beortsig had enjoyed my discomfiture and was laughing. His father frowned at him, then sat heavily. "I am sorry," he grunted.

"He'll be sorry," I said vengefully.

There was no sign of Sihtric next morning and I did not ask where Beornnoth had him hidden. We readied ourselves to leave, and Beornnoth was helped out to the courtyard by two of his men. "I fear," he said, "that I'll die before Alfred."

"I hope you live many years," I said dutifully.

"There'll be pain in Britain when Alfred goes," he said. "All the certainties will die with him." His voice faded. He was still embarrassed by the previous night's argument in his hall. He had watched one of my own men insult me, and he had prevented me from giving punishment, and the incident lay between us like a burning coal. Yet both of us pretended it had not happened.

"Alfred's son is a good man," I said.

"Edward's young," Beornnoth said scornfully, "and who knows what he'll be?" He sighed. "Life is a story without an end," he said, "but I'd like to hear a few more verses before I die." He shook his head. "Edward won't rule."

I smiled. "He may have other ideas."

"The prophecy has spoken, Lord Uhtred," he said solemnly.

I was momentarily taken aback. "The prophecy?"

"There's a sorceress," he said, "and she sees the future."

"Ælfadell?" I asked. "You saw her?"

"Beortsig did," he said, looking at his son who, hearing Ælfadell's name, made the sign of the cross.

"What did she say?" I asked the sullen Beortsig.

"Nothing good," he said curtly, and would say no more.

I climbed into my saddle. I glanced around the yard for any evidence of Sihtric, but he was still concealed and so I left him there and we rode home. Finan was puzzled by Sihtric's behavior. "He must have been drunk beyond drunkenness," he said in wonder. I answered nothing. In many ways what Sihtric had said was right, Ælfwold had died because of my carelessness, but that did not give Sihtric the right to accuse me in open hall. "He's always been a good man," Finan went on, still puzzled, "but lately he's been surly. I don't understand it."

"He's becoming like his father," I said.

"Kjartan the Cruel?"

"I should never have saved Sihtric's life."

Finan nodded. "You want me to arrange his death?"

"No," I said firmly, "only one man kills him, and that's me. You understand? He's mine, and until I rip his guts open I never want to hear his name again."

Once home I expelled Ealhswith, Sihtric's wife, and her two sons from my hall. There were tears and pleas from her friends, but I was unmoved. She went.

And next day I rode to lay my trap for Sigurd.

There was a tremulousness to those days. All Britain waited to hear of Alfred's death, in the certain knowledge that his passing would scatter the runesticks. A new pattern would foretell a new fortune for Britain, but what that fortune was, no one knew, unless the nightmare sorceress did have the answers. In Wessex they would want another strong king to protect them, in Mercia some would want the same, while other Mercians would want their own king back, while everywhere to the north, where the Danes held the land, they dreamed of conquering Wessex. Yet all that spring and summer Alfred lived and men waited and dreamed and the new crops grew and I took forty-six men east and north to where Haesten had found his lair.

I would have liked three hundred men. I had been told many years before that one day I would lead armies across Britain, but to have an army a man must have land and the land I held was only large enough to keep a single crew of men fed and armed. I collected food-rents and I took customs dues from the merchants who used the Roman road that passed Æthelflaed's estate, but that was scarcely a sufficient income and I could only lead forty-six men to Ceaster.

That was a bleak place. To the west were the Welsh, while to the east and north were Danish lords who recognized no man as king unless it were themselves. The Romans had built a fort at Ceaster, and it was in the remnants of that stronghold that Haesten had taken refuge. There had been a time when Haesten's name struck fear into every Saxon, but he was a shadow now, reduced to fewer than two hundred men, and even they were of dubious loyalty. He had begun the winter with over three hundred followers, but men expect their lord to provide more than food and ale. They want silver, they want gold, they want slaves, and so Haesten's men had trickled away in search of other lords. They went to Sigurd or to Cnut, to the men who were gold-givers.

Ceaster lay on the wild edge of Mercia and I found Æthelred's troops some three miles to the south of Haesten's fort. There were just over one hundred and fifty men whose job was to watch Haesten and keep him weak by harassing his foragers. They were commanded by a youngster called Merewalh, who seemed pleased by my arrival. "Have you come to kill the sorry bastard, lord?" he asked me.

"Only to look at him," I said.

In truth I was there to be looked at, though I dared not tell anyone my whole purpose. I wanted the Danes to know I was at Ceaster, and so I paraded my men south of the old Roman fort and flaunted my wolf's head banner. I rode in my best mail, polished to a high shine by my servant Oswi, and I went close enough to the old walls for one of Haesten's men to try his luck with a hunting arrow. I saw the feather flickering in the air and watched as the small shaft thumped into the turf a few paces from my horse's hooves.

"He can't defend all those walls," Merewalh said wistfully.

He was right. The Roman fort at Ceaster was a vast place, almost a town in itself, and Haesten's few men could never garrison the whole stretch of its decrepit ramparts. Merewalh and I might have combined our forces and attacked at night and maybe we would have found an undefended stretch of wall and then fought a bitter battle in the streets, but our numbers were too equal with Haesten's to risk such an assault. We would have lost men in defeating an enemy who was already defeated, and so I contented myself with letting Haesten know I had come to taunt him. He had to hate me. Just a year before he had been the greatest power among all the Northmen; now he was cowering like a beaten fox in his den and I had reduced him to that plight. But he was a cunning fox and I knew he would be thinking how he might regain his power.

The old fort was built inside a great curve of the River Dee. Immediately outside its southern walls were the ruins of an immense stone building that had once been an arena where, so Merewalh's priest told me, Christians had been fed to wild beasts. Some things are just too good to be true and so I was not sure I believed him. The remnants of the arena would have made a splendid stronghold for a force as small as Haesten's, but instead he had chosen to concentrate his men at the northern end of the fort where the river lay closest to the walls. He had two small ships there, nothing more than old trading boats, which, because they were obviously leaky, were half pulled onto the bank. If he were attacked and cut off from the bridge then those ships were his escape across the Dee and into the wild lands beyond.

Merewalh was puzzled by my behavior. "Are you trying to tempt him into a fight?" he asked me the third day that I rode close to the old ramparts.

"He won't want a fight," I said, "but I want him to come out and meet us. And he will, he won't be able to resist." I had paused on the Roman road that ran straight as a spear shaft to the double-arched gate that led into the fort. That gate was now blocked with vast baulks of timber. "You know I saved his life once?"

"I didn't know."

"There are times," I said, "when I think I'm a fool. I should have killed him the first time I saw him."

"Kill him now, lord," Merewalh suggested, because Haesten had just appeared from the fort's western gate and now came slowly toward us. He had three men with him, all mounted. They paused at the fort's southwestern corner, between the walls and the ruined arena, then Haesten held out both hands to show he only wanted to talk. I turned my horse and spurred toward him, but took care to stop well out of bowshot of the ramparts. I took only Merewalh with me, leaving the rest of our troops to watch from a distance.

Haesten came grinning as though this meeting was a rare delight. He had not changed much, except he now had a beard that was gray, though his thick hair was still fair. His face was misleadingly open, full of charm, with amused bright eyes. He wore a dozen arm rings and, though the spring day was warm, a cloak of sealskin. Haesten always liked to look prosperous. Men will not follow a poor lord, let alone an ungenerous one, and so long as he had hopes of recovering his wealth he had to appear confident. He also appeared overjoyed to meet me. "Lord Uhtred!" he exclaimed.

"Jarl Haesten," I said, making the title as sour as I could, "weren't you supposed to be King of Wessex by now?"

"The pleasure of that throne is delayed," he said, "but for now let me welcome you to my present kingdom."

I laughed at that, as he had meant me to. "Your kingdom?"

He swept an arm around the bleak low valley of the Dee. "No other man calls himself king here, so why not me?"

"This is Lord Æthelred's land," I said.

"And Lord Æthelred is so generous with his possessions," Haesten said, "even, I hear, with his wife's favors."

Merewalh stirred beside me and I held up a cautionary hand. "The Jarl Haesten jests," I said.

"Of course I jest," Haesten said, not smiling.

"This is Merewalh," I said, introducing my one companion, "and he serves the Lord Æthelred. He might find favor with my cousin by killing you."

"He'd gain a great deal more favor by killing you," Haesten said shrewdly.

"True," I allowed, and looked at Merewalh. "You want to kill me?"

"Lord!" he said, shocked.

"My Lord Æthelred," I said to Haesten, "wishes you to leave his land. He has enough dung without you."

"Lord Æthelred," Haesten said, "is most welcome to come and drive me away."

This was all as meaningless as it was expected. Haesten had not left the fort to listen to a string of threats, but because he wanted to know what my presence meant. "Perhaps," I said, "the Lord Æthelred has sent me to drive you away?"

"And when did you last do his bidding?" Haesten asked.

"Perhaps his wife wants you driven away," I said.

"She'd rather I were dead, I think."

"Also true," I said.

Haesten smiled. "You came, Lord Uhtred, with one crew of men. We fear you, of course, because who doesn't fear Uhtred of Bebbanburg?" He bowed in his saddle as he uttered that piece of flattery. "But one crew of men is not sufficient to give the Lady Æthelflaed her wish." He waited for my response, but I said nothing. "Shall I tell you what mystifies me?" he asked.

"Tell me," I said.

"For years now, Lord Uhtred, you have done Alfred's work. You have killed his enemies, led his armies, made his kingdom safe, yet in return for all that service you have only one crew of warriors. Other men have land, they have great halls, they have treasure piled in strongrooms, their women's necks are ringed with gold, and they can lead hundreds of oath-men into battle, yet the man who made them safe goes unrewarded. Why do you stay loyal to such an ungenerous lord?"

"I saved your life," I said, "and you are mystified by ingratitude?"

He laughed delightedly at that. "He starves you because he fears you. Have they made a Christian of you yet?"

"No."

"Then join me. You and I, Lord Uhtred. We'll tip Æthelred out of his hall and divide Mercia between us."

"I'll offer you land in Mercia," I said.

He smiled. "An estate two paces long and one pace wide?" he asked.

"And all of two paces deep," I said.

"I am a hard man to kill," he said. "The gods apparently love me, as they love you. I hear Sigurd has cursed you since Yule."

"What else do you hear?"

"That the sun rises and sets."

"Watch it well," I said, "because you may not see many more such risings and settings." I suddenly kicked my horse hard forward, forcing Haesten's stallion to back away. "Listen," I said, making my voice harsh, "you have two weeks to leave this place. Do you understand me, you ungrateful dog-turd? If you're still here in fourteen days I'll do to you what I did to your men at Beamfleot." I looked at his two companions, then back to Haesten. "Two weeks," I said, "and then the West Saxon troops come and I'll turn your skull into a drinking pot."

I lied of course, at least about the West Saxon troops coming, but Haesten knew it had been those troops who gave me the numbers to gain the victory at Beamfleot and so the lie was believable. He began to say something, but I turned and spurred away, beckoning Merewalh to follow me. "I'm leaving you Finan and twenty men," I told the Mercian when we were well out of Haesten's earshot, "and before the two weeks are up you must expect an attack."

"From Haesten?" Merewalh asked, sounding dubious.

"No, from Sigurd. He'll bring at least three hundred men. Haesten needs help, and he's going to look for favor with Sigurd by sending a message that I'm here, and Sigurd will come because he wants me dead." Of course I could not be certain that any of that would happen, but I did not think Sigurd could resist the bait I was dangling. "When he comes," I went on, "you're going to retreat. Go into the woods, keep ahead of him, and trust Finan. Let Sigurd waste his men on empty land. Don't even try to fight him, just stay ahead of him."

Merewalh did not argue. Instead, after a few moments' thought, he looked at me quizzically. "Lord," he asked, "why hasn't Alfred rewarded you?"

"Because he doesn't trust me," I said, and my honesty shocked Merewalh, who stared at me wide-eyed, "and if you have any loyalty to your lord," I went on, "you will tell him that Haesten offered me an alliance."

"And I shall tell him you refused it."

"You can tell him I was tempted," I said, shocking him again. I spurred on.

Sigurd and Eohric had laid an elaborate trap for me, one that had very nearly worked, and now I would lay a trap for Sigurd. I could not hope to kill him, not yet, but I wanted him to regret his attempt to kill me. But first I wanted to discover the future. It was time to go north.

I gave Cerdic my good mail, my helmet, my cloak, and my horse. Cerdic was not as tall as I was, but he was big enough, and, dressed in my finery and with the cheek-plates of my helmet hiding his face, he would resemble me. I gave him my shield, painted with the wolf's head, and told him to show himself every day. "Don't go too close to his walls," I said, "just let him think I'm watching him."

I left my wolf's head banner with Finan and next day, with twenty-six men, I rode east.

We rode before dawn so that none of Haesten's scouts would see us depart, and we rode into the rising sun. Once there was light in the sky we kept to wooded places, but always going east. Ludda was still with us. He was a trickster, a rogue, and I liked him. Best of all he had an extraordinary knowledge of Britain. "I'm always moving, lord," he explained to me, "that's why I know my way."

"Always moving?"

"If you sell a man two rusted iron nails for a lump of silver, then you don't want to be in arm's reach of him next morning, lord, do you? You move on, lord."

I laughed. Ludda was our guide and he led us east on a Roman road until we saw a settlement where smoke rose into the sky and then we made a wide loop southward to avoid being seen. There was no road beyond the settlement, only cattle paths that led up into the hills.

"Where's he taking us?" Osferth asked me.

"Buchestanes," I said.

"What's there?"

"The land belongs to Jarl Cnut," I said, "and you won't like what's there so I'm not going to tell you." I would rather have had Finan for company, but I trusted the Irishman to keep Cerdic and Merewalh out of trouble. I liked Osferth well enough, but there were times when his caution was a hindrance rather than an asset. If I had left Osferth at Ceaster he would have retreated from Sigurd's approach too hastily. He would have kept Merewalh far from trouble by withdrawing deep into the border forests between Mercia and Wales, and Sigurd might well have abandoned the hunt. I needed Sigurd to be taunted and tempted, and I trusted Finan to do that well.

It began to rain. Not a gentle summer rain, but a torrential downpour that was carried on a sharp east wind. It made our journey slow, miserable, and safer. Safer because few men wanted to be out in such weather. When we did meet strangers I claimed to be a lord of Cumbraland traveling to pay my respects to the Jarl Sigurd. Cumbraland was a wild place where little lords squabbled. I had spent time there once and knew enough to answer any questions, but no one we met cared enough to ask them.

So we climbed into the hills and after three days came to Buchestanes. It lay in a hollow of the hills and was a town of some size built about a cluster of Roman buildings that retained their stone walls, though their roofs had long been replaced by thatch. There was no defensive palisade, but we were met at the town's edge by three men in mail who came from a hovel to confront us. "You must pay to enter the town," one said.

"Who are you?" a second asked.

"Kjartan," I said. That was the name I was using in Buchestanes, the name of Sihtric's evil father, a name from my past.

"Where are you from?" the man asked. He carried a long spear with a rusted head.

"Cumbraland," I said.

They all sneered at that. "From Cumbraland, eh?" the first man said. "Well you can't pay in sheep dung here." He laughed, amused at his own joke.

"Who do you serve?" I asked him.

"The Jarl Cnut Ranulfson," the second man answered, "and even in Cumbraland you must have heard of him."

"He's famous," I said, pretending to be awed, then paid them with the silver shards of a chopped-up arm ring. I haggled with them first, but not too strongly because I wanted to visit this town without arousing suspicion, and so I paid silver I could scarce afford and we were allowed into the muddy streets. We found shelter in a spacious farm on the eastern side. The owner was a widow who had long abandoned raising sheep and instead made a livelihood from travelers seeking the hot springs that were reputed to have healing powers, though now, she told us, they were guarded by monks who demanded silver before anyone could enter the old Roman bathhouse. "Monks?" I asked her. "I thought this was Cnut Ranulfson's land?"

"Why would he care?" she demanded. "So long as he gets his silver he doesn't mind what god they worship." She was a Saxon, as were most of the folk in the small town, but she spoke of Cnut with evident respect. No wonder. He was rich, he was dangerous, and he was said to be the finest sword fighter in all Britain. His sword was said to be the longest and most lethal blade in the land, which gave him the name Cnut Longsword, but Cnut was also a fervent ally of Sigurd. If Cnut Ranulfson knew that I was on his land then Buchestanes would be swarming with Danes seeking my life. "So are you here for the hot springs?" the widow asked me.

"I seek the sorceress," I said.

She made the sign of the cross. "God preserve us," she said.

"And to see her," I asked, "what do I do?"

"Pay the monks, of course."

Christians are so strange. They claim the pagan gods have no power and that the old magic is as fraudulent as Ludda's bags of iron, yet when they are ill, or when their harvest fails, or when they want children, they will go to the galdricge, the sorceress, and every district has one. A priest will preach against such women, declaring them heretic and evil, yet a day later he will pay silver to a galdricge to hear his future or have the warts removed from his face. The monks of Buchestanes were no different. They guarded the Roman bathhouse, they chanted in their chapel, and they took silver and gold to arrange a meeting with the aglæcwif. An aglæcwif is a she-monster, and that is how I thought of Ælfadell. I feared her and I wanted to hear her, and so I sent Ludda and Rypere to make the arrangements, and they returned saying the enchantress demanded gold. Not silver, gold.

I had brought money on this journey, almost all the money I had left in the world. I had been forced to take the gold chains from Sigunn, and I used two of those to pay the monks, swearing that one day I would return to retrieve the precious links. Then, at dusk on our second day in Buchestanes, I walked south and west to a hill that loomed above the town and was dominated by one of the old people's graves, a green mound on a drenched hill. Those graves have vengeful ghosts and, as I followed the path into a wood of ash, beech, and elm, I felt a chill. I had been instructed to go alone and told that if I disobeyed then the sorceress would not appear to me, but now I fervently wished I had a companion to watch my back. I stopped, hearing nothing except the sigh of wind in the leaves and the drip of water and the rush of a nearby stream. The widow had told me that some men were forced to wait days to consult Ælfadell, and some, she said, paid their silver or gold, came to the wood, and found nothing. "She can vanish into air," the widow told me, making the sign of the cross. Once, she said, Cnut himself had come and Ælfadell had refused to appear.

"And Jarl Sigurd?" I had asked her. "He came too?"

"He came last year," she said, "and he was generous. A Saxon lord was with him."

"Who?"

"How would I know? They didn't rest their bones in my house. They stayed with the monks."

"Tell me what you remember," I asked her.

"He was young," she said, "he had long hair like you, but he was still a Saxon." Most Saxons cut their hair, while the Danes prefer to let it grow long. "The monks called him the Saxon, lord," the widow went on, "but who he was? I don't know."

"And he was a lord?"

"He dressed like one, lord."

I was dressed in mail and leather. I heard nothing dangerous in the wood and so went onward, stooping beneath wet leaves until I saw that the path ended at a limestone crag that was slashed by a great crevice. Water dripped down the cliff face, and the stream gushed from the crevice's base, churning itself white about fallen rocks before sluicing into the woods. I looked about and saw no one, heard no one. It seemed to me that no birds sang, though that was surely my apprehension. The stream's noise was loud. I could see footprints in the shingle and stone that edged the stream, though none looked fresh, and so I took a deep breath, clambered over the fallen stones, and stepped into the cave's slit-like mouth that was edged by ferns.

I remember the fear of that cave, a greater fear than I had felt at Cynuit when Ubba's men had made the shield wall and come to kill us. I touched Thor's hammer that hung at my neck and I said a prayer to Hoder, the son of Odin and blind god of the night, and then I groped my way forward, ducking under a rock arch beyond which the gray evening light faded fast. I let my eyes grow used to the gloom and moved on, trying to stay above the stream that scoured through the bank of pebbles and sand that grated beneath my boots. I inched my way forward through a narrow, low passage. It grew colder. I wore a helmet and it touched rock more than once. I gripped the hammer that hung about my neck. This cave was surely one of the entrances to the netherworld, to where Yggdrasil has its roots and the three fates decide our destiny. It was a place for dwarves and elves, for the shadow creatures who haunt our lives and mock our hopes. I was frightened.

I slipped on sand and blundered forward and sensed that the passage had ended and that I was now in a great echoing space. I saw a glimmer of light and wondered if my eyes played tricks. I touched the hammer again, and then put my hand on the hilt of Serpent-Breath. I was standing still, hearing the drip of water and the rush of the stream, and listening for the sound of a person. I was gripping my sword's hilt now, praying to blind Hoder to guide me in the blind darkness.

And then there was light.

Sudden light. It was only a bundle of rushlights, but they had been concealed behind screens that were abruptly lifted and their small, smoky flames seemed dazzlingly bright in the utter darkness.

The rushlights were standing on a rock that had a smooth surface like a table. A knife, a cup, and a bowl lay beside the lights, which lit a chamber as high as any hall. The cave's roof hung with pale stone that looked as if it had been frozen in midflow. Liquid stone, touched with blue and gray, and all that I saw in an instant, then I stared at the creature who watched me from behind the rock table. She was a dark cloak in the darkness, a shape in the shadows, a bent thing, the aglæcwif, but as my eyes became used to the light I saw that she was a tiny thing, frail as a bird, old as time, and with a face so dark and deep-lined that it looked like leather. Her black woolen cloak was filthy and its hood half covered her hair that was gray-streaked black. She was ugliness in human guise, the galdricge, the aglæcwif, Ælfadell.

I did not move and she did not speak. She just gazed at me, unblinkingly, and I felt the fear crawl in me, and then she beckoned to me with one clawlike hand and touched the empty bowl. "Fill it," she said. Her voice was like wind on gravel.

"Fill it?"

"Gold," she said, "or silver. But fill it."

"You want more?" I asked angrily.

"You want everything, Kjartan of Cumbraland," she said, and she had paused for the space of an eye-blink before saying that name, as if she suspected it was false, "so yes. I want more."

I almost refused, but I confess I was frightened of her power, and so I took all the silver from my pouch, fifteen coins, and put them in the wooden bowl. She smirked as the coins clinked. "What do you want to know?" she asked.

"Everything."

"There will be a harvest," she said dismissively, "and then winter, and after winter the time of sowing, and then another harvest and then another winter until time ends, and men will be born and men will die, and that is everything."

"Then tell me what I want to know," I said.

She hesitated, then gave an almost imperceptible nod. "Put your hand on the rock," she said, but when I put my left hand flat on the cold stone she shook her head. "Your sword hand," she said and I obediently laid my right hand there instead. "Turn it over," she snarled, and I turned the hand palm upward. She picked up the knife, watching my eyes. She was half smiling, daring me to withdraw my hand, and when I did not move she suddenly scored the knife across my palm. She scored it once from the ball of my thumb to the base of my small finger, then did it again, crosswise, and I watched the fresh blood well from the two cuts and I remembered the crosswise scar on Sigurd's hand. "Now," she said, putting the knife down, "slap the stone hard." She pointed with a finger to the smooth center of the stone. "Slap it there."

I slapped the stone hard and the blow left a spatter of blood drops radiating from a crude daub of a hand-print defaced by the red cross.

"Now be silent," Ælfadell said, and shrugged off her cloak.

She was naked. Thin, pale, ugly, old, shriveled, and naked. Her breasts were flaps of skin, her skin wrinkled and spotted, and her arms scrawny. She reached up and released her hair that had been twisted at the nape of her neck so that the gray-black strands fell about her shoulders in the fashion of a young unmarried girl. She was a parody of a woman, she was the galdricge, and I shuddered to look at her. She seemed unaware of my gaze, but stared at the blood, which gleamed under the flames. She touched the blood with a finger as crooked as any claw, smearing it across the smooth stone. "Who are you?" she asked, and there seemed genuine curiosity in her voice.

"You know who I am," I said.

"Kjartan of Cumbraland," she said. She made a noise in her throat that might have been laughter, then moved the bloodstained claw to touch the cup. "Drink that, Kjartan of Cumbraland," she said, saying the name with sour mockery, "drink all of it!"

I lifted the cup and drank. It tasted foul. Bitter and rank. It was throat-curdling and I drank it all.

And Ælfadell laughed.

I remember little of that night, and much of what I do remember I wish I could forget.

I woke naked, cold, and tied. My ankles and my wrists were strapped with leather thongs that had been knotted together to drag my hands down to my ankles. A faint gray light seeped through the crevice and tunnel to illuminate the big cave. The floor was pale with bat shit and my skin was smeared with my own vomit. Ælfadell, crooked and dark in her black cloak, was crouched over my mail, my two swords, my helmet, my hammer, and my clothes. "You're awake, Uhtred of Bebbanburg," she said. She pawed through my possessions. "And you are thinking," she went on, "that I would be easy to kill."

"I'm thinking you would be easy to kill, woman," I said. My voice was a dry-mouthed croak. I pulled at the leather bindings, but only managed to hurt my wrists.

"I can tie knots, Uhtred of Bebbanburg," she said. She picked up the hammer of Thor and swung it on its leather thong. "A cheap amulet for a great lord." She cackled. She was bent, stooped and disgusting. Her clawlike hand tugged Serpent-Breath from its scabbard and she carried the blade toward me. "I should kill you, Uhtred of Bebbanburg," she said. She scarcely had the strength to lift the great blade, which she rested on one of my bent knees.

"Why don't you?" I asked.

She peered at me. "Are you wiser now?" she asked. I said nothing. "You came for wisdom," she went on. "So did you find it?"

Somewhere far beyond the cave a cock crowed. I tugged at the bonds again, and again could not loosen them. "Cut the bindings," I said.

She laughed at that. "I am not a fool, Uhtred of Bebbanburg."

"You haven't killed me," I said, "and that might be foolish."

"True," she agreed. She slid the sword forward so its tip touched my breast. "Did you find wisdom in your night, Uhtred?" she asked, then smiled with her rotted teeth. "Your night of pleasure?" I tried to throw the sword off by rolling on my side, but she kept it on my skin, drawing blood with the tip. She was amused. I was on my side now and she rested the blade on my hip. "You moaned in the dark, Uhtred. You moaned with pleasure, or have you forgotten?"

I remembered the girl coming to me in the night. A dark girl, black-haired, slender and beautiful, lithe as a willow-wand, a girl who had smiled as she rode above me, her light hands touching my face and chest, a girl who had bent herself backward as my hands caressed her breasts. I remembered her thighs pressing on my hips, the touch of her fingers on my cheeks. "I remember a dream," I said surlily.

Ælfadell rocked on her heels, rocked back and forth in an obscene reminder of what the dark girl had done in the night. The flat of the sword slid on my hip bone. "It was no dream," she said, mocking me.

I wanted to kill her then, and she knew it and the knowledge made her laugh. "Others have tried to kill me," she said. "The priests came for me once. There was a score of them, led by the old abbot with a flaming torch. They were praying aloud, calling me a heathen witch, and their bones are still rotting in the valley. I have sons, you see. It is good for a mother to have sons because there is no love like a mother has for her sons. Have you forgotten that love, Uhtred of Bebbanburg?"

"Another dream," I said.

"No dream," Ælfadell said, and I remembered my mother cradling me in the night, rocking me, giving me her breast to suck, and I could remember the pleasure of that moment, and the tears when I knew it had to be a dream for my mother had died giving birth to me and I had never known her.

Ælfadell smiled. "From now on, Uhtred of Bebbanburg," she said, "I shall think of you as a son." I wanted to kill her again and she knew it and she mocked me with laughter. "Last night," she said, "the goddess came to you. She showed you all your life, and all your future, and all the wide world of men and what will happen to it. Have you forgotten already?"

"The goddess came?" I asked. I remembered talking incessantly, and I remembered the sadness when my mother left me, and I remembered the dark girl saddling me, and I remembered feeling sick and drunk, and I remembered a dream in which I had flown above the world by riding the winds as a long-hulled ship rides the waves of the sea, but I remembered no goddess. "Which goddess?" I asked.

"Erce, of course," she said as though the question were foolish. "You know of Erce? She knows you."

Erce was one of the ancient goddesses who had been in Britain when our people came from across the sea. I knew she was worshipped still in country places, an earth-mother, a giver of life, a goddess. "I know of Erce," I said.

"You know there are gods," Ælfadell said, "and in that you are not so foolish. The Christians think one god will serve all men and women, and how can that be? Could one shepherd protect every sheep in all the world?"

"The old abbot tried to kill you?" I asked. I had twisted onto my right side so my tied hands were hidden from her and I was grinding the leather bonds against a ridge of stone, hoping they would part. I could only make the smallest of movements in case she noticed, and I had to keep her talking. "The old abbot tried to kill you?" I asked again. "Yet now the monks protect you?"

"The new abbot is no fool," she said. "He knows Jarl Cnut would flay him alive if he touched me, so instead he serves me."

"He doesn't mind you're not a Christian?" I asked.

"He likes the money Erce brings him," she sneered, "and he knows Erce lives in this cave and that she protects me. And now Erce waits for your answer. Are you wiser?"

I said nothing again, puzzled by the question, and it angered her.

"Do I mumble?" she snarled. "Has stupidity furred your ears and stuffed your brain with pus?"

"I remember nothing," I said untruthfully.

That made her laugh. She squatted on her haunches, the sword still resting on my hip, and started to rock backward and forward again. "Seven kings will die, Uhtred of Bebbanburg, seven kings and the women you love. That is your fate. And Alfred's son will not rule and Wessex will die and the Saxon will kill what he loves and the Danes will gain everything, and all will change and all will be the same as ever it was and ever will be. There, you see, you are wiser."

"Who is the Saxon?" I asked. I was still dragging my bound wrists on the stone, but nothing seemed to be fraying or loosening.

"The Saxon is the king who will destroy what he rules. Erce knows all, Erce sees all."

A scuffle of feet in the entrance passage gave me a moment's hope, but instead of my men appearing it was three monks who ducked into the cave's gloom. Their leader was an elderly man with wild white hair and sunken cheeks, who stared at me, then at Ælfadell, then back to me. "It's really him?" he asked.

"It's Uhtred of Bebbanburg, it's my son," Ælfadell said, then laughed.

"Good God," the monk said. For a moment he looked frightened, and that was why I still lived. Both Ælfadell and the monk knew I was Cnut's enemy, but they did not know what Cnut wanted of me and they feared that to kill me would offend their lord. The white-haired monk came toward me, gingerly, frightened of what I might do. "Are you Uhtred?" he asked.

"I am Kjartan of Cumbraland," I said.

Ælfadell cackled. "He is Uhtred," she said. "Erce's drink does not lie. He babbled like a baby in the night."

The monk was frightened of me because my life and death were beyond his comprehension. "Why did you come here?" he asked.

"To discover the future," I said. I could feel blood between my hands. My rubbing had opened the scabs on the cuts Ælfadell had inflicted on my palm.

"He learned the future," Ælfadell said, "the future of dead kings."

"Did it tell of my death?" I asked her, and for the first time saw doubt on that wrinkled-hag face.

"We must send to Jarl Cnut," the monk said.

"Kill him," one of the younger monks said. He was a tall, strongly built man with a hard long face, a hook of a nose, and cruel unforgiving eyes. "The jarl will want him dead."

The older monk was uncertain. "We don't know the jarl's will, Brother Hearberht."

"Kill him! He'll reward you. Reward us all." Brother Hearberht was right, but the gods had filled the others with doubt.

"The jarl must decide," the older monk said.

"It will take three days to fetch an answer," Hearberht said caustically, "and what do you do with him for three days? He has his men in the town. Too many men."

"We take him to the jarl?" the older monk suggested. He was desperate for an answer, flailing at any solution that might spare him from making a decision.

"For the sake of God," Hearberht snapped. He strode to the pile of my possessions, stooped, and straightened with Wasp-Sting in his hand. The short blade caught the wan light. "What do you do with a cornered wolf?" he demanded, and came toward me.

And I used all my strength, all that strength that years of sword and shield practice had put into my bones and muscle, the years of war and readying for war, and I thrust my bent legs and pulled my arms, and I felt the bonds loosening and I was rolling back, throwing the blade off my hip, and I started to shout, a great war shout of a warrior and reached for Serpent-Breath's hilt.

Ælfadell tried to pull the sword away, but she was old and slow, and I was bellowing to fill the cave with echoes and I seized the hilt and swung the blade to drive her back, and Hearberht checked as I rose to my feet. I half stumbled, the bonds still wrapped about my ankles, and Hearberht saw his opening and came in fast, the short blade held low ready to rip up into my naked belly and I swatted it aside and fell on him. He went backward and I stood again and he hacked the blade at my bare legs, but I parried him and then stabbed down with Serpent-Breath, my sword, my lover, my blade, my war companion, and she gutted that monk like a fish under a razor-edged knife, and his blood spread on his black robe and turned the bat shit black, and I went on ripping her, unaware that I was still shouting to fill the cave with rage.

Hearberht was squealing and shaking and dying, and the other two monks were fleeing. I ripped the bonds off my ankles and pursued them. Serpent-Breath's hilt was slippery with my blood, and she was hungry.

I caught them in the woods, not fifty paces from the cave's mouth, and I felled the younger monk with a blow to the back of his head, then caught the older by his robe. I turned him to face me and smelled the fear that fouled his robe. "I am Uhtred of Bebbanburg," I said, "and who are you?"

"Abbot Deorlaf, lord," he said, falling to his knees and holding his clasped hands toward me, and I held him by the throat and buried Serpent-Breath in his belly, and I sawed her there, opening him up, and he mewed like an animal and wept like a child and called on Jesus the Redeemer as he died in his own dung. I cut the younger monk's throat, then went back to the cave where I washed Serpent-Breath's blade in the stream.

"Erce did not foretell your death," Ælfadell said. She had screamed when I tore the bonds off my wrists and seized the sword from her, yet now she was oddly calm. She just watched me and was apparently unafraid.

"Is that why you didn't kill me?"

"She didn't foretell my death either," she said.

"Then maybe she was wrong," I said, and fetched Wasp-Sting from Hearberht's dead hand.

And that was when I saw her.

From a deeper cave, from a passage that led into the netherworld, Erce came. She was a girl of such beauty that the breath stopped in my lungs. The dark-haired girl who had ridden me in the night, the long-haired girl, slender and pale, so beautiful and calm and as naked as the blade in my hand and all I could do was stare at her. I could not move, and she gazed back at me with grave, large eyes and she said nothing and I said nothing until the breath caught in me again. "Who are you?" I asked.

"Dress yourself," Ælfadell said, whether to me or the girl I could not tell.

"Who are you?" I asked the girl, but she was still and silent.

"Dress yourself, Lord Uhtred!" Ælfadell ordered, and I obeyed her. I pulled on my jerkin, my boots, and my mail, and strapped my swords at my waist, and still the girl gazed at me with her quiet, dark eyes. She was as beautiful as the summer dawn and as silent as the winter night. She did not smile, her face showed nothing. I walked toward her and sensed something strange. The Christians say we have a soul, whatever that is, and it seemed to me this girl had no soul. There was an emptiness in her dark eyes. It was frightening, making me approach her slowly.

"No!" Ælfadell called. "You cannot touch her! You have seen Erce in the daylight. No other man has."

"Erce?"

"Go," she said, "go." She dared to stand in front of me. "You dreamed last night," she said, "and in your dream you found truth. Be content with that, and go."

"Speak to me," I said to the girl, but she was unmoving and silent and empty, yet I could not take my eyes from her. I would have looked on her for all the rest of my life. The Christians talk of miracles, of men walking on water and raising the dead, and they say those miracles are proofs of their religion, though none of them can do a miracle or show us a miracle, yet here, in this damp cave beneath the hilltop grave, I saw a miracle. I saw Erce.

"Go," Ælfadell said, and though she spoke to me it was the goddess who turned and vanished into the underworld.

I did not kill the old woman. I went. I dragged the dead monks into some brambles where perhaps the wild beasts would feast on them, and then I stooped to the stream and drank like a dog.

"What did the witch tell you?" Osferth asked me when I reached the widow's farm.

"I don't know," I said, and my tone discouraged further questions, all except one. "Where are we going, lord?" Osferth asked.

"We're going south," I said, still in a daze.

And so we rode toward Sigurd's land.

Four

I had told Ælfadell my name, and what else? Had I told her my idea for revenge on Sigurd? And why had I talked so much? Ludda gave me an answer as we rode south. "There are herbs and mushrooms, lord, and there's the blight you find on ears of rye, all kinds of things can give men dreams. My mother used them."

"She was a sorceress?"

He shrugged. "A wise-woman, anyway. She told fortunes and made potions."

"And the potion Ælfadell gave me, that made me speak my name?"

"Maybe it was rye-blight? You're lucky to be alive if it was. Get it wrong and you kill the dreamer, but if she knew how to make it then you'll have gabbled like an old woman, lord."

And who knows what else I had revealed to the aglæcwif? I felt like a fool. "Does she really speak to the gods?" I had told Ludda about Ælfadell, but not about Erce. I wanted to hold that secret close, a memory to haunt me.

"Some folk claim to talk to the gods," Ludda said uncertainly.

"And see the future?"

He shifted in his saddle. Ludda was not accustomed to riding a horse, and the journey had given him a sore arse and aching thighs. "If she really saw the future, lord, would she be in a cave? She'd have a palace. Kings would crawl to her feet."

"Maybe the gods only talk to her in the cave," I suggested.

Ludda heard the anxiety in my voice. "Lord," he said earnestly, "if you roll the dice often enough you always get the numbers you want. If I tell you the sun will shine tomorrow and that it will rain and there will be snow and that clouds will cover the sky and that the wind will blow and that it will be a calm day and that the thunder will deafen us then one of those things will turn out to be true and you'll forget the rest because you want to believe that I really can tell the future." He gave me a swift smile. "Folk don't buy rusty iron because I'm persuasive, lord, but because they desperately want to believe it will turn to silver."

And I desperately wanted to believe his doubts about Ælfadell. She had said Wessex was doomed and that seven kings would die, but what did that mean? What kings? Alfred of Wessex, Edward of Cent, Eohric of East Anglia? Who else? And who was the Saxon? "She knew who I was," I said to Ludda.

"Because you had drunk her potion, lord. It was as if you were drunk and saying anything that came into your mind."

"And she tied me up," I told him, "but didn't kill me."

"God be praised," Ludda said dutifully. I doubted he was a Christian, at least not a good one, but he was too clever to fall foul of the priests. He frowned in puzzlement. "I wonder why she didn't kill you."

"She was frightened to," I said, "and so was the abbot."

"She tied you up, lord," Ludda said, "because someone had told her you were Jarl Cnut's enemy. So she knew that much, but she didn't know what Jarl Cnut wanted done with you. So she sent for the monks to find out. And they were too scared to order your death, too. It's no small thing to kill a lord, especially if his men are close by."

"One of them wasn't scared."

"And he's regretting that now," Ludda said happily, "but it's strange, lord, very strange."

"What is?"

"She can talk to the gods. And the gods didn't tell her to kill you."

"Ah," I said, seeing what he meant and not knowing what else to say.

"The gods would have known what to do with you and they would have told her what to do, yet they didn't. That tells me she's not taking commands from the gods, lord, but from Jarl Cnut. She's telling men what he wants them to hear." He shifted in the saddle again, trying to relieve the pain in his arse. "There's the road, lord," he said, pointing. He was leading us south and east and had been looking for a Roman road that crossed the hills. "It goes to some old lead mines," he had told me, "but once past the mines there's no road." I had told Ludda to take us to Cytringan where Sigurd had a feasting-hall, though I had not said what I planned to do there.

Why had I gone to find Ælfadell? To find a road, of course. The three Norns sit at the roots of Yggdrasil where they weave our fates, and at some time they will take the shears and cut our thread. We all want to know where that thread will end. We want to know the future. We want to know, as Beornnoth had said to me, how the story ends, and that was why I had gone to see Ælfadell. Alfred must die soon, maybe he was already dead, and everything would change, and I was not such a fool as to think that my part in that change would be small. I am Uhtred of Bebbanburg. Men feared me. In those days I was no great lord in terms of land or wealth or men, but Alfred had known that if he wanted victory he must lend me men, and that was how we had broken Haesten's power at Beamfleot. His son, Edward, seemed to trust me, and I knew Alfred wanted me to swear loyalty to Edward, but I had gone to Ælfadell to catch a glimpse of the future. Why ally myself to a man destined to fail? Was Edward the man whom Ælfadell called the Saxon and who was doomed to destroy Wessex? What was the safe road? Edward's sister, Æthelflaed, would never forgive me if I betrayed her brother, but perhaps she was doomed too. All my women would die. There was no great truth in that, we all die, yet why had Ælfadell said those words? Was she warning me against Alfred's children? Against Æthelflaed and Edward? We live in a world fading to darkness and I had sought a light to shine on a sure road and I had found none, except a vision of Erce, a vision that would not leave my memory, a vision to haunt me. "Wyrd bið ful āræd," I said aloud.

Fate is inexorable.

And under the influence of Ælfadell's bitter drink I had babbled my name, and what else? I had told none of my men what my plan was, but had I told Ælfadell? And Ælfadell lived on Cnut's land and under his protection. She had told me that Wessex would be destroyed and that the Danes would win everything, and of course she would say that because that was what Cnut Longsword wanted men to hear. Jarl Cnut wanted every Danish leader to visit the cave and hear that victory would be theirs because men inspired to battle by a foreknowledge of victory fought with a passion that gives them victory. Sigurd's men, attacking me on the bridge, had really believed they would win and that had encouraged them into a trap.

Now I led a few men toward what could be our deaths. Had I told Ælfadell I was planning to attack Cytringan? Because if I had blurted out that idea then she would surely be sending a message to Cnut, and Cnut would move fast to protect his friend Sigurd. I had been planning to ride home by way of Cytringan, Sigurd's feasting-hall, and had hoped to find it empty and unprotected. I had thought to burn it to the ground, then ride on fast to Buccingahamm. Sigurd had tried to kill me and I wanted him to regret that and so I had gone to Ceaster to lure him away from his heartland, and if my deceit had worked then Sigurd was going there now, thinking to trap and kill me, while I planned to burn his hall. But his friend Cnut might be sending men to Cytringan and turning that feasting-hall into a trap for me.

So I must do something different. "Forget Cytringan," I told Ludda." Take me to the valley of the Trente instead. To Snotengaham."

So we rode south beneath the wild flying clouds and after two days and nights came to the valley that brought back so many memories. The very first time I was ever in a warship I had come to this place, rowing up the Humbre and then the Trente, and it was in this valley that I had first seen Alfred. I had been a boy and he had been a young man and I had spied on him, hearing his anguish about the sin that had brought Osferth into the world. It was on the banks of the Trente that I had first encountered Ubba, who was known as Ubba the Horrible, and I had been awed and terrified by him. Later, beside a distant sea, I was to kill him. I had been a boy when I was last on the banks of this river, but now I was a man and other men feared me as I had once feared Ubba. Uhtredærwe, some men called me, Uhtred the Wicked. They called me that because I was not a Christian, but I liked the name, and one day, I thought, I would take the wickedness too far and men would die because I was a fool.

Maybe here, maybe now, for I had abandoned the idea of destroying Cytringan's feasting-hall and instead would attempt a foolish thing, but one that would have my name spoken all across Britain. Reputation. We would rather have reputation than gold, and so I left my men in a steading and rode down the river's southern bank with just Osferth for company, and I said nothing until we came to the edge of a coppiced wood from where we could see the town across the wide river's swirls. "Snotengaham," I said. "It was here I first met your father."

He grunted at that. The town lay on the river's northern bank and it had grown since I had last seen it. There were buildings outside the ramparts and the air above the roofs was thick with smoke from the kitchen fires. "Sigurd's possession?" Osferth asked.

I nodded, remembering what Beornnoth had told me, that Sigurd had laid up his war-fleet in Snotengaham. I also remembered Ragnar the Elder's words that he had spoken to me when I was a child, that Snotengaham would be Danish for ever, yet most of the folk who lived inside the walls were Saxons. This was a Mercian town, right on the northern edge of that kingdom, yet for nearly all my life it had been ruled by the Danes and now its merchants and churchmen, its whores and its tavern-keepers paid silver to Sigurd. He had built a hall on a great rock outcrop in the town's center. It was not his main dwelling, which lay far to the south, but Snotengaham was one of Sigurd's strongholds, a place he felt safe.

To reach Snotengaham from the sea a boat went up the great Humbre, then followed the Trente. That was the voyage I had made as a child in Ragnar's *Wind-Viper* and, from the coppice on the southern bank, I could see there were forty or fifty boats drawn onto the far bank. Those were the ships Sigurd had taken south to Wessex the previous year, though in the end he had achieved nothing except to lay waste to a few farmsteads outside of Exanceaster. Their presence suggested he did not plan another seaborne invasion. His next attack would be overland, a lunge into Mercia and then Wessex to take the Saxon land.

Yet a man's pride is not just his land. We measure a lord by the number of crews he leads, and those ships told me Sigurd commanded a horde. I commanded one crew. I dare say I was as famous as Sigurd, yet all my fame had not translated into wealth. I should, I thought, be called Uhtred the Foolish. I had served Alfred all these years, and to show for it I had a borrowed estate, a single crew of men, and a reputation. Sigurd owned towns and whole estates, and led an army.

It was time to taunt him.

I talked with each of my men. I told them they could become rich by betraying me, that if just one of them told some whore in the town that I was Uhtred then I would probably die, and that most of them would die with me. I did not remind them of the oath they had taken to me because not one of them would need reminding, nor did I think any of them would betray me. I had four Danes and three Frisians in that group, yet they were my men, tied to me as much by friendship as by oath. "What we're about to do," I told them, "will have men talking all over Britain. It will not make us rich, but I promise you reputation."

My name, I told them, was Kjartan. It was the name I had used with Ælfadell, a name from my past, a name I did not like, the name of Sihtric's foul father, but it would suffice for the next few days, and I would only survive those days if none of my men revealed the truth and if no one in Snotengaham recognized me. I had only met Sigurd twice, and both times briefly, but some of the men who had accompanied him to those meetings might be in Snotengaham and that was a risk I had to take. I had let my beard grow, I was wearing old mail, which I had allowed to rust, and I looked, as I wished to look, like a man on the edge of failure.

I found a tavern outside the town. It had no name. It was a

miserable place with sour ale, moldy, bread and worm-riddled cheese, but it had sufficient room for my men to sleep on its filthy straw, and the tavern's owner, a surly Saxon, was satisfied by the small amount of silver I gave him. "Why are you here?" he wanted to know.

"To buy a ship," I said, then told him we had been part of Haesten's army and that we had become tired of starving in Ceaster and only wanted to go home. "We're going back to Frisia," I said, and that was my tale and no one in Snotengaham thought it strange. The Danes follow leaders who bring them riches, and when a leader fails, his crews melt away like frost in the sun. Nor did anyone think it strange that a Frisian would lead Saxons. The crews of the Viking ships are Danish, Norse, Frisian, and Saxon. Any masterless man could go Viking, and a shipmaster did not care what language a man spoke if he could wield a sword, thrust a spear, and pull an oar.

So my tale was not questioned and, the day after we reached Snotengaham, a full-bellied Dane called Frithof came to find me. He had no left arm beneath the elbow. "Some Saxon bastard cut it off," he said cheerfully, "but I sliced off his head so it was a fair exchange." Frithof was what a Saxon would call the Reeve of Snotengaham, the man responsible for keeping the peace and serving his lord's interests in the town. "I look after Jarl Sigurd," Frithof told me, "and he looks after me."

"A good lord?"

"The very best," Frithof said enthusiastically, "generous and loyal. Why don't you swear to him?"

"I want to go home," I said.

"Frisia?" he asked. "You sound Danish, not Frisian."

"I served Skirnir Thorson," I explained. Skirnir had been a pirate on the Frisian coast and I had served him by luring him to his death.

"He was a bastard," Frithof said, "but had a pretty wife, I hear. What was his island called?" The question had no suspicion in it. Frithof was an easy, hospitable man.

"Zegge," I said.

"That was it! Nothing but sand and fish shit. So you went from

Skirnir to Haesten, eh?" He laughed, his question implying that I had chosen my lords badly. "You could do a lot worse than serve the Jarl Sigurd," Frithof assured me. "He looks after his men and there'll be land and silver soon."

"Soon?"

"When Alfred dies," Frithof said, "Wessex will fall into pieces. All we have to do is wait and then pick them up."

"I have land in Frisia," I said, "and a wife."

Frithof grinned. "There are plenty of women here," he said, "but if you really want to go home?"

"I want to go home."

"Then you need a ship," he said, "unless you plan to swim. So let's go for a walk."

Forty-seven ships had been pulled from the river and were now propped by oak shafts on a meadow close to a small shelving cove that made launching and recovering easy. Six other ships were floating. Four of those were trading boats, and two were long, sleek war boats with high prows and sterns. "*Bright-Flyer.*" Frithof pointed to one of the two fighting ships afloat in the river. "She's Jarl Sigurd's own craft."

Bright-Flyer was a beauty with a flat, sleek belly and a high prow and stern. A man was squatting on the wharf and painting a white line along her topmost strake, a line that would accentuate her sinuously threatening shape. Frithof led me down to the timber wharf and stepped over the boat's low midships. I followed him, feeling the small shiver in *Bright-Flyer* as she responded to our weight. I noted her mast was not on board, there were no oars or tholes, and the presence of two small saws, an adze, and a box of chisels showed that men were working on her. She was afloat, but she was not ready for any voyage. "I brought her here from Denmark," Frithof said wistfully.

"You're a shipmaster?" I asked.

"I was, maybe I will be again. I miss the sea." He ran his hand along the smooth wood of her top strake. "Isn't she lovely?"

"She's beautiful," I said.

"Jarl Sigurd had her built," he said, "and only the best for him!" He rapped the hull. "Green oak from Frisia. Too big for you, though."

"She's for sale?"

"Never! Jarl Sigurd would rather sell his only son into slavery! Besides, how many oars do you want? Twenty?"

"No more," I said.

"She needs fifty rowers," Frithof said, rapping the *Bright-Flyer*'s planks again. He sighed, remembering her at sea.

I looked at the carpenter's tools. "You're readying her for sea?" I asked.

"The jarl hasn't said, but I hate to see ships out of the water for too long. The timbers dry and shrink. I want to float that one next," he pointed to the head of the cove where another beauty was propped on thick oak shafts. "*Sea-Slaughterer*," Frithof said, "Jarl Cnut's ship."

"He keeps his ships here?"

"Just the two," he said, "*Sea-Slaughterer* and *Cloud-Chaser*." Men were caulking the *Sea-Slaughterer*, stuffing the plank joints with a mix of wool and pine tar. Small boys helped, or else played on the river bank. The tar braziers smoked, drifting their pungent smell across the slow river. Frithof stepped back onto the wharf and patted the head of the man who was painting the white line onto the strake. Frithof was obviously popular. Men grinned and called out respectful greetings, and Frithof responded with generous pleasure. He had a pouch at his waist filled with scraps of smoked beef that he handed to the children, all of whose names he knew. "This is Kjartan," he introduced me to the men caulking the *Sea-Slaughterer*, "and he wants to take a boat off our hands. He's going back to Frisia because his wife is there."

"Bring the woman here!" a man called to me.

"He's got more sense than letting you scum ogle her," Frithof retorted, then led me further down the bank past a huge heap of ballast stones. Frithof had Sigurd's authority to buy or sell ships, but only a half-dozen were for sale, and of those only two would suit me. One was a trading ship, broad in the beam and well made, but she was short, her length only about four times her beam, and that would make her slow. The other ship was older and much used, but she was at least seven times longer than her beam, and her sleek lines were sweet. "She belonged to a Norseman," Frithof told me, "who got himself killed in Wessex."

"Made of pine?" I asked, rapping the hull.

"She's all spruce," Frithof said.

"I'd prefer oak," I said grudgingly.

"Give me gold and I'll have a ship built for you out of the best Frisian oak," Frithof said, "but if you want to cross the sea this summer you'll do it in pine. She was well made, and she has a mast, sail, and rigging."

"Oars?"

"We've plenty of good ash oars." He ran his one hand down the stem-post. "She needs a little work," he admitted, "but she was a sweetheart in her day. *Tyr's Daughter.*"

"That's her name?"

Frithof smiled. "It is." He smiled because Tyr is the god of the warriors who fight in single combat and, like Frithof, Tyr is one-handed, having lost his right hand to the sharp fangs of Fenrir, the crazed wolf. "Her owner liked Tyr," Frithof said, still stroking the stem-post.

"She has a beast-head?"

"I can find you something."

We haggled, though good-naturedly. I offered what little silver I had left, along with all our horses, saddles, and bridles, and Frithof at first demanded a sum at least double the worth of those things, though in truth he was glad to be rid of *Tyr's Daughter*. She might have been a fine ship once, but she was old and she was small. A ship needs fifty or sixty men to be safe, and *Tyr's Daughter* would have been crowded by thirty men, but she was perfect for my purpose. If I had not bought her I suspect she would have been broken up for firewood and, in truth, I got her cheap. "She'll get you to Frisia," Frithof assured me.

We spat on our palms, shook hands, and so I became the owner of *Tyr's Daughter*. I had to buy pine tar to caulk her, and we spent two days on the river bank forcing a thick mix of hot tar, horsehair, moss, and fleece into the planking. Her mast, sails, and hemp rigging were brought from storage to the meadow where the boats were grounded, and I insisted my men leave the filthy tavern and sleep with the ship. We rigged the sail as a tent over her and slept either in or beneath her hull.

Frithof seemed to like us, or else he just approved of the notion that one of his ships was going back into the water. He would bring ale to the meadow, which lay some four or five hundred paces from the nearest part of Snotengaham's ramparts, and he would drink with us and tell old stories of long-ago fights, and in return I told him of the voyages I had made. "I miss the sea," he said wistfully.

"Come with us," I invited him.

He shook his head ruefully. "Jarl Sigurd's a good lord, he looks after me."

"Will I see him before I leave?" I asked.

"I doubt it," Frithof said, "he and his son have gone to help your old friend."

"Haesten?"

Frithof nodded. "You stayed with him through the winter?"

"He kept promising us other men would join him," I invented. "He said they'd come from Ireland, but no one did."

"He did well enough last summer," Frithof said.

"Until the Saxons took his fleet," I commented sourly.

"Uhtred of Bebbanburg," Frithof spoke just as sourly, then touched the hammer he wore about his neck. "Uhtred is besieging him now. Is that why you left?"

"I don't want to die in Britain. So, yes, that's why we left."

Frithof smiled. "Uhtred will die in Britain, my friend. Jarl Sigurd has gone to kill the bastard."

I touched my hammer. "May the gods give the jarl victory," I said piously.

"Kill Uhtred," Frithof said, "and Mercia falls, and when Alfred dies, Wessex falls." He smiled. "Why would a man want to be in Frisia when all that happens?"

"I miss home," I said.

"Make your home here!" Frithof said enthusiastically. "Join Jarl Sigurd and you can choose your own estate in Wessex, you can take a dozen Saxon wives and live like a king!"

"But I have to kill Uhtred first?" I asked lightly.

Frithof touched his amulet again. "He'll die," he said, and his voice was anything but light.

"Many men have tried to kill him," I said. "Ubba tried!"

"Uhtred has never faced Jarl Sigurd in battle," Frithof said, "nor the Jarl Cnut, and Jarl Cnut's sword is swift as the snake's tongue. Uhtred will die."

"All men die."

"His death is foretold," Frithof said, and, when he saw my interest, he touched the hammer again. "There's a sorceress," he explained, "and she has seen his death."

"Where? When?"

"Who knows?" he asked. "She knows, I suppose, and that's what she promised the jarl."

I felt a sudden, strange pang of jealousy. Had Erce straddled Sigurd in the night as she had straddled me? Then I thought Ælfadell had forecast my death to Sigurd, but had denied it to me, and that meant she either lied to one of us or that Erce, despite her loveliness, was no goddess.

"Jarl Sigurd and Jarl Cnut are doomed to fight Uhtred," Frithof went on, "and the prophecy says the jarls will win, Uhtred will die, and Wessex will fall. And that means you're missing an opportunity, my friend."

"Maybe I'll come back," I said, and I thought maybe I would return to Snotengaham one day because if Alfred's dream of uniting all the lands where the English tongue was spoken were to come true then the Danes must be driven from this and every other town between Wessex and the wild Scottish frontier.

At night, when the singing had faded from Snotengaham's taverns and the dogs had gone quiet, the sentries who watched over the ships would come to our fires and accept our food and ale. That happened for three nights, and then, in the next dawn, my men chanted as they rolled *Tyr's Daughter* down a ramp of logs and so into the Trente.

She floated. It took a day to ballast her and another half-day to distribute the stones so that she floated true, just a little down at the stern. I knew she would leak, all ships leak, but by nightfall of the second day there was no evidence of water above the newly placed ballast stones. Frithof had kept his word and brought us oars, and my men rowed the ship upstream for a few miles, then turned her and brought her back. We stowed the mast on a pair of cradles, lashed the furled sail to the mast, and stacked what meager possessions we owned beneath the small half-deck at the stern. I spent what few silver coins I had left on a barrel of ale, two of dried fish, some twice-baked bread, a flitch of bacon, and a great rock-hard cheese wrapped in canvas. At dusk Frithof brought us a sea eagle's head, carved from oak, that would fit over the prow. "It's a gift," he told me.

"You're a good man," I said, and I meant it.

He watched as his slaves carried the carved head on board my ship. "May *Tyr's Daughter* serve you well," he said, touching the hammer at his neck, "and may the wind never fail you and may the sea carry you safe home."

I told the slaves to stow the head in the prow. "You've been helpful," I told Frithof warmly, "and I wish I could thank you properly." I offered him a silver arm ring, but he shook his head.

"I've no need of it," he said, "and you might need silver in Frisia. You leave in the morning?"

"Before midday," I said.

"I'll come and say farewell," he promised.

"How long to the sea?" I asked.

"You'll make it in two days," he said, "and once out of the Humbre, head a little north. Avoid the East Anglian coast."

"Trouble there?"

He shrugged. "A few ships looking for easy prey. Eohric encourages them. Just head straight out to sea and keep going." He cocked his head at the sky that was clear of clouds. "If this fine weather lasts you'll be home in four days. Five, maybe."

"Any news from Ceaster?" I asked. I was worried that Sigurd would have learned that he had been deceived and would be returning to his heartland, but Frithof had heard nothing and I assumed that Finan was still leading the jarl a dance through the hills and woods south of the old Roman fort.

There was a full moon that night, and the watchmen again came to the wharf where *Tyr's Daughter* was tethered to *Bright-Flyer* by hemp ropes. The moon glossed the river's swirls. We gave the watchmen ale, regaled them with songs and stories, and waited. A barn owl flew low, wings white as smoke, and I took the bird's swift passage as a good omen.

When the night's heart came and the dogs were silent I sent Osferth and a dozen men to a hayrick that lay halfway to the town. "Bring back as much hay as you can carry," I said.

"Hay?" one of the watchmen asked me.

"Bedding," I explained, and told Ludda to fill the man's ale-horn. The watchmen did not seem to notice that none of my men was drinking, or sense the apprehension among my crew. They drank, and I climbed aboard *Bright-Flyer* and crossed to *Tyr's Daughter*, where I pulled my mail coat over my head and strapped Serpent-Breath to my waist. One by one my men came to the boat and dressed for war, while Osferth returned with great armfuls of hay, and only then did one of the four watchmen decide that our behavior was strange.

"What are you doing?" he asked.

"Burning your ships," I said cheerfully.

He gaped at me. "You're what?"

I drew Serpent-Breath and held her blade's tip just beneath his nose. "My name is Uhtred of Bebbanburg," I said, and watched his eyes widen. "Your lord tried to kill me," I went on, "and I'm reminding him that he failed."

I left three men to watch the prisoners on the wharf, while the rest set to work on the beached ships. We used axes to splinter rowers' benches, then piled hay and tinder in the hulls' wide bellies. I made the biggest heap in *Sea-Slaughterer*, Cnut's prized ship, for she was in the center of the stranded craft. Osferth and his half-dozen men watched the town, but no one stirred from the gates, which I assumed were barred shut. Even when we used ropes to haul away the props on some of the outer ships so that they crashed over, the noise did not carry to Snotengaham.

The town lay in the north of Sigurd's land, protected from the rest of Mercia by his large estates, while to the north was the friendly territory controlled by Cnut. Maybe no town in all Britain felt farther from trouble, which was why the boats had been brought here and why Frithof had only placed four old and half-lame men to watch them. The guards were not there to repel an attack, for no one expected Snotengaham to be assaulted, but to stop petty thieving of timbers or of the charcoal used in the braziers. That charcoal was now spread across the beached ships and I heaved one of the still smoking braziers into *Sea Slaughterer*'s belly.

We put fire into the other ships, then went back to the wharf.

Flames burst bright, faded, then burst again. Smoke thickened quickly. So far it was only the tinder and charcoal burning, the oak of the ships' timbers took longer to catch, but at last I saw the heavier flames grow and spread. The wind was light and fitful, sometimes blowing the smoke down into the fire and swirling it low before releasing it to the night air. The flames bit and spread, the heat was scorching, melting tar dripped, sparks flew high, and the noise of the fire grew.

Osferth came running, leading his men down the bank between the fire-glossed river and the flames. A boat collapsed, its burning timbers crashing onto the ground and spraying fire beneath the bellies of the neighboring craft. "Men coming!" Osferth shouted.

"How many?"

"Six? Seven?"

I took ten men up the bank while Osferth put fire into the ships that were still floating. The noise of the fire was a roar punctured by the cracks of splitting timbers. *Sea-Slaughterer* was a ship of flames now, her belly a cauldron, and her long keel broke as we passed her and she sagged with a great crash and the sparks flew outward and the flames leaped higher to show me a ragged group of men running from the town. They were not many, perhaps eight or nine, and they were not dressed, but had just pulled cloaks over their jerkins. None had a weapon and they checked when they saw me, and no wonder, for I was in mail, helmeted, with Serpent-Breath in my hand. The fire reflected from her blade. I did not speak. I had my back to the fire, which roared in the night, so my face was shadowed. The men saw a line of fire-outlined warriors ready for war and they turned back toward the town to fetch help. That help was already coming. More men were crossing the meadow and, in the fire's bright light, I saw the glint of reflected blades. "Back to the wharf," I told my men.

We retreated to the wharf, which was being scorched by the nearby flames. "Osferth! Are they all burned?" I was asking about the ships that floated, all except *Tyr's Daughter* and *Bright-Flyer*.

"They're burning," he called back.

"On board!" I shouted.

I counted my men on board *Tyr's Daughter* then, as the watchmen scuttled away from the wharf, I used an ax to sever the mooring lines that held *Bright-Flyer* to the wharf. The men from the town thought I was stealing Sigurd's boat and those with weapons came to rescue her. I jumped on board *Bright-Flyer* and chopped the ax to cut the last mooring line that held her bows to the bank. She was swinging outward, held by that last line, and my blow only half cut the hemp rope. A man took a flying leap and sprawled on the benches. He swung his sword at me and the blade struck my mail and I kicked him in the face as two more men leaped from the wharf. One missed and fell between the ship and the bank, though he managed to get one hand on the topmost strake and clung on, while the other man landed beside me and rammed a short-sword at my belly. Osferth had climbed back onto *Bright-Flyer* and was coming to help me as I parried the sword with the ax. The first man hacked at me again, slicing his sword at my legs, but the blade was stopped by the strips of iron sewn into the leather of my boots. That man had hurt himself when he jumped, maybe his ankle was broken because he seemed unable to stand. He twisted around to face Osferth who swatted the sword aside, then lunged with his own. The second man panicked, and I pushed him and he fell back into the water. I slashed the ax at the taut mooring line again and it snapped and I almost lost my footing as *Bright-Flyer* surged away from the bank. The man clinging to the strake let go. Osferth's man was dying, his blood draining into the ballast stones.

"Thank you," I said to Osferth. The river's current was carrying *Bright-Flyer* and *Tyr's Daughter* downstream away from the fire, which was brighter and fiercer than ever, its smoke filling the sky and obscuring the stars. We had put tinder, charcoal, and the last brazier into *Bright-Flyer*'s hull and I tipped the brazier over, paused long enough to see the smoldering charcoal burst into flame, then climbed onto *Tyr's Daughter*. We cut *Bright-Flyer* free. A dozen of my men already had oars and they pulled the smaller ship away from the larger. I dropped the steering oar into the slot at the stern and leaned on it to guide *Tyr's Daughter* into the river's center, and just then an ax, its blade flashing reflected firelight, flew from the bank to splash harmlessly behind us.

"Put up the eagle's head!" I shouted to my men.

"Kjartan!" Frithof, mounted on a tall black stallion, was cantering down the bank, keeping pace with us. It was one of his men who had thrown the ax, and now another launched a spear that plunged into the river. "Kjartan!"

"My name is Uhtred," I called back. "Uhtred of Bebbanburg!"

"What?" he called back.

"Uhtred of Bebbanburg! Give my greeting to Jarl Sigurd!"

"You bastard!"

"Tell that slime-eater you call a lord not to try to kill me again!"

Frithof and his men had to rein in because a tributary cut across their path. He cursed me, but his voice faded as we rowed on.

The sky behind us glowed with the fire of Sigurd's fleet burning. Not every ship had caught fire, and I did not doubt that Frithof's men would rescue one or two, maybe more, from the inferno that lit the night. They would also want to pursue us, which was why *Bright-Flyer* burned as she drifted behind us. She turned on the current, the flames cradled in her sleekly beautiful belly. She would sink eventually and the steam would replace the smoke and the wreck, I hoped, would obstruct the channel. I waved to Frithof and then laughed. Sigurd would be furious when he realized that he had been duped. Not just duped, but made into a fool. His precious fleet was ashes.

The river behind us was shimmering red, while in front of us it was moon-silvered. The current carried us swiftly and I only needed a half-dozen oars to keep us straight. I steered around the outside of the river's bends where the water was deepest, always alert for the ominous sound of our keel grinding on mud, but the gods were with us and *Tyr's Daughter* slid swiftly away from that great glow of fire that marked Snotengaham. We were traveling faster than any horse, which is why I had purchased a boat to make our escape, and we had a huge lead over any ship that might try to follow us. For a time *Bright-Flyer* drifted close behind, and then after an hour or so she stopped, though the glow of her flames still flickered above the river bends. Then that too faded and I supposed she had sunk and I hoped that her wreckage obstructed the river's channel. We journeyed on.

"What did we achieve, lord?" Osferth asked. He had come to stand beside me on the small deck at the stern of *Tyr's Daughter.*

"We made Sigurd look like a fool," I said.

"But he isn't a fool."

I knew Osferth disapproved. He was no coward, but he thought, like his father, that war would yield to intelligence and that a man could reason his way to victory. Yet war, as often as not, is about emotion. "I want the Danes to fear us," I said.

"They already did."

"Now they fear us more," I said. "No Dane can attack Mercia or Wessex in the knowledge that his home is safe. We've shown we can reach deep into their land."

"Or we've stirred them to revenge," he suggested.

"Revenge?" I asked. "You think the Danes planned to leave us in peace?"

"I fear attacks on Mercia," he said, "revenge attacks."

"Buccingahamm will be burned," I said, "but I told them all to leave the hall and go to Lundene."

"You did?" he sounded surprised, then frowned. "Then Beornnoth's hall will be burned too."

I laughed at that, then touched the silver chain Osferth wore about his neck. "You want to wager that chain?" I asked.

"Why wouldn't Sigurd burn Beornnoth's hall?" he asked.

"Because Beornnoth and his son are Sigurd's men," I said.

"Beornnoth and Beortsig?"

I nodded. I had no proof, only suspicion, but Beornnoth's lands, so close to Danish Mercia, had been left unmolested and that suggested an agreement. Beornnoth, I suspected, was too old for the troubles of continual war and so had made his peace, while his son was a bitter man and full of hatred for the West Saxons, who, in his view, had taken away Mercia's independence. "I can't prove that," I told Osferth, "but I will."

"Even so, lord," he said carefully, "what did we achieve?" He gestured toward the fading glow in the sky.

"Other than annoying Sigurd?" I asked. I leaned on the steering oar, pushing *Tyr's Daughter* to the outside of a long curve in the river. The eastern sky was luminous now, small clouds stretching bright in front of the still hidden sun. Cattle watched us pass. "Your father," I said, knowing those two words would irritate him, "has held the Danes at bay for my whole lifetime. Wessex is a fortress. But you know what your father wants."

"All the lands of the English."

"And you don't get that by building a fortress. You don't defeat the Danes by defending against them. You must attack. And your father has never attacked."

"He sent ships to East Anglia," Osferth said chidingly.

Alfred had indeed once sent an expedition to East Anglia to punish Eohric's Danes who had raided Wessex, but Alfred's ships had accomplished little. The West Saxons had built large ships and their keels were too deep to penetrate the rivers and Eohric's men had simply withdrawn into shallow water, and so Alfred's fleet had threatened and then rowed away, though the threat had been sufficient to convince Eohric to keep to the treaty between Wessex and his kingdom. "If we're to unite the Saxons," I said, "it won't be with ships. It will be with shield walls and spears and swords and slaughter."

"And God's help," Osferth said.

"Even with that," I said, "and your brother knows that, and your sister knows that, and they will look for someone to lead that shield wall."

"You."

"Us. That's why we burned Sigurd's fleet, to show Wessex and Mercia who can lead them." I slapped Osferth's shoulder and grinned at him. "I'm tired of being called the shield of Mercia. I want to be the sword of the Saxons."

Alfred, if he yet lived, was dying. And I had just made his ambition my own.

We took down the eagle's head so we would not appear hostile and, under the rising sun, slid on through England.

• • •

I had been to the land of the Danes and had seen a place of sand and thin soil and though I do not doubt that the Danes have better land than any I saw, I doubt there was any better than that through which *Tyr's Daughter* made her silent voyage. The river carried us past rich fields and deep woods. The current drew the trailing willow fronds downstream. Otters twisted in the water, sinuous as they fled the shadow of our hull. Warblers were loud on the banks where the first martins gathered mud for their nests. A swan hissed at us, wings spread, and my men all hissed back and found it funny. The trees were in their new green, spreading above meadows yellowed by cowslips, while bluebells hazed the passing woods. This was what brought the Danes here, not silver, not slaves, not even reputation, but earth; deep, rich, fertile earth where crops grew and a man could raise a family without fear of starvation. Small children weeded the fields and stopped to wave at us. I saw halls and villages and herds and flocks and knew this was the real wealth that drew men across the sea.

We looked for pursuers, but saw none. We rowed, though I was reserving my men's strength, only using a half-dozen oars on each side to keep the ship moving sleekly downriver. The mayflies were thick, and fish rose to feed, and the long weeds waved underwater and *Tyr's Daughter* passed Gegnesburh and I remembered Ragnar killing the monk there. This was the town where Alfred's wife had been raised, long before the Danes came and captured it. The town had a wall and palisade, but both were in poor repair. Much of the palisade had been torn down, presumably so men could build with the oak logs, and the earth wall had eroded into the ditch, beyond which were new houses. The Danes did not care. They felt safe here. No enemy had come in a lifetime and, as far as they were concerned, no enemy would ever come. Men called greetings to us. The only ships at Gegnesburh's wharf were traders, wide-bellied and slow. I wondered if the town had a new Danish name. This was Mercia, yet it was being turned into a kingdom of Danes.

All day we rowed until, by evening, we were in the widening Humbre and the sea was spread before us, darkening as the sun sank behind us. We stepped the mast, a job that took all my men's strength to achieve, and we tightened the hemp rigging on the boat's flanks and hauled the yard and sail up. The wool and linen bellied to the southwest wind, the rigging stretched and creaked, the ship heeled, and I felt the kick of the first waves, felt *Tyr's Daughter* shiver to that first caress, and we manned all the oars and pulled hard, fighting an incoming tide as we ran east into the shadowing night. We needed oars and sail to keep her moving against the tide, but gradually its grip weakened and we ran into the widening sea that was white flecked in the dusk as the waves fought the river, and on we went and I saw no pursuing ships as we passed the mudbanks and felt our hull lifting to the wild sea waves.

Most ships go to the coast at dusk. The shipmaster will find a creek and stay there through the dark, but we rowed eastward and, once the night fell, we shipped the oars and I let the little boat be driven by the wind. She ran well. I turned her southward sometime in the darkness, then slept when the dawn came. If we were pursued I knew nothing of it, and the ships of East Anglia did not see us as we ran southward.

I knew these waters. In the new day, under a hard bright sun, we ventured closer to the coast until I recognized a landmark. We saw two other ships, but they ignored us, and we sailed on, past the great mudflats, around Fughelness and so into the Temes. The gods loved us, the days and nights of our voyage had been undisturbed, and so we came to Lundene.

I took *Tyr's Daughter* to the dock that lay beside the house I had used in Lundene. It was a house I had never thought to see again, for it was there that Gisela had died. I thought of Ælfadell and her grim prophecy that all my women would die, then consoled myself that the sorceress had not known that Sigurd's fleet would burn, so how could she have known what would happen to my women?

I had warned my folk at Buccingahamm to expect an attack and ordered them to travel south to the safety of Lundene's defenses, and I had thought to be greeted at the house by Sigunn or even by Finan, who, his decoy work done at Ceaster, was also to meet me in the city, but the house appeared empty as we pulled the last oar strokes and nosed into the dock. Men leaped ashore with mooring lines. The oars clattered as they were laid on the thwarts, and just then the house door opened and a priest came onto the terrace. "You can't leave that boat here!" he called to me.

"Who are you?" I asked.

"This is a private house." He ignored my question. He was a lean, middle-aged man with a stern face marked by pox scars. His long black robe was spotless, woven from the finest wool. His hair was neatly trimmed. He was no ordinary priest, his clothes and demeanor both spoke of privilege. "There's wharfage downstream," he said, pointing eastward.

"Who are you?" I asked again.

"The man telling you to find another place to put this boat," he said irritably, and held his stance as I pulled myself onto the wharf and confronted him. "I'll have the boat removed," he threatened, "and you'll need to pay to recover it."

"I'm tired," I said, "and I'm not moving the boat." I smelled Lundene's familiar stench, the mix of smoke and sewage, and thought of Gisela strewing lavender on the tiled floors. The thought of her gave me the usual pang of loss and waste. She had become fond of this house that had been built by the Romans, with its rooms edging a large courtyard and its great chamber facing the river.

"You can't go in there!" the priest said sternly as I walked past him. "It belongs to Plegmund."

"Plegmund?" I asked. "Does he command the garrison here?" The house was given to whoever commanded Lundene's garrison, a job that a West Saxon called Weohstan had inherited from me, but Weohstan was a friend and I knew he would welcome me beneath his roof.

"The house was granted to the archbishop," the priest said, "by Alfred."

"Archbishop?" I asked, astonished. Plegmund was the new Archbishop of Contwaraburg, a Mercian, famously pious, a friend of Alfred's and now the evident possessor of one of Lundene's finer houses. "Did a young girl come here?" I asked. "Or an Irishman? A warrior?"

The priest blanched then. He must have remembered either Sigunn or Finan coming to the house, and that recollection told him who I was. "You're Uhtred?" he asked.

"I'm Uhtred," I said and pushed the house door open. The long room, which had been so welcoming when Gisela lived here, was now a place where monks copied manuscripts. There were six tall desks on which ink pots, quills, and parchments lay. Two of the desks were occupied by clerks. One was writing, copying a manuscript, while the other was using a ruler and a needle to prick lines on an empty parchment. The pricked lines were a guide to keep the writing straight. The two men glanced at me nervously, then went back to their copying. "So did a girl come here?" I asked the priest. "A Danish girl. Slight and pretty. She'd have had a half-dozen warriors escorting her."

"She did," he said, uncertain now.

"And?"

"She went to a tavern," he said stiffly, meaning he had rudely turned her away from the door.

"And Weohstan?" I asked. "Where's he?"

"He has quarters by the high church."

"Is Plegmund here in Lundene?" I asked.

"The archbishop is in Contwaraburg."

"And how many boats does he own?" I asked.

"None," the priest said.

"Then he doesn't need this damned dock, does he? So my boat stays there till I sell it, and if you touch it, priest, if you so much as lay one damned finger on it, if you have it moved, if you even think about moving it, I'll take you to sea and teach you to be Christ-like."

"To be Christ-like?" he asked.

"He walked on water, didn't he?"

That trivial confrontation left me dispirited because it was a reminder of how the church had placed its clammy grip on Alfred's Wessex. It seemed that the king had granted Plegmund and Werferth, who was the Bishop of Wygraceaster, half of Lundene's wharfage. Alfred wanted the church to be rich and its bishops to be powerful men because he relied on them to spread and enforce his laws and, if I helped spread Wessex's grip northward, so those bishops and priests and monks and nuns would follow to impose their joyless rules. Yet I was committed now, committed because of Æthelflaed, who was now in Wintanceaster. Weohstan told me that. "The king asked his family to gather," he said gloomily, "ready for his death." Weohstan was a stolid, bald, half-toothless West Saxon who commanded Lundene's garrison. Lundene was supposedly Mercian, but Alfred had ensured that every man of power in the city held allegiance to Wessex, and Weohstan was a good man, unimaginative but diligent. "Except I need money to repair the walls," he grumbled to me, "and they won't give it to me. They send coin to Rome to keep the pope in ale, yet they won't pay for my wall."

"Steal it," I suggested.

"Not that we've seen a Dane in months," he said.

"Except for Sigunn," I said.

"She's a pretty thing," he said, offering me one of his half-toothed smiles. He had offered her shelter while she waited for me. She had no news from Buccingahamm, but I suspected the hall there, with its barns and storehouses, would be a smoldering ruin as soon as Sigurd returned from his foray to Ceaster.

Finan arrived two days later, grinning happily and full of news. "We led Sigurd a dance," he told me, "and danced him straight into the Welsh."

"And Haesten?"

"God knows."

Finan told how he and Merewalh had retreated southward into the deep woods, and how Sigurd had followed them. "Jesus, he was eager. He sent horsemen after us on a dozen paths and we ambushed one group." He gave me a bag of silver, the spoils of the dead who had been cut down beneath the oaks. Sigurd, enraged, had become even less cautious and tried to encircle his elusive prey by sending men to the west and south, but all he had achieved was to stir up the Welsh, who never need much stirring, and a band of wild Welsh warriors came from the hills to kill the Northmen. Sigurd had held the attackers off with his shield wall, then suddenly retreated northward.

"He must have heard about his ships," I said.

"He'll be an unhappy man," Finan said happily.

"And I'm a poor one," I said. Buccingahamm was probably burned and there were no rents being paid. My men's families were all in Lundene, and *Tyr's Daughter* was sold for a pittance, and Æthelflaed was in no position to help. She was in Wintanceaster, close to her ailing father, and her husband was there too. She sent me a letter, but it was bland, even unfriendly, which made me suppose that she knew her correspondence was being read, but I had told her of my poverty and the letter suggested I go to one of her estates in the Temes valley. The steward there was a man who had fought alongside me at Beamfleot and he, at least, was pleased to see me. He had been crippled in that fight, though he could walk with a crutch and ride a horse well enough. He lent me money. Ludda stayed with me. I told him I would pay him for his services when I was wealthy again, and that he was free to go, but he wanted to stay. He was learning to use the sword and shield, and I was glad of his company. Two of my Frisians left, deciding that they could do better with another lord, and I let them go. I was in the same plight as Haesten, my men wondering whether they had sworn their oaths to the wrong man.

Then, as the summer waned, Sihtric returned.

Five

It was a summer of hunting and patrolling. Idle men are unhappy men and so I purchased horses with the silver I had borrowed and we rode north to explore the borders of Sigurd's land. If Sigurd knew I was there he did not respond, perhaps fearing another trick like the one that had led his men into a pointless fight with the savage Welsh, but we were not looking for a fight. I did not have enough men to face Sigurd. I flaunted my banner, yet in truth it was all a bluff.

Haesten was still in Ceaster, though now that garrison was five times the size that it had been in the spring. The newcomers were not Haesten's warriors, but oath-men of Sigurd and his ally Cnut Longsword, and they had come in sufficient numbers to guard the whole circuit of the old fort's walls. They had hung their shields from the palisade and put their banners on the southern gatehouse. Sigurd's badge of the flying raven was displayed next to Cnut's flag, which showed an ax and a shattered cross. There was no flag for Haesten, which told me he had submitted to one of the two greater lords.

Merewalh reckoned there were now a thousand men in the fort. "They try and provoke us," he told me. "They want a fight."

"You're not giving them one?"

He shook his head. He had only a hundred and fifty warriors and so he retreated whenever Ceaster's garrison made a sally. "I'm not sure how long we can stay here," he admitted.

"Have you asked Lord Æthelred for help?"

"I asked," he said bleakly.

"And?"

"He says we should just watch them," Merewalh said, sounding disgusted. Æthelred had enough men to provoke war, he could have taken Ceaster whenever he wished, but instead he did nothing.

I announced my presence by riding close to the walls with my wolf's head banner and, just as before, Haesten could not resist the lure. He brought a dozen men this time, but approached me on his own, hands spread wide. He was still grinning. "That was clever, my friend," he greeted me.

"Clever?"

"Jarl Sigurd was not pleased. He came to rescue me and you burned his fleet! He's not happy."

"I didn't want his happiness."

"And he's sworn you'll die."

"I think you once swore the same."

"I fulfill my oaths," he said.

"You break oaths like a clumsy child breaks eggs," I said scornfully. "So who did you bow the knee to? Sigurd?"

"To Sigurd," he admitted, "and in return he sent me his son and seven hundred men." He gestured toward the horsemen who had accompanied him and I saw the sullen young face of Sigurd Sigurdson scowling at me.

"So who commands here?" I asked. "You or the boy?"

"I do," Haesten said. "My job is to teach him sense."

"Sigurd expects you to do that?" I asked, and Haesten had the grace to laugh. He was looking beyond me, at the tree line, trying to determine how many men I might have brought to reinforce Merewalh. "Enough to destroy you," I answered his unspoken question.

"I doubt that," he said, "or else you wouldn't be talking, you'd be fighting."

That was true enough. "So what did Sigurd promise you in return for your oath?" I asked.

"Mercia," came the reply.

It was my turn to laugh. "You get Mercia? Who rules Wessex?"

"Whoever Sigurd and Cnut decide," he said airily, then smiled.

"Maybe you? I think if you grovel, Lord Uhtred, the Jarl Sigurd will forgive you. He'd rather you fought with him than against him."

"Tell him I'd rather kill him," I said. I gathered my stallion's reins. "How is your wife?"

"Brunna is well," he said, looking surprised that I had asked.

"Is she still a Christian?" I asked. Brunna had been baptized, but I suspected the whole ceremony had been a cynical exercise by Haesten to allay Alfred's suspicions.

"She believes in the Christian god," Haesten said, sounding disgusted. "She's forever wailing to him."

"I pray she has a comfortable widowhood," I said.

I turned away, but just then a man shouted and I twisted back to see Sigurd Sigurdson spurring toward me. "Uhtred!" he shouted.

I curbed the horse, turned, waited.

"Fight me," he said, dropping from the saddle and drawing his sword.

"Sigurd!" Haesten said in warning.

"I am Sigurd Sigurdson!" the pup shouted. He was glaring up at me, sword ready.

"Not now," Haesten said.

"Listen to your nursemaid," I told the boy, and that provoked him to swing the blade at me. I parried it with my right foot so that the sword struck the metal of the stirrup.

"No!" Haesten shouted.

Sigurd spat toward me. "You're old, you're frightened." He spat again, then raised his voice. "Let men say that Uhtred ran away from Sigurd Sigurdson!"

He was eager, he was young, he was a fool. He was a big enough lad, and his sword was a fine blade, but his ambition outstripped his ability. He wanted to make a reputation and I remembered how I had wanted the same at his age, and how the gods had loved me. Did they love Sigurd Sigurdson? I said nothing, but kicked my feet from the stirrups and swung myself down from the saddle. I drew Serpent-Breath slowly, smiling at the boy and seeing the first shadow of doubt in his belligerent face.

"Please, no!" Haesten called. His men had closed up, and so had mine.

I held my arms wide, inviting Sigurd to attack. He hesitated, but he had made the challenge and if he did not fight now then he would look a coward and that thought was unbearable and so he leaped toward me, his blade snake fast, and I parried it, surprised at his speed, then pushed him with my free hand so that he staggered back. He slashed again, a wild stroke, and I parried it again. I was letting him attack, doing nothing except defend myself, and that passivity drove him to a greater fury. He had been taught sword-craft, but he forgot that teaching in his rage. He swung wildly, the blows easy to block, and I heard Haesten's men calling advice. "Use the point!"

"Fight me!" he shouted, and swung again.

"Puppy," I said to him, and he was almost weeping in frustration. He sliced the sword at my head, the blade hissing in the summer air and I just leaned back and the point whipped past my eyes and I stepped forward, thrust with my free hand again, only this time I hooked a boot behind his left ankle and he went down like a hamstrung bullock and I thrust Serpent-Breath onto his neck. "Grow up before you fight me," I told him. He twisted, then went very still as he felt my sword's point digging into his neck. "Today isn't your day to die, Sigurd Sigurdson," I said. "Now let go of your sword."

He made a mewing noise.

"Let go of your sword," I snarled, and this time he obeyed me. "Was it your father's gift?" I asked him. He said nothing. "It isn't your day to die," I told him again, "but it is a day I want you to remember. The day you challenged Uhtred of Bebbanburg." I held his gaze for a few heartbeats, then slashed Serpent-Breath fast, using my wrist rather than my arm, so that the tip of her blade sliced into his sword hand. He flinched as the blood spurted, then I stepped away, stooped, and picked up his sword. "Tell his father I spared the pup's life," I told Haesten. I wiped Serpent-Breath's point on the hem of my cloak, tossed the boy's sword to Oswi, my servant, than hauled myself back into the saddle. Sigurd Sigurdson was clutching his mangled hand. "Give my greetings to your father," I told him, then spurred away. I could almost hear Haesten's sigh of relief that the boy still lived.

Why did I let him live? Because he was not worth killing. I wanted to provoke his father, and the boy's death would certainly have achieved that, but I did not have the men to fight a war against Sigurd. To do that I needed West Saxon troops. I had to wait until I was ready, until Wessex and Mercia united their forces, and so Sigurd Sigurdson lived.

We did not stay at Ceaster. We did not have enough force to capture the old fort, and the longer we stayed the more likely it was that Sigurd would arrive with overwhelming numbers, and so we left Merewalh to screen the fortress and we went back to Æthelflaed's estate in the valley of the Temes from where I sent a messenger to Alfred telling him that Haesten had sworn allegiance to Sigurd and that Ceaster was now fully garrisoned. I knew Alfred would be too sick to take much note of that news, but I assumed that Edward, or perhaps the Witan, would want to know. I received no answer. Summer slid into autumn and the silence from Wintanceaster was worrying me. We learned from travelers that the king was weaker than ever, that he scarcely left his bed these days and that his family was in constant attendance. I heard nothing at all from Æthelflaed.

"He could at least have thanked you for thwarting Eohric," Finan grumbled to me one night. He meant Alfred, of course.

"He was probably disappointed," I said.

"That you lived?"

I smiled at that. "That the treaty never happened."

Finan stared moodily down the hall. The fire in the central hearth was unlit because the evening was warm. My men were quiet at their tables, the dogs sprawled on the rushes. "We need silver," Finan said bleakly.

"I know."

How had I become so poor? I had spent most of my money on that foray north to Ælfadell and Snotengaham. I still had some silver, but nowhere near enough for my ambition, which was to retake Bebbanburg, that great fortress by the sea, and to take it I would need men, ships, weapons, food, and time. I needed a fortune, and I was living on borrowed money in a shabby hall on Mercia's southern edge. I was living on Æthelflaed's charity, and that seemed to be turning cold because I received no letter from her. I supposed she was under the baleful influence of her family and their busy priests who were ever ready to tell us how to behave. "Alfred doesn't deserve you," Finan said.

"He has other things on his mind," I said, "like his death."

"He wouldn't be alive now if it wasn't for you."

"For us," I said.

"And what has he done for us?" Finan demanded. "Jesus and his saints, we destroy Alfred's enemies and he treats us like dog shit."

I said nothing. A harpist was playing in the hall's corner, but his music was soft and plangent to match my mood. The light was fading and two servant girls brought rushlights for the table. I watched Ludda slide his hand up a skirt and wondered that he had remained with me, though when I had asked him he had said that fortunes rise and fortunes fall and he sensed mine would rise again. I hoped he was right. "What happened to that Welsh girl of yours?" I called to Ludda. "What was her name?"

"Teg, lord. She turned into a bat and flew away." He grinned, though I noted how many men made the sign of the cross.

"Maybe we should all turn into bats," I said unhappily.

Finan scowled at the tabletop. "If Alfred doesn't want you," he said uneasily, "then you should join Alfred's enemies."

"I swore an oath to Æthelflaed."

"And she swore one to her husband," he said savagely.

"I won't fight against her," I said.

"And I won't leave you," Finan said, and I knew he meant it, "but not every man here will stay through a hungry winter."

"I know," I said.

"So let's steal a ship," he urged, "and go Viking."

"It's late in the year for that," I said.

"God knows how we survive a winter," he grumbled. "We have to do something. Kill someone rich."

And just then the guards on the hall door challenged a visitor. The man arrived in mail, helmeted, and with a sheathed sword at his waist. Behind him, dim in the fast gathering darkness, was a woman and two children. "I demand entry!" he shouted.

"God alive," Finan said, recognizing Sihtric's voice.

One of the guards tried to take the sword, but Sihtric angrily slapped the man aside. "Let the bastard keep his sword," I said, standing, "and let him come in." Sihtric's wife and two sons were behind him, but they stayed at the door as Sihtric paced up the hall. There was silence.

Finan stood to confront him, but I pushed the Irishman down. "It's my duty," I told Finan quietly, then walked around the high table's end and jumped down to the rush-covered floor. Sihtric stopped when he saw me approaching. I had no sword. We did not carry weapons in hall because weapons and ale mix badly and there was a gasp as Sihtric drew his long blade. Some of my men stood to intervene, but I waved them down and kept walking toward the naked steel. I stopped just two paces from him. "Well?" I demanded harshly.

Sihtric grinned and I laughed. I embraced him, and he returned the embrace, then held the hilt of his sword to me. "Yours, lord," he said, "as it always was."

"Ale!" I shouted to the steward. "Ale and food!"

Finan was gaping as I walked Sihtric to the high table with my arm about his shoulder. Men were cheering. They had liked Sihtric and had been puzzled by his behavior, but it had all been planned between us. Even the insults had been rehearsed. I had wanted Beortsig to recruit him, and Beortsig had snapped up Sihtric like a pike attacking a duckling. And I had ordered Sihtric to stay in Beortsig's employment until he had learned what I needed to know, and now he had come back. "I didn't know where to find you, lord," he said, "so I went to Lundene first and Weohstan said to come here."

Beornnoth was dead, he told me. The old man had died in the early summer, just before Sigurd's men crossed his estates to burn Buccingahamm. "They stayed the night at the hall, lord," he told me.

"Sigurd's men?"

"And Sigurd himself, lord. Beortsig fed them."

"He's in Sigurd's pay?"

"Yes, lord," he said, and that was no surprise, "and not only Beortsig, lord. There was a Saxon with Sigurd, lord, a man Sigurd treated with honor. A long-haired man called Sigebriht."

"Sigebriht?" I asked. The name was familiar, lurking at the back of my memory, but I could not place him, though I remembered the widow in Buchestanes saying that a long-haired Saxon had visited Ælfadell.

"Sigebriht of Cent, lord," Sihtric said.

"Ah!" I poured Sihtric ale. "Sigebriht's father is Ealdorman of Cent, isn't he?"

"Ealdorman Sigelf, lord, yes."

"So Sigebriht is unhappy that Edward was named King of Cent?" I guessed.

"Sigebriht hates Edward, lord," Sihtric told me. He was grinning, pleased with himself. I had planted him as a spy in Beortsig's household and he knew he had done his work well. "And it isn't just because Edward is King of Cent, lord, it's because of a girl. The Lady Ecgwynn."

"He told you all this?" I asked, astonished.

"He told a slave girl, lord. He rutted her and he has a loose tongue when he's rutting, and he told her and she told Ealhswith." Ealhswith was Sihtric's wife. She was sitting in the hall now, eating with her two sons. She had been a whore and I had advised Sihtric not to marry her, but I had been wrong. She had proved to be a good wife.

"So who is the Lady Ecgwynn?" I asked.

"She's Bishop Swithwulf's daughter, lord," Sihtric explained. Swithwulf was Bishop of Hrofeceastre in Cent, that much I knew, but I had not met the man, nor his daughter. "And she preferred Edward to Sigebriht," Sihtric went on.

So the bishop's daughter was the girl who Edward had wanted to marry? The girl he had been ordered to abandon because his father disapproved. "I heard that Edward was forced to give the girl up," I said.

"But she ran away with him," Sihtric told me, "that's what Sigebriht said."

"Ran away!" I grinned. "So where is she now?"

"No one knows."

"And Edward," I said, "is betrothed to Ælflæd." There must have been some harsh words spoken between father and son, I thought. Edward had always been presented as the ideal heir to Alfred, the son without sin, the prince educated and groomed to be the next

King of Wessex, but a smile from a bishop's daughter had evidently undone a lifetime's preaching from his father's priests. "So Sigebriht hates Edward," I said.

"He does, lord."

"Because he took the bishop's daughter away. But would that be enough to make him swear loyalty to Sigurd?"

"No, lord." Sihtric was grinning. He had kept his biggest news back. "He's not sworn to Sigurd, lord, but to Æthelwold."

And that was why Sihtric had returned to me, because he had discovered who the Saxon was, the Saxon who Ælfadell had told me would destroy Wessex, and I wondered why I had not thought of it before. I had considered Beortsig because he wanted to be King of Mercia, but he was insignificant, and Sigebriht probably wanted to be King of Cent one day, but I could not imagine Sigebriht having the power to ruin Wessex, yet the answer was obvious. It had been there all along and I had never thought of it because Æthelwold was such a weak fool. Yet weak fools have ambition and cunning and resolve.

"Æthelwold!" I repeated the name.

"Sigebriht is sworn to him, lord, and Sigebriht is Æthelwold's messenger to Sigurd. There's something else, lord. Beortsig's priest is one-eyed, thin as a straw, and bald."

I was thinking about Æthelwold, so it took a moment for me to remember that far-off day when the fools had tried to kill me and the shepherd had saved me with his sling and his flock. "Beortsig wanted me dead," I said.

"Or his father," Sihtric suggested.

"Because Sigurd ordered it," I guessed, "or perhaps Æthelwold." And it suddenly seemed so obvious. And I knew what I had to do. I did not want to do it. I had once sworn I would never return to Alfred's court, but next day I rode to Wintanceaster.

To see the king.

Æthelwold. I should have guessed. I had known Æthelwold all my life and had despised him all that time. He was Alfred's nephew, and he was aggrieved. Alfred, of course, should have killed Æthelwold years before, but some feeling, perhaps affection for his brother's son or, more likely, the guilt that earnest Christians love to feel, had stayed his hand.

Æthelwold's father had been Alfred's brother, King Æthelred. Æthelwold, as eldest son of Æthelred, expected to be King of Wessex, but he was still a child when his father died and the Witan, the king's council of leading men, had put his uncle, Alfred, onto the throne instead. Alfred had wanted that and had worked for it, and there were men who still whispered that he was a usurper. Æthelwold had resented the usurpation ever since, but Alfred, instead of murdering his nephew as I had often recommended, indulged him. He let him keep some of his father's estates, he forgave his constant treachery, and doubtless prayed for him. Æthelwold needed a lot of prayer. He was unhappy, frequently drunk, and perhaps that was why Alfred tolerated him. It was hard to see a drunken fool as a danger to the kingdom.

But Æthelwold was now talking with Sigurd. Æthelwold wanted to be king instead of Edward, and to make himself king he had plainly sought the alliance of Sigurd, and Sigurd, of course, would like nothing better than a tame Saxon whose claim to the throne of Wessex was every bit as good as Edward's, indeed better, which meant Sigurd's invasion of Wessex would have the spurious gloss of legitimacy.

Six of us rode south through Wessex. I took Osferth, Sihtric, Rypere, Eadric, and Ludda. I left Finan in command of the rest of my men, and with a promise. "If there's no gratitude in Wintanceaster," I said, "then we go north."

"We must do something," Finan said.

"I promise," I told him. "We'll go Viking. We'll thrive. But I must give Alfred one last chance."

Finan did not much care which side we fought for, so long as we were fighting profitably, and I understood how he felt. If my ambition was to one day retake Bebbanburg, his was to return to Ireland to take revenge on the man who had destroyed his wealth and family, and for that he needed silver as much as I did. Finan, of course, was a Christian, though he never allowed that to interfere with his pleasures, and he would have happily used his sword to attack Wessex if, at the end of the fighting, there was money enough to equip an expedition back to Ireland. I knew he believed my journey to Wintanceaster was a waste of time. Alfred did not like me, Æthelflaed appeared to have distanced herself from me, and Finan believed I was going to beg from folk who should have shown gratitude from the start.

And there were times on that journey when I thought Finan was right. I had fought to help Wessex survive for so many years now, and I had put so many of her enemies beneath the ground, and to show for it I had nothing but an empty purse. Yet I also had a reluctant allegiance. I have broken oaths, I have changed sides, I have scrambled through the thorns of loyalty, yet I had meant it when I told Osferth that I wanted to be the sword of the Saxons instead of the shield of Mercia, and so I would make one last visit to the heart of Saxon Britain to discover whether they wanted my sword or not. And if not? I had friends in the north. There was Ragnar, closer than a friend, a man I loved as a brother, and he would help me, and if the price I had to pay was eternal enmity for Wessex, then so be it. I rode, not as the beggar that Finan thought I was, but vengefully.

It rained as we neared Wintanceaster, a soft rain on a soft land, on fields rich with good earth, on villages that showed prosperity and had new churches and thick thatch and no gaunt skeletons of burned house-beams. The halls grew larger, because men like to have their land near power.

There were two powers in Wessex, king and church, and the churches, like the halls, grew larger as we neared the city. No wonder the Northmen wanted this land, who would not? The cattle were plump, the barns were full, and the girls were pretty. "It's time you got married," I told Osferth as we passed an open-doored barn where two fair-haired girls winnowed grain on a threshing floor.

"I've thought of it," he said gloomily.

"Just thought?"

He half smiled. "You believe in destiny, lord," he said.

"And you don't?" I asked. Osferth and I were riding a few paces ahead of the others. "And what does destiny have to do with a girl in your bed?"

"Non ingredietur mamzer hoc est de scorto natus in ecclesiam Domini," he said, then gave me a very somber look, *"usque ad decimam generationem."*

"Both Father Beocca and Father Willibald tried to teach me Latin," I said, "and they both failed."

"It comes from the scriptures, lord," he said, "from the book of Deuteronomy, and it means a bastard isn't allowed into the church and it warns that the curse will last for ten generations."

I stared at him in disbelief. "You were training to be a priest when I met you!"

"And I left my training," he said. "I had to. How could I be a priest when God bans me from his congregation?"

"So you can't be a priest," I said, "but you can be married!"

"Usque ad decimam generationem," he said. "My children would be cursed, and their children too, and every child for ten generations."

"So every bastard is doomed?"

"God tells us that, lord."

"Then he's a bloody-minded god," I said savagely, then saw that his distress was real. "It wasn't your fault that Alfred played piggyback with a servant girl."

"True, lord."

"So how can his sin affect you?"

"God is not always fair, lord, but he is just within his rules."

"Just! So if I can't catch a thief I should whip his children instead and you'd call me just?"

"God abhors sin, lord, and what better way to avert sin than threaten it with the direst punishment?" He edged his horse to the left side of the road to allow a string of packhorses to pass by. They were traveling northward, carrying sheepskins. "If God didn't punish us severely," Osferth went on, "then what is to stop sin spreading?"

"I like sin," I said and nodded to the horseman whose servants led the packhorses. "Does Alfred live?" I asked him.

"Scarcely," the man said. He made the sign of the cross and nodded thanks when I wished him a safe journey.

Osferth frowned at me. "Why did you bring me here, lord?" he asked.

"Why not?"

"You could have brought Finan, but you chose me."

"You don't want to see your father?"

He said nothing for a while, then turned to me and I saw there were tears in his eyes. "Yes, lord."

"That's why I brought you," I said, and just then we turned a bend in the road and Wintanceaster was beneath us, its new church rearing high above the huddle of roofs.

Wintanceaster was, of course, the chief of Alfred's burhs, those towns fortified against the Danes. It was surrounded by a deep ditch, flooded in places, beyond which was a high earthen bank topped by a palisade of oak trunks. There are few things worse than assaulting such a place. The defenders, like Haesten's men at Beamfleot, hold all the advantage and can rain weapons and stones on the attackers, who have to struggle through obstacles and try to climb ladders that are being hacked apart by axes. Alfred's burhs were what had made Wessex safe. The Danes could still ravage the countryside, but everything of value would be pulled inside the burh walls and the Danes could only ride around those walls and make empty threats. The surest way to capture a burh was to starve its garrison into submission, but that could take weeks or months, and for all that time the besiegers would be vulnerable to troops coming from other fortresses. The alternative was to throw men at the walls and watch them die in the ditch and the Danes were never profligate with men. The burhs were strongholds, too strong for the Danes, and Bebbanburg, I thought, was tougher than any burh.

The northern gateway to Wintanceaster was now made of stone and guarded by a dozen men who barred the open arch. Their leader was a small grizzled man with fierce eyes who waved his troops away when he saw me. "It's Grimric, lord," he said, obviously expecting to be recognized.

"You were at Beamfleot," I guessed.

"I was, lord!" he said, pleased that I remembered.

"Where you did great slaughter," I said, hoping it was true.

"We showed the bastards how Saxons fight, lord, didn't we?" he said, grinning. "I keep telling these lily boys that you know how to give a man a real fight!" He jerked a thumb at his men, all of whom were youngsters pulled away from their farms or shops to serve their term of weeks in the burh's garrison. "They're still wet with mama's milk, lord," Grimric said.

I gave him a coin I could scarce afford to give, but such things are expected of a lord. "Buy them ale," I told Grimric.

"That I shall, lord," he said, "and I knew you'd come! I have to tell them you're here, of course, but I knew everything would be all right."

"All right?" I asked, puzzled by his words.

"I knew it would be, lord!" He grinned, then waved us on. I went to the Two Cranes, where the owner knew me. He shouted at his servants to look after our horses, brought us ale, and gave us a large chamber at the back of the tavern where the straw was clean.

The landlord was a one-armed man with a beard so long that he tucked its lower end into a wide leather belt. He was named Cynric, had lost his lower left arm fighting for Alfred, and had owned the Two Cranes for over twenty years, and there was not much that went on in Wintanceaster that he did not know about. "The churchmen rule," he told me.

"Not Alfred?"

"Poor bastard's sick as a drunken dog. It's a miracle he still lives."

"And Edward's under the thumb of the clergy?" I asked.

"The clergy," Cynric said, "his mother, and the Witan. But he's not nearly as pious as they think. You heard about the Lady Ecgwynn?"

"The bishop's daughter?"

"That's the one, and she was a lovely thing, God knows. Just a little girl she was, but so beautiful."

"She's dead?"

"Died giving birth."

I stared at him, the implications tumbling in my head. "Are you sure?"

"God's teeth, I know the woman who midwifed her! Ecgwynn produced twins, a boy called Æthelstan and a girl called Eadgyth, but the poor mother died that same night."

"Edward was the father?" I asked and Cynric nodded. "Twin royal bastards," I said softly.

Cynric shook his head. "But are they bastards?" He kept his voice low. "Edward claims he married her, his father says it wasn't legal, and his father wins that argument. And they kept the whole thing quiet! God knows they paid the midwife well enough."

"The children lived?"

"They're in Saint Hedda's nunnery, with the Lady Æthelflaed."

I stared into the fire. So the perfect heir had proved as sinful as the next man. And Alfred was sweeping away the fruits of that sin, tucking them into a nunnery in hope no one would notice them. "Poor Edward," I said.

"He's marrying Ælflæd now," Cynric said, "which pleases Alfred."

"And he already has two children," I said in wonderment. "That's a royal mess. You say Æthelflaed is in Saint Hedda's?"

"Locked away there," Cynric said. He knew of my attachment to Æthelflaed, and his tone suggested she had been locked away to keep her from me.

"Her husband's here?"

"In Alfred's palace. The whole family is here, even Æthelwold."

"Æthelwold!"

"Came here two weeks back, weeping and wailing for his uncle."

Æthelwold was braver than I thought. He had made his alliance with the Danes, yet was brazen enough to come to his dying uncle's court. "Is he still drunk?" I asked.

"Not that I know of. He hasn't been in here. They say he spends his time praying." He spoke scornfully, and I laughed. "We're all praying," he finished glumly, meaning that everyone worried about what happened when Alfred died.

"And Saint Hedda's?" I asked. "Is it still Abbess Hildegyth?"

"She's a saint herself, lord, yes, she's still there."

I took Osferth to Saint Hedda's. The rain was spitting, making the streets greasy. The convent lay on the northern edge of the town, close by the earthen bank with its high palisade. The only door to the nunnery lay at the end of a long, muddy alley that, just like the last time I had visited, was crowded with beggars who were waiting for the alms and food that the nuns distributed morning and evening. The beggars shuffled out of our way. They were nervous because Osferth and I were both in mail and both carrying swords. Some held out hands or wooden bowls, but I ignored them, puzzled by the presence of three soldiers at the nunnery door. The three wore helmets and carried spears, swords, and shields, and as we approached they stepped away from the door to bar our path. "You can't go inside, lord," one of them said.

"You know who I am?"

"You're the Lord Uhtred," the man said respectfully, "and you can't go inside."

"The abbess is an old friend," I said, and that was true. Hild was a friend, a saint, and a woman I had loved, but it seemed I was not allowed to visit her. The leader of the three soldiers was a well-set man, not young, but with broad shoulders and a confident face. His sword was sheathed, and I did not doubt he would draw it if I tried to force my way past him, but nor did I doubt that I could beat him down into the mud. Yet there were three of them, and I knew Osferth would not fight against West Saxon soldiers who guarded a convent. I shrugged. "You can give the Abbess Hild a message?" I asked.

"I can do that, lord."

"Tell her Uhtred came to visit her."

He nodded, and I heard the beggars gasp behind me and turned to see even more soldiers filing up the alley. I recognized their commander, a man called Godric who had served under Weohstan. He led seven helmeted men who, like those guarding the convent, had shields and spears. They were ready for battle. "I'm asked to take you to the palace, lord," Godric greeted me.

"You need spears to do that?"

Godric ignored the question, gesturing back down the alley instead. "You'll come?"

"With pleasure," I said, and followed him back through the town. The people in the streets watched us pass in silence. Osferth and I had kept our swords, but we still looked as though we were prisoners under escort and, when we reached the palace gate, a steward insisted we give up those weapons. That was normal. Only the king's bodyguards were allowed to carry weapons inside the palace precincts and so I handed Serpent-Breath to the stewards, then followed Godric past Alfred's private chapel to a small low thatched building.

"You're asked to wait inside, lord," he said, indicating the door.

We waited in a windowless room that was furnished with two benches, a reading desk, and a crucifix. Godric's men stayed outside and, when I tried to leave, spears barred my way. "We want food," I said, "and ale. And a bucket to piss in."

"Are we under arrest?" Osferth asked me after the food and bucket had been brought.

"It looks that way."

"Why?"

"I don't know," I said. I ate the bread and hard cheese and then, though the room's earth floor was damp, I lay down and tried to sleep.

It was dusk before Godric returned. He was still courteous. "You'll come with me, lord," he said, and Osferth and I followed him through familiar courtyards to one of the smaller halls where a fire burned bright in the hearth. There were painted leather hangings on the wall, each showing a different West Saxon saint, while at the hall's high end, at a table spread with a blue-dyed cloth, sat five churchmen. Three were strangers to me, but I recognized the other two and neither was a friend. Bishop Asser, the poisonous Welsh priest who was Alfred's closest confidant was one, while Bishop Erkenwald was the other. They flanked a thin-shouldered man whose tonsured hair was white above a face as lean as a starving weasel's. He had a blade for a nose, intelligent eyes, and pinched, narrow lips that could not hide his crooked teeth. The two priests at either end of the table were much younger and each had a quill, an ink pot, and a sheet of parchment. They were there, it seemed, to take notes.

"Bishop Erkenwald," I greeted him, then looked at Asser. "I don't think I know you."

"Take that hammer from his neck," Asser said to Godric.

"Touch that hammer," I told Godric, "and I'll dump your arse in the fire."

"Enough!" The starving weasel slapped the table. The ink pots jumped. The two clerk-priests were scratching away. "I am Plegmund," the man told me.

"High sorcerer of Contwaraburg?" I asked.

He stared at me with obvious dislike, then drew a sheet of parchment toward him. "You have some explaining to do," he said.

"And no lies this time!" Asser spat. Years before, in this same hall, I had been tried by the Witan for offenses of which, in truth, I was wholly guilty. The chief witness of my crimes had been Asser, but I had lied my way out and he had known I had lied and he had despised me ever since.

I frowned at him. "What is your name?" I asked. "You remind me of someone. He was a Welsh earsling, a ratlike little shit, but I killed him, so you can't be the same man."

"Lord Uhtred," Bishop Erkenwald said tiredly, "please do not insult us."

Erkenwald and I were not fond of each other, but in his time as Bishop of Lundene he had proved an efficient ruler and he had not stood in my way before Beamfleot, indeed his skills as an organizer had contributed mightily to that victory. "What do you want explained?" I asked.

Archbishop Plegmund pulled a candle across the table to illuminate the parchment. "We have been told of your activities this summer," he said.

"And you want to thank me," I said.

The cold, sharp eyes stared at me. Plegmund had become famous as a man who denied himself every pleasure, whether it was food, women, or luxury. He served his god by being uncomfortable, by praying in lonely places, and by being a hermit priest. Why folk think that admirable, I do not know, but he was held in awe by the Christians, who were all delighted when he abandoned his hermit's discomfort to become archbishop. "In the spring," he said in a thin, precise voice, "you had a meeting with the man who calls himself Jarl Haesten, following which meeting you rode north into the country possessed by Cnut Ranulfson where you consulted the witch, Ælfadell. From there you went to Snotengaham, presently occupied by Sigurd Thorrson, and thereafter to the Jarl Haesten again."

"All true," I said easily, "only you've left some things out."

"Here come the lies," Asser sneered.

I frowned at him. "Was your mother straining at stool when you were born?"

Plegmund slapped the table again. "What have we left out?"

"The small truth that I burned Sigurd's fleet."

Osferth had been looking increasingly alarmed at the hostility in the room and now, without a word to me, and without any demurral from the clerics at the linen-covered table, he edged back to the door. They let him go. It was me they wanted.

"The fleet was burned, we know," Plegmund said, "and we know the reason."

"Tell me."

"It was a sign to the Danes that there can be no retreat across the water. Sigurd Thorrson is telling his followers that their fate is to capture Wessex, and as proof of that fate he burned his own ships to demonstrate that there can be no withdrawal."

"You believe that?" I asked.

"It is the truth," Asser snapped.

"You wouldn't know the truth if it was rammed down your throat with an ax-handle," I said, "and no northern lord will burn his ships. They cost gold. I burned them, and Sigurd's men tried to kill me when I did."

"Oh, no one doubts that you were there when they were burned," Erkenwald said.

"And you do not deny consulting the witch Ælfadell?" Plegmund asked.

"No," I said, "nor do I deny destroying the Danish armies at Fearnhamme and at Beamfleot last year."

"No one denies that you have done past service," Plegmund said.

"When it suited you," Asser added acidly.

"And do you deny slaying the Abbot Deorlaf of Buchestanes?" Plegmund asked.

"I gutted him like a plump fish," I said.

"You don't deny it?" Asser sounded astonished.

"I'm proud of it," I said, "and of the other two monks I killed."

"Note that!" Asser hissed at the clerk-priests who hardly needed his encouragement. They were scribbling away.

"Last year," Bishop Erkenwald said, "you refused to give an oath of loyalty to the ætheling Edward."

"True."

"Why?"

"Because I'm tired of Wessex," I said, "tired of priests, tired of being told what your god's will is, tired of being told that I'm a sinner, tired of your endless damned nonsense, tired of that nailed tyrant you call god who only wants us to be miserable. And I refused to give the oath because my ambition is to go back north, to Bebbanburg, and to kill the men who hold it, and I cannot do that if I am sworn to Edward and he wants something different of me."

That might not have been the most tactful speech, but I was not feeling tactful. Someone, I assumed Æthelred, had done their best to destroy me and had deployed the power of the church to do that and I was determined to fight the miserable bastards. It seemed I was succeeding, at least in making them even more miserable. Plegmund was grimacing, Asser making the sign of the cross, and Erkenwald's eyes were closed. The two young priests were writing faster than ever. "Nailed tyrant," one of them repeated slowly as his quill scratched on the parchment.

"And who had the clever idea to send me to East Anglia so Sigurd could kill me?" I demanded.

"King Eohric assures us that Sigurd went without his invitation, and that had he known he would have launched an attack on those forces," Plegmund said.

"Eohric is an earsling," I said, "and in case you didn't know, archbishop, an earsling is a thing like Bishop Asser that is squirted out of an arse."

"You will be respectful!" Plegmund snarled, glaring at me.

"Why?" I demanded.

He blinked at that. Asser was whispering in his ear, the sibilance urgent and demanding, while Bishop Erkenwald tried to discover something useful from me. "What did the witch Ælfadell tell you?" he asked.

"That the Saxon would destroy Wessex," I said, "and that the Danes would win and Wessex would be no more."

All three were checked by that. They might have been Christians, and important Christians at that, but they were not immune to the real gods and their magic. They were scared, though none made the sign of the cross because to have done so would have been an admission that the pagan prophetess might have some access to the truth, a thing they would want to deny to each other. "And who is the Saxon?" Asser hissed the question.

"That," I said, "is what I came to Wintanceaster to tell the king."

"So tell us," Plegmund demanded.

"I'll tell the king," I said.

"You snake," Asser said, "you thief in the night! The Saxon who will destroy Wessex is you!"

I spat to show my derision, but the spittle did not reach the table.

"You came here," Erkenwald said wearily, "because of a woman."

"Adulterer!" Asser snapped.

"That is the only explanation for your presence here," Erkenwald said, then looked at the archbishop. "*Sicut canis qui revertitur ad vomitum suum.*"

"*Sic inprudens qui iterat stultitiam suam,*" the archbishop intoned.

I thought for a moment they were cursing me, but little Bishop Asser could not resist demonstrating his learning by providing me with a translation. "As the dog returns to its vomit, so the fool returns to his filth."

"The words of God," Erkenwald said.

"And we must decide what to do with you," Plegmund said, and at those words Godric's men moved closer. I was aware of their spears behind me. A log cracked in the fire, shooting sparks onto the rushes that began to smoke. Normally a servant, or one of the soldiers, would have rushed forward to stamp out the tiny fire, but no one moved. They wanted me dead. "It has been demonstrated to us," Plegmund broke the silence, "that you have been consorting with our king's enemies, that you have conspired with them, that you have eaten their bread and taken their salt. Worse, you have admitted to slaying the holy Abbot Deorlaf and two of his brethren and . . ."

"The holy Abbot Deorlaf," I interrupted him, "was in league with the witch Ælfadell, and the holy Abbot Deorlaf wished to kill me. What was I supposed to do? Turn the other cheek?"

"You will be silent!" Plegmund said.

I took two steps forward and ground out the burning rushes with my boot. One of Godric's soldiers, thinking I was about to attack the clergymen, had drawn back his spear and I turned and looked at him. Just looked. He reddened and, very slowly, the spear went down. "I have fought your king's enemies," I said, still gazing at the spearman, but then, turning toward Plegmund, "as Bishop Erkenwald well knows. While other men cowered behind burh walls I was leading your king's army. I stood in the shield wall. I cut down foemen, I reddened the soil with the blood of your enemies, I burned ships, I took the fort at Beamfleot."

"And you wear the hammer!" Asser's voice was shrill. He was pointing at my amulet with a shaking finger, saying, "It is the symbol of our enemies, the very sign of those who would torture Christ again, and you wear it even in the court of our king!"

"What did your mother do?" I asked. "Fart like a mare? And there you were?"

"Enough," Plegmund said tiredly.

It was not hard to guess who had dripped poison in their ears; my cousin Æthelred. He was the titular Lord of Mercia, the closest thing that country had to a king, yet every man knew that he was a puppy on a West Saxon leash. He wanted that leash cut, and when Alfred died he would doubtless look for a crown. And for a new wife, the old being Æthelflaed who had added horns to his leash. A leashed and horned puppy who wanted revenge, and wanted me dead because he knew there were too many men in Mercia who would follow me rather than him.

"It is our duty to decide your fate," Plegmund said.

"The Norns do that," I said, "at Yggdrasil's root."

"Heathen," Asser hissed.

"The kingdom must be protected," the archbishop went on,

ignoring both of us, "it must have the shield of faith and the sword of righteousness, and there is no place in God's kingdom for a man of no faith, a man who could turn against us at any moment. Uhtred of Bebbanburg, I must tell you . . ."

But whatever he was about to tell me went untold because the door at the hall's end creaked open. "The king wants to see him," a familiar voice said.

I turned to see Steapa standing there. Good Steapa, commander of Alfred's household troops, a peasant slave who had risen to become a great warrior, a man daft as a barrel of loam and strong as an ox, a friend, a man as true as any I have known. "The king," he said in his stolid voice.

"But . . ." Plegmund began.

"The king wants me, you snaggle-toothed bastard," I told him, then looked at the spearman who had threatened me. "If you ever point a blade at me again," I promised him, "I'll rip your belly open and feed your entrails to my dogs."

The Norns were probably laughing, and I went to see the king.

PART TWO

DEATH OF A KING

Six

Alfred lay swathed in woolen blankets and propped against a great cushion. Osferth sat on the bed, his hand held by his father. The king's other hand lay on a bejeweled book, I assumed a gospel book. Just outside the room, in a long passageway, Brother John and four members of his choir were singing a doleful chant. The room stank, despite the herbs scattered on the floor and the great candles that burned in tall wooden sticks. Some of them were Alfred's prized candle clocks, their bands marking the hours as the king's life leaked away. Two priests stood against one wall of Alfred's chamber, while opposite them was a great panel of leather on which the crucifixion was painted.

Steapa pushed me into the room and shut the door on me.

Alfred looked dead already. Indeed, I might have thought him a corpse if he had not pulled his hand away from Osferth, who was in tears. The king's long face was pale as fleece, with sunken eyes, sunken cheeks, and dark shadows. His hair had thinned and gone white. His gums had pulled back from his remaining teeth, his unshaven chin was stained with spittle, while the hand on the book was mere skin-covered bones on which a great ruby shone, the ring too big now for his skeletal finger. His breath was shallow, though his voice was remarkably strong. "Behold the sword of the Saxons," he greeted me.

"I see your son has a loose tongue, lord King," I said. I went onto one knee until he feebly gestured for me to stand.

He looked at me from his pillow and I looked at him and the monks chanted beyond the door and a candle guttered to spew a thick twist of smoke. "I'm dying, Lord Uhtred," Alfred said.

"Yes, lord."

"And you look healthy as a bullock," he said with a grimace that was meant to be a smile. "You always had the capacity to irritate me, didn't you? It isn't tactful to look healthy in front of a dying king, but I rejoice for you." His left hand stroked the gospel book. "Tell me what will happen when I'm dead," he commanded me.

"Your son Edward will rule, lord."

He gazed at me and I saw the intelligence in those sunken eyes. "Don't tell me what you think I want to hear," he said with a touch of his old asperity, "but what you believe."

"Your son Edward will rule, lord," I repeated.

He nodded slowly, believing me. "He's a good son," Alfred said, almost as if he were trying to persuade himself of that.

"He fought well at Beamfleot. You would have been proud of him, lord."

Alfred nodded tiredly. "So much is expected of a king," he said. "He must be brave in battle, wise in council, just in judgment."

"You have been all those things, lord," I said, not flattering him, but telling the truth.

"I tried," he said, "God knows I did try." He closed his eyes and was silent for so long that I wondered if he had fallen asleep and whether I should leave, but then his eyes opened and he gazed at the smoke-darkened ceiling. Somewhere deep in the palace a hound barked shrilly, then suddenly stopped. Alfred frowned in thought, then turned his head to look at me. "You spent time with Edward last summer," he said.

"I did, lord."

"Is he wise?"

"He's clever, lord," I said.

"Many folk are clever, Lord Uhtred, but very few are wise."

"Men learn wisdom through experience, lord," I said.

"Some do," Alfred said tartly, "but will Edward learn?" I shrugged because it was not a question I could answer. "I worry," Alfred said, "that his passions will rule him."

I glanced at Osferth. "As yours ruled you, lord, once."

"Omnes enim peccaverunt," Alfred said softly.

"All have sinned," Osferth translated and received a smile from his father.

"I worry that he is headstrong," Alfred said, talking of Edward again. I was surprised that he talked so openly of his heir, but of course it was the one thing that preyed on his mind in those last days. Alfred had dedicated his life to the preservation of Wessex, and he desperately wanted reassurance that all his achievements would not be thrown away by his successor, and so deep was that worry that he could not let the subject alone. He wanted that reassurance so badly.

"You leave him with good counsel, lord," I said, not because I believed it, but because he wanted to hear it. Many men of the Witan were indeed good counselors, but there were too many churchmen like Plegmund, whose advice I would never trust.

"And a king can reject all counsel," Alfred said, "because in the end it is always the king's decision, it is the king's responsibility, it is the king who is wise or foolish. And if the king is foolish, what will happen to the kingdom?"

"You worry, lord," I said, "because Edward did what all young men do."

"He is not like other young men," Alfred said sternly, "but born to privilege and duty."

"And a girl's smile," I said, "can erode duty faster than flame melts frost."

He stared at me. "So you know?" he said, after a long while.

"Yes, lord, I know."

Alfred sighed. "He said it was passion, that it was love. Kings don't marry for love, Lord Uhtred, they marry to make their kingdom safe. And she wasn't right," he said firmly, "she was brazen! She was shameless!"

"Then I wish I'd known her, lord," I said, and Alfred laughed, though the effort hurt him and the laugh turned to a groan. Osferth had no idea what we talked about and I gave him the slightest shake of my head to show that he should not ask, and then I thought of the words that would give Alfred the reassurance he wanted. "At Beamfleot, lord," I said, "I stood beside Edward in a shield wall and a man cannot hide his character in a shield wall, and I learned that your son is a good man. I promise you, he is a man to be proud of." I hesitated, then nodded at Osferth. "As are all your sons."

I saw the king's hand tighten on Osferth's fingers. "Osferth is a good man," Alfred said, "and I am proud of him." Alfred patted his bastard son's hand and looked back to me. "And what else will happen?" he asked.

"Æthelwold will make an attempt to take the throne," I said.

"He swears not."

"He swears easily, lord. You should have cut his throat twenty years ago."

"People said the same about you, Lord Uhtred."

"Maybe you should have taken their advice, lord?"

His mouth showed the ghost of a smile. "Æthelwold is a sorry creature," he said, "without discipline or sense. He's not a danger, just a reminder of our fallibility."

"He's talked to Sigurd," I said, "and he has disaffected allies in both Cent and Mercia. That's why I came to Wintanceaster, lord, to warn you of this."

Alfred gazed at me for a long time, then sighed. "He's always dreamed of being king," he said.

"Time to kill him and his dream, lord," I said firmly. "Give me the word and I'll rid you of him."

Alfred shook his head. "He's my brother's son," Alfred said, "and a weak man. I don't want my family's blood on my hands when I stand before God at the judgment seat."

"So you let him live?"

"He's too weak to be dangerous. No one in Wessex will support him."

"Very few will, lord," I said, "so he'll go back to Sigurd and Cnut. They will invade Mercia and then Wessex. There will be battles." I hesitated. "And in those battles, lord, Cnut, Sigurd, and Æthelwold will die, but Edward and Wessex will be safe."

He considered that glib statement for a moment, then sighed. "And Mercia? Not every man in Mercia loves Wessex."

"The Mercian lords must choose sides, lord," I said. "Those who support Wessex will be on the winning side, the others will be dead. Mercia will be ruled by Edward."

I had told him what he wanted to hear, but also what I believed. Strange, that. I had been left confused by Ælfadell's predictions, yet when I was asked to foretell the future I had no hesitation.

"How can you be so sure?" Alfred asked. "Did the witch Ælfadell tell you all that?"

"No, lord. She told me the very opposite, but she was only telling me what Jarl Cnut wanted her to say."

"The gift of prophecy," Alfred said sternly, "would not be given to a pagan."

"Yet you ask me to tell the future, lord?" I asked mischievously, and was rewarded by another grimace that was intended as a smile.

"So how can you be sure?" Alfred asked.

"We've learned how to fight the Northmen, lord," I said, "but they haven't learned how to fight us. When you have burhs, then the defender has all the advantages. They will attack, we will defend, they will lose, we shall win."

"You make it sound simple," Alfred said.

"Battle is simple, lord, maybe that's why I'm good at it."

"I have been wrong about you, Lord Uhtred."

"No, lord."

"No?"

"I love the Danes, lord."

"But you are the sword of the Saxons?"

"Wyrd bið ful āræd, lord," I said.

He closed his eyes momentarily. He lay so still that for a few heartbeats I feared he was dying, but then he opened his eyes again and frowned toward the smoke-blackened rafters. He tried to suppress a moan, but it escaped anyway and I saw the pain pass across his face. "That is so hard," he said.

"There are potions that help with pain, lord," I said helplessly.

He shook his head slowly. "Not pain, Lord Uhtred. We are born to pain. No, fate is difficult. Is all ordained? Foreknowledge is not fate, and we may choose our paths, yet fate says we may not choose them. So if fate is real, do we have choice?" I said nothing, letting him puzzle that unanswerable question for himself. He looked at me. "What would you have your fate be?" he asked.

"I would recapture Bebbanburg, lord, and when I find myself on my deathbed I want it to be in Bebbanburg's high hall with the sound of her sea filling my ears."

"And I have Brother John filling my ears," Alfred said, amused. "He tells them they must open their mouths like hungry little birds, and they do." He put his right hand back on Osferth's hand. "They want me to be a hungry little bird. They feed me thin gruel, Lord Uhtred, and insist that I eat, but I don't want to eat." He sighed. "My son," he meant Osferth, "tells me you are a poor man. Why? Did you not capture a fortune at Dunholm?"

"I did, lord."

"You wasted it?"

"I wasted it in your service, lord, on men, mail, and weapons. On guarding the frontier of Mercia. On equipping an army to defeat Haesten."

"*Nervi bellorum pecuniae,*" Alfred said.

"Your scriptures, lord?"

"A wise Roman, Lord Uhtred, who said that money is the sinews of war."

"He knew what he was talking about, lord."

Alfred closed his eyes and I could see the pain cross his face again. His mouth tightened as he suppressed a groan. The smell in the room grew ranker. "There is a lump in my belly," he said, "like a stone." He paused and again tried to stifle a groan. A single tear escaped. "I watch the candle clocks," he said, "and wonder how many bands will burn before—" He hesitated. "I measure my life by inches. You will come back tomorrow, Lord Uhtred."

"Yes, lord."

"I have given my"—he paused, then patted Osferth's hand—"my son," he said, "a charge." He opened his eyes and looked at me. "My son is charged with converting you to the true faith."

"Yes, lord," I said, not knowing what else to say. I saw the tears on Osferth's face.

Alfred looked at the great leather panel that showed the crucifixion. "Do you notice anything strange about that painting?" he asked me.

I stared at it. Jesus hung from the cross, blood streaked, the sinews in his arms stretching against the dark sky behind. "No, lord," I said.

"He's dying," Alfred said. That seemed obvious and so I said nothing. "In every other depiction I have seen of our Lord's death," the king went on, "he is smiling on the cross, but not in this one. In this painting his head is hanging, he is in pain."

"Yes, lord."

"Archbishop Plegmund reproved the painter," Alfred said, "because he believes our Lord conquered pain and so would have smiled to the end, but I like the painting. It reminds me that my pain is as nothing compared to his."

"I would you had no pain, lord," I said awkwardly.

He ignored that. He still gazed at the agonized Christ, then grimaced. "He wore a crown of thorns," he said in a tone of wonderment. "Men want to be king," he went on, "but every crown has thorns. I told Edward that wearing the crown is hard, so hard. One last thing"—he turned his head from the painting and raised his left hand, and I saw what an effort it took to lift that pathetic hand from the gospel book—"I would have you swear an oath of loyalty to Edward. That way I can die in the knowledge that you will fight for us."

"I will fight for Wessex," I said.

"The oath," he said sternly.

"And I will give an oath," I said. His shrewd eyes stared at me.

"To my daughter?" he asked, and I saw Osferth stiffen.

"To your daughter, lord," I agreed.

He seemed to shudder. "In my laws, Lord Uhtred, adultery is not just a sin, but a crime."

"You would make criminals of all mankind, lord."

He half smiled at that. "I love Æthelflaed," he said, "she was always the liveliest of my children, but not the most obedient." His hand dropped back onto the gospel book. "Leave me now, Lord Uhtred. Come back tomorrow."

If he was still alive, I thought. I knelt to him, then to Osferth, and I left. We walked in silence to a cloistered courtyard where the last roses of summer had dropped their petals on the damp grass. We sat on a stone bench and listened to the mournful chants echoing from the passageway. "The archbishop wanted me dead," I said.

"I know," Osferth said, "so I went to my father."

"I'm surprised they let you see him."

"I had to argue with the priests who guard him," he said with a half-smile, "but he heard the argument."

"And called you to see him?"

"He sent a priest to summon me."

"And you told him what was happening to me?"

"Yes, lord."

"Thank you," I said. "And you made your peace with Alfred?"

Osferth gazed unseeing into the dark. "He said he was sorry, lord, that I am what I am, and that it was his fault, and that he would intervene for me in heaven."

"I'm glad," I said, not sure how else to respond to such nonsense.

"And I told him, lord, that if Edward were to rule, then Edward needed you."

"Edward will rule," I said, then I told him about the Lady Ecgwynn and the twin babies hidden away in the nunnery. "Edward was only doing what his father did," I said, "but it will cause problems."

"Problems?"

"Are the babies legitimate?" I asked. "Alfred says not, but once Alfred dies, then Edward can declare otherwise."

"Oh, God," Osferth said, seeing the difficulties so far in the future.

"What they should do, of course," I said, "is strangle the little bastards."

"Lord!" Osferth said, shocked.

"But they won't. Your family was never ruthless enough."

It had begun to rain harder, the drops beating on the tile and thatch of the palace roofs. There was no moon, no stars, only clouds in darkness and the hard rain teeming and the wind sighing about the scaffolded tower of Alfred's great new church. I went to Saint Hedda's. The guards were gone, the alleyway dark, and I beat on the convent door till someone answered.

Next day the king and his bed had been moved to the larger hall where Plegmund and his colleagues had thought to condemn me. The crown was on the bed, its bright emeralds reflecting the fire that filled the high chamber with smoke and heat. The room was crowded, stinking of men and the king's decay. Bishop Asser was there, as was Erkenwald, though the archbishop had evidently found other business to keep him from the king's presence. A score of West Saxon lords were there. One of them was Æthelhelm, whose daughter was to marry Edward. I liked Æthelhelm, who now stood close behind Ælswith, Alfred's wife, who did not know which she resented more, my existence or the strange truth that Wessex did not recognize the rank of queen. She watched me balefully. Her children flanked her. Æthelflaed, at twenty-nine, was the eldest, then came her brother, Edward, then Æthelgifu, and lastly Æthelweard, who was just sixteen. Ælfthryth, Alfred's third daughter, was not there because she had been married to a king across the water in Frankia. Steapa was there, looming above my dear old friend, Father Beocca, who was now stooped and white-haired. Brother John and his monks sang softly. Not all of the choir were monks, some were small boys robed in pale linen and, with a shock, I recognized my son Uhtred as one of them.

I have been, I confess, a bad father. I loved my two youngest children, but my eldest who, in the tradition of my family, had taken my name, was a mystery. Instead of wishing to learn sword-craft and spear-skill, he had become a Christian. A Christian! And now, with the other boys of the cathedral choir, he sang like a little bird. I glared at him, but he resolutely avoided my gaze.

I joined the ealdormen who stood at one side of the hall. They, with the senior clerics, formed the king's council, the Witan, and they had business to discuss, though none did it with any enthusiasm. A grant of land was given to a monastery, and payment authorized for the masons who were working on Alfred's new church. A man who had failed to pay his fine for the crime of manslaughter was pardoned because he had done good service with Weohstan's forces at Beamfleot. Some men looked at me when that victory was mentioned, but no one asked if I remembered the man. The king took little part, except to raise a weary hand to signify his assent.

All this while a clerk was standing behind a desk where he wrote a manuscript. I thought at first he was making a record of the proceedings, but two other clerks were clearly doing that, while the man at the desk was mainly copying from another document. He seemed very conscious of everyone's gaze and was red in the face, though perhaps that was the heat from the great fire. Bishop Asser was scowling, Ælswith looked ready to kill me with anger, but Father Beocca was smiling. He bobbed his head to me and I winked at him. Æthelflaed caught my eye and smiled so mischievously that I hoped her father had not seen it. Her husband was standing not far away from her and, like my son, he studiously avoided my gaze. Then, to my astonishment, I saw Æthelwold standing at the back of the hall. He looked at me defiantly, but could not hold my stare and stooped instead to talk with a companion I did not recognize.

A man complained that his neighbor, Ealdorman Æthelnoth, had taken fields that did not belong to him. The king interrupted the complaint, whispering to Bishop Asser who gave the king's judgment. "Will you accept the arbitration of Abbot Osburh?" he asked the man.

"I will."

"And you, Lord Æthelnoth?"

"Gladly."

"Then the abbot is charged with discovering the boundaries according to the proper writs," Asser said, and the clerks scratched his words, and the council moved on to discuss other matters and I saw Alfred look wearily toward the man copying the document at the desk. The man had finished, because he sanded the parchment, waited a few heartbeats, and then blew the sand into the fire. He folded the parchment and wrote something on the folded side, then sanded and blew again. A second clerk brought a candle, wax, and a seal. The finished document was then carried to the king's bed, and Alfred, with great effort, signed his name and then beckoned that Bishop Erkenwald and Father Beocca should add their signatures as witnesses to whatever it was he had signed.

The council fell silent as this was done. I assumed the document was the king's will, but once the wax had been impressed with the great seal, the king beckoned to me.

I went to his bedside and knelt. "I have been granting small gifts as remembrances," Alfred said.

"You were ever generous, lord King," I lied, but what else does one say to a dying man?

"This is for you," he said, and I heard Ælswith's sharp intake of breath as I took the newly written parchment from her husband's feeble hand. "Read it," he said. "You can still read?"

"Father Beocca taught me well," I said.

"Father Beocca does all things well," the king said, then moaned with pain, which caused a monk to go to his side and offer him a cup.

The king sipped, and I read. It was a charter. The clerk had copied much of it, for one charter is much like another, but this one took my breath away. It granted me land, and the grant was not conditional, like that which Alfred had once used to give me an estate at Fifhiden. Instead it conveyed the land freely to me and to my heirs or to whoever else I chose to grant that land, and the charter laboriously described the boundaries of the land, and the length of that description told me that the estate was wide and deep. There was a river and orchards and meadows and villages, and a hall at a place called Fagranforda, and all of it in Mercia. "The land belonged to my father," Alfred said.

I did not know what to say, except to utter thanks.

The feeble hand stretched toward me and I took it. I kissed the ruby. "You know what I want," Alfred said. I kept my head bowed over his hand. "The land is given freely," he said, "and it will give you wealth, much wealth."

"Lord King," I said, and my voice faltered.

His feeble fingers tightened on my hand. "Give something back to me, Uhtred," he said, "give me peace before I die."

And so I did what he wanted, and what I did not wish to do, but he was dying, and he had been generous at the end, and how can you slap a man who is in his last days of life? And so I went to Edward and I knelt to him, and I put my hands between his and I swore the oath of loyalty. And some in the hall applauded while some stayed resolutely silent. Æthelhelm, the chief adviser in the Witan, smiled, for he knew I would now fight for Wessex. My cousin Æthelred shuddered, for he knew he would never call himself king in Mercia so long as I did Edward's will, while Æthelwold must have wondered if he would ever take Alfred's throne if he had to fight his way past Serpent-Breath. Edward pulled me to my feet and embraced me. "Thank you," he whispered. That was Wednesday, Woden's Day, in October, the eighth month of the year, which was 899.

The next day belonged to Thor. The rain did not stop, coming in huge swaths that swept across Wintanceaster. "Heaven itself is weeping," Beocca told me. He was crying himself. "The king asked me to give him the last rites," he said, "and I did, but my hands were shaking." It seemed Alfred received the last rites at intervals through the day, so intent was he on making a good end, and the priests and bishops vied with each other for the honor of anointing the king and placing a piece of dry bread between his lips. "Bishop Asser was ready to give the *viaticum*," Beocca said, "but Alfred asked for me."

"He loves you," I said, "and you've served him well."

"I have served God and the king," Beocca said, then let me guide him to a seat beside the fire in the great room of the Two Cranes. "He took some curds this morning," Beocca told me earnestly, "but not many. Two spoonfuls."

"He doesn't want to eat," I said.

"He must," Beocca said. Poor dear Beocca. He had been my father's priest and clerk, and my childhood tutor, though he had abandoned Bebbanburg when my uncle usurped its lordship. He was lowborn and ill-born, with a pathetic squint, a misshapen nose, a palsied left hand, and a clubfoot. It was my grandfather who saw the boy's cleverness and had him educated by the monks at Lindisfarena, and Beocca became a priest and then, following my uncle's treachery, an exile. His cleverness and his devotion had attracted Alfred, whom Beocca had served ever since. He was old now, almost as old as the king, and his straggly red hair had turned white, his back was bent, yet he still had a keen mind and a strong will. He also had a Danish wife, a true beauty, who was the sister of my dearest friend, Ragnar.

"How is Thyra?" I asked him.

"She is well, thanks be to God, and the boys! We're blessed."

"You'll be blessed and dead if you insist on walking the streets in this rain," I said. "No fool like an old fool."

He chuckled at that, then made a small impotent protest when I insisted on taking his sopping wet cloak and placing a dry one around his shoulders. "The king asked me to come to you," he said.

"Then the king should have told me to go to you," I said.

"Such a wet season!" Beocca said. "I haven't seen rain like this since the year Archbishop Æthelred died. The king doesn't know it's raining. Poor man. He strives against the pain. He can't last long now."

"And he sent you," I reminded him.

"He asks a favor of you," Beocca said, with a touch of his old sternness.

"Go on."

"Fagranforda is a great estate," Beocca said. "The king was generous."

"I have been generous to him," I said.

Beocca waved his crippled left hand as if to dismiss my remark. "There are presently four churches and a monastery on the estate," he went on crisply, "and the king has asked for your assurance that you will maintain them as they should be maintained, as their charters demand, and as is your duty."

I smiled at that. "And if I refuse?"

"Oh please, Uhtred," he said wearily. "I have struggled with you my whole life!"

"I will tell the steward to do all that is necessary," I promised.

He looked at me with his one good eye as if judging my sincerity, but seemed pleased with what he saw. "The king will be grateful," he said.

"I thought you were going to ask me to abandon Æthelflaed," I said mischievously. There were few people I would ever talk to about Æthelflaed, but Beocca, who had known me since I was a stripling, was one.

He shuddered at my words. "Adultery is a grievous sin," he said, though without much passion.

"A crime too," I said, amused. "Have you told that to Edward?"

He flinched. "That was a young man's foolishness," he said, "and God punished the girl. She died."

"Your god is so good," I said caustically, "but why didn't he think to kill her royal bastards as well?"

"They have been put away," he said.

"With Æthelflaed."

He nodded. "They kept her from you," he said. "You know that?"

"I know that."

"Locked her away in Saint Hedda's," he said.

"I found the key," I said.

"God preserve us from wickedness," Beocca said, making the sign of the cross.

"Æthelflaed," I said, "is loved in Mercia. Her husband is not."

"This is known," he said distantly.

"When Edward becomes king," I said, "he will look to Mercia."

"Look to Mercia?"

"The Danes will come, father," I said, "and they'll begin with Mercia. You want the Mercian lords fighting for Wessex? You want the Mercian fyrd fighting for Wessex? The one person who can inspire them is Æthelflaed."

"You can," he said loyally.

I gave that statement the scorn it deserved. "You and I are Northumbrians, father. They think we're barbarians who eat our children for breakfast. But they love Æthelflaed."

"I know," he said.

"So let her be a sinner, father, if that is what makes Wessex safe."

"Am I supposed to tell the king that?"

I laughed. "You're supposed to tell Edward that. And tell him more. Tell him to kill Æthelwold. No mercy, no family sentimentality, no Christian guilt. Just give me the order and he's dead."

Beocca shook his head. "Æthelwold is a fool," he said accurately, "and most of the time a drunken fool. He flirted with the Danes, we cannot deny it, but he has confessed all his sins to the king and been forgiven."

"Forgiven?"

"Last night," Beocca said, "he shed tears at the king's bedside and swore allegiance to the king's heir."

I had to laugh. Alfred's response to my warning had been to summon Æthelwold and believe the fool's lies. "Æthelwold will try to take the throne," I said.

"He swore the opposite," Beocca said earnestly. "He swore on Noah's feather and on the glove of Saint Cedd."

The feather had supposedly belonged to a dove that Noah had released from the ark back in the days when it rained as heavily as the downpour that now drummed on the roof of the Two Cranes. The feather and the saint's glove were two of Alfred's most precious relics, and doubtless he would believe anything that was sworn in their presence. "Don't believe him," I said, "kill him. Or else he'll make trouble."

"He has sworn his oath," Beocca said, "and the king believes him."

"Æthelwold is a treacherous earsling," I said.

"He's just a fool," Beocca said dismissively.

"But an ambitious fool, and a fool with a legitimate claim to the throne, and men will use that claim."

"He has relented, he has made confession, he has been absolved, and he is penitent."

What fools we all are. I see the same mistakes being made, time after time, generation after generation, yet still we go on believing what we wish to believe. That night, in the wet darkness, I repeated Beocca's words. "He has relented," I said, "he has made confession, he has been absolved, and he is penitent."

"And they believe him?" Æthelflaed asked bleakly.

"Christians are fools," I said, "ready to believe anything."

She prodded me hard in the ribs, and I chuckled. The rain fell on Saint Hedda's roof. I should not have been there, of course, but the abbess, dear Hild, pretended not to know. I was not in that part of the nunnery where the sisters lived in seclusion, but in a range of buildings about the outer courtyard where lay folk were permitted. There were kitchens where food was prepared for the poor, there was a hospital where the indigent could die, and there was this attic room, which had been Æthelflaed's prison. It was not uncomfortable, though small. She was attended by maidservants, but this night they had been told to make themselves beds in the storerooms beneath. "They told me you were negotiating with the Danes," Æthelflaed said.

"I was. I was using Serpent-Breath."

"And negotiating with Sigunn too?"

"Yes," I said, "and she's well."

"God knows why I love you."

"God knows everything."

She said nothing to that, but just stirred beside me and pulled the fleece higher about her head and shoulders. The rain beat on. Her hair was golden in my face. She was Alfred's eldest child and I had watched her grow to become a woman, had watched the joy in her face fade to bitterness when she was given as wife to my cousin, and I had seen the joy return. Her blue eyes were flecked with brown, her nose was small and upturned. It was a face I loved, but a face that now had lines of worry. "You should talk to your son," she said, her voice muffled by the fleece bedcover.

"Uhtred spouts pious nonsense to me," I said, "so I'd rather talk to my daughter."

"She's safe, and your other son too, in Cippanhamm."

"Why is Uhtred here?" I asked.

"The king wanted him here."

"They're turning him into a priest," I said angrily.

"And they want to turn me into a nun," she said just as angrily.

"They do?"

"Bishop Erkenwald administered the oath to me, I spat at him."

I pulled her head out from under the fleece. "They really tried?"

"Bishop Erkenwald and my mother."

"What happened?"

"They came here," she said in a very matter-of-fact voice, "and insisted I go to the chapel, and Bishop Erkenwald said a great deal of angry Latin, then held a book to me and told me to put my hand on it and swear to keep the oath he'd just said."

"And you did?"

"I told you what I did. I spat at him."

I lay in silence for a while. "Æthelred must have persuaded them," I said.

"Well I'm sure he'd like to put me away, but Mother said it was Father's wish I take the vows."

"I doubt that," I said.

"So then they went back to the palace and announced I had taken the vow."

"And put guards on the gate," I said.

"I think that was to keep you out," Æthelflaed said, "but you say the guards are gone?"

"They're gone."

"So I can leave?"

"You left yesterday."

"Steapa's men escorted me to the palace," she said, "then brought me back here."

"There are no guards now."

She frowned in thought. "I should have been born a man."

"I'm glad you weren't."

"And I would be king," she said.

"Edward will be a good king."

"He will," she agreed, "but he can be indecisive. I would have made a better king."

"Yes," I said, "you would."

"Poor Edward," she said.

"Poor? He'll be king soon."

"He lost his love," she said.

"And the babies live."

"The babies live," she agreed.

I think I loved Gisela best of all the women in my life. I mourn her still. But of all those women, Æthelflaed was always the closest. She thought like me. I would sometimes start to say something and she would finish the sentence. In time we just looked at each other and knew what the other was thinking. Of all the friends I have made in my life, I loved Æthelflaed the best.

Sometime in that wet darkness, Thor's Day turned into Freya's Day. Freya was Woden's wife, the goddess of love, and for all of her day the rain continued to fall. A wind rose in the afternoon, a high wind that tore at Wintanceaster's thatch and drove the rain in malevolent spite, and that same night King Alfred, who had ruled in Wessex for twenty-eight years and was in the fiftieth year of his life, died.

The next morning there was no rain and little wind. Wintanceaster was silent, except for the pigs rooting in the streets, the cockerels crowing, the dogs howling or barking, and the thud of the sentries' boots on the waterlogged planks of the ramparts. Folk seemed dazed. A bell began to toll in midmorning, just a single bell struck again and again, and the sound faded down the river valley where floods sheeted the meadows, then came again with brutal force. The king is dead, long live the king.

Æthelflaed wanted to pray in the nuns' chapel, and I left her in Saint Hedda's and walked through the silent streets to the palace, where I surrendered my sword at the gatehouse and saw Steapa sitting alone in the outer courtyard. His grim, skin-stretched face that had terrified so many of Alfred's enemies was wet with tears. I sat on the bench beside him, but said nothing. A woman hurried past carrying a stack of folded linens. The king dies, yet still sheets must be washed, rooms swept, ashes thrown out, wood stacked, grain milled. A score of horses had been saddled and were waiting at the courtyard's farther end. I supposed they were for messengers who would carry the news of the king's death to every corner of his kingdom, but instead a troop of men, all in mail and all helmeted, appeared from a doorway and were helped up into their saddles. "Your men?" I asked Steapa.

He gave them a sour glance. "Not mine."

They were Æthelwold's men. Æthelwold himself was the last to appear and, like his followers, he was dressed for war in a helmet and mail. Three servants had brought the troops' swords from the gatehouse and men milled about in search of their own blade, then strapped the swords and belts about their waists. Æthelwold took his own long-sword, let a servant buckle the belt, then was helped up onto his horse, a big black stallion. He saw me then. He kicked the horse toward me and pulled the blade out of its scabbard. I did not move, and he curbed the stallion a few paces away. The horse flailed a hoof at the cobblestones, striking a spark. "A sad day, Lord Uhtred," Æthelwold said. The bare sword was at his side, pointing down. He wanted to use it and he dared not use it. He had ambition and he was weak.

I looked up into his long face, once so handsome, now ravaged by drink and anger and disappointment. There was gray at his temples. "A sad day, my prince," I agreed.

He was measuring me, measuring the distance his sword needed to travel, measuring the chance he would have to escape through the gate arch after striking the blow. He glanced around the courtyard to see how many of the royal bodyguard were in sight. There were only two. He could have struck me, let his followers take care of the two men, and be gone, all in a moment, but still he hesitated. One of his followers pushed his horse close. The man wore a helmet with closed cheek-plates, so all I could see of his face were his eyes. A shield was slung on his back and on it was painted the head of a bull with bloodied horns. His horse was nervous and he slapped its neck hard. I saw the scars on the beast's flanks where he had used his spurs deep and hard. He leaned close to Æthelwold and said something under his breath, but was interrupted by Steapa, who simply stood up. He was a huge man, frighteningly tall and broad and, as commander of the royal bodyguard, permitted to wear his sword throughout the palace. He grasped his sword's hilt and Æthelwold immediately pushed his own blade halfway back into its scabbard. "I was worried," he said, "that the damp weather would have rusted the sword. It seems not."

"You put fleece-grease on the blade?" I asked.

"My servant must," he said airily. He pushed the blade home. The man with the bloodied bull's horns on his shield stared at me from the shadows of his helmet.

"You'll return for the funeral?" I asked Æthelwold.

"And for the coronation too," he said slyly, "but till then I have business at Tweoxnam." He offered me an unfriendly smile. "My estate there is not so large as yours at Fagranforda, Lord Uhtred, but large enough to need my attention in these sad days." He gathered the reins and rammed back his spurs so that the stallion leaped forward. His men followed, their horses' hooves loud on the stone.

"Who shows a bull's head on his shield?" I asked Steapa.

"Sigebriht of Cent," Steapa said, watching the men disappear through the arch. "A young rich fool."

"Were they his followers? Or Æthelwold's?"

"Æthelwold has men," Steapa said. "He can afford them. He owns his father's estates at Tweoxnam and Wimburnan, and that makes him wealthy."

"He should be dead."

"It's family business," Steapa said, "nothing to do with you and me."

"It's you and me who'll be doing the killing for the family," I said.

"I'm getting too old for it," he grumbled.

"How old are you?"

"No idea," he said. "Forty?"

He led me through a small gate in the palace wall, then across a patch of waterlogged grass toward Alfred's old church that stood beside the new minster. Scaffolding spiderwebbed the sky where the great stone tower was unfinished. Townsfolk stood by the old church door. They did not speak, but stood and looked bereft, shuffling aside as Steapa and I approached. Some bowed. The door was guarded today by six of Steapa's men, who pulled their spears aside when they saw us.

Steapa made the sign of the cross as we entered the old church. It was cold inside. The stone walls were painted with scenes from the Christian scriptures, while gold, silver, and crystal glinted from the altars. A Dane's dream, I thought, because there was enough treasure here to buy a fleet and fill it with swords. "He thought this church was too small," Steapa said in wonderment as he gazed up at the high roof beams. Birds flew there. "A falcon nested up there last year," he said.

The king had already been brought to the church and laid in front of the high altar. A harpist played and Brother John's choir sang from the shadows. I wondered if my son was among them, but did not look. Priests muttered in front of side-altars or knelt beside the coffin where the king lay. Alfred's eyes were closed and his face tied with a white cloth that compressed his lips between which I could just see a crust, presumably because a priest had placed a piece of the Christians' holy bread in the dead man's mouth. He was dressed in a penitent's white robe, like the one he had once forced me to wear. That had been years before, when Æthelwold and I had been commanded to abase ourselves before an altar, and I had been given no choice but to agree, but Æthelwold had turned the whole miserable ceremony into a farce. He had pretended to be full of remorse, and shouted that remorse to the sky, "No more tits, God! No more tits! Keep me from tits!" and I remembered how Alfred had turned away in frustrated disgust.

"Exanceaster," Steapa said.

"You were remembering the same day," I said.

"It was raining," he said, "and you had to crawl to the altar in the field. I remember."

That had been the very first time I had seen Steapa, so baleful and frightening, and later we had fought and then become friends, and it was all such a long time ago, and I stood beside Alfred's coffin and thought how life slipped by, and how, for nearly all my life, Alfred had been there like a great landmark. I had not liked him. I had struggled against him and for him, I had cursed him and thanked him, despised him and admired him. I hated his religion and its cold disapproving gaze, its malevolence that cloaked itself in pretended kindness, and its allegiance to a god who would drain the joy from the world by naming it sin, but Alfred's religion had made him a good man and a good king.

And Alfred's joyless soul had proved a rock against which the Danes had broken themselves. Time and again they had attacked, and time and again Alfred had out-thought them, and Wessex grew ever stronger and richer and all that was because of Alfred. We think of kings as privileged men who rule over us and have the freedom to make, break, and flout the law, but Alfred was never above the law he loved to make. He saw his life as a duty to his god and to the people of Wessex and I have never seen a better king, and I doubt my sons, my grandsons, and their children's children will ever see a better one. I never liked him, but I have never stopped admiring him. He was my king and all that I now have I owe to him. The food that I eat, the hall where I live, and the swords of my men all started with Alfred, who hated me at times, loved me at times, and was generous with me. He was a gold-giver.

Steapa had tears on his cheeks. Some of the priests kneeling about the coffin were openly weeping. "They'll make a grave for him tonight," Steapa said, pointing toward the high altar that was heaped with the glittering reliquaries that Alfred had loved.

"They're burying him in here?" I asked.

"There's a vault," he said, "but it has to be opened. Once the new church is finished he'll be taken there."

"And the funeral is tomorrow?"

"Maybe a week. They need time so folk can travel here."

We stayed a long time in the church, greeting men who came to mourn, and at midday the new king arrived with a group of nobles. Edward was tall, long-faced, and thin-lipped, and had very black hair that he wore brushed back. He looked so young to me. He wore a blue robe that was belted with a gold-paneled strip of leather, and over it a black cape that hung to the floor. He wore no crown, for he was not yet crowned, but had a bronze circlet about his skull.

I recognized most of the ealdormen who accompanied him, Æthelnoth, Wilfrith and, of course, Edward's future father-in-law,

Æthelhelm, who walked beside Father Coenwulf who was Edward's confessor and guardian. There were a half-dozen younger men I did not know, and then I saw my cousin, Æthelred, and he saw me at the same moment and checked. Edward, walking toward his father's coffin, beckoned him on. Steapa and I both went down on one knee and stayed there as Edward knelt at the foot of his father's coffin and put his hands together in prayer. His guard all knelt. No one spoke. The choir was chanting interminably as incense smoke drifted in the sun-shafted air.

Æthelred's eyes were closed in pretend prayer. The look on his face was bitter and strangely aged, perhaps because he had been ill and was, as Alfred his father-in-law had been, prone to bouts of sickness. I watched him, wondering. He must have hoped that Alfred's death would loosen the leash that tied Mercia to Wessex. He must have been hoping that there would be two coronations, one in Wessex and another in Mercia, and he must have known that Edward knew all that. What stood in his way was his wife, who was beloved in Mercia, and who he had tried to make powerless by immuring her in Saint Hedda's convent, and the other obstacle was his wife's lover.

"Lord Uhtred." Edward had opened his eyes, though his hands were still clasped in prayer.

"Lord?" I asked.

"You will stay for the burial?"

"If you wish, lord."

"I do wish," he said.

"And then you must go to your estate in Fagranforda," he went on. "I am sure you have much to do there."

"Yes, lord."

"The Lord Æthelred," Edward spoke firmly and loudly, "will stay to counsel me for a few weeks. I have need of wise counsel and I can think of none more able to deliver it."

That was a lie. A spavined idiot could give better counsel than Æthelred, but of course Edward did not want my cousin's advice. He wanted Æthelred where he could see him, where it would be difficult for Æthelred to foment unrest, and he was sending me to Mercia because he trusted me to keep Mercia on the West Saxon leash. And because he knew that if I went to Mercia so would his sister. I kept a very straight face.

A sparrow flew in the high church roof and its dropping, wet and white, fell on Alfred's dead face, spattering messily from his nose to his left cheek.

An omen so bad, so terrible, that every man about the coffin held his breath.

And just then one of Steapa's guards came into the church and hurried up the long nave, but did not kneel. Instead he looked from Edward to Æthelred, and from Æthelred to me, and he seemed not to know what to say until Steapa growled at him to speak.

"The Lady Æthelflaed," the man said.

"What of her?" Edward asked.

"The Lord Æthelwold took her by force, lord, from the convent. Took her, lord. And they've gone."

So the struggle for Wessex had begun.

Seven

Æthelred laughed. Perhaps it was a nervous reaction, but in that old church the sound echoed mockingly from the lower walls that were made of stone. When the sound died away all I could hear was water dripping onto the floor from the rain-soaked thatch.

Edward looked at me, then at Æthelred, finally at Æthelhelm. He appeared confused.

"Where did Lord Æthelwold go?" Steapa asked usefully.

"The nuns said he was going to Tweoxnam," the messenger said.

"But he gave me his oath!" Edward protested.

"He was always a lying bastard," I said. I looked at the man who had brought the news. "He told the nuns he was going to Tweoxnam?"

"Yes, lord."

"He said the same to me," I said.

Edward gathered himself. "I want every man armed and mounted," he told Steapa, "and ready to ride to Tweoxnam."

"Is that his only estate, lord King?" I asked.

"He owns Wimburnan," Edward said. "Why?"

"Isn't his father buried at Wimburnan?"

"Yes."

"Then that's where he's gone," I said. "He told us Tweoxnam because he wants to confuse us. If you abduct someone you don't tell your pursuers where you're taking them."

"Why abduct Æthelflaed?" Edward was looking lost again.

"Because he wants Mercia on his side," I said. "Is she friendly to him?"

"Friendly? We all tried to be," Edward said. "He's our cousin."

"He thinks he can persuade her to bring Mercia to his cause," I suggested, and did not add that it would not just be Mercia. If Æthelflaed declared for her cousin then many in Wessex would be persuaded to support him.

"We go to Tweoxnam?" Steapa asked uncertainly.

Edward hesitated, then shook his head and looked to me. "The two places are very close," he said, still hesitant, but then remembered he was a king and made up his mind. "We ride to Wimburnan," he said.

"And I go with you, lord King," I said.

"Why?" Æthelred blurted the question before he had the sense or time to think what he was asking. The king and the ealdormen looked embarrassed.

I let the question hang till its echo had faded, then smiled. "To protect the honor of the king's sister, of course," I said, and I was still laughing when we rode out.

It took time, it always takes time. Horses had to be saddled, mail donned, and banners fetched, and while the royal housecarls readied themselves I went with Osferth to Saint Hedda's where Abbess Hildegyth was in tears. "He said she was wanted at the church," she explained to me, "that the family was praying together for her father's soul."

"You did nothing wrong," I told her.

"But he's taken her!"

"He won't hurt her," I reassured her.

"But . . ." Her voice faded, and I knew she was remembering the shame of being raped by the Danes so many years before.

"She's Alfred's daughter," I said, "and he wants her help, not her enmity. Her support gives him legitimacy."

"She's still a hostage," Hild said.

"Yes, but we'll get her back."

"How?"

I touched Serpent-Breath's hilt, showing Hild the silver cross embedded in the pommel, a cross she had given me so long ago. "With this," I said, meaning the sword, not the cross.

"You shouldn't wear a sword in a nunnery," she said with mock sternness.

"There are many things I shouldn't do in a nunnery," I told her, "but I did most of them anyway."

She sighed. "What does Æthelwold hope to gain?"

Osferth answered. "He hopes to persuade her that he should be the king. And he hopes she will persuade Lord Uhtred to support him." He glanced at me and, at that moment, looked astonishingly like his father. "I've no doubt," he went on drily, "he'll offer to make it possible for the Lord Uhtred and the Lady Æthelflaed to marry, and will probably hold out the throne of Mercia as an enticement. He doesn't just want the Lady Æthelflaed's support, he wants Lord Uhtred's too."

I had not thought of that and it took me by surprise. There had been a time when Æthelwold and I had been friends, but that was long ago when we were both young and a shared resentment of Alfred had brought us together. Æthelwold's resentment had soured into hatred, while mine had turned into reluctant admiration, and so we were friends no longer. "He's a fool," I said, "and he always was a fool."

"A desperate fool," Osferth added, "but a fool who knows this is his last chance to gain the throne."

"He'll not have my help," I promised Hild.

"Just bring her back," Hild said, and we rode to do just that.

A small army went westward. At its heart was Steapa and the king's bodyguard, and every warrior in Wintanceaster who possessed a horse joined in. It was a bright day, the sky clearing of the clouds that had brought so much rain. Our route took us across the wild lands of southern Wessex, where the deer and wild ponies ranged across forest and moor and where the hoofprints of Æthelwold's band were easy to follow because the ground was so damp. Edward rode a little behind the vanguard, and with him was a standard-bearer flying the white dragon banner. Edward's priest, Father Coenwulf, his black skirts draped on his horse's rump, kept pace with the king, as did two ealdormen, Æthelnoth and

Æthelhelm. Æthelred came too, he could hardly avoid an expedition to rescue his wife, but he and his followers stayed with the rearguard, well away from where Edward and I rode, and I remember thinking that we were too many, that a half-dozen men were enough to cope with a fool like Æthelwold.

Other men joined us, leaving their halls to follow the king's standard, and by the time we left the moorland we must have numbered over three hundred horsemen. Steapa had sent scouts ahead, but they sent no news back, which suggested Æthelwold was waiting behind his hall's palisade. At one point I spurred my horse off the road and up a low hill to look ahead and Edward pointedly joined me, leaving his guard behind. "My father," he said, "told me I can trust you."

"Do you doubt his word, lord King?" I asked.

"While my mother says you can't be trusted."

I laughed at that. Ælswith, Alfred's wife, had always hated me, and it was a mutual feeling. "Your mother has never approved of me," I said mildly.

"And Beocca tells me you want to kill my children," he spoke resentfully.

"That isn't my decision, lord King," I said, and he looked surprised. "Your father," I explained, "should have slit Æthelwold's throat twenty years ago, but he didn't. Your worst enemies, lord King, aren't the Danes. They're the men closest to you who want your crown. Your illegitimate children will be a problem for your legitimate sons, but it isn't my problem. It's yours."

He shook his head. This was our first moment alone together since his father's death. I knew he liked me, but he was also nervous of me. He had only ever known me as a warrior and, unlike his sister, he had never been close to me as a child. He said nothing for a while, but watched the small army file westward beneath us, its banners bright in the sun. The land gleamed from all the rain. "They're not illegitimate," he finally said softly. "I married Ecgwynn. I married her in a church, before God."

"Your father disagreed," I said.

Edward shuddered, "He was angry. So was my mother."

"And Ealdorman Æthelhelm, lord King?" I asked. "He can't be happy that his daughter's children won't be the eldest."

His jaw tightened. "He was assured I didn't marry," he said distantly.

So Edward had surrendered to his parents' anger. He had agreed to the fiction that his children by Lady Ecgwynn were bastards, but it was apparent that he was unhappy with that surrender. "Lord," I said, "you're king now. You can raise the twins as your legitimate children. You're king."

"I offend Æthelhelm," he asked plaintively, "and how long do I stay king?" Æthelhelm was the wealthiest of Wessex's nobles, the most powerful voice in the Witan, and a man much liked in the kingdom. "My father always insisted that the Witan could make or unmake a king," Edward said, "and my mother insists I listen to their advice."

"You're the eldest son," I said, "so you're king."

"Not if Æthelhelm and Plegmund refuse to support me," Edward said.

"True," I agreed grudgingly.

"So the twins must be treated as though they're illegitimate," he said, still unhappy, "and stay bastards until I have the power to decree otherwise. And till then they must be kept safe, so they're going to my sister's care."

"To my care," I said flatly.

"Yes," he said. He looked at me searchingly. "So long as you promise not to kill them."

I laughed. "I don't kill babies, lord King. I wait till they grow up."

"They must grow up," he said, then frowned. "You don't condemn me for sin, do you?"

"Me! I'm your pagan, lord," I said, "what do I care about sin?"

"Then care for my children," he said.

"I will, lord King," I promised.

"And tell me what I do about Æthelred," he said.

I stared down at my cousin's troops, who rode together as the rearguard. "He wants to be King of Mercia," I said, "but he knows he needs Wessex's support if he's to survive, so he won't take the throne without your permission, and you won't give that."

"I won't," Edward said. "But my mother insists I need his support too."

That wretched woman, I thought. She had always liked Æthelred and disapproved of her daughter. Yet what she said was partly true. Æthelred could bring at least a thousand men to a battlefield, and if Wessex were ever to strike against the powerful Danish lords to the north, then those men would be invaluable, but as I had told Alfred a hundred times, it was always best to reckon that Æthelred would find a thousand excuses to keep his warriors at home. "So what is Æthelred asking of you?"

Edward did not answer directly. Instead he looked up at the sky, then westward again. "He hates you."

"And your sister," I said flatly.

He nodded. "He wants Æthelflaed returned to . . ." he began, but then stopped speaking because a horn sounded.

"He wants Æthelflaed in his hall or else locked away in a convent," I said.

"Yes," Edward said, "that's what he wants." He stared down at the road from where the horn had sounded a second time. "But they want me," he said, looking to where Father Coenwulf waved toward us. I could see a couple of Steapa's men galloping toward the vanguard. Edward dug in his spurs and we cantered to the head of the column, where we discovered the two scouts had brought in a priest who half fell from his saddle to kneel before the king.

"Lord, lord King!" the priest gasped. He was out of breath.

"Who are you?" Edward asked.

"Father Edmund, lord."

He had come from Wimburnan, where he was the priest, and he told how Æthelwold had raised his banner in the town and declared himself King of Wessex.

"He did what?" Edward asked.

"He made me read a proclamation, lord, outside Saint Cuthberga's."

"He's calling himself king?"

"He says he's King of Wessex, lord. He's demanding that men come and swear allegiance to him."

"How many men were there when you left?" I asked.

"I don't know, lord," Father Edmund said.

"Did you see a woman?" Edward asked. "My sister?"

"The Lady Æthelflaed? Yes, lord, she was with him."

"Does he have twenty men?" I asked. "Or two hundred?"

"I don't know, lord. A lot."

"He sent messengers to other lords?" I asked.

"To his thegns, lord. He sent me. I'm supposed to bring him men."

"And you found me instead," Edward said warmly.

"He's raising an army," I said.

"The fyrd," Steapa said scornfully.

Æthelwold was doing what he thought wise, but he had no wisdom. He had inherited wide estates from his father, and Alfred had been foolish enough to leave those estates untouched, and now Æthelwold was demanding that his tenants come with weapons to make an army that he presumably believed would march on Wintanceaster. But the army would be the fyrd, the citizen army, the laborers and carpenters and thatchers and plowmen, while Edward had his royal bodyguard, who were all trained warriors. The fyrd was good for defending a burh, or for impressing an enemy with numbers, but to fight, to face a sword-Dane or a raving Northman, a warrior was needed. What Æthelwold should have done was stay in Wintanceaster, murder all Alfred's children, and then raise his standard, but like a fool he had gone to his own home and now we rode there with warriors.

The day was dying as we neared Wimburnan, the sun was low in the west and the shadows long on the rich slopes, where Æthelwold's sheep and cattle had their grazing. We came from the east and no one tried to prevent us reaching the small town that lay cradled between two rivers that joined close to where a stone church loomed above the shadowed thatch of the roofs. King Æthelred, Alfred's brother and Æthelwold's father, lay buried in that church, and beyond it, and surrounded by a tall palisade, was Æthelwold's hall, where a great flag flew. It showed a prancing white stag with fierce eyes and two Christian crosses for antlers, and the low sun was catching the linen that was spread by a small wind and the banner's dark red field seemed to smolder like boiling blood in the late daylight.

We rode north around the town, crossing the smaller river and then climbing a shallow slope that led to one of those forts that the ancient people had built all across Britain. This fort had been hacked out of a chalk hilltop, and Father Edmund told me it was called Baddan Byrig and that the local people believed the devil danced there on winter nights. It had three walls of heaped chalk, all overgrown with grass, and two intricate entrances where sheep grazed, and it overlooked the road that Æthelwold must take if he wanted to go north to his Danish friends. Edward's first instinct had been to block the road to Wintanceaster, but that town was protected by its walls and garrison and I persuaded him that the greater danger was that Æthelwold would escape Wessex altogether.

Our army spread along the skyline beneath its royal banners. Wimburnan lay just a couple of miles south and east of us and we must have looked formidable to anyone watching from the town. We were sunlit by the low rays that reflected the glint of our mail and weapons and that made the bare chalk patches of Baddan Byrig's walls glow white. That low sun made it difficult to see what was happening in the small town, but I glimpsed men and horses by Æthelwold's hall and could see people gathered in the streets, yet there was no shield wall defending the road that led to that great hall. "How many men does he have?" Edward asked. He had asked that question a dozen times since we had met Father Edmund, and a dozen times he had been told we did not know, that no one knew, and that it might be forty men or it might be four hundred.

"Not enough men, lord," I said now.

"What . . ." he began, then abruptly checked. He had been about to ask what we should do, then had remembered that he was the king, and was supposed to supply the answer himself.

"Do you want him dead or alive?" I asked.

He looked at me. He knew he must make decisions, but did not know what decision to make. Father Coenwulf, who had been his tutor, began to offer advice, but Edward cut him short with a wave of his hand. "I want him to stand trial," he said.

"Remember what I told you," I said. "Your father could have

saved us a lot of trouble by just killing Æthelwold, so why don't you let me go and slaughter the bastard?"

"Or let me, lord," Steapa volunteered.

"He must stand trial before the Witan," Edward decided. "I do not wish to begin my reign with slaughter."

"Amen and God be praised," Father Coenwulf said.

I gazed into the valley. If Æthelwold had raised any kind of army, it was not in evidence. All I could see was a handful of horses and an undisciplined rabble. "Just let me kill him, lord," I said, "and the problem will be solved by sundown."

"Let me talk to him," Father Coenwulf urged.

"Reason with him," Edward said to the priest.

"Do you reason with a cornered rat?" I demanded.

Edward ignored that. "Tell him he must surrender to our mercy," he told Father Coenwulf.

"And suppose he decides to kill Father Coenwulf instead, lord King?" I asked.

"I am in God's hands," Coenwulf said.

"You'd be better in Lord Uhtred's hands," Steapa growled.

The sun was just above the horizon now, a dazzling red globe suspended in the autumn sky. Edward looked confused, but still wanted to appear decisive. "The three of you will go," he announced firmly, "and Father Coenwulf will do the talking."

Father Coenwulf lectured me as we rode downhill. I was not to threaten anyone, I was not to speak unless spoken to, I was not to touch my sword, and the Lady Æthelflaed, he insisted, was to be escorted back to her husband's protection. Father Coenwulf was pale-skinned and stern, one of those rigid men that Alfred had loved to appoint as tutors or counselors. He was clever, of course, all Alfred's favored priests were sharp-witted, but all too ready to condemn sin or, indeed, to define it, which meant he disapproved of me and of Æthelflaed. "Do you understand me?" he demanded as we reached the road, which was little more than a rutted track between untrimmed hedges. Wagtails flocked in the fields and far off, beyond the town, a great cloud of starlings wheeled and faded in the sky.

"I'm not to threaten anyone," I said cheerfully, "not to speak to anyone, and not to touch my sword. Wouldn't it be easier if I just stopped breathing?"

"And we shall restore the Lady Æthelflaed to her proper place," Coenwulf said firmly.

"What is her proper place?" I asked.

"Her husband will decide that."

"But he wants her in a nunnery," I pointed out.

"If that is her husband's decision, Lord Uhtred," Coenwulf said, "then that is her fate."

"I think you'll learn," I said mildly, "that the lady has a mind of her own. She might not do what any man wants."

"She will obey her husband," Coenwulf insisted and I just laughed at him, which annoyed him. Poor Steapa looked confused.

There were half a dozen armed men at the outskirts of the town, but they made no attempt to stop us. There was no wall, this was no burh, and we plunged straight into a street that smelled of dung and woodsmoke. The folk in the town were worried, and silent. They watched us, and some made the sign of the cross as we passed. The sun had gone now, it was twilight. We skirted a comfortable-looking tavern, and a man sitting with a horn of ale raised it to us as we rode past. I noted that few men had weapons. If Æthelwold could not raise the fyrd in his own home town, then how could he hope to raise the county against Edward? The gate to Saint Cuthberga's nunnery opened a crack as we came near and I saw a woman peer out, and then the gate slammed shut. There were more guards at the door to the church, but again they made no effort to stop us. They just watched us pass, their faces sullen. "He's already lost," I said.

"He has," Steapa agreed.

"Lost?" Father Coenwulf asked.

"This is his stronghold," I said, "and no one wants to defy us."

At least no one wanted to defy us until we reached the entrance to Æthelwold's hall. The gate was decorated with his flag and guarded by seven spearmen and blocked by a pathetic barricade of barrels on which two logs had been placed. One of the spearmen strode toward us and leveled his weapon. "No further," he announced.

"Just take away the barrels," I said, "and open the gate."

"State your names," he said. He was a middle-aged man, solidly built, gray-bearded and dutiful.

"That's Matthew," I said, pointing at Father Coenwulf, "I'm Mark, he's Luke, and the other fellow got drunk and stayed behind. You know damn well who we are, so open the gate."

"Let us in," Father Coenwulf said sternly, after giving me a foul look.

"No weapons," the man said.

I looked at Steapa. He had his long-sword at his left side, his short-sword on the right, and a war ax looped across his back. "Steapa," I asked him, "just how many men have you killed in battle?"

He was puzzled by the question, but thought about his answer. In the end he had to shake his head. "I lost count," he said.

"Me too," I said, and looked back to the man who faced us. "You can take the weapons from us," I told him, "or you can live and let us through the gate."

He decided he wanted to live and so ordered his men to remove the barrels and logs, then pull the gates wide, and we rode into the courtyard, where torches had just been lit and their wild flames cast fluttering shadows from saddled horses that waited for riders. I counted about thirty men, some in mail and all armed, waiting with the horses, but not one challenged us. Instead they looked nervous. "He's getting ready to flee," I said.

"You are not to talk here," Father Coenwulf said testily.

"Be quiet, you dull priest," I told him.

Servants came to take our horses and, as I expected, a steward demanded that Steapa and I give up our swords before we went into the great hall. "No," I said.

"My sword stays," Steapa said menacingly.

The steward looked flustered, but Father Coenwulf just pushed past the man and we followed him into the great hall that was lit by a blazing fire and by candles arrayed on two tables between which was a throne. There was no other word to do justice to that great chair, which reared high above the massed candles and in which Æthelwold sat, though the moment we appeared he jumped to his feet and strode to the edge of the dais on which the throne had pride of place. There was a second chair on the dais, much smaller and pushed to one side, and Æthelflaed sat there, flanked by two men carrying spears. She saw me, smiled wryly, and raised a hand to indicate that she was unharmed.

Over fifty men were in the hall. Most were armed, despite the steward's efforts, but again no one threatened us. Our appearance seemed to have caused a sudden silence. These men, like those in the courtyard, were nervous. I knew a few of them and sensed that the hall was in two minds. The youngest men closest to the dais were Æthelwold's supporters, while the older men were his thegns, and they were the ones who were plainly unhappy at what was unfolding. Even the dogs in the hall looked whipped. One whined as we entered, then slunk to the hall's edge, where he then lay shivering. Æthelwold was standing at the dais's edge with folded arms, trying to look regal, but to me he seemed as nervous as the dogs, though a fair-haired young man beside him was full of energy. "Take them prisoner, lord," the young man urged Æthelwold.

There is no cause so hopeless, no creed so mad, no idea so ludicrous that it will not attract some believers, and the fair-haired youngster had plainly adopted Æthelwold's cause as his own. He was a handsome brute, bright-eyed, strong-jawed, and strongly built. He wore his hair long and tied behind his neck with a leather ribbon. A second ribbon was around his neck like a thin scarf and it looked oddly feminine because it was pink and made of the precious and delicate silk that is brought to Britain by traders from some far-off land. The tails of the silk ribbon hung over his mail, which was finely wrought, probably made by the expensive smiths in Frankia. His belt was paneled with gold squares and the hilt of his sword was decorated by a crystal pommel. He was rich, he was confident, and he faced us belligerently. "Who are you?" Father Coenwulf demanded of the youngster.

"My name is Sigebriht," the young man said proudly, "Lord Sigebriht to you, priest." So that was the young man who had carried messages between Æthelwold and the Danes, Sigebriht of Cent, who had loved the Lady Ecgwynn and lost her to Edward. "Don't let them talk," Sigebriht urged his patron. "Kill them!"

Æthelwold did not know what to do. "Lord Uhtred," he greeted me, for want of anything else to say. He should have ordered his men to chop us to pieces, then led his forces out to attack Edward, but he was not man enough, and he probably knew that only a handful of the men in the hall would follow him.

"Lord Æthelwold," Father Coenwulf spoke sternly, "we are here to summon you to the court of King Edward."

"There is no such king," Sigebriht yapped.

"You will be accorded the dignity of your rank," Father Coenwulf ignored Sigebriht and spoke directly to Æthelwold, "but you have disturbed the king's peace and for that you must answer to the king and his Witan."

"I am king here," Æthelwold said. He drew himself up in an attempt to look regal. "I am king," he said, "and I shall live or die here in my kingdom!"

For a moment I almost felt sorry for him. He had indeed been cheated of the throne of Wessex, thrust aside by his uncle Alfred and forced to watch as Alfred made Wessex into the most powerful kingdom of Britain. Æthelwold had found consolation in ale, mead, and wine, and in his cups he could be good company, yet always there had been that ambition to right what he saw was the great wrong done to him in childhood. Now he tried so hard to be kingly, yet even his own followers were not prepared to follow him, all but for a handful of young fools like Sigebriht.

"You are not king, lord," Father Coenwulf said simply.

"He is king!" Sigebriht insisted and stepped toward Father Coenwulf as if he would beat the priest down, and Steapa took one pace forward.

I have seen many formidable men in my life, and Steapa was the most frightening. In truth he was a gentle soul, kind and endlessly considerate, but he was a head taller than most men and blessed with a bony face over which the skin seemed to be stretched into a permanently bleak expression that suggested ferocity without pity. At one time men had called him Steapa Snotor, which meant Steapa the Stupid, but it was years since I had heard that jibe. Steapa had been born a slave, but had risen to become the head of the royal bodyguard, and though he was not swift of thought, he was loyal, painstaking, and thorough. He was also the most feared warrior of all Wessex and now, as he put one hand on the hilt of his enormous sword, Sigebriht just stopped and I saw the sudden fear on that arrogant young face.

I also saw Æthelflaed smile.

Æthelwold knew he had lost, but he still tried to hold on to his dignity. "Father Coenwulf, isn't it?" he asked.

"Yes, lord."

"Your counsel will be wise, I am sure. Perhaps you would give it to me?"

"That is why I am here," Coenwulf said.

"And say a prayer in my chapel?" Æthelwold gestured to a door behind him.

"It would be a privilege," Coenwulf said.

"You too, my dear," Æthelwold said to Æthelflaed. He sounded resigned. He beckoned a half-dozen others, his closest companions, who included the abashed Sigebriht, and they all went through the small door at the back of the dais. Æthelflaed looked quizzically at me and I nodded because I had every intention of going to the chapel with her and so she followed Sigebriht, but as soon as we started toward the dais Æthelwold raised a hand. "Just Father Coenwulf," he said.

"Where he goes, we go," I said.

"You want to pray?" Father Coenwulf asked me sarcastically.

"I want you safe," I said, "though only your god knows why."

Coenwulf looked at Æthelwold. "I have your word that I am safe in your chapel, lord?"

"You are my safety, father," Æthelwold said with surprising humility, "and I want your counsel, I want your prayers, and yes, you have my word that you are safe."

"Then wait here," Coenwulf snapped at me, "both of you."

"You trust the bastard?" I asked, loud enough for Æthelwold to hear.

"I trust in Almighty God," Coenwulf said grandly, and climbed nimbly onto the dais and followed Æthelwold out of the hall.

Steapa put his hand on my arm. "Let him go," he said, and so he and I waited. Two of the older men came to us and said this had not been their idea and that they had believed Æthelwold when he had assured them that the Witan of Wessex had agreed to his assumption of the throne, and I told them they had nothing to fear so long as they had not raised a weapon against their rightful king. That king, so far as I knew, was still waiting on the old chalk-walled fort to the north of the town, waiting as the long night fell and the stars appeared. And we waited too. "How long does a prayer take?" I asked.

"I've known them to last two hours," Steapa said gloomily, "and the sermons can take even longer."

I turned to the steward who had tried to take our swords. "Where is the chapel?" I asked him.

The man looked terrified, then stammered, "There is no chapel, lord."

I swore, hurried to the door at the rear of the hall, and pushed it open to see a sleeping chamber. There were fur rugs, woolen blankets, a wooden bucket, and a tall unlit candle in a silver holder, beyond which was a second door that led to a smaller courtyard. It was an empty courtyard with an open gate guarded by a lone spearman. "Which way did they go?" I shouted at the guard who answered by pointing west down the street outside.

We ran back to the larger courtyard where our horses were waiting. "Go to Edward," I suggested to Steapa, "tell him the bastard's running."

"And you?" he asked, hauling himself into the saddle.

"I'll go west."

"Not on your own," he said chidingly.

"Just go," I said.

Steapa was right, of course. There was really little sense in riding alone into the night's chaos, but I did not want to return to the chalk slopes of Baddan Byrig where, inevitably, the next two hours would be spent discussing what to do. I wondered what had happened to Father Coenwulf, and hoped he was alive, then I was through the gate and scattering the people in the torch-lit street as I spurred the horse down a lane that led eastward.

Æthelwold had lost his pitiable attempt to be acknowledged King of Wessex, but he had not given up. The folk of his own county had failed to support him, he had only the smallest band of supporters, and so he was fleeing to where he could find swords, shields and spears. He wanted to go north to the Danes, and he had only two choices that I could see. He could ride overland, hoping to circle around the small army that Edward had brought to Wimburnan, or he could go south to where a boat might be waiting for him. I dismissed that last thought. The Danes had not known when Alfred would die, and no Danish boat dared linger in West Saxon waters, which made it more than unlikely that any ship was waiting to rescue Æthelwold. He was on his own for now, and that meant he was trying to ride across country.

And I pursued him, or rather I groped my way into the darkness. There was a moon that night, but the shadows it cast were black on the road and neither I nor the horse could see well and so we went slowly. In places I thought I could detect the fresh hoofprints, but I could not be sure. The road itself was mud and grass, wide between hedges and tall trees, a drover's road that followed the river valley as it curved northward. Sometime in the night I came to a village where light showed in a blacksmith's hut. A boy was feeding the furnace. That was his job, to keep the fire alight through the darkness, and he cowered when he saw me in my war splendor, my helmet, mail, and scabbard lit by the flames that brightened the muddy street.

I stopped the horse and gazed at the boy. "When I was your age," I spoke from behind my helmet's cheek-plates, "I used to watch a charcoal fire. My job was to stuff the holes with moss and wet earth if any smoke escaped. I watched all night. It can be lonely."

He nodded, still too terrified to say anything.

"But I had a girl who used to watch with me," I said, remembering Brida in the darkness. "You don't have a girl?"

"No, lord," he said, on his knees now.

"Girls are the best company on lonely nights," I said, "even if they do talk too much. Look at me, boy." He had lowered his head, perhaps out of awe. "Now tell me something," I went on, "did some men ride through here? They would have had a woman with them." The boy said nothing, just stared at me. My horse did not like the heat of the furnace, or perhaps its pungent smell upset him, and so I patted his neck to quieten him. "The men told you to keep silent," I said to the boy. "They said you must keep a secret. Did they threaten you?"

"He said he was the king, lord," the boy almost whispered those words.

"The real king is close by," I said. "What's the name of this place?"

"Blaneford, lord."

"It looks a good place to live. So they rode north?"

"Yes, lord."

"How long ago?"

"Not long, lord."

"And this road goes to Sceaftesburi?" I asked, trying to remember these heartlands of rich Wessex.

"Yes, lord."

"How many men were there?" I asked.

"Dick and mimp, lord," he said, and I realized that was his way of counting, different to the ways I was used to, and he was smart enough to realize it too and held up all his fingers once and then just one hand. Fifteen.

"Was there a priest?"

"No, lord."

"You're a good lad," I said, and he was, because he had possessed the wit to count. I tossed him a scrap of silver. "In the morning," I said, "tell your father that you met Uhtred of Bebbanburg and that you did your duty to your new king."

He gazed at me with very wide eyes as I turned and rode into the ford where I let the horse drink very little, then spurred uphill.

I remember thinking I could have died that night. Æthelwold had fourteen companions, not counting Æthelflaed, and he must have known he would be pursued. I assume he thought all of Edward's army would blunder through the night, but if he had known it was a single horseman he would surely have set an ambush and I would have been beaten down by the blades and so hacked to death in the moonlight. A better death, I thought, than Alfred's. Better than lying in a stinking room with the pain conquering the body, with a lump in the belly like a stone, with dribble and tears and shit and stench. But then comes the relief of the afterlife, the rebirth into joy. The Christians call it heaven and try to scare us into its marble halls with tales of a hell hotter than the blacksmith's furnace in Blaneford, but I will go with a burst of light in the arms of a Valkyrie to the great hall of Valhalla, where my friends will wait for me, and not only my friends but my enemies too, the men I have killed in battle, and there will be feasting and drinking and fighting and women. That is our fate, unless we die badly, when we live forever in the frigid halls of the goddess Hel.

I thought that was strange as I followed Æthelwold through the night. The Christians say that our punishment is hell and the Danes say that those who die badly go to Hel, where the goddess of the same name rules. Hell and Hel sound the same, yet they are not the same. Hel is not hell. Hel does not burn people, they just live in misery. Die with a sword in your hand and you will never see Hel's decaying body or feel hunger in her vast cold caverns, but there is no punishment about Hel's domain of Hel. It is just ordinary life forever. The Christians promise punishment or reward as if we are small children, but in truth what comes after is just what went before. All will change, as Ælfadell had told me, and all will be the same as ever it was and ever shall be. And remembering Ælfadell made me think of Erce, of that slim body undulating on mine, of the guttural sounds she had made, of the memory of joy.

Dawn brought the sound of stags roaring. This was the rutting season when starlings blacken the sky and the leaves begin to fall. I paused my tired horse at a rise in the road and looked about me, but saw no one. I seemed to be alone in a misted dawn, suspended in a gold and yellow world that was silent except for the roar of the stags, and even that sound vanished as I looked eastward and southward for any sign of Edward's men, but still saw nothing. I kicked the horse on north toward the smoke-smear in the sky that betrayed the town of Sceaftesburi beyond the hills.

Sceaftesburi was one of Alfred's burhs, a fortress town that protected both a royal mint and a nunnery that had been beloved of Alfred. Æthelwold would never dare demand entrance to such a town, or risk waiting for its gates to open so that he could ride through the streets. The burh's commander, whoever he was, would be too curious, which meant Æthelwold must have circled Sceaftesburi. But which way? I searched for tracks and saw nothing obvious. I was tempted to abandon the pursuit, which had been a foolish idea in the first place. I wanted to find a tavern in the burh and eat a meal and find a bed and pay a whore to warm it, but then a hare ran across my path, east to west, and that was surely a sign from the gods. I turned west off the road.

And moments later the mist cleared and I saw the horses on a chalk hill. Between me and the hill was a wide, thickly wooded valley and I spurred into it even as I saw the horsemen had noticed me. They were in a group, staring my way and I saw one point at me, then they turned and went on northward. I counted only nine men, yet surely it had to be Æthelwold, but once I dropped into the trees I could not look for the remaining horsemen because the mist thickened here and I had to go slowly because the branches dipped low and I needed to duck. Ferns grew thick. A small stream tumbled across my path. A dead tree was layered with fungi and moss. Brambles, ivy, and holly choked the undergrowth either side of the path, a path pocked with fresh hoofprints. It was silent among the trees and in the silence I felt the fear, the prickling, the knowledge born of nothing but experience that danger was close.

I dismounted and tied the horse's reins to an oak. What I should do, I thought, was remount the horse and ride straight to Sceaftesburi and raise the alarm. I should requisition a fresh horse and lead the garrison's men in pursuit of Æthelwold, but to do that was to turn my back on whatever threatened me. I drew Serpent-Breath. There was comfort in the feel of her familiar hilt.

I walked on, slowly.

Had the horsemen on the hill seen me before I saw them? That seemed likely. I had been lost in thought as I followed the road, half dreaming, half thinking. Suppose they had seen me? They knew I was alone, they probably knew who I was, and I had only seen nine men, which suggested the others had been left in the wood to ambush me. So go back, I told myself, go back and rouse the burh's garrison, and just as I had decided that was both my duty and the prudent thing to do, two horsemen burst out of cover fifty paces away and charged up the path toward me. One carried a spear, the other a sword. Both had helmets with face-plates, both were in mail, both had shields, and both were fools.

A man cannot fight on horseback in a deep, old wood. There are too many obstacles. They could not ride abreast because the path was too narrow and the undergrowth too thick on either side, and so the spearman led and he, like his companion, was right-handed, which meant the spear was on the right side of his tired horse and to my left. I let them come, wondering why only two were attacking, but put that mystery to one side as they got close and I could see the man's eyes in the slit of his helmet, and I simply stepped to my right, into brambles and behind an oak's trunk and the spearman galloped past helplessly and I stepped back out and swung Serpent-Breath with all my strength so that she slammed the second horse in the mouth, splintering teeth and scattering blood, and the beast screamed and swerved and the rider was falling, tangled in the reins and stirrups as the first man tried to turn.

"No!" a voice shouted from deeper in the trees. "No!"

Was he talking to me? Not that it mattered. The swordsman was on his back now, struggling to rise, while the spearman was struggling to turn his horse on the narrow path. The swordsman's shield was looped to his left forearm so I simply stood on the willow boards, trapping him, and plunged Serpent-Breath down. Hard down. Once.

And there was blood in the leaf-mold and a choking sound and a body shaking beneath me and a dying man's sword arm going limp as the spearman kicked his horse back toward me. He lunged with the spear, but it was simple to avoid by swaying to one side, and I seized the ash shaft and tugged hard and the man had to let go or else be pulled from the saddle, and his horse was backing away as the rider tried to draw his sword and he was still trying when I slid Serpent-Breath up his right thigh, beneath his mail, opening his skin and muscle with her point and edge and then finding the bone of his hip and thrusting harder and shouting with all my breath to scare him and to give the lunge force. The sword was in his body and I was grinding it, turning it, pushing it, and the voice from deep in the wood shouted again, "No!"

But yes. The man had half drawn his sword, but the blood was dripping from his boot and stirrup and I simply caught his right elbow with my left hand and pulled so that he came off his horse. "Idiot," I snarled at him, and killed him as I had killed his companion, then turned fast toward the place from where the voice had sounded.

Nothing.

Somewhere far off a horn sounded, then was answered by another. The sounds came from the south and told me Edward's forces were coming. A bell began to toll, presumably from Sceaftesburi's convent or church. The wounded horse whinnied. The second man died and I pulled Serpent-Breath's tip from his throat. My boots were dark with new blood. I was tired. I wanted that meal and bed and whore, but instead I walked down the path toward the place where the two fools had come from.

The path turned where thick foliage screened the view, then it opened into a glade around a wide stream. The day's first sunlight flickered through leaves to make the grass very green. There were daisies in the grass and Sigebriht was there with three men and with Æthelflaed, all of them mounted. It was one of these men who had shouted at his two dead companions, but which man, or why, I could not tell.

I walked out of the shadow. The helmet's face-plates were closed, my mail and boots were blood-spattered, Serpent-Breath was reddened. "Who's next?" I asked.

Æthelflaed laughed. A kingfisher, all red and blue and bright, darted down the stream behind her and vanished in the shadows. "Lord Uhtred," she said, and kicked her heels so that her horse came toward me.

"You're unhurt?" I asked.

"They were all very polite," she said, looking back at Sigebriht with a mocking expression.

"There's only four of them," I said, "so which one do you want me to kill first?"

Sigebriht drew his crystal-pommeled sword. I was ready to step back among the trees, where the trunks would give me an advantage against a mounted man, but to my surprise he threw the sword so that it landed heavily in the dewy grass a few paces from me. "I yield to your mercy," Sigebriht said. His three men followed his example and threw their swords onto the ground.

"Off your horses," I said, "all of you." I watched them dismount. "Now kneel." They knelt. "Give me one reason not to kill you," I said as I walked toward them.

"We have yielded to you, lord," Sigebriht said, head lowered.

"You yielded," I said, "because your two fools failed to kill me."

"They were not my fools, lord," Sigebriht said humbly. "They were Æthelwold's men. These three are my men."

"Did he order those two idiots to attack me?" I called back to Æthelflaed.

"No," she said.

"They wanted glory, lord," Sigebriht said. "They wanted to be known as the slayers of Uhtred."

I touched the bloodied tip of Serpent-Breath to his cheek. "And what do you want, Sigebriht of Cent?"

"To make my peace with the king, lord."

"Which king?"

"There is only one king in Wessex, lord. King Edward."

I let Serpent-Breath's tip lift the long tail of fair hair tied with leather. The blade, I thought, would cut through his neck so easily. "Why do you seek peace with Edward?"

"I was wrong, lord," Sigebriht said humbly.

"Lady?" I called, not taking my eyes from him.

"They saw you following," Æthelflaed explained, "and this man," she pointed at Sigebriht, "offered to bring me back to you. He told Æthelwold that I would persuade you to join him."

"Did he believe that?"

"I told him I would try and persuade you," she said, "and he believed me."

"He's a fool," I said.

"And instead I told Sigebriht to make his peace," Æthelflaed went on, "and that his best hope of living beyond today's dusk was to abandon Æthelwold and swear allegiance to Edward."

I put the sword under Sigebriht's clean-shaven chin and tilted his face up toward me. He was so handsome, so bright-eyed, and in those eyes I could see no guile, only the eyes of a frightened man. Yet I knew I should kill him. I touched the sword-blade to the silk ribbon around his neck. "Tell me why I shouldn't cut through your miserable neck," I ordered him.

"I've yielded, lord," he said, "I beg mercy."

"What's the ribbon?" I asked, flicking the pink silk with Serpent-Breath's tip and leaving a smear of blood.

"It was a gift from a girl," he said.

"The Lady Ecgwynn?"

He gazed up at me. "She was beautiful," he said wistfully, "she was like an angel, she drove men to madness."

"And she preferred Edward," I said.

"And she's dead, lord," Sigebriht said, "and I think King Edward regrets that as much as I do."

"Fight for someone who lives," Æthelflaed said, "not for the dead."

"I was wrong, lord," Sigebriht said, and I was not sure I believed him, and so I pressed the sword against his neck and saw the fear in his blue eyes.

"It is my brother's decision," Æthelflaed said gently, knowing what was in my mind.

I let him live.

That night, so we heard later, Æthelwold crossed the border into Mercia and kept riding north until he reached the safety of Sigurd's hall. He had escaped.

Eight

Alfred was buried.

The burial took five hours of praying, chanting, weeping, and preaching. The old king had been placed in an elm coffin painted with scenes from the lives of the saints, while the lid depicted a surprised-looking Christ ascending into heaven. A splinter of the true cross was placed in the dead king's hands and his head was pillowed by a gospel book. The elm coffin was sheathed in a lead box, which in turn was enclosed by a third casket, this one of cedar and carved with pictures of saints defying death. One saint was being burned, though the flames could not touch her, a second was being tortured yet was smiling forgiveness on her hapless tormentors, while a third was being pierced by spears and still was preaching. The whole cumbersome coffin was carried down to the crypt of the old church, where it was sealed in a stone chamber where Alfred rested until the new church was finished, and then he was carried to the vault where he still lies. I remember Steapa weeping like a child. Beocca was in tears. Even Plegmund, that stern archbishop, was crying as he preached. He talked of Jacob's ladder, which appeared in a dream described in the Christian scriptures, and Jacob, as he lay on his stony pillow beneath the ladder, heard the voice of God. "The land on which you lie shall be given to your children and to their children's children," Plegmund's voice broke as he read the words, "and your children shall be like the dust of the earth and they shall spread abroad to the west and to the east and to the north and to the south, and by you and your children shall all the families of the world bless themselves."

"Jacob's dream was Alfred's dream." Plegmund's voice was hoarse by this point in his long sermon. "And Alfred now lies here, in this place, and this land shall be given to his children and to his children's children till the day of judgment itself! And not just this land! Alfred dreamed that we Saxons should spread the light of the gospel through all Britain, and all other lands, until every voice on earth is lifted in praise of God Almighty."

I remember smiling to myself. I stood at the back of the old church, watching the smoke from the incense burners swirl around the gilded rafters, and it amused me that Plegmund believed that we Saxons should spread like the dust of the earth to the north, south, east, and west. We would be lucky if we kept what land we had, let alone spread, but the congregation was moved by Plegmund's words. "The pagans press upon us," Plegmund declared, "they persecute us! Yet we shall preach to them and we shall pray for them, and we shall see them bow their knee to Almighty God and then Alfred's dream will come true and there shall be rejoicing in heaven! God will preserve us!"

I should have listened more carefully to that sermon, but I was thinking of Æthelflaed and Fagranforda. I had asked Edward's permission to go to Mercia, and his reply was to send Beocca to the Two Cranes. My old friend sat by the hearth and chided me for ignoring my eldest son. "I don't ignore him," I said. "I'd like him to come to Fagranforda as well."

"And what will he do there?"

"What he should do," I said, "train as a warrior."

"He wants to be a priest," Beocca said.

"Then he's no son of mine."

Beocca sighed. "He's a good boy! A very good boy."

"Tell him to change his name," I said. "If he becomes a priest he's not worthy to be called Uhtred."

"You're so like your father," he said, which surprised me because I had been frightened of my father. "And Uhtred is so like you!" Beocca went on. "He looks like you, and he has your stubbornness." He chuckled. "You were a most stubborn child."

I am often accused of being Uhtredærwe, the wicked enemy of Christianity, yet so many I have loved and admired have been

Christians, and Beocca was chief among them. Beocca and his wife, Thyra, Hild, Æthelflaed, dear Father Pyrlig, Osferth, Willibald, even Alfred, the list is endless, and I suppose they were all good people because their religion insists they must behave in a certain way, which mine does not. Thor and Woden demand nothing of me except respect and some sacrifice, but they would never be so foolish as to insist that I love my enemy or turn the other cheek. Yet the best Christians, like Beocca, struggle daily to be good. I have never tried to be good, though nor do I think I am wicked. I am just me, Uhtred of Bebbanburg. "Uhtred," I said to Beocca, talking of my eldest son, "will be Lord of Bebbanburg after me. He can't hold that fortress by prayer. He needs to learn how to fight."

Beocca stared into the fire. "I always hoped I would see Bebbanburg again," he said wistfully, "but I doubt that will happen now. The king says you may go to Fagranforda."

"Good," I said.

"Alfred was generous to you," Beocca said sternly.

"I don't deny it."

"And I had some influence there," Beocca said with a little pride.

"Thank you."

"You know why he agreed?"

"Because Alfred owed me," I said, "because without Serpent-Breath he wouldn't have remained king for twenty-eight years."

"Because Wessex needs a strong man in Mercia," Beocca said, ignoring my boasting.

"Æthelred?" I suggested mischievously.

"He's a good man, and you've wronged him," Beocca said fiercely.

"Maybe," I said, avoiding a quarrel.

"Æthelred is Lord of Mercia," Beocca said, "and the man with the best claim to the throne of that land, yet he has not tried to take that crown."

"Because he's frightened of Wessex," I said.

"He has been loyal to Wessex," Beocca corrected me, "but he cannot appear too subservient or the Mercian lords who crave their own country will turn against him."

"Æthelred rules in Mercia," I said, "because he's the richest man in the country, and whenever a lord loses cattle, slaves, or a hall to the Danes he knows that Æthelred will reimburse him. He pays for his lordship, but what he should be doing is crushing the Danes."

"He watches the Welsh frontier," Beocca said, as if dealing with the Welsh was an adequate excuse for being somnolent with the Danes, "but it is appreciated." He hesitated over the word, as if it had been carefully selected, "appreciated that he is not a natural warrior. He is a superb ruler," he hurried on after those words to stifle any laugh he suspected I would give, "and his administration is admirable, but he has no talent for warfare."

"And I do," I said.

Beocca smiled. "Yes, Uhtred, you do, but you have no talent for respect. The king expects you to treat Lord Æthelred with respect."

"All the respect he deserves," I promised.

"And his wife will be permitted to return to Mercia," Beocca said, "upon the understanding that she endows, indeed that she builds, a nunnery."

"She's to be a nun?" I asked, angry.

"Endows and builds!" Beocca said. "And she will be free to choose wherever she so wishes to endow and to build the nunnery."

I had to laugh. "I'm to live next door to a nunnery?"

Beocca frowned. "We cannot know where she will choose."

"No," I said, "of course not."

So the Christians had swallowed the sin. I assumed that Edward had learned a new tolerance for sin, which was no bad thing and it meant Æthelflaed was free to live more or less as she wished, though the nunnery would serve as an excuse for Æthelred to claim that his wife had chosen a life of holy contemplation. In truth Edward and his council knew they needed Æthelflaed in Mercia, and they needed me too. We were the shield of Wessex, but it seemed we were not to be the sword of the Saxons because Beocca gave me a stern warning before he left the tavern. "The king expressly wishes that the Danes be left in peace," he said. "They are not to be provoked! That is his command."

"And if they attack us?" I asked, annoyed.

"Of course you may defend yourself, but the king does not wish to start a war. Not before he is crowned."

I growled acceptance of the policy. I supposed it made sense that Edward wanted to be left in peace while he established his authority over his new kingdom, but I doubted the Danes would oblige him. I was certain they wanted war, and would want it before Edward's coronation.

That ceremony would not take place until the new year, giving time for honored guests to arrange their travel and so, as the autumn mists turned colder and the days shrank, I went at last to Fagranforda.

That was a blessed place of sweet low hills, slow rivers, and rich earth. Alfred had indeed been generous. The steward was a morose Mercian named Fulk who did not welcome a new lord, and no wonder, for he had lived well off the estate's income, helped in that by the priest who kept the accounts. That priest, Father Cynric, tried to persuade me that the harvests had been poor of late, and that the stumps in the woodland were there because the trees had died of disease rather than been felled for the value of their timber. He laid out the documents that matched the receipts I had brought from the treasury in Wintanceaster, and Father Cynric smiled happily at that coincidence. "As I told you, lord," he said, "we held the estate in sacred trust, as it were, for King Alfred." He beamed at me. He was a plump man, full-faced, with a quick smile.

"And no one ever came from Wessex to examine your accounts?"

"What need was there?" he asked, sounding surprised and amused at such a thought. "The church teaches us to be honest laborers in the Lord's vineyard."

I took all the documents and put them on the hall fire. Father Cynric and Fulk watched in speechless surprise as the parchments scorched, curled, cracked, and burned. "You've been cheating," I said, "and now it stops." Father Cynric opened his mouth to protest, but then thought better of it. "Or do I have to hang one of you?" I asked. "Maybe both?"

Finan searched both Fulk's and Father Cynric's houses and found some of their hoarded silver, which I used to buy timber and to pay back the steward who had lent me money. I have always loved to build, and Fagranforda needed a new hall, new storehouses, and a palisade, all projects for the winter. I sent Finan north to patrol the lands between the Saxons and the Danes, and he took new men with him, men who came to me because they heard I was wealthy and gave silver. Finan sent messages every few days, and they all said that the Danes were surprisingly quiet. I had been certain that Alfred's death would provoke an attack, but none came. Sigurd, it seemed, was sick, and Cnut had no desire to attack southward without his friend. I thought it an opportunity for us to attack northward and said so in a message to Edward, but the suggestion went unanswered. We heard rumors that Æthelwold had gone to Eoferwic.

Gisela's brother had died and been succeeded as king in Northumbria by a Dane who ruled only because Cnut allowed it. Cnut, for whatever reason, had no wish to be king, but his man occupied the throne and Æthelwold was sent to Eoferwic presumably because it was so far from Wessex and so deep inside Danish land, and was thus a safe place. Cnut must have believed that Edward might send a force to destroy Æthelwold, and so hid his prize behind Eoferwic's formidable Roman walls.

So Æthelwold cowered, Cnut waited, and I built. I made a hall as high as a church with stout beams and a tall palisade. I nailed wolf skulls to the gable, which faced the rising sun, and I hired men to make tables and benches. I had a new steward, a man called Herric who had been wounded in the hip at Beamfleot and could no longer fight, but Herric was energetic and mostly honest. He suggested we build a mill on the stream, a good suggestion.

It was while I was searching for a good place to make the mill that the priest arrived. It was a cold day, as cold as the day on which Father Willibald had found me in Buccingahamm, and the edges of the stream were crackling with thin ice. A wind came cold from the northern uplands, while from the south came a priest. He rode a mule, but scrambled out of the saddle when he came close to me. He was young and even taller than I was. He was skeletally thin, his black robe was filthy and its hems caked with dried mud. His face was long, his nose like a beak, his eyes bright and very green, his fair hair straggly and his chin nonexistent. He had the wispiest, most pathetic beard, which dangled halfway down a long, thin neck around which he wore a large silver cross which was missing one of its arms. "You are the great Lord Uhtred?" he inquired earnestly.

"I am," I said.

"And I am Father Cuthbert," he introduced himself, "and so very pleased to meet you. Do I bow?"

"Grovel, if you like."

To my surprise he went down on his knees. He bowed his head almost to the frost-whitened grass, then unfolded and stood. "There," he said, "I groveled. Greetings, lord, from your new chaplain."

"My what?"

"Your chaplain, your own priest," he said brightly. "It's my punishment."

"I don't need a chaplain."

"I'm sure you don't, lord. I'm unnecessary, I know. I am not needed, I am a mere blight on the eternal church. Cuthbert the Unnecessary." He smiled suddenly as an idea struck him. "If I'm ever made into a saint," he said, "I shall be Saint Cuthbert the Unnecessary! It would distinguish me from the other Saint Cuthbert, would it not? It would, indeed it would!" He capered a few steps of gangling dance. "Saint Cuthbert the Unnecessary!" he chanted. "Patron saint of all useless things. Nevertheless, lord," he composed his face into a serious expression, "I am your chaplain, a burden upon your purse, and I require food, silver, ale, and especially cheese. I'm very fond of cheese. You say you don't need me, lord, but I am here nonetheless, and at your humble service." He bowed again. "You wish to say confession? You want me to welcome you back into the bosom of Mother Church?"

"Who says you're my chaplain?" I asked.

"King Edward. I'm his gift to you." He smiled beatifically, then made a sign of the cross toward me. "Blessings on you, lord."

"Why did Edward send you?" I asked.

"I suspect, lord, because he has a sense of humor. Or," he frowned, thinking, "perhaps because he dislikes me. Except I don't think he does, in fact he doesn't dislike me at all, he's very fond of me, though he believes I need to learn discretion."

"You're indiscreet?"

"Oh, lord, I am so many things! A scholar, a priest, an eater of cheese, and now I am chaplain to Lord Uhtred, the pagan who slaughters priests. That's what they tell me. I'd be eternally grateful if you refrained from slaughtering me. May I have a servant, please?"

"A servant?"

"To wash things? To do things? To look after me? A maid would be a blessing. Something young with nice breasts?"

I was grinning by then. It was impossible not to like Saint Cuthbert the Unnecessary. "Nice breasts?" I asked sternly.

"If it pleases you, lord. I was warned you were more likely to slaughter me, to make me into a martyr, but I would much prefer breasts."

"Are you really a priest?" I asked him.

"Oh indeed, lord, I am. You can ask Bishop Swithwulf! He made me a priest! He laid his hands on me and said all the proper prayers."

"Swithwulf of Hrofeceastre?" I asked.

"The very same. He's my father and he hates me!"

"Your father?"

"My spiritual father, yes, not my real father. My real father was a stonemason, bless his little hammer, but Bishop Swithwulf educated me and raised me, God bless him, and now he detests me."

"Why?" I asked, already suspecting the answer.

"I'm not allowed to say, lord."

"Say it anyway, you're indiscreet."

"I married King Edward to Bishop Swithwulf's daughter, lord."

So the twins who were now in Æthelflaed's care were legitimate, a fact that would upset Ealdorman Æthelhelm. Edward was pretending otherwise in case the Witan of Wessex decided to offer the throne elsewhere, and the evidence of his first marriage had been sent to my care.

"God, you're a fool," I said.

"So the bishop tells me. Saint Cuthbert the Foolish? But I was a friend of Edward, and he begged me, and she was a delightful little thing. So pretty." He sighed.

"She had nice breasts?" I asked sarcastically.

"They were like two young fawns, lord," he said earnestly.

I'm sure I gaped at him. "Two young fawns?"

"The holy scriptures describe perfect breasts as being like two young fawns, lord. I have to say I've researched the matter thoroughly." He paused to consider what he had just said, then nodded approval. "Very thoroughly! Yet still the similarity escapes me, and who am I to question the holy scriptures?"

"And now," I said, "everyone is saying the marriage never happened."

"Which is why I can't tell you that it did," Cuthbert said.

"But it did," I said, and he nodded. "So the twin babies are legitimate," I went on, and he nodded again. "Didn't you know Alfred would disapprove?" I asked.

"Edward wanted the marriage," he said simply and seriously.

"And you're sworn to silence?"

"They threatened to send me to Frankia," he said, "to a monastery, but King Edward preferred I come to you."

"In hope that I'd kill you?"

"In hope, lord, that you would protect me."

"Then for God's sake don't go around telling people that Edward was married."

"I shall keep silence," he promised, "I shall be Saint Cuthbert the Silent."

The twins were with Æthelflaed, who was building her convent in Cirrenceastre, a town not far from my new estate. Cirrenceastre had been a great place when the Romans ruled in Britain and Æthelflaed lived in one of their houses, a fine building with large rooms enclosing a pillared courtyard. The house had once belonged to the older Æthelred, Ealdorman of Mercia and husband to my father's sister, and I had known it as a child, when I fled south from my other uncle's usurpation of Bebbanburg. The older Æthelred had expanded it so that Saxon thatch was joined to Roman tile, but it was a comfortable house and well protected by Cirrenceastre's walls. Æthelflaed had men pulling down some ruined Roman houses and was using the stone to make her convent. "Why bother?" I asked her.

"Because it was my father's wish," she said, "and because I promised to do it. It will be dedicated to Saint Werburgh."

"She's the woman who frightened the geese?"

"Yes."

Æthelflaed's household was loud with children. There was her own daughter, Ælfwynn, and my two youngest, Stiorra and Osbert. My oldest, Uhtred, was still at school in Wintanceaster from where he wrote me dutiful letters that I did not bother to read because I knew they were filled with tedious pieties. The youngest children at Cirrenceastre were Edward's twins who were just babies. I remember looking at Æthelstan in his swaddling clothes and thinking that so many problems could be solved with one plunge of Serpent-Breath. I was right in that, but wrong too, and little Æthelstan would grow into a young man I loved. "You know he's legitimate?" I asked Æthelflaed.

"Not according to Edward," she said tartly.

"I have the priest who married them in my household," I told her.

"Then tell him to keep his mouth shut," she said, "or he'll be buried with it open."

We were in Cirrenceastre, which lay not that far from Gleawecestre where Æthelred had his hall. He hated Æthelflaed, and I worried he would send men to capture her, then either simply kill her or immure her in a nunnery. She no longer had the protection of her father, and I doubted Edward frightened Æthelred nearly as much as Alfred had, but Æthelflaed dismissed my fears. "He might not be worried by Edward," she said, "but he's terrified of you."

"Will he make himself King of Mercia?" I asked.

She watched a mason chip at a Roman statue of an eagle. The poor man was attempting to make it look like a goose, and so far had only managed to make it resemble an indignant chicken. "He won't," Æthelflaed said.

"Why not?"

"Too many powerful men in southern Mercia want Wessex's protection," she said, "and Æthelred really is not interested in power."

"He's not?"

"Not now. He used to be. But he falls ill every few months and he fears death. He wants to fill what time he has with women." She gave me a very tart look. "He's like you in some ways."

"Nonsense, woman," I said, "Sigunn is my housekeeper."

"Housekeeper," Æthelflaed said scornfully.

"And terrified of you."

She liked that and laughed, then she sighed as an unwise blow of the mason's mallet knocked off the sad chicken's beak. "All I asked for," she said, "was a statue of Werburgh and one goose."

"You want too much," I teased her.

"I want what my father wanted," she said quietly, "England."

In those days I was always surprised when I heard that name. I knew Mercia and Wessex, and I had been to East Anglia and reckoned Northumbria was my homeland, but England? It was a dream back then, a dream of Alfred's, and now, after his death, that dream was as vague and faraway as ever. It seemed likely that if ever the four kingdoms were to be joined then they would be called Daneland rather than England, yet Æthelflaed and I shared Alfred's dream. "Are we English?" I asked her.

"What else?"

"I'm Northumbrian."

"You're English," she said firmly, "and have a Danish bed-warmer." She prodded me hard in the ribs. "Tell Sigunn I wish her a good Christmas."

I celebrated Yule with a feast at Fagranforda. We made a great wheel from timber, more than ten paces wide, and we wrapped it in straw and mounted it horizontally on an oak pillar and greased the spindle with fleece-oil so that the wheel could revolve. Then, after dark, we set fire to it. Men used rakes or spears to turn the wheel, which whirled about spewing sparks. My two youngest children were with me, and Stiorra held my hand and gazed wide-eyed at the huge burning wheel. "Why did you set fire to it?" she asked.

"It's a sign to the gods," I said, "it tells them that we remember them, and it begs them to bring new life to the year."

"It's a sign to Jesus?" she asked, not quite comprehending.

"Yes," I said, "and to the other gods."

There was a cheer when the wheel collapsed and then men and women competed to jump over the flames. I held my two children in my arms and leaped with them, flying through the smoke and sparks. I watched those sparks fly into the cold night and I wondered how many other wheels were burning in the north, where the Danes dreamed of Wessex.

Yet if they dreamed they did nothing about those dreams. That, of itself, was surprising. Alfred's death, it seemed to me, should have been a signal to attack, but the Danes had no one leader to unite them. Sigurd was still sick, we heard Cnut was busy beating the Scots into submission, and Eohric did not know whether his loyalties were to the Christian south or to the Danish north and so did nothing. Haesten still lurked in Ceaster, but he was weak. Æthelwold remained in Eoferwic, but he was helpless to attack Wessex until Cnut allowed it and so we were left in peace, though I was sure that could not last.

I was tempted, so tempted, to go north and consult Ælfadell again, yet I knew that was stupid, and I knew it was not Ælfadell I wished to see, but Erce, that strange, silent beauty. I did not go, but I had news when Offa came to Fagranforda and I sat him in my new hall and piled the fire high to warm his old bones.

Offa was a Mercian who had once been a priest, but whose faith had weakened. He abandoned the priesthood and instead walked about Britain with a pack of trained terriers who amused folk at fairs by walking on their hind legs and dancing. The few coins those dogs collected would never have paid for Offa's fine house in Liccelfeld, but his real talent, the skill that had made him wealthy, was his ability to learn about men's hopes, dreams, and intentions. His ludicrous dogs were welcome in every great hall, whether Dane or Saxon, and Offa was sharp-eared and sharp-minded, and he listened, he questioned, and then he sold what he had learned. Alfred had used him, but so did Sigurd and Cnut. It was Offa who told me what happened in the north. "Sigurd's sickness doesn't seem fatal," he told me, "just weakening. He has fevers, he recovers, then they come back."

"Cnut?"

"He won't attack south till he knows Sigurd will join him."

"Eohric?"

"Pisses himself with worry."

"Æthelwold?"

"Drinks and humps servant girls."

"Haesten?"

"Hates you, smiles, dreams of revenge."

"Ælfadell?"

"Ah," he said, and smiled. Offa was a lugubrious man who rarely smiled. His long, deep-lined face was guarded and shrewd. He cut a slice of the cheese made in my dairy. "I hear you're building a mill?"

"I am."

"Sensible, lord. A good place for a mill. Why pay a miller when you can grind your own wheat?"

"Ælfadell?" I asked again, placing a silver coin on the table.

"I hear you visited her?"

"You hear too much," I said.

"You compliment me," Offa said, scooping up the coin. "So you met her granddaughter?"

"Erce."

"So Ælfadell calls her," he said, "and I envy you."

"I thought you had a new young wife?"

"I do," he said, "but old men shouldn't take young wives."

I laughed. "You're tired?"

"I'm getting too old to keep straying the roads of Britain."

"Then stay home in Liccelfeld," I said. "You don't need the silver."

"I have a young wife," he said, amused, "so I need the peace of constant travel."

"Ælfadell?" I asked yet again.

"She was a whore in Eoferwic," he said, "years ago. That's where Cnut found her. She told fortunes as well as whoring, and she must have told Cnut something that turned out to be true because he took her under his shield."

"He gave her the cave at Buchestanes?"

"It's his land, so yes."

"And she tells folk what he wants them to hear?"

Offa hesitated, always a sign that whatever answer was required needed a little more money. I sighed and placed another coin on the table. "She speaks his words," Offa confirmed.

"So what's she saying now?" I asked, and he hesitated again. "Listen," I went on, "you wizened piece of goat gristle, I've paid enough. So tell me."

"She's saying that a new king of the south will arise in the north."

"Æthelwold?"

"They'll use him," Offa said bleakly. "He is, after all, the rightful King of Wessex."

"He's a drunken idiot."

"When did that make a man unfit to be king?"

"So the Danes will use him to placate the Saxons," I said, "then kill him."

"Of course."

"Then why wait?"

"Because Sigurd is sick, because the Scots are threatening Cnut's land, because the stars aren't aligned propitiously."

"So Ælfadell can only tell men to wait for the stars?"

"She's saying that Eohric will be King of the Sea, that Æthelwold will be King of Wessex, and that all the great lands of the south will be given to the Danes."

"King of the Sea?"

"Just a fancy way of saying that Sigurd and Cnut won't take Eohric's throne. They worry that he'll ally himself with Wessex."

"And Erce?"

"Is she as beautiful as men say?" he asked.

"You haven't seen her?"

"Not in her cave."

"Where she's naked," I said and Offa sighed. "She is more than beautiful," I said.

"So I hear. But she's a mute. She can't speak. Her mind is touched. I don't know if she's mad, but she is like a child. A beautiful, dumb, half-mad child who drives men wholly mad."

I thought about that. I could hear the sound of blades on blades outside the hall, the sound of steel hammering linden-wood shields. My men were practicing. All day, every day, men rehearse warfare, using sword and shield, ax and shield, spear and shield, readying themselves for the day when they must face Danes who practice just as much. That day, it seemed, was being delayed by Sigurd's bad health. We should attack instead, I thought, but to invade northern Mercia I needed troops from Wessex, and Edward had been advised by the Witan to keep Britain's fragile peace.

"Ælfadell is dangerous," Offa interrupted my thoughts.

"An old woman babbling her master's words?"

"And men believe her," he said, "and men who believe they know fate do not fear risk."

I thought of Sigurd's foolhardy attack on the bridge at Eanulfsbirig and knew Offa was right. The Danes might be waiting to attack, but all the time they were hearing magical prophecies that told them they would win. And rumors of those prophecies were spreading through the Saxon lands. Wyrd bið ful āræd. I had an idea, and opened my mouth to speak, then thought better of it. If a man wants to keep a secret, then Offa was the last man to tell, because he made his living betraying other men's secrets. "You were about to speak, lord?" he asked.

"What do you hear about the Lady Ecgwynn?" I asked.

He looked surprised. "I thought you knew more about her than I do."

"I know she died," I said.

"She was frivolous," Offa said disapprovingly, "but very lovely. Elfin."

"And married?"

He shrugged. "I hear a priest performed a ceremony, but there was no contract between Edward and her father. Bishop Swithwulf's no fool! He refused to allow it. So was the marriage legal?"

"If a priest performed it."

"Marriage requires a contract," Offa said sternly. "They weren't two peasants humping like pigs in a mud-floored hut, but a king and a bishop's daughter. Of course there must be a contract, and a bride-price! Without those? It's just a royal rut."

"So the children are illegitimate?"

"That's what the Witan of Wessex says, so it must be true."

I smiled. "They're sickly children," I lied, "and most unlikely to live."

Offa could not hide his interest. "Truly?"

"Æthelflaed can't persuade the boy to suckle his wet nurse," I lied again, "and the girl is frail. Not that it matters if they die, they're illegitimate."

"Their deaths would solve many problems," Offa said.

So I had done Edward one small service by spreading a rumor that would please Æthelhelm, his father-in-law. In truth the twins were healthy, squalling babies, and problems in the making, but problems that could wait, just as Cnut had decided that his invasion of southern Mercia and Wessex must wait.

There are seasons of our lives when nothing seems to be happening, when no smoke betrays a burned town or homestead and few tears are shed for the newly dead. I have learned not to trust those times, because if the world is at peace then it means someone is planning war.

Spring came and with it Edward's coronation at Cyninges Tun, the King's town, which lay just west of Lundene. I thought it a strange choice. Wintanceaster was the main town of Wessex where Alfred had built his great new church and where the largest royal palace stood, but Edward had chosen Cyninges Tun. It was true that it was a great royal estate, but of late it had been ignored because it was too close to Lundene and, before I captured that city from the Danes, Cyninges Tun had been plundered again and again. "The archbishop says it's where some of the old monarchs were crowned," Edward explained to me, "and there's a stone here."

"A stone, lord?"

He nodded. "It's a royal stone. The old kings either stood on it or sat on it, I'm not sure which." He shrugged, evidently confused by the stone's purpose. "Plegmund thinks it's important."

I had been summoned to the royal estate a week before the

ceremonies and ordered to bring as many household warriors as I could muster. I had seventy-four men, all mounted, all well equipped, and Edward added a hundred of his own men and asked that we protect Cyninges Tun during his crowning. He feared that the Danes would attack and I gladly agreed to keep guard. I would much rather have been on horseback under the open skies than sitting and standing through hours of Christian ceremony, and so I rode the empty countryside while Edward sat or stood on the royal stone and had his head anointed with holy oil and then crowned with his father's emerald-studded crown.

No Danes attacked. I had been so sure that Alfred's death would mean war, but it brought one of those strange periods during which swords rested in their scabbards, and Edward was crowned in peace and afterward he went to Lundene and summoned me there to a great council. The streets of the old Roman city were hung with banners, all in celebration of Edward's coronation, while the formidable ramparts were thick with troops. None of that was surprising, but what was astonishing was to find Eohric there.

King Eohric of East Anglia, who had conspired to kill me, was in Lundene by invitation of Archbishop Plegmund, who had sent two of his own nephews as hostages to guarantee the king's safety. Eohric and his followers had come up the Temes in three lion-prowed boats and were now quartered in the great Mercian palace that crowned the hill at the center of the old Roman city. Eohric was a big man, bellied like a pregnant sow, strong as a bullock, with a suspicious, small-eyed face. I first saw him on the ramparts, where he was walking with a group of his men along the old Roman defenses. He had three wolfhounds on leashes and their presence on the ramparts was provoking the dogs in the city beneath to howl. Weohstan, the commander of the garrison, was Eohric's guide, presumably because Edward had ordered him to show the East Anglian king whatever he wanted to see.

I was with Finan. We climbed to the ramparts up a Roman stair built into one tower of the gate that men called the Bishop's Gate. It was morning, and the sun was warming the old stone. It stank because the ditch outside the wall was filling with refuse and offal. Children were scavenging there.

A dozen West Saxon soldiers were clearing the way for Eohric's men, but they let me alone, and Finan and I just waited as the East Anglians approached us. Weohstan looked alarmed, perhaps because Finan and I were both wearing swords, though neither of us had mail or helmets or shields. I bowed to the king. "You've met the Lord Uhtred?" Weohstan asked Eohric.

The small eyes stared at me. One of the wolfhounds snarled and was quietened. "The burner of boats," Eohric said, clearly amused.

"He burns towns too," Finan could not resist saying, reminding Eohric that I had burned his fine port at Dumnoc.

Eohric's mouth tightened, but he did not rise to the bait. Instead he glanced south at the city. "A fine place, Lord Uhtred."

"May I ask what brings you here, lord King?" I asked respectfully.

"I am a Christian," Eohric said. His voice was a rumble, impressive and deep, "and the Holy Father in Rome tells me that Plegmund is my spiritual father. The archbishop invited me, I came."

"We're honored," I said, because what else do you say to a king?

"Weohstan tells me you captured the city," Eohric said. He sounded bored, like a man who knows he must make conversation, but is not interested in what is being said.

"I did, lord."

"At the gate over there?" he gestured west toward Ludd's Gate.

"Yes, lord King."

"You must tell me the tale," he said, though he was only being polite. We were both being polite. This was a man who had tried to kill me and neither of us acknowledged that, but instead made stilted conversation. I knew what he was thinking. He was thinking that the wall beside the Bishop's Gate was the most vulnerable place in the whole three miles of Roman ramparts. It offered the easiest approach, though the rubbish-stinking ditch was a formidable obstacle, but east of the gate the wall's ragstone had crumbled in places and been replaced with a palisade of oak trunks. A whole stretch of wall between the Bishop's Gate and the Old Gate was derelict. When I had commanded the garrison I had made the palisade, but it needed repair and if Lundene could be captured then this was the easiest place to attack, and Eohric was thinking the same thing. He gestured to a man beside him. "This is the Jarl Oscytel," he said.

Oscytel was the commander of Eohric's household troops. He was what I expected, big and brutal, and I nodded to him and he nodded back. "You've come to pray too?" I asked him.

"I come because my king ordered me to come," Oscytel said.

And why, I thought angrily, had Edward allowed this nonsense? Eohric and Oscytel could well become Wessex's enemies, yet here they were being welcomed to Lundene and treated as honored guests. There was a great feast that night and one of Edward's harpists chanted a great poem in praise of Eohric, celebrating his heroism, though in truth Eohric had never made any great reputation in battle. He was a sly, clever man, who ruled by force, who avoided battle, who survived because his kingdom lay at the edge of Britain and so no armies needed to cross his land to reach their enemies.

Yet Eohric was not negligible. He could lead at least two thousand well-equipped warriors to war and if the Danes were ever to make a wholehearted assault on Wessex then Eohric's men would be a valuable addition. Equally, if the Christians were ever to make an assault on the northern pagans they would welcome those two thousand troops. Both sides tried to seduce Eohric and Eohric received the gifts, made promises, and did nothing.

Eohric did nothing, but he was the key to Plegmund's grand idea to unite all Britain. The archbishop claimed it had come to him in a dream after Alfred's funeral, and he had persuaded Edward that the dream was from God. Britain would be united by Christ, not by the sword, and there was something propitious in the year, 900. Plegmund believed, and convinced Edward, that Christ would return in the year 1000, and that it was the divine will that the last hundred years of the Christian millennium should be spent converting the Danes in readiness for the second coming. "War has failed," Plegmund thundered from his pulpit, "so we must put our faith in peace!" He believed the time had come to convert the pagans and he wanted Eohric's Christian Danes to be his missionaries to Sigurd and Cnut.

"He wants what?" I asked Edward. I had been summoned to

the king's presence on the morning after the great feast and had listened as Edward explained the archbishop's hopes.

"He wants the conversion of the heathen," Edward said stiffly.

"And they want Wessex, lord."

"Christian will not fight Christian," Edward said.

"Tell that to the Welsh, lord King."

"They keep the peace," he said, "mostly."

He was married by then. His bride, Ælflæd, was little more than a child, perhaps thirteen or fourteen, already pregnant, and she was playing with her companions and a kitten in the small garden where I had so often met Æthelflaed. The window in the king's chamber looked down on that small garden and Edward saw where I was looking. He sighed. "The Witan believes Eohric will prove an ally."

"Your father-in-law believes that?"

Edward nodded. "We've had war for three generations," he said sternly, "and still it has not brought peace. Plegmund says we must try prayer and preaching. My mother agrees."

I laughed at that. So we were to defeat our enemies with prayer? Cnut and Sigurd, I thought, would welcome that tactic. "And what does Eohric want from us?" I asked.

"Nothing!" Edward seemed surprised by the question.

"He wants nothing, lord?"

"He wants the archbishop's blessing."

Edward, in those first years of his reign, was under the influence of his mother, his father-in-law, and the archbishop, and all three resented the cost of war. Building the burhs and equipping the fyrd had taken huge sums of silver, while to put an army into the field cost even more, and that money came from the church and from the ealdormen. They wanted to keep their silver. War is expensive, but prayer is free. I scoffed at the idea, and Edward cut me off with an abrupt gesture. "Tell me about the twins," he said.

"They thrive," I said.

"My sister said the same, but I heard Æthelstan won't suckle?" he sounded anguished.

"Æthelstan sucks like a bull calf," I said. "I started a rumor that he's weak. It's what your mother and your father-in-law want to hear."

"Ah," Edward said, and smiled. "I'm forced to deny their legitimacy," he went on, "but they are dear to me."

"They're safe and well, lord," I assured him.

He touched my forearm. "Keep them that way! And, Lord Uhtred," his hand tightened on my forearm to emphasize his next words, "I don't want the Danes provoked! You understand me?"

"Yes, lord King."

He suddenly realized he was gripping my arm and pulled his hand away. He was awkward with me, I assumed because he was embarrassed that he had made me nursemaid to his royal bastards, or perhaps because I was his sister's lover, or perhaps because he had ordered me to keep the peace when he knew I believed that peace was fraudulent. But the Danes were not to be provoked, and I was sworn to obey Edward.

So I set out to provoke the Danes.

PART THREE

ANGELS

Nine

"Edward's under the thumb of the priests," I grumbled to Ludda, "and his damned mother is worse. Stupid bitch." We had returned to Fagranforda and I had taken him northward to the edge of the hills from where a man can stare across the wide Sæfern into the hills of Wales. It was raining in that far west, but a watery sun reflected like beaten silver from the river in the valley beneath us. "They think they can avoid war by praying," I went on, "and all because of that fool Plegmund. He thinks God will geld the Danes."

"Prayer might work, lord," Ludda said cheerfully.

"Of course it won't work," I snarled, "if your god wanted it to work then why didn't he do it twenty years ago?"

Ludda was too sensible to offer an answer. There were just the two of us. I was seeking something, and I did not want folk to know what I sought, and so Ludda and I rode the crestline alone. We were searching, talking to slaves in the fields and to thegns in their halls, and on the third day I found what I sought. It was not perfect. It was too near to Fagranforda for my liking and not close enough to Danish land.

"But there's nothing like this to the north," Ludda said, "not that I know of. There are plenty of weird stones up north, but not any buried stones."

Weird stones are strange circles of great boulders placed by the old people, presumably in honor of their gods. Usually, when we find such a place, we dig at the base of the stones, and I have found treasure at one or two. The buried stones are in mounds, some of which are round heaps and some like long ridges, and both are the old people's graves. We dig into them too, though some folk believe the skeletons inside are protected by spirits or even by dragons with fiery breath, but I once uncovered a jar filled with jet, amber, and golden ornaments inside just such a grave. The mound we discovered that day was on a high ridge with views stretching all around. Looking north, we could see into the far-off Danish land, though that was a long way off, too far off, but nevertheless I thought this ancient tomb would suit us.

The place was called Natangrafum and it belonged to a Mercian thegn named Ælwold, who was happy that I should dig into his mound. "I'll lend you slaves to do the work," he told me, "bastards don't have enough to do until the harvest."

"I'll use my own," I said.

Ælwold was immediately suspicious, but I was Uhtred and he did not want to antagonize me. "You'll share anything you find?" he asked anxiously.

"I will," I said, then put gold on his table. "That gold," I said, "is for your silence. No one knows I'm here and you tell no one. If I find you break that silence I'll come back and I'll bury you in that mound."

"I'll say nothing, lord," he promised. He was older than I, with pendulous jowls and long gray hair. "God knows I don't want trouble," he went on, "last year's harvest was bad, the Danes aren't that far away, and I just pray for a quiet life." He took the gold. "But you'll find nothing in that mound, lord. My father dug it out years ago and there's nothing there but skeletons. Not even a bead."

There were two graves on the ridge top, one built upon the other. A circular mound lay in the center and athwart it and beneath it, running east and west, was a long mound some ten feet high and over sixty paces long. Much of that long mound was just that, a mound of earth and chalk, but at its eastern end were man-made caves that were entered through a boulder-clad doorway that faced toward the rising sun.

I sent Ludda to fetch a dozen slaves from Fagranforda and they moved the boulder, and cleared the entrance of earth so that we were able to stoop into the long, stone-lined passageway. Four chambers, two on either side, opened from that tunnel. We lit the tomb with pitch-soaked torches and pulled down the heavy rocks that blocked the chamber entrances and found, as Ælwold had said, nothing but skeletons.

"Will it do?" I asked Ludda.

He did not answer at first. He was staring at the skeletons and there was fear on his face. "They'll come back to haunt us, lord," he said softly.

"No," I said, yet felt a cold shiver in my blood. "No," I said again, though I did not believe it.

"Don't touch them, lord," he pleaded.

"Ælwold said his father disturbed them," I said, trying to convince myself, "so we should be safe."

"He disturbed them, lord, and that means he woke them. Now they're waiting to take revenge." The skeletons lay in untidy heaps, adults and children together. Their skulls grinned at us. One bony head had a great gash in its left side and there were vestiges of hair on another. A child lay curled in a skeleton's lap. Another corpse reached a bony arm toward us, its finger bones spread on the stony floor. "Their spirits are here," Ludda whispered, "I can feel them, lord."

I felt the cold shiver again. "Ride back to Fagranforda," I told Ludda, "and bring Father Cuthbert and my best hound."

"Your best hound?"

"Lightning, bring him. I'll expect you tomorrow."

We crept back out of the passage and the slaves put back the great boulder that sealed the dead from the living, and that night the sky was lit with great curtains of pale blue and glowing white that shivered high to hide the stars. I have seen those lights before, usually in the depths of winter and always in the northern sky, but it was surely no coincidence that they shimmered the heavens on the day I had let light fall on the dead beneath the earth.

I had rented a house from Ælwold. It was a Roman house, mostly in ruins, which lay a small distance from a village called Turcandene, which was a short ride south of the tomb. Brambles choked most of the house and ivy wriggled up its broken walls, but the two largest rooms, from where the Romans had once lorded the nearby countryside, had been used as a cattle shed and were protected by crude rafters and stinking thatch. We cleared those rooms and I slept under the thatch that night and next morning went back to the tomb. A mist hovered about the long mound. I waited there with the slaves squatting a few paces away. Ludda returned about midday and the mist still lingered. He had Lightning, my good deerhound, on a leash, and with him was Father Cuthbert. I took Lightning's leash from Ludda. The hound whimpered and I ruffled his ears. "What you have to do now," I told Cuthbert, "is make certain that the spirits in this grave don't interfere with us."

"May I ask, lord, what it is you do here?"

"What did Ludda tell you?"

"Just that you needed me, and to bring the doggy."

"Then that's all you need to know. And make sure you drive those spirits away."

We took the great entrance stone away and Cuthbert went into the grave where he chanted prayers, sprinkled water, and planted a cross he made from tree branches. "We must wait till the night's heart, lord," he told me, "to make sure the prayers have worked." He looked distraught and waved his hands in gestures that suggested hopelessness. He had the hugest hands and never seemed to know quite what to do with them. "Will the spirits obey me?" he asked. "I don't know! They sleep during the day and should wake to find themselves chained and helpless, but perhaps they're stronger than we know? We'll discover tonight."

"Why tonight? Why not now?"

"They sleep in the daytime, lord, then they'll wake tonight and scream like souls in torment. If they break the chains?" He shuddered. "But I shall stay through the night and summon angels."

"Angels?"

He nodded seriously. "Yes, lord, angels." He saw my puzzlement and smiled. "Oh don't think of angels as pretty girls, lord. Simple folk believe angels are lovely bright things with wonderful," he paused, his huge hands fluttering over his chest, "fawns," he finally said, "but in truth they're the shield-warriors of God. Fiercely formidable creatures!" He flapped his hands, to suggest wings, then went very still as he became aware of my gaze. I stared at him so long that he became nervous. "Lord?" he asked tremulously.

"You're clever, Cuthbert," I said.

He looked pleased and bashful. "I am indeed, lord."

"Saint Cuthbert the Clever," I said in admiration. "A fool," I went on, "but such a clever fool!"

"Thank you, lord, you're so kind."

That night Cuthbert and I stayed in the tomb's entrance and watched the stars grow bright. Lightning lay with his head on my lap as I stroked him. He was a great hound, full of running, fierce as a warrior, and fearless. A quarter moon climbed above the hills. The night was filled with noises, the rustle of creatures in nearby woods, the haunting call of a hunting owl, the cry of a vixen far away. When the moon had climbed to its height Father Cuthbert faced the tomb, went to his knees, and began to pray silently, his lips moving and his hands clasping the broken cross. If angels came, I did not see them, but perhaps they were there; the bright-winged and beautiful shield-warriors of the Christian god.

I let Cuthbert pray as I took Lightning to the top of the mound where I knelt and cuddled the hound. I told him how good he was, how loyal and how brave. I stroked his coarse pelt and I buried my head in his fur and I told him he was the greatest hound I had ever known, and I was still cuddling him as I cut his throat with one hard tug of a knife I had sharpened that afternoon. I felt his huge body struggle and lurch, the sudden howl fading fast, the blood soaking my mail and knees, and I was crying because of his death, and I held his shivering body and I told Thor I had made the sacrifice. I did not want to, but it is the sacrifice of things dear to us that touches the minds of the gods, and I held Lightning until he died. It was mercifully swift. I begged Thor to accept the sacrifice and in return to keep the dead silent in their grave.

I carried Lightning's body to some nearby trees and I used the knife and a shard of stone to make a grave. I laid the hound inside, put the knife beside him, then wished him happy hunting in the next world. I filled in the grave and heaped rocks over it to preserve his body from the carrion-eaters. It was almost dawn by the time I had finished and I was dirty, blood-soaked, and miserable.

"Dear God, what happened?" Father Cuthbert stared aghast at me.

"I prayed to Thor," I said curtly.

"The dog?" he whispered the question.

"Is hunting in the next world," I said.

He shuddered. Some priests would have chided me for sacrificing to false gods, but Cuthbert just made the sign of the cross. "The spirits have been quiet," he told me.

"So one of the prayers worked," I said, "either yours or mine."

"Or both, lord," he said.

And when the sun rose the slaves came and I had them open the tomb and then move the dead from one of the two deeper chambers. They piled the bones in the opposite chamber, and then we sealed that corpse-crowded space with a slab of rock. We put skulls in the two cavities nearest the entrance, so that any visitor, stooping into the passageway, would be greeted by the grinning dead. The hardest work was disguising the entrance of the northernmost chamber, the one we had cleared of bones, because Ludda needed to be able to get in and out of that artificial cave. Father Cuthbert found the solution. His father had taught him the stonemason's trade, and Cuthbert clumsily chipped away at a limestone slab until it resembled a thin shield. It took him two days, but he managed it, and we balanced the thin slab on a flat rock, and Ludda found he could tip it easily enough. He could pull it outward and crawl past it into the chamber, and then another man could push it back upright so that Ludda was hidden behind the shield-like slab. When he spoke from behind the slab his voice was muffled but audible.

We sealed the grave again, piling earth over the entrance boulder and then went back to Fagranforda. "Now we go to Lundene," I told Ludda. "You, me, and Finan."

"Lundene!" He liked that. "Why are we going, lord?"

"To find two whores, of course."

"Of course," he said.

"I can help!" Father Cuthbert said eagerly.

"I thought I'd make you responsible for collecting the goose feathers," I told Cuthbert.

"Goose feathers?" He stared at me, appalled. "Oh, lord, please!"

Whores and goose feathers. Plegmund was praying for peace and I was planning for war.

I took thirty men to Lundene, not because I needed them, but because a lord should travel in style. We found quarters for men and horses in the Roman fort that guarded the old city's north-western corner, then I walked with Finan and Weohstan along the remnants of the Roman wall. "When you commanded here," Weohstan asked, "did they starve you of money?"

"No," I said.

"I have to beg for every coin," he grumbled. "They're building churches, but I can't persuade them to repair the wall."

And the wall needed repair more than ever. A great stretch of the Roman battlements between the Bishop's Gate and the Old Gate had fallen into the stinking ditch beyond. It was not a new problem. Back when I had been commander of the garrison, I had filled the gap with a massive oak palisade, but those trunks were dark now and some of them were rotting. King Eohric had seen this decayed stretch and I did not doubt he had noted it, and after his visit to Lundene I had suggested that repairs be made urgently, but nothing had been done. "Just look," Weohstan said, and scrambled awkwardly down the slope of rubble that marked the ruined wall's end. He pushed on an oak trunk and I saw it move like a dead tooth. "They won't pay to replace them," Weohstan said gloomily. He kicked the base of the trunk and soft dark lumps of fungus-ridden wood exploded from his boot.

"We're at peace," I said sarcastically, "hadn't you heard?"

"Tell that to Eohric," Weohstan said, climbing back to join me. All the land to the northeast was Eohric's land, and Weohstan told of Danish patrols coming close to the city. "They're watching us," he said, "and all I'm allowed to do is wave at them."

"They don't need to come close," I said, "their traders will have told them everything they want to know." Lundene was always busy with traders, Danish, Saxon, Frankish, and Frisian, and such merchants carried news back to their homelands. Eohric, I was certain, knew just how vulnerable Lundene's defenses were, indeed he had seen them for himself. "But Eohric's a cautious bastard," I said.

"Sigurd isn't."

"He's still sick."

"Pray God he dies," Weohstan said savagely.

I learned more news in the city's taverns. There were shipmasters from the whole coast of Britain who, for the price of an ale, offered rumors, some of them true. And not one rumor spoke of war. Æthelwold was still sheltered in Eoferwic, and still claimed to be King of Wessex, but he had no power until the Danes gave him an army. Why were they so quiet? It puzzled me. I had been so confident they would attack at the news of Alfred's death, but instead they did nothing. Bishop Erkenwald knew the answer. "It's God's will," he told me. We had met by chance in a street. "God commanded us to love our enemies," he explained, "and by love we shall make them Christian and peaceable."

I remember staring at him. "Do you really believe that?" I asked.

"We must have faith," he said fiercely. He made the sign of the cross toward a woman who had curtseyed to him. "So," he asked me, "what brings you to Lundene?"

"We're looking for whores," I said. He blinked. "Do you know any good ones, bishop?" I asked.

"Oh, dear God," he hissed, and went on his way.

In truth I had decided against finding whores in Lundene's taverns because there was always a chance that the girls might be recognized, and so I led Finan, Ludda, and Father Cuthbert down to the slave dock that lay upriver of the old Roman bridge. Lundene had never possessed a thriving slave market, but there was always some small trade in young folk captured from Ireland or Wales or Scotland. The Danes kept more slaves than the Saxons, and those that we did possess were usually farm laborers. A man who cannot afford an ox could harness a pair of slaves to a plow, though the furrow would never be as deep as that made by an ox-drawn blade. Oxen were less trouble too, though in the old days a man could kill a slave who proved a nuisance, and face no penalty. Alfred's laws changed that. And many men liked to release their slaves, believing it earned them God's approval, and so there was no great demand in Lundene, though there were usually a few slaves for sale at the dock beside the Temes. The traders came from Ratumacos, a town in Frankia, and almost all those traders were Northmen because the Viking crews had conquered all the region about that town. They came to buy the young folk captured in our border skirmishes, and some also brought slaves to sell, knowing that the wealthy men of Wessex and Mercia appreciated an exotic girl. The church frowned on that trade, but it thrived anyway.

The wharf lay not far beyond the river wall and the slaves were kept in dank wooden huts inside the wall. There were four traders in Lundene that day and their guards saw us coming and warned their masters that rich men were approaching. The traders came into the street and bowed low. "Wine, my lords?" one asked. "Ale, perhaps? Or whatever your lordships desire."

"Women," Father Cuthbert said.

"Be quiet," I growled at him.

"Jesus and Joseph," Finan said under his breath and I knew he was remembering the long months he and I had spent as slaves, chained to Sverri's oars, our arms branded with the S of slavery. Sverri had died, as had his henchman, Hakka, both slaughtered by Finan, but the Irishman had never lost his hatred of slavers.

"You're looking for women?" one of the traders asked. "Or for girls? Something young and tender? I have just what you need. Unspoilt goods! Juicy and precious! Gentlemen?" He bowed, gesturing us toward a crude door inserted into a Roman arch.

I looked at Father Cuthbert. "Take the grin off your face," I snarled at him, then lowered my voice, "and go and find Weohstan. Tell him to bring ten or a dozen men. Quickly."

"But, lord . . ." he began, wanting to stay.

"Go!" I shouted.

He fled. "Always wise to lose the priests, lord," the trader said, assuming I had sent Cuthbert away because the church frowned on his business. I tried to make a friendly response, but the same anger that was seething in Finan was now curdling my belly. I remembered the humiliation of slavery, the misery. Finan and I had once been chained in a dank building exactly like this. The scar on my upper arm seemed to smart as I followed the trader through the low door. "I brought a half-dozen girls across the water," he said, "and I assume you're not wanting dairymaids or kitchen drabs?"

"We want angels," Finan said tightly.

"That's what I supply!" the man said cheerfully.

"What's your name?" I asked.

"Halfdan," he said. He was in his thirties, I guessed, burly and tall with a head as bald as an egg, and a beard that reached to his waist, where a silver-hilted sword was strapped. The room we entered had four guards, two armed with cudgels and two with swords. They watched a score of slaves who sat chained in the floor's sewage-stinking sludge. The back wall of the hut was the city-side of the river rampart, its stones green and black in the small light that came through chinks in the rotting thatch roof. The slaves watched us sullenly. "They're mostly Welsh," Halfdan said carelessly, "but there's a couple from Ireland."

"You'll take them to Frankia?" Finan asked.

"Unless you want them," Halfdan said. He unbolted another door, then rapped on its dark wood, and I heard a second bolt being drawn on the further side. The door was pulled open to reveal another man waiting there, this one with a sword. He guarded Halfdan's most valuable merchandise, the girls. The man grinned a welcome as we stooped through the doorway.

It was difficult to see what the girls looked like in the gloom. They huddled in a corner, and one appeared to be sick. I could see that one girl was very dark-skinned while the others were fair. "Six of them," I said.

"You can count, lord," Halfdan said in jest. He bolted the door that led back into the larger room, where the men slaves were kept.

Finan knew what I meant. Two of us and six slavers, and we were angry, and we had not been given a chance to fight anyone for too long, and we were restless. "Six is nothing," Finan said. Ludda sensed an undertone and looked nervous.

"You want more than six?" Halfdan asked. He banged open a recalcitrant shutter to let in some light from the street and the girls blinked, half dazzled. "Six beauties," Halfdan said proudly.

The six beauties were thin, bedraggled, and terrified. The dark-skinned girl turned her face away, but not before I saw that she was indeed beautiful. Two of the others were very fair-haired. "Where are they from?"

"Mostly from north of Frankia," Halfdan said, "but that one?" He pointed to the cringing girl. "She's from the ends of the earth. The gods alone know where she sprang from. Could have dropped from the moon for all I know. I bought her off a trader from the south. She speaks some weird tongue, but she's a pretty enough thing if you like your meat dark."

"Who doesn't?" Finan asked.

"I was going to keep her," Halfdan said, "but the bitch won't stop crying and I can't abide a weepy bitch."

"They were whores?" I asked.

"They're not virgins," Halfdan said, amused. "I won't lie to you, lord, if that's what you want then I can find some for you, but it might take a month or two? But not these girls. The dark one and the Frisian were put to work in a tavern for a time, but they weren't overused, just broken in. They're still pretty. Let me show you." He reached down with a massive hand and pulled the dark girl out of the huddle. She screamed as he pulled, and he slapped her hard around the head. "Stop crying, you silly bitch," he snapped. He turned her face toward me. "What do you think, lord? She's a weird color, but a lovely girl."

"She is," I agreed.

"Same color all over," he said, grinning, and to prove it he yanked her dress down to reveal her breasts. "Stop whimpering, bitch," he said, slapping her again. He lifted one of her breasts. "See, lord? Brown tits."

"Let me," I said. I had drawn my knife and Halfdan assumed I was going to cut off the remains of the girl's dress, and so he stepped away.

"Have a good look, lord," he said.

"I will," I promised, and the girl was still whimpering as I turned and drove the blade up into Halfdan's belly, but there was metal beneath his tunic and the blade was stopped dead. I could hear the whisper of Ludda's sword sliding from the scabbard as Halfdan tried to head-bang me, but I already had hold of his beard with my left hand and I pulled it down hard. I had turned the knife upright and I pulled Halfdan's head down onto the point. The girls were screaming and one of the guards in the other room was hammering the bolted door. Halfdan was bellowing and then the bellow turned to a gurgle as the blade tore into his lower jaw and throat. There was blood brightening the room. Finan's man was already dead, killed by the Irishman's lightning speed, and then Finan slashed the blade across the back of Halfdan's legs, hamstringing him, and the big man went to his knees and I finished the job properly by slitting his throat. His big beard soaked up most of the blood.

"You took your time," Finan said, amused.

"I'm out of practice," I said. "Ludda, tell the girls to be quiet."

"Four more," Finan said.

I sheathed the knife, wiped the blood from my hand on Halfdan's tunic, and drew Serpent-Breath. Finan unbolted the door and it burst open. A guard ducked inside, saw the blade waiting for him, and tried to back away, but Finan pulled him inside and I drove the sword deep into his belly, then brought a knee into his face as he buckled. He went down on the blood-soaked floor. "Finish him off, Ludda," I ordered.

"Jesus," he murmured.

The other three guards were more cautious. They waited at the long room's farther end and they had already called for help from the other slavers. It was in the traders' interest to help each other, and their appeal brought still more men into the room. Four more, then five, all armed, and all eager for a fight. "Osferth always says we don't think enough before we start a fight," Finan said.

"He's right, isn't he?" I said, but then there was a huge shout from the street. Weohstan had arrived with some of his garrison troops. Those troops forced their way into the shack and herded the slavers out into the street, where two traders were complaining to Weohstan that we were murderers. Weohstan bellowed for quiet, then explored the shack. He wrinkled his nose at the stench in the large room, then ducked into the smaller room and looked at the two corpses. "What happened?"

"These two had an argument," I said, pointing to Halfdan and the guard Finan had slaughtered so quickly, "and they killed each other."

"And that one?" Weohstan nodded at the third man who was curled on the floor and whimpering.

"I told you to finish him," I said to Ludda, then did the job myself. "He was overcome with grief at their deaths," I explained to Weohstan, "so tried to kill himself."

Two of the other slave traders had followed us into the shed and they protested fiercely that we were liars and murderers. They pointed out that their trade was legal and that they had been promised the protection of the laws. They demanded that I stand trial for manslaughter and that I pay a huge price in silver for the lives I had taken. Weohstan listened to them patiently. "You'd swear an oath at his trial?" he asked the two men.

"We will!" one of the traders said.

"You'll tell what happened and swear to it on oath?"

"He must compensate us!"

"Lord Uhtred," Weohstan turned to me, "you'll bring oath-givers to contest the evidence?"

"I will," I said, but the mention of my name had been enough to drain the belligerence from the two men. They stared at me for an eyeblink, then one of them muttered that Halfdan had always been an argumentative fool.

"So you won't swear in court?" Weohstan asked, but the two men were already backing away. They fled.

Weohstan grinned. "What I'm supposed to do," he said, "is arrest you for manslaughter."

"I didn't do anything," I said.

He looked at Serpent-Breath's reddened blade. "I can see that, lord," he said.

I stooped to Halfdan's body and slit his tunic open to find a mail coat, but also, as I expected, a pouch at his waist. It was the pouch that had stopped my first knife thrust and it was crammed with coins, many of them gold.

"What do we do with the slaves?" Weohstan wondered aloud.

"They're mine," I said, "I just bought them." I handed him the pouch after taking a few coins for myself. "That should buy oak trunks for a palisade."

He counted the coins and looked delighted. "You're an answer to prayer, lord," he said.

We took the slaves to a tavern in the new city, the Saxon settlement that lay to the west of Roman Lundene. The coins I had taken from Halfdan's purse paid for food, ale, and clothing. Finan talked to the men and reckoned a half-dozen would make good warriors. "If we ever need warriors again," he grumbled.

"I hate peace," I said, and Finan laughed.

"What do we do with the others?" he asked.

"Let the men go," I said, "they're young, they'll survive."

Ludda and I spoke with the girls while Father Cuthbert just stared at them wide-eyed. He was entranced by the dark-skinned girl, whose name appeared to be Mehrasa. She looked the oldest of the six, she was perhaps sixteen or seventeen while the others were all three or four years younger. Once they realized they were safe, or at least not in any immediate danger, they began to smile. Two were Saxon girls, taken from the coast of Cent by Frankish raiders, and two were Franks. Then there was the mysterious Mehrasa, and the sick girl who was a Frisian. "The Centish girls can go home," I said, "but you take the others to Fagranforda." I was speaking to Ludda and Father Cuthbert. "Choose a pair of them. Teach them what they need to know. The other two can work in the dairy or kitchens."

"A pleasure, lord," Father Cuthbert said.

I looked at him. "If you mistreat them," I said, "I'll hurt you."

"Yes, lord," he said humbly.

"Now go."

I sent Rypere and a dozen men to protect the girls on their journey, but Finan and I stayed in Lundene. I have always liked that city and there was nowhere better to discover what happened in the rest of Britain. I talked to traders and travelers and even listened to one of Erkenwald's interminable sermons, not because I needed his advice, but to hear what the church was telling its people. The bishop preached well and his message was exactly what Archbishop Plegmund wanted. It was a plea for peace, to give the church time to enlighten the heathen. "We have been oppressed by war," Erkenwald said, "and we have been soaked by the tears of widows and of mothers. Every man who kills another man breaks a mother's heart." He knew I was in the church and was staring into the shadows where I stood, then he pointed at a fresh painting on the wall that showed Mary, Christ's mother, weeping at the foot of the cross. "What guilt those Romans had to bear, and what guilt we bear when we kill! We are the children of God, not lambs to be slaughtered."

There had been a time when Erkenwald preached slaughter, urging us to ravage the pagan Danes, but the coming of the year 900 had somehow persuaded the church to enjoin peace on us, and it seemed their prayers were being answered. There were cattle raids on the borderlands, yet no Danish armies came to conquer. Later that summer Finan and I went aboard one of Weohstan's ships and were rowed downriver to the wide estuary where I had spent so much time. We went close to Beamfleot and I saw that no Danes had tried to rebuild the burned forts and no ships lay in the Hothlege Creek, though we could see the blackened ribs of the vessels we had burned there. We went further east to where the Temes widened into the great sea and we nosed the boat across the shallows at Sceobyrig, another place where Danish crews liked to wait in ambush for trading ships traveling to and from Lundene, but the anchorage was empty. It was the same on the estuary's southern bank. Nothing but wild birds and wet mud.

We rowed up the curving River Medwæg to the burh at Hrofeceastre, where I saw that the timber palisade atop the mighty earth bank was rotting like the one in Lundene, but a great heap of newly felled oak trunks suggested that someone here was ready to repair the defenses. Finan and I went ashore at the wharf by the Roman bridge and walked to the bishop's house beside the great church. The steward bowed to us and, when he heard my name, did not dare ask for my sword. Instead he took us to a comfortable room and had servants bring us ale and food.

Bishop Swithwulf and his wife arrived an hour later. The bishop was a worried-looking man, gray-haired, with a long face and twitching hands, while his wife was small and nervous. She must have bowed to me ten times before sitting. "What brings you here, lord?" Swithwulf asked.

"Curiosity," I said.

"Curiosity?"

"I'm wondering why the Danes are so quiet," I said.

"God's will," the bishop's wife said timidly.

"Because they're planning something," Swithwulf said. "Never trust a Dane when he's silent." He looked at his wife. "Don't the cooks need your advice?"

"The cooks? Oh!" She stood, fluttered for a moment, then fled.

"Why are the Danes quiet?" Swithwulf asked me.

"Sigurd's ill," I suggested, "Cnut's busy on his northern border."

"And Æthelwold?"

"Getting drunk in Eoferwic," I said.

"Alfred should have strangled him," Swithwulf growled.

I was warming to the bishop. "You're not preaching peace like the rest?" I asked.

"Oh, I preach what I'm told to preach," he said, "but I'm also deepening the ditch and rebuilding the wall."

"And Ealdorman Sigelf?" I asked. Sigelf was the ealdorman of Cent, the county's military leader and its most prominent noble.

The bishop looked at me suspiciously. "What of him?"

"He wants to be King of Cent, I hear."

Swithwulf was taken aback by that statement. He frowned. "His son had that idea," he said cautiously. "I'm not sure if Sigelf thinks the same way."

"And Sigebriht was talking to the Danes," I said. Sigebriht, who had surrendered to me outside Sceaftesburi, was Sigelf's son.

"You know that?"

"I know that," I said. The bishop sat silent. "What's going on in Cent?" I asked, and still he was silent. "You're the bishop," I said, "you hear things from your priests. So tell me."

He still hesitated, but then, like a millpond's dam bursting, he told me of the unhappiness in Cent. "We were our own kingdom once," he said. "Now Wessex treats us as runts of the litter. Look what happened when Haesten and Harald landed! Were we protected? No!"

Haesten had landed on Cent's northern coast while Jarl Harald

Bloodhair had brought more than two hundred ships to the southern shore where he had stormed a half-built burh and slaughtered the men inside, then spread across the county in an orgy of burning, killing, enslaving, and robbing. Wessex had sent an army led by Æthelred and Edward to oppose the invaders, but the army had done nothing. Æthelred and Edward had placed their men on the great wooded ridge at the center of Cent and then argued whether to strike north toward Haesten or south toward Harald, and all the while Harald had burned and killed.

"I killed Harald," I said.

"You did," the bishop allowed, "but not till after he'd ravaged the county!"

"So men want Cent to be its own kingdom again?" I asked.

He hesitated a long time before answering, and even then he was evasive. "No one wanted that while Alfred lived," he said, "but now?"

I stood and walked to a window from where I could stare down at the wharves. Gulls screamed and wheeled in the summer sky. There were two cranes on the wharf and they were lifting horses into a wide-bellied trading ship. The ship's hold had been divided into stalls where the frightened beasts were being tethered. "Where are the horses going?" I asked.

"Horses?" Swithwulf asked, puzzled, then realized why I had asked the unexpected question. "They send them to market in Frankia. We breed good horses here."

"You do?"

"Ealdorman Sigelf does," he said.

"And Sigelf rules here," I said, "and his son talks to the Danes."

The bishop shuddered. "So you say," he said cautiously.

I turned to him. "And his son was in love with your daughter," I said, "and for that reason hates Edward."

"Dear God," Swithwulf said quietly and made the sign of the cross. There were tears in his eyes. "She was a silly girl, a silly girl, but joyous."

"I'm sorry," I said.

He blinked away the tears. "And you look after my grandchildren?"

"They're in my care, yes."

"I hear the boy is sickly." He sounded anxious.

"That's just a rumor," I reassured him. "They're both healthy, but it's better for their health if Ealdorman Æthelhelm believes the contrary."

"Æthelhelm's not a bad man," the bishop said grudgingly.

"But he'd still cut your grandchildren's throats if he had the chance."

Swithwulf nodded. "What color do they have?"

"The boy's dark like his father, the girl is fair."

"Like my daughter," he said in a whisper.

"Who married the ætheling of Wessex," I said, "who now denies it. And Sigebriht, her rejected lover, went to the Danes out of hatred for Edward."

"Yes," the bishop said quietly.

"But then swore an oath to Edward when Æthelwold fled north."

Swithwulf nodded. "I heard."

"Can he be trusted?"

The directness of the question unsettled Swithwulf. He frowned and shifted uncomfortably, then gazed through a window to where crows were loud on the grass. "I would not trust him," he said softly.

"I couldn't hear you, bishop."

"I would not trust him," he said more loudly.

"But his father is ealdorman here, not Sigebriht."

"Sigelf is a difficult man," the bishop said, his voice low again, "but not a fool." He looked at me with unhappy appeal. "I'll deny this conversation," he said.

"Have you heard us having a conversation?" I asked Finan.

"Not a word," he said.

We stayed that night in Hrofeceastre and next day went back to Lundene on the flooding tide. There was a chill on the water, the first taste of autumn coming, and I rousted my men from the new town's taverns and saddled horses. I was deliberately staying away from Fagranforda because it was so close to Natangrafum and so I took my small troop south and west along familiar roads until we reached Wintanceaster.

Edward was surprised and pleased to see me. He knew I had not been in Fagranforda for most of the summer so did not ask me about the twins, instead telling me that his sister had sent news of them. "They're well," he said. He invited me to a feast. "We don't serve my father's food," he assured me.

"That's a blessing, lord," I said. Alfred had ever served insipid meals of weak broths and limp vegetables, while Edward, at least, knew the virtues of meat. His new wife was there, plump and pregnant, while her father, Ealdorman Æthelhelm, was plainly Edward's most trusted counselor. There were fewer priests than in Alfred's day, but at least a dozen were at the feast, including my old friend Willibald.

Æthelhelm greeted me jovially. "We feared you'd be provoking the Danes," he said.

"Who? Me?"

"They're quiet," Æthelhelm said, "and best not to wake them."

Edward looked at me. "Would you wake them?" he asked.

"What I would do, lord," I told him, "is send a hundred of your best warriors to Cent. Then I'd send another two or three hundred to Mercia and build burhs there."

"Cent?" Æthelhelm asked.

"Cent is restless," I said.

"They've always been troublesome," Æthelhelm said dismissively, "but they hate the Danes as much as the rest of us."

"The Centish fyrd must protect Cent," Edward said.

"And Lord Æthelred can build burhs," Æthelhelm declared. "If the Danes come we'll be ready for them, but there's no point in poking them with a sharp stick. Father Willibald!"

"Lord?" Willibald half stood at one of the lower tables.

"Have we heard from our missionaries?"

"We will, lord!" Willibald said, "I'm sure we will."

"Missionaries?" I asked.

"Among the Danes," Edward said. "We will convert them."

"We shall beat Danish swords into plowshares," Willibald said, and it was just after those hopeful words were said that a messenger arrived. He was a mud-spattered priest who had come from Mercia, and he had been sent to Wessex by Werferth, who was the

Bishop of Wygraceaster. The man had plainly ridden hard and there was a hush in the hall as we waited to hear his news. Edward raised a hand and the harpist lifted his fingers from the strings.

"Lord." The priest went on his knees before the dais on which the high table was bright with candles. "Great news, lord King."

"Æthelwold's dead?" Edward asked.

"God is great!" the priest said. "The age of miracles is not over!"

"Miracles?" I asked.

"It seems there is an ancient tomb, lord," the priest explained, looking up at Edward, "a tomb in Mercia, and angels have appeared there to foretell the future. Britain will be Christian! You will rule from sea to sea, lord! There are angels! And they have brought the prophecy from heaven!"

There was a sudden spate of questions that Edward silenced. Instead he and Æthelhelm questioned the man, learning that Bishop Werferth had sent trusted priests to the ancient tomb and they had confirmed the heavenly visitation. The messenger could not contain his joy. "The angels say the Danes will turn to Christ, lord, and you shall rule one kingdom of all the Angelcynn!"

"You see?" Father Coenwulf, who had survived being locked in a stable on the night he had gone to pray with Æthelwold, could not resist the temptation to be triumphant. He was looking at me. "You see, Lord Uhtred! The age of miracles is not over!"

"Glory be to God!" Edward said.

Goose feathers and tavern whores. Glory be to God.

Natangrafum became a place of pilgrimage. Hundreds of people went there, and most were disappointed because the angels did not appear every night, indeed whole weeks went by with no lights showing at the tomb and no strange singing sounding from its stony depths, but then the angels would come again and the valley beneath Natangrafum's sepulchre would echo with the prayers of folk seeking help.

Only a few were permitted into the tomb, and those were chosen by Father Cuthbert, who led them past the armed men who protected the ancient mound. Those men were mine, led by Rypere, but the banner planted on the hill's top, close to the tomb's entrance, was Æthelflaed's flag, which showed a rather ungainly goose that was somehow holding a cross in one webbed foot and a sword in the other. Æthelflaed was convinced Saint Werburgh protected her, just as the saint had once protected a wheatfield by driving out a flock of hungry geese. That was supposed to be a miracle, in which case I am a miracle worker too, but I was also too sensible to tell that to Æthelflaed. The goose banner suggested that the guards belonged to Æthelflaed, and anyone invited into the tomb would assume that it was under Æthelflaed's protection, and that was believable because no one would credit Uhtred the Wicked with guarding a place of Christian pilgrimage. The visitor, led past the guards, would come to the tomb entrance, which, at night, was lit by dim rushlights that showed two heaps of skulls, one on each side of the low, cavelike opening. Cuthbert would kneel with them, pray with them, then command them to take off their weapons and mail. "No one can go into the angelic presence with war gear," he would say sternly and, once they had obeyed him, he offered them a potion in a silver cup. "Drink it all down," he would order them.

I never tried that liquid, which was cooked up by Ludda. My memory of Ælfadell's drink was more than sufficient. "It gives them dreams, lord," Ludda explained when I made one of my rare visits to Turcandene.

Æthelflaed had come with me and insisted on sniffing the potion. "Dreams?" she asked.

"One or two vomit as well, lady," Ludda said, "but, yes, dreams."

Not that they needed dreams for, once they had drunk, and when Cuthbert saw the vagueness in their eyes, he let them crawl into the tomb's long passage. Inside they saw the stone walls, floor, and ceiling, and on either side the chambers heaped with bones, all lit by rushlights, but ahead of them were the angels. Three angels, not two, huddled together at the passage's end, where they were surrounded by the glorious feathers of their wings. "I chose three, as three is a sacred number, lord," Cuthbert explained, "an angel for each member of the Trinity."

The goose feathers were glued to the rock. They formed fans, which, in the dim light, could easily be mistaken for wings. It had taken Ludda a whole day to place the feathers, then the three girls had to be coached in their duties, which had taken the best part of a month. They sang softly when a visitor came. Cuthbert had taught them the music, which was soft and dreamlike, not much above a hum and with no words, just sounds that echoed in that small stone space.

Mehrasa was the central angel. Her dark skin, black hair, and jet eyes made her mysterious, and Ludda had added to the mystery by pasting some raven feathers among the white. All three girls were simply robed in white linen, while the dark Mehrasa had a chain of gold about her neck. Men gazed in awe, and no wonder, for the three girls were beautiful. The two Franks were both very fair-haired with wide blue eyes. They were visions in that dark tomb, though both, Ludda told me, were prone to bouts of giggling when they should have been at their most solemn.

The visitor probably never noticed the giggles. A strange voice, Ludda's, seemed to come from the solid rock. Ludda chanted that the visitor had come before the angel of death and the two angels of life, and that they should address their questions to all three and wait for an answer.

Those questions were all important because they told us what men wanted to know, and most of that, of course, was trivial. Would they inherit from a relative? What was the prospect of the harvest? Some were heartbreaking pleas for the life of a child or a wife, some were prayers to be helped in a lawsuit or in a quarrel with a neighbor, and all those Ludda dealt with as best he could, while the three girls crooned their soft, low and plangent melody. Then came the more interesting questions. Who would rule Mercia? Would there be war? Would the Danes come south and take the land of the Saxons? The whores, the feathers, and the tomb were a net and we caught some interesting fish there. Beortsig, whose father had paid money to Sigurd, had come to the tomb and wanted to know if the Danes would take over Mercia and place a tame Mercian on the throne and then, more interesting still, Sigebriht of Cent had crawled up the dim stone passage that was pungent with the smell of burning incense, and had asked about Æthelwold's fate.

"And what did you tell him?" I asked Ludda.

"What you ordered me to tell him, lord, that all his hopes and dreams would come true."

"And did they come true that night?"

"Seffa did her duty," Ludda said with a straight face. Seffa was one of the two Franks.

Æthelflaed glanced over at the girl. Ludda, Father Cuthbert, and the three angels were living in the Roman house at Turcandene. "I like this house," Father Cuthbert had greeted me. "I think I should live in a large house."

"Saint Cuthbert the Comfortable?"

"Saint Cuthbert the Content," he said.

"And Mehrasa?"

He gave her an adoring look. "She really is an angel, lord."

"She looks happy," I said, and so she did. I doubted she fully understood the strange things she was asked to do, but she was learning English fast and she was a clever girl. "I could find her a wealthy husband," I teased Cuthbert.

"Lord!" He looked hurt, then frowned. "If I have your permission, lord, I would take her as my wife."

"Is that what she wants?"

He giggled, he really giggled, then nodded. "Yes, lord."

"So she's not as clever as she looks," I said sourly. "But she must finish here first. And if she gets pregnant I'll seal you up with the other bones."

The tomb was doing exactly what I had wished it to do. The questions men asked told us what was on their minds, thus Sigebriht's anxious inquiries about Æthelwold confirmed that he had not abandoned his hopes of becoming King of Cent if Æthelwold were to topple Edward from the throne. The angel's second task was to fight the rumors that came south from Ælfadell's prophecies that the Danes would gain the overlordship of all Britain. Those rumors had dispirited men in both Mercia and Wessex, but now they heard a different prophecy, that the Saxons would be the victors, and that message, I knew, would encourage the Saxons, just as it would intrigue and irritate the Danes. I wanted to goad them. I wanted to defeat them.

I suppose that one day, long after I am dead, the Danes will find a leader who can unite them, and then the world will be consumed by flames and the halls of Valhalla will fill with the feasting dead, but so long as I have known, loved, and fought the Danes they have been quarrelsome and divided. My present wife's priest, an idiot, says that is because God has sown dissension among them, but I have always thought it was because the Danes are a stubborn, proud, and independent people, unwilling to bend their knees to a man simply because he wears a crown. They will follow a man with a sword, but as soon as he fails they drift away to find another leader, and so their armies come together, fall apart, and then re-form. I have known Danes who almost succeeded in keeping a mighty army together and leading it to complete triumph. There were Ubba, Guthrum, even Haesten: all of them tried, yet in the end they all failed. The Danes did not fight for a cause or even for a country and certainly not for a creed, but only for themselves, and when they suffered a defeat their armies vanished as men went to find another lord who might lead them to silver, women, and land.

And my angels were a lure to persuade them that there was reputation to be made in war. "Have any Danes visited the tomb?" I asked Ludda.

"Two, lord," he said, "both merchants."

"And you told them?"

Ludda hesitated, glanced at Æthelflaed, then back to me. "I told them what you ordered me to tell them, lord."

"You did?"

He nodded, then made the sign of the cross. "I told them you would die, lord, and that a Dane would earn great renown by slaying Uhtred of Bebbanburg."

Æthelflaed drew in a sharp breath and then, like Ludda, made the sign of the cross. "You told them what?" she asked.

"What Lord Uhtred told me to tell them, lady," Ludda said nervously.

"You're risking fate," Æthelflaed told me.

"I want the Danes to come," I said, "and I need to offer them a bait."

Because Plegmund was wrong, and Æthelhelm was wrong, and Edward was wrong. Peace is a fine thing, but we only have peace when our enemies are too scared to make war. The Danes were not quiet because the Christian god had silenced them, but because they were distracted by other things. Edward wanted to believe they had abandoned their dreams of conquering Wessex, yet I knew they would come. Æthelwold had not abandoned his dream either. He would come, and with him would come a savage horde of sword-Danes and spear-Danes, and I wanted them to come. I wanted to get it over. I wanted to be the sword of the Saxons.

And still they did not come.

I never did understand why it took the Danes so long to take advantage of Alfred's death. I suppose if Æthelwold had been a more inspirational leader instead of being a weak man then they might have come sooner, but they waited so long that all Wessex was convinced that their god had answered their prayers and made the Danes peaceable. And all the while my angels sang their two songs, one to the Saxons and one to the Danes, and perhaps they made a difference. There were plenty of Danes who wanted to nail my skull to their gable, and the song of the tomb was an invitation.

Yet they hesitated.

Archbishop Plegmund was triumphant. Two years after Edward's coronation I was summoned to Wintanceaster and had to endure a sermon in the new great church. Plegmund, stern and fierce, claimed that God had conquered when all the swords of man had failed. "We are in the last days," he said, "and we see the dawning of Christ's kingdom."

I remember that visit because it was the last time I saw Ælswith, Alfred's widow. She was retiring to a convent, driven there, I heard, by Plegmund's insistence. It was Offa who told me that. "She supports the archbishop," Offa said, "but he can't stand her! She nags."

"I pity the nuns," I said.

"Oh Lord alive, she'll have them hopping," Offa said with a smile. He was old. He still had his dogs, but he trained no new ones. "They're companions now," he told me, stroking the ears of a terrier, "and we're growing old together." He sat with me in the Two Cranes tavern. "I'm in pain, lord," he said.

"I'm sorry."

"God will take me soon," he said, and in that he was right.

"Have you traveled this summer?"

"It was hard," he said, "but yes, I went north and I went east. Now I'm going home."

I put money on the table. "Tell me what's happening."

"They're going to attack," he said.

"I know that."

"Jarl Sigurd is recovered," Offa said, "and boats are coming across the sea."

"Boats are always crossing the sea," I said.

"Sigurd has let it be known there will be land to possess."

"Wessex."

He nodded. "And so the crews are coming, lord."

"Where?"

"They're assembling at Eoferwic," Offa said. I had already heard that news from traders who had been in Northumbria. New ships had come, filled with ambitious and hungry warriors, but the traders all claimed that the army was being assembled to attack the Scots. "That's what they want you to think," Offa said. He touched one of the silver coins on the table, tracing his finger over the outline of Alfred's head. "It's a clever thing you're doing at Natangrafum," he said slyly.

I said nothing for a moment. A flock of geese was driven past the tavern and there were angry shouts as a dog barked at them. "I don't know what you're talking about," I said, a feeble response.

"I've told no one," Offa said.

"You're dreaming, Offa," I said.

He looked at me and made the sign of the cross on his skinny chest. "I promise you, lord, I told no one. But it was clever, I salute you. It annoyed Jarl Sigurd!" He chuckled, then used the bone handle of a knife to crack open a hazelnut. "What did one of your angels say? That Sigurd was a small man, badly endowed." He chuckled again and shook his head. "It annoyed him a lot, lord. And maybe that is why Sigurd is giving Eohric money, a great deal of money. Eohric will join the other Danes."

"Edward says he has a pledge of peace from Eohric," I pointed out.

"And you know what Eohric's pledges are worth," Offa retorted. "They're going to do what they should have done twenty years ago, lord. They're going to unite against Wessex. All the Danes, and all the Saxons who hate Edward, all of them."

"Ragnar?" I asked. Ragnar was my old dear friend, a man I thought of as a brother, a man I had not seen in years.

"He's not well," Offa said gently, "not well enough to march."

That saddened me. I poured ale and one of the tavern girls hurried over to see if the jug was empty, but I waved her away. "And what about Cent?" I asked Offa.

"What about Cent, lord?"

"Sigebriht hates Edward," I said, "and he wants his own kingdom."

Offa shook his head. "Sigebriht is a young fool, lord, but his father has reined him in. The whip has been used and Cent will stay loyal." He sounded very certain.

"Sigebriht isn't talking to the Danes?" I asked.

"If he is, I haven't heard a whisper," Offa said. "No, lord, Cent is loyal. Sigelf knows he can't hold Cent by himself, and Wessex is a better ally for him than the Danes."

"Have you told Edward all this?"

"I told Father Coenwulf," he said. Coenwulf was now Edward's closest adviser and constant companion. "I even told him where the attack will come from."

"Which is?"

He looked at my coins on the table and said nothing. I sighed and added two more. Offa drew the coins to his side of the table and made a neat line of them. "They'll want you to believe their attack will come from East Anglia," he said, "but it won't. The real attack will be from Ceaster."

"How can you possibly know that?" I asked.

"Brunna," he said.

"Haesten's wife?"

"She's a real Christian," he said.

"Truly?" I asked. I had always believed the baptism of Haesten's wife was a cynical ploy to deceive Alfred.

"She has seen the light," Offa said in a mocking tone. "Yes, lord, truly, and she confided in me." He looked at me with his sad eyes. "I was a priest once and perhaps you never really stop being a priest and she wanted to make confession and receive the sacraments and so, God help me, I gave her what she wanted, and now, God help me, I have betrayed the secrets she told me."

"The Danes will make an army in East Anglia?"

"You'll see that happening, I'm sure, but you won't see the army gathering behind Ceaster, and that's the army that will march south."

"When?"

"After the harvest," Offa spoke confidently, his voice so low that only I could hear. "Sigurd and Cnut want the biggest army seen in Britain. They say it's time to end the war forever. They will come when they have the harvest to feed their horde. They want the largest army ever to invade Wessex."

"You believe Brunna?"

"She resents her husband, so, yes, I believe her."

"What is Ælfadell saying these days?" I asked.

"She's saying what Cnut tells her to say, that the attack will come from the east and that Wessex will fall." He sighed. "I wish I could live long enough to see the end of this, lord."

"You're good for another ten years, Offa," I told him.

He shook his head. "I feel the angel of death close behind me, lord." He hesitated. "You've always been good to me, lord." He bowed his head. "I owe you for your kindness."

"You owe me nothing."

"I do, lord." He looked up at me and, to my surprise, there were tears in his eyes. "Not everyone has been kind to me, lord," he said, "but you have always been generous."

I was embarrassed. "You've been very useful," I muttered.

"So in respect for you, lord, and in gratitude to you, I give you my last advice." He paused and to my surprise pushed the coins back toward me.

"No," I said.

"Give me the pleasure, lord," he said. "I want to thank you." He pushed the coins still closer to me. A tear rolled down his cheek and he cuffed it away. "Trust no one, lord," he said softly, "and beware Haesten, lord, beware the army in the west." He looked up at me and dared touch my hand with a long finger. "Beware the army at Ceaster, and don't let the pagans destroy us, lord."

He died that summer.

Then the harvest came, and it was good.

And after it the pagans came.

Ten

I worked it out later, though the knowledge was small consolation. A war-band rode to Natangrafum and because so many of the warriors were Saxons no one thought their presence strange. They arrived on an evening when the tomb was empty, because by then the peace had lasted so long that the angels rarely appeared, but the raiders knew exactly where to go. They rode directly to the Roman house outside Turcandene where they took the handful of guards by surprise and then killed fast and efficiently. When I arrived the next day I saw blood, a lot of blood.

Ludda was dead. I assumed he had tried to defend the house, and his eviscerated body lay sprawled across the doorway. His face was a grimace of pain. Eight others of my men were dead, their bodies stripped of mail, arm rings, and anything else of value. On one wall, where the Roman plaster still clung to the bricks, a man had used blood to make a crude drawing of a flying raven. The drips had run down the wall and I could see the print of the man's hand beneath the raven's savagely hooked beak. "Sigurd," I said bitterly.

"His symbol, lord?" Sihtric asked me.

"Yes."

None of the three girls was there. I supposed the attackers must have taken them, but they had failed to find Mehrasa, the dark girl. She and Father Cuthbert had hidden in some nearby woods and only emerged when they were certain it was my men who now ringed the slaughterhouse. Cuthbert was crying. "Lord, lord," was all he could say to me at first. He fell to his knees in front of me and wrung his big hands. Mehrasa was steadier, though she refused to cross the house's blood-reeking threshold where the flies buzzed around Ludda's opened gut.

"What happened?" I asked Cuthbert.

"Oh God, lord," he said, his voice quavery.

I slapped him hard around the face. "What happened?"

"They came at dusk, lord," he said, his hands shaking as he tried to clasp them, "there were a lot of them! I counted twenty-four men." He had to pause, he was shaking so much, and when he next tried to speak he just made a mewing noise. Then he saw the anger on my face and took a deep breath. "They hunted us, lord."

"What do you mean?"

"They searched around the house, lord. In the old orchard, down by the pond."

"You were hidden."

"Yes, lord." He was crying and his voice was scarce above a whisper. "Saint Cuthbert the Cowardly, lord."

"Don't be a fool," I snarled, "what could you do against so many?"

"They took the girls, lord, and killed everyone else. And I liked Ludda."

"I liked Ludda too," I said, "but now we bury him." I did like Ludda. He was a clever rogue and he had served me well, and worse, he had trusted me and now he was cut from the groin to the ribs and the flies were thick about his entrails. "So what were you doing while he died?" I asked Cuthbert.

"We were watching the sunset from the hill, lord."

I laughed without mirth. "Watching the sunset!"

"We were, lord!" Cuthbert said, hurt.

"And you've been hiding ever since?"

He looked around at the red mess and his body shook with a sudden spasm. He vomited.

By now, I thought, the two angels would have confessed the whole deception and the Danes were laughing at us. I looked north and east for smoke in the sky, the sure sign that a war had broken out, but I saw none. The temptation was to assume that the killers had been a small raiding party who, their revenge taken, had headed back to safer land, but was the raid just that? A revenge for the ships of Snotengaham? And if it were such a revenge, how did the raiders know the angels were my idea? Or was Plegmund's peace breaking into a thousand bloody pieces? The raiders had not fired the Roman building, suggesting they did not want to draw attention to their presence. "You say there were Saxons among the war-band?" I asked Cuthbert.

"I heard them talking, lord," he said, "and yes, there were Saxons."

Æthelwold's men? If it was Æthelwold's followers then it was surely war, and that meant an attack from Ceaster if Offa was right. "Dig graves," I told my men. We would begin by burying our dead, but I sent Sihtric and three men back to Fagranforda. They carried orders that my whole household should retreat into Cirrenceastre, and to take the livestock with them. "Tell the Lady Æthelflaed she's to go south into Wessex," I said, "and tell her to pass the news to Æthelred and to her brother. Make sure King Edward knows! Tell her I need men, and that I've gone north toward Ceaster. Have Finan bring every man here."

It took a day to assemble my men. We buried Ludda and the others in Turcandene's churchyard and Cuthbert said prayers over the fresh mounds. I still watched the sky and saw no great plumes of smoke. It was high summer, the sky a clear blue in which lazy clouds drifted, and as we rode north I did not know whether we rode to war or not.

I led only a hundred and forty-three men, and if the Danes were coming then I could expect thousands of them. We rode first to Wygraceaster, the northernmost burh in Saxon Mercia, and the bishop's steward was surprised by our arrival. "I've heard no news of a Danish attack, lord," he told me. The street outside the bishop's large house was busy with a market, though the bishop himself was in Wessex.

"Make sure your storehouses are full," I told the steward, who bowed, but I could see he was unconvinced. "Who commands the garrison here?" I asked.

It was a man called Wlenca, one of Æthelred's followers, and he bridled when I told him to assume the war had started. He looked north from the burh's ramparts and saw no smoke. "We'd have heard if there was war," he said in a surly tone, and I noted he did not call me "lord."

"I don't know if it has started or not," I confessed, "but assume it has."

"Lord Æthelred would send me notice if the Danes attacked," he insisted loftily.

"Æthelred's scratching his arse in Gleawecestre," I said. "Is that what you did when Haesten invaded last?" He looked at me angrily, but said nothing. "How do I reach Ceaster from here?" I asked him.

"Follow the Roman road," he said, pointing.

"Follow the Roman road, *lord*," I said.

He hesitated, plainly wanting to defy me, but good sense won. "Yes, lord," he said.

"And tell me a good defensive place a day's ride away."

He shrugged. "You can try Scrobbesburh, lord?"

"Rouse the fyrd," I told him, "and make sure the walls are manned."

"I know my duty, lord," he said, yet it was plain from his truculence that he had no intention of reinforcing the men who lazed on the ramparts. That empty, innocent sky persuaded him that there was no danger, and doubtless the moment I left he sent a messenger to Æthelred saying I was panicking unnecessarily.

And perhaps I was panicking. The only evidence of war was the slaughter at Turcandene and the sixth sense of a warrior. War had to come, it had been hiding away for too long, and I was convinced the raid that had killed Ludda was the first spark of a great fire.

We rode on north, following the Roman road that led through the valley of the Sæfern. I missed Ludda and his astonishing knowledge of Britain's pathways. We had to ask our way, and most folk we questioned could only give us guidance to the next village or town. Scrobbesburh lay to the west of what seemed the quickest way north and so I did not go there, instead we spent a night amidst towering Roman ruins at a place called Rochecestre, a village that astonished me. It had been a vast Roman town, almost as large as Lundene, but now it was a ruin of ghosts, crumbling walls, broken pavements, fallen pillars, and shattered marble. A few folk lived there, their wattle-and-straw huts propped against the Roman stone and their sheep and goats grazing amidst the broken glory. A scrawny priest was the only man who made sense, and he nodded dumbly when I told him I feared the Danes were coming. "Where would you go if they came?" I asked him.

"I'd go to Scrobbesburh, lord."

"Then go there now," I ordered him, "and tell the rest of the village to go. Is there a garrison there?"

"Just whoever lives there, lord. There's no thegn. The Welsh killed the last one."

"And if I want to reach Ceaster from here? What road do I take?"

"Don't know, lord."

Places like Rochecestre fill me with despair. I love to build, yet I look at what the Romans did and know we cannot construct anything half so beautiful. We build sturdy halls of oak, we make stone walls, we bring masons from Frankia who raise churches or feast-halls with crude pillars of ill-dressed stone, yet the Romans built like gods. All across Britain their houses, bridges, halls, and temples still stand, and they were made hundreds of years ago! Their roofs have fallen and the plaster is flaked, but still they stand, and I wonder how people who were able to make such marvels could have been defeated. The Christians tell us we move inexorably toward better times, toward their god's kingdom on earth, but my gods only promise the chaos of the world's ending, and a man only has to look around him to see that everything is crumbling, decaying, proof that the chaos is coming. We are not climbing Jacob's ladder to some heavenly perfection, but stumbling downhill toward Ragnarok.

The next day brought heavier clouds that shadowed the land as we climbed the small hills and left the Sæfern's valley behind. If there was smoke we saw none except the tendrils from cooking fires in small villages. Off to our west the peaks of the Welsh hills vanished in the clouds. If there had been an attack, I thought, we would surely have heard by now. We would have met messengers riding away from the carnage or refugees fleeing the invaders. Instead we rode through peaceful villages, past fields where the first harvesters swung their sickles, and always following the Roman road with its mile-marked stones. The land sloped down to the north now, toward the Dee. It began to rain as the day wore on and we found shelter that evening in a hall close to the road. The hall was a poor place, its oak walls scorched by a fire that had evidently failed to burn the place down. "They tried," the owner, a widow whose husband had been killed by Haesten's men, told us, "but God sent rain and they failed. Didn't keep me from harm, though." The Danes, she said, were never far away. "And if it's not the Danes it's the Welsh," she said bitterly.

"Then why stay here?" Finan asked her.

"And where do I go? I've lived here more than forty years, so where do I start again? You'll buy this land from me?"

Rain dripped through the thatch all night, but the dawn brought a chill clearing wind. We were hungry because the widow could not spare food for all my men, not unless she killed the cockerels that were crowing and the pigs that were being driven to the nearby beech wood as we threw saddles over our horses' backs. Oswi, my servant, was tightening my stallion's girth strap as I wandered to the ditch on the north side of the hall. I gazed ahead as I pissed. The clouds were low and dark, but was there a darker smudge there? "Finan," I called, "is that smoke?"

"God knows, lord. Let's hope so."

I laughed. "Hope so?"

"If peace lasts much longer I'll go mad."

"If it lasts into the autumn we'll go to Ireland," I promised him, "and break some of your enemies' heads."

"Not to Bebbanburg?" he asked.

"I need at least a thousand more men for that, and to get a thousand men I need the profits of a war."

"We all suffer from dreams," he said wistfully. He stared northward. "I'm thinking that is smoke, lord." He frowned. "Or maybe just a thundercloud."

And then the horsemen came.

There were three of them, riding hard from the north and when they saw us they slewed off the road and spurred their mud-spattered, tired horses toward the hall. They were Merewalh's men, sent south to warn Æthelred that the Danes had attacked. "Thousands of them, lord," one told me excitedly.

"Thousands?"

"Couldn't count them, lord."

"Where are they?"

"Westune, lord."

The name meant nothing to me. "Where's that?"

"Not far."

"Two hours' ride, lord," another man said more helpfully.

"And Merewalh?"

"Retreating, lord."

They told me the message Merewalh was sending to Æthelred, which was simply that an army of Danes had streamed out of Ceaster, far too many for Merewalh's small force to contain or even face. The Danes were coming south, and Merewalh, remembering the tactics I had used against Sigurd, was retreating down the Welsh border in hopes that the savage tribesmen would come from the hills to attack the invaders. "When did they attack?" I asked.

"Last night, lord. At twilight."

A strange time, I thought, yet on the other hand it had probably been intended to take Merewalh's force off-guard, and if so it had failed. Merewalh had been alert, his scouts had warned him, and so far he had escaped. "How many men does he have now?" I asked.

"Eighty-three, lord."

"And who's leading the Danes? What banners did you see?"

"A raven, lord, another with an ax breaking a cross, and a skull."

"There were dragons as well," the second man put in.

"And two with wolves," the third man added.

"And a stag with crosses on its head," the first man said. He struck me as intelligent and thoughtful, and he had told me what I needed to know. "A flying raven?" I asked him.

"Yes, lord."

"That's Sigurd," I said, "the ax is Cnut, and the skull is Haesten."

"And the stag, lord?" he asked.

"Æthelwold," I said bitterly. So it seemed Offa had been right and the Danes were attacking from Ceaster, and that surely meant they were heading southward, ostensibly led by Æthelwold. I gazed northward, thinking that the Danes could not be far away. "Lord Æthelred," I spoke to the first man, "will probably send you to King Edward."

"Probably, lord."

"Because you've seen the Danes," I said. "So tell King Edward I need men. Tell him—" I paused, trying to make a decision that would not be destroyed by the passage of time. "Tell him they should meet me at Wygraceaster. And if Wygraceaster is under siege, tell them to look for me at Cirrenceastre." I already knew we would have to retreat and by the time Edward responded and sent men, if he sent any at all, I could well have been pushed south of the Temes.

The three men rode on south and we probed cautiously north, our scouts ahead and to the flanks. And I saw that the darkness in the morning sky was not a thundercloud, it was the smoke of burning thatch.

How often I have seen the war-smoke smearing the sky, dark and roiling, rising from beyond trees or from some valley, and knowing that another steading or village or hall was being reduced to ashes. We rode slowly north and I saw for myself that Plegmund's peace was ended and I thought how it had been the peace that passeth understanding. That is a phrase from the Christians' holy book, and certainly Plegmund's peace passed all understanding. The Danes had been quiet for so long and that had led Plegmund to believe his god had gelded his enemies, but now they had broken the incomprehensible peace, and the villages and farms and ricks and mills were burning.

It was an hour before we saw the Danes. Scouts rode back to tell us where the enemy was, though the smoke in the sky was indication enough and already the road was crowded by folk trying to escape the invaders. We rode to the crest of a low wooded hill and watched the steadings burn. Immediately beneath us was a hall with barns and storehouses. It swarmed with men. A wagon stood by the hall, and I watched the newly gathered harvest being piled onto the wagon's bed. "How many?" I asked Finan.

"There's three hundred men there," he said, "at least three hundred."

And more men were in the wide vale beyond. Bands of Danes crossed the meadows, looking for fugitives or more places to ravage. I could see a small huddle of women and children who had been spared and who were being guarded by sword-Danes and doubtless they were on their way to the slave market across the sea. A second wagon, piled with cooking pots, spits, a loom, rakes, hoes, and anything else that could be useful, was whipped northward. The captured women and children, along with a great herd of livestock, followed, and a man tossed a burning brand up onto the hall's thatch. A horn sounded from somewhere in the valley and gradually the Danes obeyed its insistent call and the horsemen moved toward the road. "Jesus," Finan said, "but there are hundreds of the bastards."

"See the skull," I said. I could see a human skull held aloft on a pole.

"Haesten," Finan said.

I looked for Haesten himself, but there were too many horsemen. I did not see any other banners, at least none that I recognized. For a few moments I was tempted to take my men to the east and gallop down the hill to cut off a few of the enemy stragglers, but I resisted the temptation. Those stragglers were not far from the larger bands, and we would be pursued immediately and overwhelmed by numbers. The Danes were not moving fast, their horses were rested and well fed, and my task now was to stay ahead of them to watch what they did and where they went.

We went back down the road. All day we retreated, and all day the Danes came on behind us. I watched the widow's hall burn, saw the smoke rise to east and west, and the great plumes in the sky suggested there were three war-bands harrying the country. The Danes were not even bothering to use scouts, they knew their numbers were sufficient to crush any enemy, while my scouts were forever being pushed back. In truth I was blind. I had no real idea how many Danes we faced, I just knew there were hundreds of them and that the smoke was rising and I was angry, so angry that most of my men avoided my gaze. Finan did not care. "We need a prisoner," he said, but the Danes were being careful. They stayed in large troops, always too many for my few men. "They're in no hurry," Finan observed in a puzzled tone, "and that's strange. No hurry at all."

We were on another low hill, still watching. We had left the road because the Danes were following it and too many folk were using it to escape southward, and those folk wanted to stay close to us, but their presence only made us more vulnerable. I told those fugitives to keep going south and we watched the Danes from the hills east of the road and as the day wore on I became ever more baffled. As Finan had said, the Danes were in no hurry. They were scavenging like rats in a bare granary, exploring every hovel, hall, and farm, taking anything useful, yet this was country that had been harried before, part of the dangerous land between Saxon and Danish Mercia, and the pickings had to be slight. The real plunder lay southward, so why were they not hurrying? The smoke was warning the countryside of their coming and folk had time to bury their valuables or else carry them away. It made small sense. The Danes were picking up scraps while the feast lay unguarded, so what were they doing?

They knew we were watching them. It is impossible to hide a hundred and forty-three men in half-wooded country and they must have glimpsed us in the distance, though they could not have known who we were because I deliberately did not fly my banner. If they had known Uhtred of Bebbanburg was so close and so outnumbered they might have made a greater effort, but it was not until late in the afternoon that they tried to lure us into battle and even then it was a halfhearted effort. Seven Danish horsemen headed south on the now empty road. They were ambling, but I could see them glancing nervously toward the woods that hid us. Sihtric grinned. "They're lost."

"They're not lost," Finan said wryly.

"Bait," I said. It was too obvious. They wanted us to attack and as soon as we did they would turn and gallop north to lead us into an ambush.

"Ignore them," I ordered, and we went south again, crossing the watershed so that ahead of us in the deceptively peaceful evening shadows I could see a glint of the Sæfern. I was hurrying a little, wanting to find a place where we could spend the night in relative safety and far from the Danes. Then I saw another glint, a glimmer, a mere flash amidst the long shadows, and it was away to our left and I stared a long time and wondered if I had imagined it, then saw the prick of light again. "Bastards," I said, because I knew why the Danes had been so sluggish in their pursuit of us. They had sent men looping around our eastern flank, a war party to cut us off, but the low sun had reflected from a helmet or a spear-point, and now I could see them, far far off, mailed men among the trees. "Ride!" I called to my men.

Spurs and fear. A mad gallop down the long slope, hooves thudding, shield banging against my back, Serpent-Breath's scabbard flapping against the saddle, and off to my left I saw the Danes come from the trees, far too many Danes. They were spurring their horses into a reckless gallop, hoping to cut us off. I could have swerved west away from them, but I reckoned a second Danish party might have gone that way and we could have ridden straight into their swords, so the only hope was to go south, hard and fast, riding to escape the jaws that I sensed were closing on us.

I was riding toward the river. We could not ride faster than our slowest horses, not without sacrificing men, and the Danes were spurring hard, but if I could reach the Sæfern then there was a chance. Drive the horses straight into the water and make them swim, then defend the farther bank if we survived the mad crossing, and so I told Finan to head toward the last place we had seen a sliver of reflected sunlight from water while I rode at the back of my men, where I was pelted by clods of damp earth slung up by the heavy hooves.

Then Finan shouted a warning and I saw horsemen ahead of us. I cursed, but kept riding. I drew Serpent-Breath. "Just charge them!" I shouted. There could be nothing clever to do. We were trapped, and our only hope was to fight through the men ahead and I reckoned we outnumbered them. "Kill and keep going!" I shouted at my men and spurred the horse so I could lead the charge. We were close to a road now, its muddy surface pitted by hooves and wheel ruts. There were cottages, small plots of vegetables, manure heaps, and pigpens. "Straight down the road," I called as I reached the head of our small column. "Kill them and keep going!"

"They're ours!" Finan called urgently. "Lord, they're ours! They're ours!"

It was Merewalh who spurred to meet us. "That way, lord," he shouted at me, pointing down the road, and his men joined mine, hooves thudding on the turf either side of the Roman road's broken stones. I looked over my left shoulder and saw Danes not far behind, but ahead of us was a low hill and at the top of the hill was a palisade. A fort. It was old, it was in ruins, but it was there and I swerved toward it, then glanced behind again and saw that a half-dozen Danes had far outstripped their companions.

"Finan!" I shouted, hauled on a rein, and turned the stallion. A dozen of my men saw what I was doing and their horses also slewed around, throwing up gobbets of mud. I kicked the horse and slapped its rump with the flat of Serpent-Breath and to my astonishment the six Danes turned almost as fast. One of their horses slipped and fell in a great flail of hooves and the man sprawled onto the road, scrambled up, seized one of his companions' stirrups, and ran alongside the horse as they rode away. "Stop!" I shouted, not to the Danes, but to my own men because the greater body of Danes was now in sight and coming fast. "Back!" I called. "Back and up the hill!"

The hill, with its dilapidated fort, stood on a neck of land made by a great loop of the Sæfern. There was a village inside the loop with a church and a huddle of houses, though most of the land was scrub or marsh. Fugitives had come here, and their cattle, pigs, geese, and sheep crowded about the small thatched houses. "Where are we?" I called to Merewalh.

"It's called Scrobbesburh, lord," he called back.

It was made for defense. The neck was about three hundred paces wide and to defend it I had my one hundred and forty-three men, now joined by Merewalh's, but a good number of the fugitives were men who served in the fyrd and they had axes, spears, hunting bows, and even a few swords. Merewalh had already lined them across the neck. "How many men do you have?" I asked him.

"Three hundred, lord, besides my eighty-three warriors."

The Danes were watching. There were perhaps a hundred and fifty of them now, and many more were coming from the north. "Put a hundred fyrd in the fort," I told Merewalh. The fort lay on the southern side of the neck, leaving the long northern stretch to be defended. Close to the river the land was marshy and I doubted any Dane could cross that land, so I made my shield wall between the fort's low hill and the marsh's edge. The sun was sinking. The Danes, I thought, should attack now, but though they arrived in ever greater numbers they did not try. Our deaths, it seemed, must wait till morning.

There was little sleep. I lit fires across the neck so that we could see if the Danes made an attack in the night, and we watched the Danish campfires spread to the north as more men arrived and more fires were lit until the sky was a glow of flame reflected from low clouds. I ordered Rypere to explore the village and find whatever food he could. There were at least eight hundred people trapped in Scrobbesburh and I had no idea how long we would be there, but I doubted we would find provisions for more than a few days, even after we had slaughtered the livestock. Finan had a dozen men dismantling the houses so their timbers could be used to make a barrier across the neck. "The sensible thing," Merewalh said to me sometime during that long nervous night, "would be to swim the horses across the river and keep going south."

"So why don't you do that?"

He smiled and nodded toward some children sleeping on the ground. "And leave them to the Danes, lord?"

"I don't know how long we can hold here," I warned him.

"Lord Æthelred will send an army," Merewalh answered.

"You believe that?"

He half smiled. "Or maybe King Edward?"

"Maybe," I said, "but it will take two or three days for your messengers to reach Wessex and they'll talk for another two or three days, and by then we'll be dead." Merewalh flinched at that brutal truth, but unless help was already on the way we were doomed. The fort was a pathetic thing, a remnant from some ancient war against the Welsh who were forever harrying Mercia's western lands. It had a ditch that would not have stopped a cripple, and the palisade was so rotten that it could be pushed over with one hand. The barrier we made was risible, just a straggling line of roof timbers that might trip a man, but would never stop a determined assault. I knew Merewalh was right, that our duty was to cross the Sæfern and keep riding south until we reached a place where an army could assemble, but to do that would be to abandon all the folk who had taken refuge in the river's great loop.

And the Danes would probably be over the river already. There were fords to the west and they would want to surround Scrobbesburh to stop reinforcements reaching us. In truth, I thought, our best hope was that the Danes would want to keep their invasion moving and so, rather than lose men defeating us, they would ride on south. It was a thin and unconvincing hope, and in the late night, just before the gray of dawn stained the eastern sky, I felt the despair of the doomed. The three Norns had given me no choice except to plant my banner and die with Serpent-Breath in my hand. I thought of Stiorra, my daughter, and wished I could see her one more time, and then the gray light came, and with it a mist, and the clouds were low again and brought a small rain spitting from the west.

Through the mist I could see the Danish banners. At their center was Haesten's symbol, the skull on its long pole. The wind was too light to flaunt the flags and so I could not see whether they showed eagles, ravens, or boars. I counted the banners. I could see at least thirty, and the mist hid some, and beneath those damp flags the Danes were making a shield wall.

We had two banners. Merewalh was showing Æthelred's flag of a prancing white horse, which he had placed in the fort. It hung limp from its long pole. My banner of the wolf's head was in the lower land to the north and I ordered Oswi, my servant, to cut down a sapling to make a second pole so that I could spread the flag and show the Danes who it was they faced. "That's just an invitation, lord," Finan said. He stamped his feet in the wet ground. "Remember the angels said you'd die. They all want your skull nailed to their gable."

"I'm not going to hide from them," I said.

Finan made the sign of the cross and stared bleakly at the enemy ranks. "At least it will be quick, lord," he said.

The mist slowly lifted, though the small rain drizzled on. The Danes had formed a line between two copses a half-mile away. The line, thick with painted shields, filled the space between the trees and I had the impression the line continued on into the woods. That was strange, I thought, but then nothing about this sudden war had been predictable. "Seven hundred men?" I guessed.

"About that," Finan said, "plenty enough of them. And there's more in the trees."

"Why?"

"Maybe the bastards want us to attack them?" Finan suggested. "Then close on us from either side?"

"They know we won't attack," I said. We were fewer in number and most of our men were not trained warriors. The Danes would know that, simply because the fyrd was rarely equipped with shields. They would see my shield wall at the center of our line, but on either side, that shield wall was flanked by men carrying no protection. Easy meat, I thought, and I did not doubt the fyrd would break like a twig when the Danes advanced.

Except they stayed between the trees as the mist vanished and the rain thickened. At times the Danes beat swords against shields to make the war-thunder, and I half heard men shouting, though they were too far away for me to hear the words. "Why don't they come?" Finan asked plaintively.

I could not answer because I had no idea what the Danes were doing. They had us at their mercy and they were standing instead of charging. They had advanced so slowly the previous day, now they were immobile, and this was their great invasion? I remember staring at them, wondering, and two swans flew overhead, wings beating the rain. A sign, but what did it mean? "If they kill us to the last man," I asked Finan, "how many of them will die?"

"Two hundred?" he guessed.

"That's why they're not attacking," I suggested, and Finan looked at me, puzzled. "They're hiding men in the trees," I said, "not in hope we attack, but so we don't know how many they are." I paused, sensing an idea taking shape in my mind. "Or more accurately," I went on, "how few they are."

"Few?" Finan asked.

"This isn't their great army," I said, suddenly sure of it. "This is a feint. Sigurd's not there, nor is Cnut." I was guessing, but it was the only explanation I could find. Whoever commanded these Danes had fewer than a thousand men and did not want to lose two or three hundred in a fight that was not part of the main invasion. His job was to hold us here and draw other Saxon troops to the valley of the Sæfern, while the real invasion came. From where? From the sea?

"I thought Offa told you . . ." Finan began.

"That bastard was crying," I said savagely, "he was weeping to convince me that he spoke the truth. He told me he was repaying my kindness, but I was never kind to him. I paid him, just like everyone else. And the Danes must have paid him more to tell me a pack of lies." Again I did not know whether that was true, but why were these Danes not coming to slaughter us?

Then there was movement in the center of their line and the shields parted to let three horsemen through. One carried a leafy branch, a sign that they wanted to talk, while another wore a high, silver-crested helmet from which trailed a plume of raven feathers. I called to Merewalh, then walked with him and Finan past our feeble barrier and across the wet grassland toward the approaching Danes.

Haesten was the man in the raven-plumed helmet. It was a magnificent piece of workmanship, decorated by the Midgard serpent that twisted around the crown, its tail protecting the nape of his neck while the mouth formed the crest that held the raven plumes. The cheek-pieces were incised with dragons, between which Haesten's face grinned at me. "The Lord Uhtred," he said happily.

"You're wearing your wife's bonnet," I said.

"It was a gift from the Jarl Cnut," he said, "who will be here by nightfall."

"I wondered why you were waiting," I said. "Now I know. You need help."

Haesten smiled as if he indulged my insults. The man with the green branch was a few paces behind him, while next to him was a warrior wearing another ornate helmet, this one with its cheek-pieces laced together so I could not see his face. His mail was expensive, his saddle and belt decorated with silver, and his arms thick with precious rings. His horse was nervous and he struck it hard on the neck, which only made it sidestep in the soft ground. Haesten leaned over and stroked the skittery stallion. "Jarl Cnut is bringing Ice-Spite," he said to me.

"Ice-Spite?"

"His sword," Haesten explained. "You and he, Lord Uhtred, will fight in the hazel branches. That's my gift to him."

Cnut Ranulfson was reputed to be the greatest swordsman among all the sword-Danes, a magician with a blade, a man who smiled as he killed and was proud of his reputation. I confess I felt a tremor of fear at Haesten's words. A fight contained in a space marked by hazel branches was a formal fight, and always to the death. It would be a demonstration of skill by Cnut. "It will be a pleasure killing him," I said.

"But didn't your angels say you were to die?" Haesten asked, amused.

"My angels?"

"A clever idea," Haesten said. "Young Sigurd here brought them back to us. Two such pretty girls! He enjoyed them! So did most of our men."

So the horseman with Haesten was Sigurd's son, the puppy who had wanted to fight me at Ceaster, and the raid on Turcandene had been his doing, his initiation as a leader, though I did not doubt his father had sent older and wiser men to make sure his son made no fatal errors. I remembered the flies around Ludda's body and the crudely drawn raven on the Roman plaster. "When you die, puppy," I told him, "I'll make sure you have no sword in your hand. I'll send you to Hel's rotten flesh instead. See how you enjoy that, you dribble of bat shit."

Sigurd Sigurdson drew his sword, he drew it very slowly as if to demonstrate that he was not issuing an immediate challenge. "She is called Fire-Dragon," he said, holding the blade upright.

"A puppy's blade," I scoffed.

"I want you to know the name of the sword that will kill you," he said, then wrenched his stallion's head around as if to drive the beast into me, but the horse half reared and young Sigurd had to cling to the mane to stay in the saddle. Haesten again leaned over and took hold of the stallion's bridle.

"Put the sword away, lord," he told the boy, then smiled at me. "You have till evening to surrender," he said, "and if you do not surrender," his voice was harder now, riding over the comment I had been about to make, "then every one of you will die. But if you yield, Lord Uhtred, we shall spare your men. Till evening!" He turned his horse, dragging young Sigurd with him. "Till evening!" he called again as he rode away.

This was the war that passeth understanding, I thought. Why wait? Unless Haesten so feared losing a quarter or a third of his force. But if this truly was the vanguard of a great Danish army, then it had no business loitering at Scrobbesburh. They should be pushing fast and hard into the soft underbelly of Saxon Mercia, then crossing the Temes to ravage Wessex. Every day that the Danes waited now was a day to assemble the fyrd and bring house-warriors from the Saxon shires, unless my suspicion was right and this Danish thrust was intended to deceive because the real attack was taking place somewhere else.

There were more Danes nearby. Late in the morning, as the rain at last ended and a watery sun showed weak through the clouds, we saw more smoke in the eastern sky. The smoke was thin at first, but thickened fast, and within an hour two more plumes appeared. So the Danes were harrying the nearby villages, and another band had crossed the river and were patrolling the great loop that trapped us. Osferth had found two boats, just skins stretched over willow frames, and had wanted to make a big raft like the one we had found to cross the Use, but the presence of the Danish horsemen ended that idea. I ordered my men to stiffen the barricade across the neck, raising it with beams and rafters to protect the men of the fyrd and channel any attack into my shield wall. I had small hope of surviving a determined assault, but men must be kept busy and so they pulled down six of the cottages and carried the timbers to the neck, where the barrier slowly became more formidable. A priest who had taken refuge in Scrobbesburh walked along my defensive line giving men small scraps of bread. They knelt before him, he placed the crumbs on their lips, then added a pinch of soil. "Why's he doing that?" I asked Osferth.

"We come from the earth, lord, and that's where we'll go."

"We'll go nowhere unless Haesten attacks," I said.

"He fears us?"

I shook my head. "It's a trap," I said, and there had been so many traps, from the moment the men tried to kill me on Saint Alnoth's day and the summons to seal a treaty with Eohric, and my burning of Sigurd's ships, and the creation of the angels, but now I suspected the Danes had sprung the largest trap and it had worked because in the afternoon there was a sudden flurry of panic on the river's far bank as the patrolling Danes spurred their horses westward. Something had frightened them, and a few moments later a much larger band of horsemen appeared and these men were flaunting two banners, one with a cross and the other a dragon. They were West Saxons. Haesten was drawing men to Scrobbesburh, and I was convinced we were all needed in some place far away where the real Danish attack must be unfolding.

Steapa led the newcomers. He dismounted and clambered down the riverbank to a small shelf of mud where he cupped his hands. "Where can we cross?"

"To the west," I shouted back. "How many are you?"

"Two hundred and twenty!"

"We've got seven hundred Danes here," I called, "but I don't think this is their great army!"

"More of our people are coming!" he called, ignoring my last words, and I watched him clamber back up the bank.

He went west, vanishing in the trees as he sought a ford or bridge. I went back to the neck and saw the Danes still sitting in their line. They had to be bored, but they made no effort to provoke us, even when evening came and went. Haesten must have known I would not meekly surrender, yet he made no move to enforce his morning threat. We watched the Danish campfires spring up again, we watched westward for the arrival of Steapa, we watched and we waited. Night fell.

And in the dawn the Danes were gone.

Æthelflaed arrived an hour after the sun rose, bringing almost one hundred and fifty warriors. Like Steapa she had to ride west to find a ford and it was midday before we were all together. "I thought you were going south," I greeted her.

"Someone has to fight them," she retorted.

"Except they've gone," I said. The land to the north of the neck was still dotted with smoldering campfires, but there were no Danes, only hoof tracks going eastward. We now had an army, but no one to fight. "Haesten never meant to fight me," I said, "he just wanted to draw men here."

Steapa looked at me with a puzzled expression, but Æthelflaed understood what I was saying. "So where are they?"

"We're in the west," I said, "so they must be in the east."

"And Haesten's gone to join them?"

"I'd think so," I said. We knew nothing for certain, of course, except that Haesten's men had attacked south from Ceaster and then, mysteriously, ridden eastward. Edward, like Æthelflaed, had responded to my very first warnings, sending men north to discover whether there was an invasion or not. Steapa was supposed to confirm or deny my first message, then ride back to Wintanceaster. Æthelflaed had ignored my orders to shelter in Cirrenceastre and instead brought her own house-warriors north. Other Mercian troops, she said, had been summoned to Gleawecestre. "That's a surprise," I said sarcastically. Æthelred, just as he had the last time Haesten invaded Mercia, would protect his own lands and let the rest of the country fend for itself.

"I should go back to the king," Steapa said.

"What are your orders?" I asked him. "To find the Danish invasion?"

"Yes, lord."

"Have you found it?"

He shook his head. "No."

"Then you and your men come with me," I said, "and you," I pointed to Æthelflaed, "should go to Cirrenceastre or else join your brother."

"And you," she said, pointing back at me, "do not command me, so I'll do what I wish." She stared at me challengingly, but I said nothing. "Why don't we destroy Haesten?" she asked.

"Because we don't have enough men," I said patiently, "and because we don't know where the rest of the Danes are. You want to start a battle with Haesten and then discover three thousand mead-crazed Danes are in your rear?"

"Then what do we do?" she asked.

"What I tell you to do," I said, and so we went eastward, following Haesten's hoofprints, and it was noticeable that no more steadings had been burned and no villages sacked. That meant Haesten had been traveling fast, ignoring the chances for enrichment because, I assumed, he was under orders to join the Danish great army, wherever that was.

We hurried too, but on the second day we were close to Liccelfeld and I had business there. We rode into the small town that had no walls, but boasted a great church, two mills, a monastery, and an imposing hall, which was the bishop's house. Many of the folk had fled southward, seeking the shelter of a burh, and our arrival caused panic. We saw folk running toward the nearest woods, assuming we were Danes.

We watered the horses in the two streams that ran through the town and I sent Osferth and Finan to buy food while Æthelflaed and I took thirty men to the town's second largest hall, a magnificent and new building that stood at Liccelfeld's northern edge. The widow who lived there had not fled from our arrival. Instead she waited in her hall, accompanied by a dozen servants.

Her name was Edith. She was young, she was pretty, and she was hard, though she looked soft. Her face was round, her curly red hair was springy, and her figure was plump. She wore a gown of linen dyed gold and around her neck was a looped golden chain.

"You're Offa's widow," I said, and she nodded without speaking. "Where are his dogs?"

"I drowned them," she said.

"How much did Jarl Sigurd pay your husband to lie to us?" I asked.

"I don't know what you're talking about," she said.

I turned to Sihtric. "Search the place," I told him. "Take all the food you need."

"You can't . . ." Edith began.

"I can do what I want!" I snarled at her. "Your husband sold Wessex and Mercia to the Danes."

She was stubborn, admitting nothing, yet there was too much evident wealth in the newly built hall. She screamed at us, clawed at me when I took the gold from around her neck, and spat curses when we left. I did not leave the town straightaway, instead I went to the graveyard by the cathedral where my men dug Offa's body from its grave. He had paid silver to the priests so that he could be buried close to the relics of Saint Chad, believing that proximity would hasten his ascent into heaven on the day of Christ's return to earth, but I did my best to consign his filthy soul to the Christian hell. We carried his rotting body, still in its discolored winding sheet, to the edge of town and there threw it into a stream.

Then we rode on eastward to discover whether his treachery had doomed Wessex.

PART FOUR

DEATH IN WINTER

Eleven

The village was no more. The houses were smoldering piles of charred timbers and ash, the corpses of four hacked dogs lay in the muddy street, and the stink of roasted flesh was mingling with the sullen smoke. A woman's body, naked and swollen, floated in a pond. Ravens were perched on her shoulders, tearing at the bloated flesh. Blood had dried black in the grooves of the flat washing-stone beside the water. A great elm tree towered above the village, but its southern side had been set alight by flames from the church roof and had burned so that the tree appeared lightning-blasted, one half in full green leaf, the other half black, shriveled, and brittle. The ruins of the church still burned and there was not one person alive to tell us the name of the place, though a dozen smears of smoke told us that this was not the only village to be reduced to charred ruin.

We had ridden eastward, again following the tracks of Haesten's band, then those hoofprints had turned south to join a larger burned and beaten path. That path had been made by hundreds of horses, probably thousands, and the smoke trails in the sky suggested that the Danes were journeying south toward the valley of the Temes and the rich pickings of Wessex beyond.

"There are corpses in the church," Osferth told me. His voice was calm, yet I could tell he was angry. "Many corpses," he said. "They must have locked them inside and burned the church around them."

"Like a hall-burning," I said, remembering Ragnar the Elder's hall blazing in the night and the screams of the people trapped inside.

"There are children there," Osferth said, sounding angrier. "Their bodies shriveled to the size of babies!"

"Their souls are with God," Æthelflaed tried to comfort him.

"There's no pity anymore," Osferth said, looking at the sky, which was a mix of gray cloud and dark smoke.

Steapa also glanced at the sky. "They're going south," he said. He was thinking of his orders to return to Wessex and worrying that I was keeping him in Mercia while a Danish horde threatened his homeland.

"Or maybe to Lundene?" Æthelflaed suggested. "Maybe south to the Temes, then downriver to Lundene?" She was thinking the same thoughts as me. I remembered the city's decayed wall, and Eohric's scouts watching that wall. Alfred had known the importance of Lundene, which is why he had asked me to capture it, but did the Danes know? Whoever garrisoned Lundene controlled the Temes, and the Temes led deep into Mercia and Wessex. So much trade went through Lundene and so many roads led there and whoever held Lundene held the key to southern Britain. I looked southward where the great plumes of smoke drifted. A Danish army had passed this way, probably only a day before, but was it their only army? Was another besieging Lundene? Had another already captured the city? I was tempted to ride straight for Lundene to ensure that it would be well defended, but that would mean abandoning the burning trail of the great army.

Æthelflaed was watching me, waiting for an answer, but I said nothing. Six of us sat on our horses in the center of that burned village while my men watered their horses in the pond where the swollen corpse floated. Æthelflaed, Steapa, Finan, Merewalh, and Osferth were all looking to me, and I was trying to place myself in the mind of whoever commanded the Danes. Cnut? Sigurd? Eohric? We did not even know that.

"We'll follow these Danes," I finally decided, nodding toward the smoke in the southern sky.

"I should join my lord," Merewalh said unhappily.

Æthelflaed smiled. "Let me tell you what my husband will do," she said, and the scorn in the word "husband" was as pungent as the stench from the burning church. "He will keep his forces in

Gleawecestre," she went on, "just as he did when the Danes last invaded." She saw the struggle on Merewalh's face. He was a good man, and like all good men he wanted to do his oath-duty, which was to be at his lord's side, but he knew Æthelflaed spoke the truth. She straightened in her saddle. "My husband," she said, though this time without any scorn, "gave me permission to give orders to any of his followers that I encountered. So now I order you to stay with me."

Merewalh knew she was lying. He looked at her for an instant, then nodded. "Then I shall, lady."

"What about the dead?" Osferth asked, staring at the church.

Æthelflaed leaned over and gently touched her half-brother's arm. "The dead must bury their dead," she said.

Osferth knew there was no time to give the dead a Christian burial. They must be left here, but the anger was tight in him and he slid from his saddle and walked to the smoking church where small flames licked from the burning timbers. He pulled two charred lengths of wood from the ruin. One was about five feet long, the other much shorter, and he scavenged among the ruined cottages until he found a strip of leather, perhaps a belt, and he used the leather to lash the two pieces of timber together. He made a cross. "With your permission, lord," he told me, "I want my own standard."

"The son of a king should have a banner," I said.

He rammed the butt of the cross on the ground so that it shed ash, and the crosspiece tilted crookedly. It would have been funny if he had not been so bitterly enraged. "This is my standard," he said, and called for his servant, a deaf-mute named Hwit, to carry the cross.

We followed the hoof tracks south through more burned villages, past a great hall that was now ashes and blackened rafters, and by fields where cattle lowed miserably because they needed milking. If the Danes had left cows behind then they must already have a vast herd, too big to manage, and they must have collected women and children for the slave markets as well. They were encumbered by now. Instead of being a fast, dangerous, well-mounted army of savage raiders they had become a lumbering procession of captives, wagons, herds, and flocks. They would still be spewing out vicious raid parties, but each of those would bring back further plunder to slow the main army even more.

They had crossed the Temes. We discovered that next day when we reached Cracgelad where I had killed Aldhelm, Æthelred's man. The small town was now a burh, and its walls were of stone, not earth and wood. The fortifications were Æthelflaed's doing, and she had ordered the work done, not only because the small town guarded a crossing of the Temes, but because she had witnessed a small miracle there; touched, she believed, by a dead saint's hand. So Cracgelad was now a formidable fortress, with a flooded ditch fronting the new stone wall and it was hardly surprising that the Danes had ignored the garrison and instead had headed for the causeway that led across the marshes on the north bank of the Temes to the Roman bridge, which had been repaired at the same time that Cracgelad's walls had been rebuilt. We also followed the causeway and stood our horses on the northern bank of the Temes and watched the skies burn above Wessex. So Edward's kingdom was being ravaged.

Æthelflaed might have made Cracgelad into a burh, but the town still flew her husband's banner of the white horse above its southern gate rather than her flag of the cross-grasping goose. A dozen men now appeared at that gate and walked to join us. One was a priest, Father Kynhelm, and he gave us our first reliable news. Æthelwold, he said, was with the Danes. "He came to the gate, lord, and demanded we surrender."

"You recognized him?"

"I've never seen him before, lord, but he announced himself, and I assume he told the truth. He came with Saxons."

"Not Danes?"

Father Kynhelm shook his head. "The Danes stayed away. We could see them, but as far as I could tell the men at the gate were all Saxons. A lot of them shouted at us to surrender. I counted two hundred and twenty."

"And one woman," a man added.

I ignored that. "How many Danes?" I asked Father Kynhelm.

He shrugged. "Hundreds, lord, they blackened the fields."

"Æthelwold's banner is a stag," I said, "with crosses for antlers. Was that the only flag?"

"They showed a black cross as well, lord, and a boar flag."

"A boar?" I said.

"A tusked boar, lord."

So Beortsig had joined his masters, which meant that the army plundering Wessex was part Saxon. "What answer did you give Æthelwold?" I asked Father Kynhelm.

"That we served Lord Æthelred, lord."

"You have news of Lord Æthelred?"

"No, lord."

"You have food?"

"Enough for the winter, lord. The harvest was adequate, God be praised."

"What forces do you have?"

"The fyrd, lord, and twenty-two warriors."

"How many fyrd?"

"Four hundred and twenty, lord."

"Keep them here," I said, "because the Danes will probably be back." When Alfred was on his deathbed I had told him that the Northmen had not learned how to fight us, but we had learned how to fight them, and that was true. They had made no attempt to capture Cracgelad, except for a feeble summons for the town to surrender, and if thousands of Danes could not capture one small burh, however formidable its walls, then they had no chance against Wessex's larger garrisons, and if they could not capture the large burhs and so destroy Edward's forces inside, then eventually they must retreat. "What Danish banners did you see?" I asked Father Kynhelm.

"None plainly, lord."

"What is Eohric's banner?" I asked everyone in earshot.

"A lion and a cross," Osferth said.

"Whatever a lion is," I said. I wanted to know if Eohric's East Anglians had joined the Danish horde, but Father Kynhelm did not have the answer.

Next morning it was raining again, the drops pitting the Temes as it slid past the burh's walls. The low cloud made it hard to distinguish the smoke plumes, but my impression was that the fires were not far south of the river. Æthelflaed went to Saint Werburgh's convent and prayed, Osferth found a carpenter in the town who jointed his cross properly and fixed it with nails, while I summoned two of Merewalh's men and two of Steapa's troops. I sent the Mercians to Gleawecestre with a message for Æthelred. I knew that if the message came from me he would ignore it utterly, and so I ordered them to say it was a request from King Edward that he bring his troops, all his troops, to Cracgelad. The great army, I explained, had crossed the Temes at the burh and would almost certainly withdraw the same way. They could, of course, choose another ford or bridge, but men have a habit of using the roads and tracks they already know. If Mercia assembled its army on the northern bank of the Temes then Edward could bring the West Saxons from the south and we would trap them between us. Steapa's men carried the same message to Edward, except that message came from me and was merely a strong suggestion that as the Danes withdrew he should concentrate his army and follow them, but not attack until they were already crossing the Temes.

It was around midmorning that I gave the order to saddle the horses and be ready to ride, though I did not say to where, then just as we were about to depart two messengers arrived from Bishop Erkenwald in Lundene.

I never liked Erkenwald, while Æthelflaed had hated him ever since he had preached a sermon on adultery and stared at her throughout, but the bishop knew his business. He had sent messengers along every Roman road from Lundene with orders to seek out Mercian or West Saxon forces. "He said to keep a watchful eye for you, lord," one of the two men said. He was from Weohstan's garrison and told us that the Danes were outside Lundene's walls, but not in any great force. "If we threaten them, lord, they retreat."

"Whose men are they?"

"King Eohric's, lord, and a few follow Sigurd's banner too."

So Eohric had joined the Danes and not the Christians. Erkenwald's messengers said they had heard that the Danes had assembled at Eoferwic, and from there they had taken ship to East Anglia, and while I had been lured to Ceaster, that great army, reinforced by Eohric's warriors, had launched themselves across the Use and started their path of fire and death. "What are Eohric's men doing at Lundene?" I asked.

"They just watch, lord. There aren't enough of them to make an assault."

"But enough to keep troops inside the walls," I said. "So what does Bishop Erkenwald want?"

"He hoped you would go to Lundene, lord."

"Tell him to send me half of Weohstan's men instead," I said.

Bishop Erkenwald's request—I suspected it had been couched as an order that the messengers had softened into a suggestion—made small sense to me. True, Lundene needed to be defended, but the army that threatened that city was here, south of the Temes, and if we moved fast we could trap it here. The enemy force at Lundene was probably only there to keep the city's large garrison from sallying out to confront the great army. My expectation was that the Danes would plunder and burn, but eventually they would either have to besiege a burh or else be fought in the open country by a West Saxon army, and it was more important to know where they were and what they intended than to gather in far Lundene. To defeat the Danes we had to meet them in open battle. There could be no escape from the horrors of the shield wall. The burhs might stave off defeat, but victory came in face-to-face combat, and my thought was to force a battle when the Danes were recrossing the Temes. The one thing I did know was that we had to choose the battlefield, and Cracgelad, with its river, causeway, and bridge, was as good a place as any, as good as the bridge at Fearnhamme where we had slaughtered the army of Harald Bloodhair after trapping it when only half his troops were across the river.

I gave Erkenwald's messengers fresh horses and sent them back to Lundene, though without much hope that the bishop would dispatch reinforcements unless he received a direct order from Edward, then I led most of our force across the river. Merewalh stayed in Cracgelad, and I had told Æthelflaed to remain with him, but she ignored the order and rode beside me. "Fighting," I growled at her, "is not women's business."

"What is women's business, Lord Uhtred?" she asked with mock sweetness. "Oh, please, please! Tell me!"

I looked for the trap hidden in the question. There obviously was a trap, though I could not see it. "A woman's business," I said stiffly, "is to look after the household."

"To clean? To sweep? To spin? To cook?"

"To supervise the servants, yes."

"And to raise the children?"

"That too," I agreed.

"In other words," she said tartly, "women are supposed to do all that a man can't do. And right now it seems men can't fight, so I'd better do that too." She smiled triumphantly, then laughed when I scowled. In truth I was glad of her company. It was not just that I loved her, but Æthelflaed's presence always inspired men. The Mercians adored her. She might have been a West Saxon, but her mother was a Mercian, and Æthelflaed had adopted that country as her own. Her generosity was famous, there was hardly a convent in Mercia that did not depend on the income from the wide estates Æthelflaed had inherited to help their widows and orphans.

Once across the Temes we were in Wessex. The same hoof-scarred path showed where the great army had spread out as they went southward, and the first villages we passed were burned, their ashes now turned to a gray sludge by the night's rain. I sent Finan and fifty men ahead to act as scouts, warning them that the smoke trails in the sky were much closer than I had expected. "What did you expect?" Æthelflaed asked me.

"That the Danes would go straight to Wintanceaster," I said.

"And attack it?"

"They should," I said, "or ravage the country around the city and hope they can lure Edward out for a fight."

"If Edward's there," she said uncertainly.

But instead of attacking Wintanceaster, the Danes seemed to be scouring the land just south of the Temes. It was good land with plump farms and rich villages, though much of its wealth would have been driven or carried into the closest burhs. "They have to besiege a burh or leave," I said, "and they don't usually have the patience for a siege."

"Then why come in the first place?"

I shrugged. "Maybe Æthelwold thought folk would support him?

Maybe they hope Edward will lead an army against them and they can defeat him?"

"Will he?"

"Not till he has enough strength," I said, hoping that was true. "But right now," I said, "the Danes are being slowed by captives and by plunder and they'll send some of that back to East Anglia." That was what Haesten had done during his great ravaging of Mercia. His forces had moved swiftly, but he had constantly detached bands of men to escort his captive slaves and loaded pack mules back to Beamfleot. If my suspicion was right, the Danes would be sending men back along the route they had come, and that was why I rode south, looking for one of those Danish bands taking plunder back to East Anglia.

"It would make more sense for them to use another route," Æthelflaed observed.

"They have to know the country to do that. Following your own tracks home is much easier."

We did not need to ride far from the bridge because the Danes were surprisingly close, indeed they were very close. Within an hour Finan had returned to me with news that large bands of Danes were spread all across the nearer country. The land rose gradually toward the south and the fires of destruction were burning on the far skyline while men brought captives, livestock, and plunder to the lower ground. "There's a village on the road ahead," Finan told me, "or rather there was a village, and they're collecting the plunder there, and there's not more than three hundred of the bastards."

I worried that the Danes had not guarded the bridge at Cracgelad, but the only answer to that worry was to assume they had no fear of any attack from Mercia. I had sent scouts along the riverbank to east and west, but none reported any news of a Danish presence. It seemed the enemy was intent on amassing plunder and was not watching for an attack from across the Temes. That was either carelessness, or else a careful trap.

We numbered almost six hundred men. If it was a trap then we would be a hard beast to kill, and I decided to lay a trap of our own. I was beginning to think the Danes were being careless, overconfident of their overwhelming numbers, and we were in their rear and we had a safe route of escape, and the opportunity was simply too good.

"Can those trees hide us?" I asked Finan, nodding toward some thick woodland to the south.

"You could hide a thousand men in there," he said.

"We'll wait in the trees," I said. "You're going to lead all our men," I told him, meaning the men sworn to me, "and attack the bastards. Then you lead them back toward the rest of us."

It was a simple ambush, so simple I did not really believe it could work, but this was still the war that passed understanding. First, it was happening three years too late and now, after attempting to lure me to Ceaster, the Danes seemed to have forgotten all about me. "They have too many leaders," Æthelflaed suggested as we walked our horses south along the Roman road that led from the bridge, "and they're all men, so not one of them will give in. They're arguing among themselves."

"Let's hope they go on arguing," I said. Once among the trees we spread out. Æthelflaed's men were on the right, and I sent Osferth to keep her safe. Steapa's men went to the left, while I stayed in the center. I dismounted, giving my horse's reins to Oswi, and walked with Finan to the wood's southern edge. Our arrival in the trees had sent pigeons clattering through the branches, but no Danes took any notice. The nearest were some two or three hundred paces away, close to a mixed herd of sheep and goats. Beyond them was a steading, still unburned, and I could see a crowd of people there.

"Captives," Finan said, "women and children."

There were Danes there too, their presence betrayed by a large herd of saddled horses in a hedged paddock. It was hard to tell how many horses, but it was at least a hundred. The steading was a small hall beside a pair of newly thatched barns, their roofs bright in the sun. There were more Danes beyond the hall, out in fields, where I assumed they were collecting livestock. "I'd suggest riding for the hall," I said, "kill as many as you can, bring me a captive, and take their horses."

"About time we had a fight," Finan said wolfishly.

"Lead them onto us," I said, "and we'll kill every last mother's son." He turned to go, but I put a hand on his mailed arm. I was still staring south. "It isn't a trap, is it?"

Finan gazed south. "They reached this far without a fight," he said, "and they think no one dares face them."

I felt a moment's frustration. If I had Mercia's army at Cracgelad, and Edward could bring the men of Wessex from the south, we could have crushed this careless army, but so far as I knew we were the only Saxon troops anywhere near the Danes. "I want to keep them here," I said.

"Keep them here?" Finan asked.

"Near the bridge, so King Edward can bring men to crush them." We had more than enough men to hold the bridge against as many attacks as the Danes could make. We did not even need Æthelred's Mercians to make this trap work. This, then, was the battleground I wanted. "Sihtric!"

The choice of this place as the ground to destroy the Danes was so obvious, so tempting, and so advantageous that I did not want to wait before Edward knew of my certainty. "I'm sorry you'll miss the fight," I told Sihtric, "but this is urgent." I was sending him with three other men to ride westward and then south. They were to follow my first messengers and tell the king where the Danes were, and how they could be beaten. "Tell him the enemy is just waiting to be killed. Tell him this can be his first great victory, tell him the poets will sing of it for generations, and above all tell him to hurry!" I waited until Sihtric was gone, then looked back to the enemy. "Bring me as many horses as you can," I told Finan.

Finan led my men southward, keeping to some woods east of the road, while I brought up all the remaining horsemen. I rode along our line, ducking under the low branches, and told men they should not only kill the enemy, but wound them. Wounded men slow an army. If Sigurd, Cnut, and Eohric had badly wounded troops, then they could not ride fast and loose. I wanted to slow this army, to trap it, to keep it in place till the forces of Wessex could come from the south to kill it.

I watched the birds fly from the trees where Finan was leading my men. Not one Dane noticed, or took any interest if he did see the birds. I waited beside Æthelflaed and felt a sudden exhilaration.

The Danes were trapped. They did not know it, but they were doomed. Bishop Erkenwald's sermon was right, of course, and war is a dreadful thing, but it could also be so enjoyable, and there was no part more enjoyable than forcing an enemy to do your bidding. This enemy was where I wanted him, and where he would die, and I remember laughing aloud and Æthelflaed looked at me curiously. "What's funny?" she asked, but I did not answer because just then Finan's men broke cover.

They charged from the east. They went fast and for a moment the Danes seemed stunned by their sudden appearance. Hoof-thrown clods of earth flecked the air behind my men, I could see the light reflected from their blades, and I watched Danes running toward the hall, and then Finan's men were among them, riding them down, horsemen overtaking fugitives, blades falling, blood coloring the day, men falling, bleeding, panicking, and Finan drove them on, aiming for the field where the Danish horses were penned.

I heard a horn call. Men were gathering at the hall, men snatching up shields, but Finan ignored them. A hurdle lay across the hedge opening and I saw Cerdic lean down and pull it away. The Danish horses surged through the opened gap to follow my men. More Danes were galloping from the south, called by the urgent horn, while Finan led a wild charge of riderless horses toward our trees. The path where he had galloped was strewn with bodies, I counted twenty-three, and not all dead. Some were wounded, writhing on the ground as their lifeblood stained the grass. Panicked sheep milled, a second horn joined its summons to the first, the noise harsh in the afternoon air. The Danes were gathering, but they had still not seen the rest of us among the trees. They saw a herd of their horses being driven northward and they must have assumed Finan was from Cracgelad's garrison and that the horses were being taken across the Temes into the safety of those stone walls, and some Danes set off in pursuit. They spurred their horses as Finan vanished among the trees. I drew Serpent-Breath and my stallion's ears pricked back as he heard the hiss of the blade through the scabbard's fleece-lined throat. He was trembling, pawing the ground with one heavy hoof. He was called Broga, and he was excited by the horses crashing through the trees. He whinnied and I loosened the reins to let him go forward.

"Kill and wound!" I shouted. "Kill and wound!"

Broga, the name meant terror, leaped forward. All along the wood's edge the horsemen appeared, blades gleaming, and we charged at the scattered Danes, shouting, and the world was the drumbeat of hooves.

Most Danes turned to flee. The sensible ones kept charging toward us, knowing that their best chance of survival lay in crashing through our ranks and escaping behind us. My shield banged on my back, Serpent-Breath was raised, and I swerved toward a man on a gray horse and saw him ready to swing his sword at me, but one of Æthelflaed's men speared him first, and he twisted in the saddle, sword falling, and I left him behind and caught up with a Dane fleeing on foot and slammed Serpent-Breath across his shoulders, drew her back along his neck, saw him stagger, left him, swung the sword at a running man, and laid his scalp open so that his long hair was suddenly wet with blood.

The dismounted Danes by the hall had made a shield wall, perhaps forty or fifty men who faced us with their round shields overlapping, but Finan had turned and brought his men back, savaging his way up the road and leaving bodies behind him and he now brought his men behind the shield wall. He screamed his Irish challenge, words that meant nothing to any of us, but curdled the blood all the same, and the shield wall, seeing horsemen in front and behind, broke apart. Their captives were cowering in the yard, all women and children, and I shouted at them to head north toward the river. "Go, go!" Broga had charged two men. One swung his sword at Broga's mouth, but he was trained well and reared up, hooves flailing, and the man ducked away. I clung to him, waited till he came down, and brought Serpent-Breath hard down onto the second man's head, splitting helmet and skull. I heard a scream and saw that Broga had bitten off the first man's face. I spurred on. Dogs were howling, children screaming, and Serpent-Breath was feeding. A naked woman stumbled from the hall, her hair unbound, her face smeared with blood. "Go that way!" I shouted at her, pointing my red blade north.

"My children!"

"Find them! Go!"

A Dane came from the hall, sword in hand, stared in horror, and turned back, but Rypere had seen him and galloped by him, seized him by his long hair, and dragged him away. Two spears gouged his belly and a stallion trampled him and he writhed, bloody and moaning, and we left him there.

"Oswi!" I shouted for my servant. "Horn!"

More Danes were showing in the south now, many more Danes, and it was time to go. We had hurt the enemy badly, but this was no place to fight against an outnumbering horde. I just wanted the Danes to stay here, trapped by the river, so that Edward could bring the army of Wessex against them and drive them like cattle onto my swords. Oswi kept sounding the horn, the noise frantic.

"Back!" I shouted. "All of you! Back!"

We went back slowly enough. Our wild charge had killed and wounded at least a hundred men so that the small fields were dotted with bodies. The injured lay in ditches or by hedges, and we left them there. Steapa was grinning, a fearsome sight, his big teeth bared and his sword reddened. "Your men are the rearguard," I told him, and he nodded. I looked for Æthelflaed and was relieved to see her unharmed. "Look after the fugitives," I told her. The escaped captives had to be shepherded back. I saw the naked woman dragging two small children by their hands.

I formed my men at the edge of the trees where our charge had started. We waited there, shields on our arms now, swords bright with enemy blood, and we dared the Danes to come at us, but they were disorganized and they were hurt, and they would not risk a charge until they had more men, and once I saw that the fugitives were safely gone north I shouted at my men to follow them.

We had lost five men; two Mercians and three West Saxons, but we had savaged the enemy. Finan had two captives, and I sent them ahead with the fugitives. The bridge was crowded with horses and fleeing people, and I stayed with Steapa, guarding the southern end until I was certain the last of our people was across the river.

We barricaded the northern end of the bridge, heaping logs

across the road and inviting the Danes to come and be killed between the Roman parapets. But none did. They watched us work, they gathered in ever greater numbers on the West Saxon side of the river, but they did not come for their revenge. I left Steapa and his men to guard the barricade, certain that no Dane would cross while he was there.

Then I went to question the captives.

The two Danes were being guarded by six of Æthelflaed's Mercians, who protected them from the fury of a crowd that had gathered in the space before Saint Werburgh's convent. The crowd fell silent when I arrived, cowed perhaps by Broga whose mouth was still stained with blood. I slid from the saddle and let Oswi take the reins. I still carried Serpent-Breath in my hand, her blade unwashed.

There was a tavern hung with the sign of a goose next to the convent and I had the two men taken into its yard. Their names were Leif and Hakon, both were young, both were frightened, and both were trying not to show it. I had the yard gates closed and barred. The two stood in the yard's center, surrounded by six of us. Leif, who did not look a day over sixteen, could not take his eyes from Serpent-Breath's blood-caked blade. "You have a choice," I told the pair. "You can answer my questions and you'll die with swords in your hands, or you can be obstinate and I'll strip you both naked and throw you to the folk outside. First, who is your lord?"

"I serve Jarl Cnut," Leif said.

"And I serve King Eohric," Hakon said, his voice so low I almost could not hear him. He was a sturdy, long-faced boy with straw-colored hair. He wore an old mail coat, ripped at the elbows and too big for him and I suspected it had been his father's. He also wore a cross about his neck, while Leif had a hammer.

"Who commands your army?" I asked them.

They both hesitated. "King Eohric?" Hakon suggested, but he did not sound sure.

"Jarl Sigurd and Jarl Cnut," Leif said, just as uncertainly and almost at the same moment.

And that explained a great deal, I thought. "Not Æthelwold?" I asked.

"Him too, lord," Leif said. He was trembling.

"Is Beortsig with the army?"

"Yes, lord, but he serves Jarl Sigurd."

"And Jarl Haesten serves Jarl Cnut?"

"He does, lord," Hakon said.

Æthelflaed was right, I thought. Too many masters, and no one man in command. Eohric was weak, but he was proud, and he would not be subservient to Sigurd or Cnut, while those two probably despised Eohric, yet had to treat him as a king if they were to have his troops. "And how big is the army?" I asked.

Neither of them knew. Leif thought it was ten thousand strong, which was ludicrous, while Hakon just said they had been assured it was the largest army ever to attack the Saxons. "And where is it going?" I asked.

Again neither knew. They had been told that they would make Æthelwold the King of Wessex and Beortsig the King of Mercia, and those two monarchs would reward them with land, but when I asked if they were going to Wintanceaster they both looked blank and I realized neither had even heard of that city.

I let Finan kill Leif. He died bravely and swiftly, a sword in his hand, but Hakon begged to see a priest before he died. "You're a Dane," I told him.

"And a Christian, lord."

"Does no one worship Odin in East Anglia?"

"Some, lord, but not many."

That was worrying. Some Danes, I knew, converted because it was convenient. Haesten had insisted his wife and daughters were baptized, but that was only because it yielded better terms from Alfred, though if Offa had not lied about everything before he died, then Haesten's wife was a true believer. These days, as I face my own death and my old age dims the glories of this world, I see nothing but Christians. Perhaps in the far north where the ice grips the summer land there are some folk left who sacrifice to Thor, Odin, and Freya, but I know of none in Britain. We slide into darkness, toward the final chaos of Ragnarok, when the seas will burn in turmoil and the land will break and even the gods will die. Hakon did not care whether he held a sword or not, he just wanted to say his prayers, and when they were said we took his head from his shoulders.

I sent more messengers to Edward, only this time I sent Finan because I knew the king would listen to the Irishman, and I sent him with seven other men. They were to ride west before crossing the Temes, then go fast toward Wintanceaster or to wherever else the king might be, and they carried a letter I wrote myself. Men are always surprised that I can read and write, but Beocca taught me when I was a child and I have never lost the skills. Alfred, of course, insisted that all his lords should learn to read, mainly so that he could write his chiding letters to us, but since his death not many bother to learn, yet I still have the skills. I wrote that the Danes were cursed with too many leaders, that they were lingering too long just south of the Temes, that I had slowed them by taking horses and leaving them with a mass of wounded men. Come toward Cracgelad, I urged the king. Collect every warrior, I urged him, call the fyrd, and advance on the Danes from the south and I would be the anvil against which he could beat the enemy into blood, bones, and raven-food. If the Danes moved, I said, I would shadow them on the northern bank of the Temes to block their escape, but I doubted they would move far. "We have them in our hand, lord King," I wrote, "and now you must close the fist."

And then I waited. The Danes did not move. We saw the smoke pyres in the distant southern sky that told us they were scouring a wider area of Wessex, but their main encampment was still not far south of Cracgelad's bridge, which we now had made into a fortress. No one could cross the bridge unless we allowed it. I went over each day, taking fifty or sixty men to patrol a short distance on the southern bank to make certain the Danes were not moving, and each day I returned to Cracgelad astonished that the enemy was making it so easy for us. At night we could see the glow of their campfires lighting the southern sky and by day we watched the smoke, and in four days nothing changed except the weather. Rain came and went, the wind stirred the river, and an early autumn mist obscured the ramparts one morning, and when the mist lifted the Danes were still there.

"Why aren't they moving?" Æthelflaed asked me.

"Because they can't agree where to go."

"And if you led them," she asked, "where would they go?"

"To Wintanceaster," I said.

"And besiege it?"

"Capture it," I said, and that was their difficulty. They knew men would die in the burh's ditch and on its high wall, but that was no reason not to try. Alfred's burhs had given the enemy a riddle they could not solve, and I would have to find a solution if I was to retake Bebbanburg, a fortress that was more formidable than any burh. "I'd go to Wintanceaster," I told her, "and I'd hurl men at the wall until it fell, and then I'd make Æthelwold king there and demand that West Saxons follow me, and then we'd march on Lundene."

Yet the Danes did nothing. They argued instead. We heard later that Eohric wanted the army to march on Lundene, while Æthelwold reckoned it should assault Wintanceaster, and Cnut and Sigurd were all for recrossing the Temes to capture Gleawecestre. So Eohric wanted to bring Lundene into his kingdom's boundaries, Æthelwold wanted what he believed was his birthright, while Cnut and Sigurd simply wanted to extend their lands southward to the Temes, and their arguments left the great army drifting in indecision, and I imagined Edward's messengers riding between the burhs, gathering the warriors, bringing together a Saxon army that could destroy the Danish power in Britain for ever.

Then Finan returned with all the messengers I had sent to Wintanceaster. They crossed the Temes well to the west, looping about the Danes, and came to Cracgelad on horses that were sweat-whitened and dust-covered. They brought a letter from the king. A priestly clerk had written it, but Edward had signed it and the letter bore his seal. It greeted me in the name of the Christian god, thanked me effusively for my messages, and then ordered me to leave Cracgelad immediately and to take all the forces under my command to meet the king in Lundene. I read it in disbelief. "Did you tell the king we have the Danes trapped on the river?" I asked Finan.

Finan nodded, "I told him, lord, but he wants us in Lundene."

"Doesn't he understand the opportunity?"

"He's going to Lundene, lord, and he wants us to join him there," Finan said flatly.

"Why?" And that was a question no one could answer.

I could do no good on my own. I had men, true, but not nearly enough. I needed two or three thousand warriors to come from the south, and that was not going to happen. Edward, it seemed, was taking his army to Lundene, going by a route that kept him well clear of any Danish outriders. I swore, but I had sworn an oath to obey King Edward and my oath-lord had given me an order.

So we unlocked the trap, let the Danes live, and rode to Lundene.

King Edward was already in Lundene and the streets were filled with warriors, every courtyard was being used as a stable, even the old Roman amphitheater was crammed with horses.

Edward was in the old Mercian royal palace. Lundene was properly in Mercia, though it had been under West Saxon rule ever since I had captured it for Alfred. I found Edward in the big Roman chamber with its pillars, dome, cracked plaster, and shattered tile floor. A council was in session, and the king was flanked by Archbishop Plegmund and by Bishop Erkenwald, while facing them, in a semicircle of benches and chairs, sat more churchmen and a dozen ealdormen. The banners of Wessex were propped at the back of the chamber. A lively discussion was under way as I entered, and the voices fell silent as my feet sounded loud on the broken floor. Scraps of tile skittered away. There had been a picture made with the tiles, but it had vanished by now.

"Lord Uhtred," Edward greeted me warmly, though I noted a slight nervousness in his voice.

I knelt to him. "Lord King."

"Welcome," he said, "and join us."

I had not cleaned my mail. There was blood in the gaps between the tight rings and men noticed it. Ealdorman Æthelhelm ordered a chair brought next to him and invited me to sit there. "How many men do you bring us, Lord Uhtred?" Edward asked.

"Steapa is with me," I said, "and, counting his men, we have five hundred and sixty-three." I had lost some in the fighting at Cracgelad, and others had fallen behind because of lamed horses as we rode to Lundene.

"Which makes a total of?" Edward asked a priest seated at a table to the side of the chamber.

"Three thousand, four hundred and twenty-three men, lord King."

He obviously meant household warriors, not the fyrd, and it was a respectable army. "And the enemy?" Edward asked.

"Four to five thousand men, lord, as best we may judge."

The stilted conversation was plainly meant for my ears. Archbishop Plegmund, face as sour as a shriveled crab apple, watched me closely. "So you see, Lord Uhtred," Edward turned back to me, "we did not have enough men to force an encounter on the banks of the Temes."

"The men of Mercia would have joined you, lord King," I said. "Gleawecestre is not so far away."

"Sigismund has landed from Ireland," Archbishop Plegmund took up the tale, "and has occupied Ceaster. The Lord Æthelred needs to watch over him."

"From Gleawecestre?" I asked.

"From wherever he decides," Plegmund said testily.

"Sigismund," I said, "is a Norseman who's been run out of Ireland by the native savages, and he's hardly a threat to Mercia." I had never heard of Sigismund before and had no idea why he had chosen to occupy Ceaster, but it seemed a likely explanation.

"He has brought crews of pagans," Plegmund said. "A host!"

"He is not our business," Edward intervened, obviously unhappy at the sharp tone of the last few statements. "Our business is to defeat my cousin Æthelwold. Now"—he looked at me—"you will agree our burhs are well defended?"

"I hope so, lord."

"And it is our belief," Edward went on, "that the enemy will be frustrated by the burhs and so will withdraw soon."

"And we shall fight them as they withdraw," Plegmund said.

"So why not fight them south of Cracgelad?" I asked.

"Because the men of Cent could not have reached that place in a timely fashion," Plegmund said, sounding irritated by my question, "and Ealdorman Sigelf has promised us seven hundred warriors. Once they have joined us," he went on, "we shall be ready to confront the enemy."

Edward looked at me expectantly, plainly wanting my agreement. "It's surely sensible," he finally spoke after I had made no comment, "to wait until we have the men of Cent? Their numbers will make our army truly formidable."

"I have a suggestion, lord King," I said respectfully.

"All your suggestions are welcome, Lord Uhtred," he said.

"I think that instead of bread and wine the church should serve ale and old cheese," I said, "and I propose that the sermon should be at the beginning of the service instead of at the end, and I think priests should be naked during the ceremonies, and . . ."

"Silence!" Plegmund shouted.

"If your priests are going to conduct your wars, lord King," I said, "then why shouldn't your warriors run the church?" There was some nervous laughter at that, but as the council went on it was clear that we were as leaderless as the Danes. The Christians talk about the blind leading the blind, and now the blind were fighting the blind. Alfred would have dominated such a council, but Edward deferred to his advisers, and men like Æthelhelm were cautious. They preferred to wait until Sigelf's Centish troops had joined us.

"Why aren't the men of Cent here now?" I asked. Cent was close to Lundene and in the time it had taken my men to cross and recross half of Saxon Britain the men of Cent had failed to complete a two-day march.

"They will be here," Edward said. "I have Ealdorman Sigelf's word."

"But why has he delayed?" I insisted.

"The enemy went to East Anglia in ships," Archbishop Plegmund supplied the answer, "and we feared they might use those ships to descend on the coast of Cent. Ealdorman Sigelf preferred to wait until he was sure that the threat was not real."

"And who commands our army?" I asked, and that question caused embarrassment.

There was silence for a few heartbeats, then Archbishop Plegmund scowled. "Our lord King commands the army, of course," he said.

And who commands the king, I wondered, but said nothing. That evening Edward sent for me. It was dark when I joined him. He dismissed his servants so we were alone. "Archbishop Plegmund is not in charge," he chided me, obviously remembering my final question in the council, "but I find his advice is good."

"To do nothing, lord King?"

"To gather all our forces before we fight. And the council agrees." We were in the large upper room, where a great bed stood between two candle-lanterns. Edward was standing in the large window that overlooked the old city, the window where Æthelflaed and I had stood so often. It looked west toward the new city, where soft firelight glimmered. Farther west it was dark, a black land. "The twins are safe?" Edward asked me.

"They're in Cirrenceastre, lord King," I said, "so, yes, they're safe." The twins, Æthelstan and Eadgyth, were with my daughter and younger son, all in good hands inside Cirrenceastre, a burh that was as well defended as Cracgelad. Fagranforda had been burned as I had expected, but my people were all safe inside Cirrenceastre.

"And the boy is in good health?" Edward asked anxiously.

"Æthelstan's a lusty baby," I said.

"I wish I could see them," he said.

"Father Cuthbert and his wife are looking after them," I said.

"Cuthbert's married?" Edward asked, surprised.

"To a very pretty girl," I said.

"Poor woman," Edward said, "she'll be riddled to death by him." He smiled, and looked unhappy when I did not return the smile. "And my sister's here?"

"Yes, lord King."

"She should be looking after the children," he said sternly.

"You tell her, lord King," I said, "and she's brought you almost a hundred and fifty Mercian warriors," I went on. "Why hasn't Æthelred sent any?"

"He's worried about the Irish Norsemen," he said, then shrugged when I made a dismissive noise. "Why didn't Æthelwold go deeper into Wessex?" he asked me.

"Because they're leaderless," I said, "and because no one came to his banner." Edward looked puzzled. "I think their plan was to reach Wessex, proclaim Æthelwold king, and wait for men to join them, but no one did."

"So what will they do?"

"If they can't take a burh," I said, "they'll go back where they came from."

Edward turned to the window. Bats flitted in the darkness, sometimes showing briefly in the light of the lanterns that lit the high room. "There are too many of them, Lord Uhtred," he said, talking of the Danes, "just too many. We must be sure before we attack."

"If you wait for certainty in war, lord King," I said, "you'll die waiting."

"My father advised me to hold on to Lundene," he said. "He told me we should never relinquish the city."

"And let Æthelwold have the rest?" I asked sourly.

"He will die, but we need Ealdorman Sigelf's men."

"He's bringing seven hundred?"

"So he promised," Edward said, "which will give us over four thousand men." He took comfort in that number. "And, of course," he went on, "we now have your men and the Mercians too. We should be strong enough."

"And who commands us?" I asked in a gruff voice.

Edward looked surprised at the question. "I do, of course."

"Not Archbishop Plegmund?"

Edward stiffened. "I have advisers, Lord Uhtred," he said, "and it's a foolish king who doesn't listen to his advisers."

"It's a foolish king," I retorted, "who doesn't know which advisers to trust. And the archbishop has advised you to mistrust me. He thinks I'm sympathetic to the Danes."

Edward hesitated, then nodded. "He worries about that, yes."

"Yet so far, lord King, I'm the only one of your men who has killed any of the bastards. For a man who can't be trusted that's strange behavior, is it not?"

Edward just looked at me, then flinched as a large moth fluttered close to his face. He called for servants to close the big shutters. Somewhere in the dark I could hear men singing. A servant took the robe from Edward's shoulders, then lifted the gold chain from around his neck. Beyond the arch, where the door stood open, I could see a girl waiting in the dark shadows. It was not Edward's wife. "Thank you for coming," he said, dismissing me.

I bowed to him, then went.

And next day Sigelf arrived.

Twelve

The fight began in the street below the big church next to the old Mercian palace where Edward and his entourage were quartered. The men of Cent had arrived that morning, streaming across the Roman bridge and beneath the broken arch that led through Lundene's river wall. Six hundred and eighty-six men, led by their ealdorman, Sigelf, and his son, Sigebriht, rode beneath banners showing Sigelf's crossed swords and Sigebriht's bloody-horned bull's head. They had dozens of other flags, most with crosses or saints, and the horsemen were accompanied by monks, priests, and wagons loaded with supplies. Not all Sigelf's warriors were mounted, at least one hundred came without horses, and those men straggled into the city for a long while after the horsemen had arrived.

Edward ordered the Centishmen to find quarters in the eastern part of the city, but of course the newcomers wanted to explore Lundene and the fight started when a dozen of Sigelf's men demanded ale in a tavern called the Red Pig, which was popular with Ealdorman Æthelhelm's men. The fight began over a whore and soon spilled from the tavern door and spread down the hill. Mercians, West Saxons, and Centishmen were brawling in the street and within minutes swords and knives were drawn.

"What's happening?" Edward, his council interrupted, stared aghast from a palace window. He could hear shouts and blades clashing, and see dead and wounded men on the stone-paved hill. "Is it the Danes?" he asked, appalled.

I ignored the king. "Steapa!" I called, then ran down the steps and shouted at the steward to bring me Serpent-Breath. Steapa was calling his men together. "You!" I grabbed one of the king's bodyguard. "Find a rope. A long one."

"A rope, lord?"

"There are masons repairing the palace roof. They have rope! Fetch it! Now! And find someone who can blow a horn!"

A dozen of us strode into the street, but there were at least a hundred men fighting there, and twice that many watching and calling encouragement. I slammed a man across the head with the flat of Serpent-Breath, kicked another one down, bellowed for men to stop, but they were oblivious. One man even ran at me, screaming, his sword lifted, then seemed to realize his mistake and curved away.

The man I had sent to find a rope brought one with a heavy wooden bucket attached, and I used the pail as a weight to hurl the rope over the projecting inn sign of the Red Pig. "Find me a man, any man, one who's fighting," I told Steapa.

He stomped off while I made a noose. A wounded man, guts hanging, crawled down the hill. A woman was screaming. The gutter was running with ale-diluted blood. One of the king's men arrived with a horn. "Sound it," I said, "and keep blowing it."

Steapa dragged a man to me, we had no idea whether he was from Wessex or Mercia, but it did not matter. I tightened the noose around his neck, slapped him when he begged for mercy, and hauled him into the air where he hanged, legs kicking. The horn blew on, insistent, unignorable. I handed the rope's end to Oswi, my servant. "Tie it to something," I said, then turned and bellowed at the street. "Anyone else want to die?"

The sight of a man dancing on a rope while he chokes to death has a calming influence on a crowd. The street went quiet. The king and a dozen men had appeared at the palace door and men bowed or knelt in homage.

"One more fight," I shouted, "and you'll all die!" I looked for one of my men. "Pull on the bastard's ankles," I said, pointing at the hanged man.

"You just killed one of my men," a voice said, and I turned to see a slight man with a sharp foxlike face and long red plaited mustaches. He was an older man, perhaps close to fifty, and his red hair was graying at the temples. "You killed him without trial!" he accused me.

I towered over him, but he faced me pugnaciously. "I'll hang a dozen more of your men if they fight in the street," I said. "And who are you?"

"Ealdorman Sigelf," he said, "and you call me lord."

"I'm Uhtred of Bebbanburg," I said and was rewarded by a blink of surprise, "and you can call me lord."

Sigelf evidently decided he did not want to fight me. "They shouldn't have been fighting," he acknowledged grudgingly. He frowned. "You met my son, I believe?"

"I met your son," I said.

"He was a fool," Sigelf said in a voice as sharp as his face, "a young fool. He's learned his lesson."

"The lesson of loyalty?" I asked, looking across the street to where Sigebriht was bowing low to the king.

"So they both liked the same bitch," Sigelf said, "but Edward was a prince and princes get what they want."

"So do kings," I said mildly.

Sigelf caught my meaning and gave me a very hard glance. "Cent doesn't need a king," he said, clearly trying to scotch the rumor that he wanted the throne for himself.

"Cent has a king," I said.

"So we hear," he spoke sarcastically, "but Wessex needs to take more care of us. Every damned Northman who gets his arse kicked in Frankia comes to our shores, and what does Wessex do? It scratches its own arse then sniffs its fingers while we suffer." He watched his son bow a second time and spat, though whether that was because of his son's obeisance or because of Wessex it was hard to tell. "Look what happened when Harald and Haesten came!" he demanded.

"I defeated both of them," I said.

"But not before they'd raped half of Cent and burned fifty or more villages. We need more defenses." He glared at me. "We need some help!"

"At least you're here," I said emolliently.

"We'll help Wessex," Sigelf said, "even if Wessex doesn't help us."

I had thought that the arrival of the Centishmen would provoke some action from Edward, but instead he waited. There was a council of war every day, but it decided nothing except to wait and see what the enemy would do. Scouts were watching the Danes and sent reports back every day and those reports said the Danes were still not moving. I urged the king to attack them, but I might as well have begged him to fly to the moon. I begged him to let me lead my own men to scout the enemy, but he refused.

"He thinks you'll attack them," Æthelflaed told me.

"Why doesn't he attack?" I asked, frustrated.

"Because he's frightened," she said, "because there are too many men giving him advice, because he's scared of doing the wrong thing, because he only has to lose one battle and he's no longer king."

We were on the top floor of a Roman house, one of those astonishing buildings that had stairs climbing to floor after floor. The moon shone through a window, and through the holes in the roof where the slates had fallen. It was cold and we were wrapped in fleeces. "A king shouldn't be frightened," I said.

"Edward knows men compare him to his father. He wonders what Father would have done now."

"Alfred would have called for me," I said, "preached to me for ten minutes, then given me the army."

She lay silent in my arms. She was gazing at the moon-speckled roof. "Do you think," she asked, "that we'll ever have peace?"

"No."

"I dream of a day when we can live in a great hall, go hunting, listen to songs, walk by the river, and never fear an enemy."

"You and me?"

"Just you and me," she said. She turned her head so that her hair hid her eyes. "Just you and me."

Next morning Edward ordered Æthelflaed to return to Cirrenceastre, an order she pointedly ignored. "I told him to give you the army," she said.

"And he said?"

"That he was king and he would lead the army."

Her husband had also ordered Merewalh back to Gleawecestre, but Æthelflaed persuaded the Mercian to stay. "We need every good man," she told him, and so we did, but not to rot inside Lundene. We had a whole army there, over four thousand five hundred men, and all it did was guard the walls and gaze out at the unchanging countryside beyond.

We did nothing and the Danes ravaged the Wessex countryside, but made no attempt to storm a burh. The autumn days shrank and still we remained indecisive in Lundene. Archbishop Plegmund returned to Contwaraburg and I thought his departure might embolden Edward, but Bishop Erkenwald stayed with the king and counseled caution. So did Father Coenwulf, Edward's mass priest and closest adviser. "It's not like the Danes to be supine," he told Edward, "so I fear a trap. Let them make the first move, lord King. They surely cannot stay forever." In that, at least, he was right, for as the autumn slid cold into winter the Danes at last moved.

They had been as indecisive as us, and now they simply recrossed the river at Cracgelad and went back the way they had come. Steapa's scouts told us of their retreat, and day by day the reports came that they were heading back toward East Anglia, taking slaves, livestock, and plunder. "And once they're back there," I told the council, "the Northumbrian Danes will go home in their ships. They've achieved nothing, except taking a lot of slaves and cattle, but we've done nothing either."

"King Eohric has broken his treaty," Bishop Erkenwald pointed out indignantly, though what use that observation was escaped me.

"He promised to be at peace with us," Edward said.

"He must be punished, lord King," Erkenwald insisted. "The treaty was solemnized by the church!"

Edward glanced at me. "And if the Northumbrians go home," he said, "Eohric will be vulnerable."

"When they go home, lord King," I pointed out. "They might wait till spring."

"Eohric can't feed that many," Ealdorman Æthelhelm pointed out. "They'll leave his kingdom quickly! Look at the problems we have in feeding an army."

"So you'll invade in winter?" I asked scornfully. "When the rivers are flooding, the rain is falling, and we're wading in freezing mud?"

"God is on our side!" Erkenwald declared.

The army had been in Lundene for almost three months now, and the food supplies of the city were running low. There was no enemy at the gates, so more food was constantly being carted into the storehouses, but that took an immense number of wagons, oxen, horses, and men. And the warriors themselves were bored. Some blamed the men of Cent for delaying their arrival and, despite my having hanged a man, there were frequent fights in which dozens of men died. Edward's army was querulous, underemployed, and hungry, but Bishop Erkenwald's indignation at Eohric's betrayal of a sacred trust somehow invigorated the council and persuaded the king to make a decision. For weeks we had the Danes at our mercy and granted them mercy, but now they had left Wessex, the council suddenly discovered courage. "We shall follow the enemy," Edward announced, "take back what they have stolen from us, and revenge ourselves on King Eohric."

"If we're following them," I said, looking at Sigelf, "we all need horses."

"We have horses," Edward pointed out.

"Not all the men of Cent do," I said.

Sigelf bridled at that. He was a man, it seemed to me, ready to take offense at the slightest suggestion of criticism, but he knew I was right. The Danes always moved on horseback, and an army slowed by foot soldiers would never catch them or be able to react quickly to an enemy move. Sigelf scowled at me, but resisted the temptation to snap at me, instead he looked to the king. "You could lend us horses?" he asked Edward. "What about the horses of the garrison here?"

"Weohstan won't like that," Edward said unhappily. A man's horse was one of his most valuable possessions, and not one that was casually lent to a stranger going to war.

No one spoke for a moment, then Sigelf shrugged. "Then let a hundred of my men stay here as garrison troops and your, what was his name, Weohstan? He can send a hundred horsemen to replace them."

And that was how it was decided. Lundene's garrison would give the army a hundred horsemen and Sigelf's men would replace them on the walls, and then at last we could march, and so next morning the army left Lundene by the Bishop's Gate and by the

Old Gate. We followed the Roman roads north and east, but it could hardly be called a pursuit. Some of the army, those with experience, traveled light, but too many contingents had brought wagons, servants, and too many spare horses, and we were lucky to travel three miles in an hour. Steapa led half the king's warriors as a vanguard with orders to stay within sight of the army, and he grumbled that he was forced to travel so slowly. Edward had ordered me to stay with the rearguard, but I disobeyed and went far ahead of Steapa's men. Æthelflaed and her Mercians came with me. "I thought your brother insisted you stayed in Lundene?" I told her.

"No," she said, "he ordered me to go to Cirrenceastre."

"So why aren't you obeying him?"

"I am obeying him," she said, "but he didn't tell me which road to take." She smiled at me, daring me to send her away.

"Just stay alive, woman," I growled.

"Yes, lord," she said with mocking humility.

I sent my scouts far ahead, but all they discovered were the hoofprints of the Danish retreat. Nothing, I thought, made sense. The Danes had assembled an army that probably numbered over five thousand men, they had crossed Britain, invaded Wessex, and then done nothing except take plunder. Now they were retreating, but it could hardly have been a profitable summer for them. Alfred's burhs had done their work by protecting much of Wessex's wealth, but staving off the Danes was not the same as defeating them. "So why didn't they attack Wintanceaster?" Æthelflaed asked me.

"It's too strong."

"So they just walk away?"

"Too many leaders," I said. "They're probably having councils of war just like us. Everyone has a different idea, they talk, and now they're going home because they can't make a decision."

Lundene lies on the border of East Anglia so on our second day we were deep inside Eohric's territory and Edward released the army to take its revenge. The troops spread out, plundering farmsteads, rounding up cattle, and burning villages. Our progress slowed to a crawl, our presence signified by the great pillars of smoke from burning houses. The Danes did nothing. They had retreated far beyond the frontier and we followed them, dropping from the low hills into the wide East Anglian plain. This was a country of damp fields, wide marshes, long dikes, and slow rivers, of reeds and wildfowl, of morning mists and eternal mud, of rain and bitter cold winds from the sea. Roads were few and tracks were treacherous. I told Edward time and again to keep the army closed up, but he was eager to ravage Eohric's land and so the troops spread wider, and my men, still acting as scouts, had a hard time staying in touch with the farthest-flung men. The days were shortening, the nights became colder, and there were never enough trees to make all the campfires we needed, so instead men used the timber and thatch from captured buildings, and at night those fires spread across a great swath of land, yet the Danes still did nothing to take advantage of our dispersal. We went ever farther into their realm of water and mud, and still we saw no Danes. We skirted Grantaceaster, heading toward Eleg, and on the higher patches of land we found huge, great-raftered feast-halls, thick-thatched with reed that burned with a hard, bright crackle, but the inhabitants of the halls had retreated ever farther from us.

On the fourth day I realized where we were. We had been following the remnants of a Roman road that ran straight as a spear across the low land, and I scouted westward and found the bridge at Eanulfsbirig. It had been repaired with great lengths of rough-cut timber laid across the fire-blackened stonework of the Roman piers. I was on the Use's western bank, where Sigurd had challenged me, and the road from the bridge ran toward Huntandon. I remembered Ludda telling me there was higher ground on the far side of the river there, and that was where Eohric's men had planned to ambush me, and it seemed likely that Eohric would have the same thought now, and so I sent Finan and fifty men to scout that farther bridge. They returned in the middle of the afternoon. "Hundreds of Danes," Finan said laconically, "a fleet of ships. They're waiting for us."

"Hundreds?"

"Can't cross the river to count them properly," he said, "not without getting killed, but I saw a hundred and forty-three ships."

"So thousands of Danes," I said.

"Just waiting for us, lord."

I found Edward in a convent to the south. Ealdorman Æthelhelm and Ealdorman Sigelf were with him, as were Bishop Erkenwald and Father Coenwulf, and I interrupted their supper to give them the news. It was a cold night, and a wet wind was rattling the shutters of the convent's hall.

"They want battle?" Edward asked.

"What they want, lord," I said, "is for us to be stupid enough to offer them battle."

He looked puzzled at that. "But if we've found them," he began.

"We must destroy them," Bishop Erkenwald declared.

"They're on the far side of a river we cannot cross," I explained, "except by the bridge that they are defending. They will slaughter us one by one until we withdraw, and then they'll follow us like wolves behind a flock. That's what they want, lord King. They've chosen the battlefield and we're fools to accept their choice."

"Lord Uhtred is right," Ealdorman Sigelf snapped. I was so surprised that I said nothing.

"He is," Æthelhelm agreed.

Edward plainly wanted to ask what we should do, but he knew the question would make him look weak. I could see him working out the alternatives and was pleased that he chose the right one. "The bridge you spoke of," he said. "Eanulfsbirig?"

"Yes, lord King."

"We can cross it?"

"Yes, lord King."

"So if we cross it we can destroy it?"

"I would cross it, lord King," I said, "and march on Bedanford. Invite the Danes to attack us there. That way we choose the battlefield, not them."

"That makes sense," Edward said hesitantly, looking toward Bishop Erkenwald and Father Coenwulf for support. They both nodded. "Then that's what we'll do," Edward said more confidently.

"I ask a favor of you, lord King," Sigelf said, sounding unnaturally humble.

"Whatever you wish," Edward said graciously.

"Allow my men to be the rearguard, lord King? If the Danes attack, let my shields take their assault and let the men of Cent defend the army."

Edward looked surprised and pleased at the request. "Of course," he said, "and thank you, Lord Sigelf."

And so the orders were sent to all the scattered troops, summoning them to the bridge at Eanulfsbirig. They were to march at first light, and at the same time Sigelf's Centishmen would advance up the road to confront the Danes just south of Huntandon. We were doing exactly what the Danes had done. We had invaded, destroyed, and now we would withdraw, only we withdrew in chaos.

The dawn brought a bitter cold. Hoarfrost touched the fields, and the ditches had a skin of ice. I remember that day so well because half the sky was a bright, glittering blue and the other half, all to the east, was gray clouds. It was as though the gods had half dragged a blanket across the world, dividing the sky, and the edge of the clouds was as straight as a blade. That edge was silvered by the sun and beneath it the land was dark, and it was across that land that Edward's troops straggled westward. Many had plunder and wanted to use the Roman road, the same road up which Sigelf's men were advancing. I saw a broken wagon loaded with a millstone. A man was shouting at his warriors to mend the wagon and at the same time was whipping the two helpless oxen. I was with Rollo and twenty-two men and we simply cut the two oxen out of their harness, then pushed the broken wagon with its immense burden into the ditch, shattering the thin ice. "That's my stone," the angry man yelled.

"And this is my sword," I snarled back, "now get your men west."

Finan had most of my men close to Huntandon, while I had ordered Osferth to take twenty horsemen and to escort Æthelflaed west of the river. She had obeyed me meekly, which surprised me. I remembered Ludda telling me that there was another road that ran from Huntandon to Eanulfsbirig outside of the great river bend, and so I had warned Edward of that route and then sent Merewalh and his Mercians to guard it. "The Danes could try to cut off our retreat," I told Edward. "They could send ships upriver or use the smaller road, but Merewalh's scouts should see them if they try either of those things."

He had nodded. I was not sure he entirely understood what I was saying, but he was now so grateful for my advice that he would probably have nodded if I had told him to send men to guard the dark half of the moon.

"I can't be certain they'll try to cut our retreat," I told the king, "but as your army crosses the bridge just keep them there. No one marches on Bedanford till we're all across the river! Draw them up for battle. Once we have every man safe across we can march on Bedanford together. What we don't do is string the army out along the road."

We should have had everyone across the river by midday, but chaos ruled. Some troops were lost, others were so laden with plunder that they could only move at a snail's pace, and Sigelf's men became entangled with those coming the other way. The Danes should have crossed the river and attacked, but instead they stayed at Huntandon, and Finan watched them from the south. Sigelf did not reach Finan till midafternoon, and then he arrayed his men across the road about half a mile south of the river. It was a well-chosen position. A straggly stand of trees hid some of his men who were protected on either flank by stretches of marsh, and in front by a flooded ditch. If the Danes crossed the bridge they could draw up their shield wall, but to attack Sigelf they must cross the deep, flooded ditch behind which the Centish shields, swords, axes, and spears were waiting.

"They might try to go around the marshes to attack you from behind," I told Sigelf.

"I've fought before," he snapped at me.

I did not care if I was offending him. "So don't stay here if they do cross the bridge," I told him, "just back away. And if they don't cross I'll send word when you should rejoin us."

"Are you in command?" he demanded. "Or Edward?"

"I am," I said, and he looked startled.

His son, Sigebriht, had listened to the exchange and now accompanied me as I rode north to look at the Danes. "Will they attack, lord?" he asked me.

"I understand nothing about this war," I told him, "nothing. The bastards should have attacked us weeks ago."

"Perhaps they're frightened of us," he said, then laughed, which I thought curious, but ascribed to youthful foolishness. He was indeed foolish, yet such a handsome fool. He still wore his hair long, tied at the nape of his neck with a leather strip, and around his neck was the pink silk ribbon that still had the faint bloodstain from that morning outside Sceaftesburi. His expensive mail was polished, his gold-paneled belt shone, and his crystal-pommeled sword was sheathed in a scabbard decorated with writhing dragons made from finely twisted gold wire. His face was strong-boned, bright-eyed, and his skin reddened by the cold. "So they should have attacked us," he said, "but what should we have done?"

"Attacked them at Cracgelad," I said.

"Why didn't we?"

"Because Edward was frightened of losing Lundene," I said, "and he was waiting for your father."

"He needs us," Sigebriht said with evident satisfaction.

"What he needed," I said, "was an assurance of Cent's loyalty."

"He doesn't trust us?" Sigebriht asked disingenuously.

"Why should he?" I asked savagely. "You supported Æthelwold and sent messengers to Sigurd. Of course he didn't trust you."

"I submitted to Edward, lord," Sigebriht said humbly. He glanced at me and decided he needed to say more. "I admit all you say, lord, but there is a madness in youth, is there not?"

"Madness?"

"My father says young men are bewitched to madness." He fell silent a moment. "I loved Ecgwynn," he said wistfully. "Did you ever meet her?"

"No."

"She was small, lord, like an elf, and as beautiful as the dawn. She could turn a man's blood to fire."

"Madness," I said.

"But she chose Edward," he said, "and it maddened me."

"And now?" I asked.

"The heart mends," he said feelingly, "it leaves a scar, but I'm not foolish-mad. Edward is king and he's been good to me."

"And there are other women," I said.

"Thank God, yes," he said and laughed again.

I liked him at that moment. I had never trusted him, but he was surely right that there are women who drive us to madness and to foolishness, and the heart does mend, even if the scar remains, and then we ended the conversation because Finan was galloping toward us and the river was before us and the Danes were in sight.

The Use was wide here. The clouds had slowly covered the windless sky so that the river was gray and flat. A dozen swans moved slow on the slow-moving water. It seemed to me that the world was still, even the Danes were quiet and they were there in their hundreds, their thousands, their banners bright beneath the darkening cloud. "How many?" I asked Finan.

"Too many, lord," he said, an answer I deserved because it was impossible to count the enemy who were hidden by the houses of the small town. More were spread along the riverbanks either side of the town. I could see Sigurd's flying raven banner on the higher ground at the town's center, and Cnut's flag of the ax and broken cross at the far side of the bridge. There were Saxons there too, because Beortsig's symbol of the boar was displayed alongside Æthelwold's stag. Downriver of the bridge was a fleet of Danish ships moored thick along the farther bank, but only seven had been dismasted and brought beneath the bridge, which suggested the Danes had no thought of using their boats to advance upriver to Eanulfsbirig.

"So why aren't they attacking?" I asked.

None had crossed the bridge, which, of course, had been made by the Romans. I sometimes think that if the Romans had never invaded Britain we would never have managed to cross a river. On the southern bank, close to where we stood our horses, was a dilapidated Roman house and a huddle of thatched cottages. It would have been a fine place for the Danish vanguard, but for some reason they seemed content to wait on the far northern bank.

It began to rain. It was a thin, sharp rain, and it brought a gust of wind that rippled the river about the swans. The sun was low in the west, the sky there still free of cloud, so that it seemed to me that the land across the river and the bright-shielded Danes glowed in a world of gray shadow. I could see a smoke plume much farther north, and that was strange because whatever burned was in Eohric's territory and we had no men that far north. Perhaps, I thought, it was just a trick of the clouds or an accidental fire. "Does your father listen to you?" I asked Sigebriht.

"Yes, lord."

"Tell him we'll send a messenger when he can begin to withdraw."

"Till then we stay?"

"Unless the Danes attack, yes," I said, "and one other thing. Watch those bastards." I pointed to the Danes who were farthest west. "There's a road that goes outside the river bend and if you see the enemy using that road, send us a message."

He frowned in thought. "Because they might try to block our retreat?"

"Exactly," I said, pleased he had understood, "and if they manage to cut the road to Bedanford then we'll have to fight them back and front."

"And that's where we're going?" he asked. "To Bedanford?"

"Yes."

"And that's to the west?" he asked.

"To the west," I told Sigebriht, "but you won't have to find your own way there. You'll be back with the army this evening." What I did not tell him was that I was leaving most of my men not far behind the Centish troops. Sigebriht's father, Sigelf, was such a proud man and so difficult to deal with that he would have immediately accused me of not trusting him if he had known my men were close. In truth I wanted my own eyes close to Huntandon, and Finan had the keenest eyes of anyone I knew.

I left Finan on the road a half-mile south of Sigelf, then took a dozen men back to Eanulfsbirig. It was dusk as I arrived and the chaos was at last subsiding. Bishop Erkenwald had ridden back up the road and ordered the slowest, heaviest wagons abandoned, and Edward's army was now gathering in the fields across the river. If the Danes did attack they would be forced to cross the bridge into an army, or else march around by the bad road that skirted the outside of the river bend. "Is Merewalh still guarding that road, lord King?" I asked Edward.

"He is, he says there's no sign of the enemy."

"Good. Where's your sister?"

"I sent her back to Bedanford."

"And she went?"

He smiled. "She did!"

It was now plain that the whole army, except for my men and Sigelf's rearguard, would be safe across the Use before nightfall and so I sent Sihtric back up the road with a message for both forces to retire as fast as possible. "Tell them to come to the bridge and cross it." Once that was done, and so long as no Danes tried to outflank us, then we would have escaped the Danish choice of battlefield. "And tell Finan to let Sigelf's men go first," I told Sihtric. I wanted Finan as the real rearguard, because no other warrior in the army was so reliable.

"You look tired, lord," Edward said sympathetically.

"I am tired, lord King."

"It'll be at least an hour before Ealdorman Sigelf reaches us," Edward said, "so rest."

I made sure my dozen men and horses were resting, then ate a poor meal of hard bread and pounded beans. The rain was falling harder now, and an east wind made the evening cruelly cold. The king had his quarters in one of the cottages we had half destroyed to burn the bridge, but somehow his servants had found a piece of sailcloth with which to make a roof. A fire burned in the hearth, swirling smoke under the makeshift canopy. Two priests were arguing quietly as I settled close to the fire. Against the far wall was a pile of precious boxes, silver, gold, and crystal, which held the relics that the king would take on campaign to ensure his god's favor. The priests were disagreeing over whether one of the reliquaries contained a splinter from Noah's ark or a toenail of Saint Patrick, and I ignored them.

I half dozed, and I was thinking how strange it was that all the people who had affected my life over the last three years were suddenly in one place, or close to one place. Sigurd, Beortsig, Edward, Cnut, Æthelwold, Æthelflaed, Sigebriht, all of them gathered in this cold, wet corner of East Anglia and surely, I thought, that was significant. The three Norns were weaving the threads close together, and that had to be for a purpose. I looked for a pattern in the weave, but saw none, and my thoughts drifted as I half fell asleep. I woke when Edward stooped through the low door. It was dark outside now, black dark. "Sigelf isn't retreating," he said to the two priests, his tone querulous.

"Lord King?" one of them asked.

"Sigelf is being stubborn," the king said, holding his hands to the fire. "He's staying where he is! I've told him to retreat, but he won't."

"He's what?" I asked, suddenly fully awake.

Edward seemed startled to see me. "It's Sigelf," he said. "He's ignoring my messengers! You sent a man to him, didn't you? And I've sent five more! Five! But they come back telling me he's refusing to retreat! He says it's too dark and he's waiting for the dawn, but God knows he's risking his men. The Danes will be awake at first light." He sighed. "I've just sent another man with orders that they must retreat." He paused, frowning. "I'm right, aren't I?" he asked me, needing reassurance.

I did not answer. I stayed silent because at last I saw what the Norns were doing. I saw the pattern in the weave of all our lives and I understood, finally, the war that passed all understanding. My face must have looked shocked because Edward was staring at me. "Lord King," I said, "order the army to march back across the bridge, then join Sigelf. Do you understand?"

"You want me to . . ." he began, confused.

"The whole army!" I shouted. "Every man! March them to Sigelf now!" I shouted at him as though he were my underling and not my king, because if he disobeyed me now he would not be a king much longer. Maybe it was already too late, but there was no time to explain it to him. There was a kingdom to be saved. "March them now," I snarled at him, "back the way we came, back to Sigelf, and hurry!"

And I ran for my horse.

I took my twelve men. We led the horses over the bridge, then mounted and followed the road toward Huntandon. It was a black night, black and cold, rain spitting into our faces and we could not ride fast. I remember being assailed by doubt. Suppose I was wrong? If I was wrong then I was leading Edward's army back into the battleground the Danes had chosen. I was stranding them in the river loop, perhaps with Danes on every side, but I resisted the doubt. Nothing had made sense, and now it all made sense, all except for the fires that burned far to the north. There had been one smoke plume in the afternoon, now I could see three huge blazes, betrayed by their reflected glow on the low clouds. Why would the Danes be burning halls or villages in King Eohric's land? It was another mystery, but not one I worried about because the fires were far off, a long way beyond Huntandon.

It was an hour before a sentry challenged us. It was one of my men and he led us to where Finan had the remainder in a patch of woodland. "I didn't retreat," Finan explained, "because Sigelf isn't moving. God knows why."

"You remember when we were in Hrofeceastre," I asked him, "talking to Bishop Swithwulf?"

"I remember."

"What were they loading onto the ships?"

There was a moment's pause as Finan realized what I was saying. "Horses," he said quietly.

"Horses for Frankia," I said, "and Sigelf comes to Lundene and claims he doesn't have enough horses for his men."

"So now a hundred of his men are part of Lundene's garrison," Finan said.

"And ready to open the gates when the Danes arrive," I continued, "because Sigelf is sworn to Æthelwold or to Sigurd or to whoever has promised him the throne of Cent."

"Jesus and Joseph," Finan said.

"And the Danes haven't been indecisive," I said, "they were waiting for Sigelf to declare his loyalty. Now they have it, and the Centish bastard isn't retreating because he expects the Danes to join him, and maybe they already have, and they think we're going west and they'll march fast southward and Sigelf's men in Lundene will open the gates and the city will fall while we're still waiting for the earslings in Bedanford."

"So what do we do?" Finan asked.

"Stop them, of course."

"How?"

"By changing sides, of course," I said.

How else?

Thirteen

Doubt weakens the will. Suppose I was wrong? Suppose Sigelf was simply a stubborn and stupid old man who really did think it was too dark to retreat? But though the doubts assailed me I kept on, leading my men east around the marshland that anchored the right of Sigelf's line.

The wind was sharp, the night was freezing, the rain malevolent, and the darkness absolute, and if it had not been for the Centish campfires we would surely have been lost. A slew of fires marked Sigelf's position, and there were still more just to the north, which told me that at least some Danes had now crossed the river and were sheltering from the weather in the hovels around the old Roman house. Those mysterious great fires, the big glow of burning halls, also showed much farther north, and those three I could not explain.

So much, and not just those distant fires, defied understanding. Some Danes had crossed the river, but the glow of fires on the northern bank told me that most still remained in Huntandon, which was strange if they intended to move southward. Sigelf's men had not moved from where I had left them, which meant there was a gap between his men and the nearest Danes, and that gap was my opportunity.

I had left our horses behind, all of them tethered in woodland, and my men were on foot and carrying shields and weapons. The fires guided us, but for a long time we were so far from the nearest blaze that we could not see the ground and so we stumbled, fell, struggled, waded, and forced our way through the marsh. At least once I was up to my waist in water, the mud was clinging to my boots and the tussocks were tripping me, while startled birds screamed as they flew into the night, and that noise, I thought, must surely warn our enemies that we were on their flank, yet they seemed oblivious.

I sometimes lie awake in the long nights of old age and I think of the mad things I have done, the risks, the dice throws that challenged the gods. I remember assaulting the fort at Beamfleot, or facing Ubba, or creeping up the hill at Dunholm, yet almost none of those lunacies rivaled that cold, wet night in East Anglia. I led one hundred and thirty-four men through the winter darkness, and we were attacking between two enemy forces that together numbered at least four thousand. If we were caught, if we were challenged, if we were defeated then we would have nowhere to run and no place to hide except in our graves.

I had ordered all my Danes to be the vanguard. Men like Sihtric and Rollo, whose native tongue was Danish, men who had come to serve me after losing their lords, men who were sworn to me even though we fought against other Danes. I had seventeen such men, and to them I added my dozen Frisians. "When we attack," I had told them, "you shout Sigurd."

"Sigurd," one of them said.

"Sigurd!" I repeated. "Sigelf's men must think we're Danes." I gave the same instruction to my Saxons. "You shout Sigurd! That's your war cry till the horn sounds. You shout and you kill, but be ready to pull back when the horn sounds."

This was going to be a dance with death. For some reason I thought of poor Ludda, slaughtered in my service, and how he had told me that all magic is making someone think one thing while, in truth, another is happening. "You make them watch your right hand, lord," he told me once, "while your left is picking their purse."

So now I would make the men of Cent believe they had been betrayed by their allies, and if the trick worked I hoped to turn them back into good men of Wessex. And if it failed then Ælfadell's prophecy would come true and Uhtred of Bebbanburg would die in this miserable winter swamp and I would kill most of my men alongside me. And how I loved those men! On that miserable cold night as we advanced to a desperate fight they were full of enthusiasm. They trusted me as I trusted them. Together we would make reputation, we would have men in halls across Britain telling the story of our exploit. Or of our deaths. They were friends, they were oath-men, they were young, they were warriors, and with such men it might be possible to storm the gates of Asgard itself.

It seemed to take forever to make that short journey through the marshland. I kept glancing anxiously eastward, hoping the dawn would not break, then looking northward, hoping the Danes would not join Sigelf's men. As we drew closer I saw two horsemen on the road, and that took away my doubts. Messengers were traveling between the two forces. The Danes, I supposed, were waiting for the first light before they left the shelter of Huntandon's houses and moved south, but once they did move they would march swiftly on Lundene unless we stopped them.

And then, at last, we were close to Sigelf's fires. His men were sleeping or just sitting close to the flames. I had forgotten the ditch that protected them and slid into it, my shield clattering as I fell. Ice cracked as I slithered into the water. A dog barked from the Centish lines, and a man glanced in our direction, but saw nothing to worry him. Another man hit the dog and someone laughed.

I hissed at four of my men to join me in the ditch. They stood there, making a line across it, and those four guided the rest down the treacherously slippery bank, through the water and up the farther side. My boots squelched as I climbed the far bank. I crouched there as my men came over the ditch and as they spread into a battle line. "Shield wall!" I hissed the order at my vanguard of Danes and Frisians. "Osferth?"

"Lord?"

"You know what to do."

"Yes, lord."

"Then do it."

I had given Osferth almost half my men and careful instructions. He hesitated. "I've prayed for you, lord," he said.

"Then let's hope the damned prayers work," I whispered, and touched the hammer around my neck.

My men were forming the shield wall. Any moment, I thought, someone would see us, and the enemy, because for the moment Sigelf's men were our enemy, would make their own shield wall and would outnumber us by four or five to one, but victory does not come to men who listen to their fears. My shield touched Rollo's and I drew Serpent-Breath. Her long blade sighed through the scabbard's throat. "Sigurd!" I hissed. Then louder, "Forward!"

We charged. We bellowed our enemy's name as we ran. "Sigurd!" we shouted, "Sigurd! Sigurd!"

"And kill!" I shouted in Danish. "Kill!"

We killed. We were killing Saxons, men of Wessex, though this night they had been betrayed by their ealdorman into serving the Danes, yet we killed them and ever since there have been rumors of what we did that night. I deny them, of course, but few believe my denials. At first the killing was easy. The Centishmen were half asleep, off-guard, their sentries looking toward the south instead of guarding against an attack from the north, and we sliced and hacked our way deep into their encampment. "Sigurd!" I shouted, and stabbed Serpent-Breath into a waking man, then kicked him into the campfire and heard him scream as I backswung the blade against a youngster, and we were not taking the time to finish off the men we attacked, but leaving that to the rank behind us. We crippled the men of Cent, wounded them, downed them, and the men who followed stabbed down with sword or spear and I heard men shouting for mercy, shouting that they were on our side, and I bellowed our war cry even louder. "Sigurd! Sigurd!"

That first charge took us a third of the way into their encampment. Men fled from us. I heard a man bellowing to form a shield wall, but panic had spread through Sigelf's men. I watched a man trying to find his own shield from a pile, desperately tugging at the arm straps and watching us with terrified eyes. He abandoned the shields and ran. A spear arced through the firelight, vanishing over my shoulder. Our shield wall had lost its cohesion, but it did not need to be tight because the enemy was scattering, though it would only be moments before they realized how ridiculously small my attacking force was, but then the gods proved they were on our side because Ealdorman Sigelf himself galloped toward us on horseback.

"We're with you!" he shouted. "For God's sake, you damned fools, we're with you!"

My helmet cheek-pieces were closed. We carried no banner, because that had gone with Osferth. Sigelf had no idea who I was, though he undoubtedly saw the richness of my helmet and the finely forged links of my mud-spattered mail. I held up my sword, checking my men.

Sigelf was shaking with fury. "You damned fools," he snarled, "who are you?"

"You're on our side?" I asked.

"We're allied with Jarl Sigurd, you damned fool, and I'll have your head for this!"

I smiled, though he did not see my smile behind the glinting steel of the cheek-pieces. "Lord," I said humbly, then backswung Serpent-Breath into his horse's mouth and the beast reared up, screaming, blood frothing in the night, and Sigelf fell backward from the saddle. I hauled him down to the mud, slapped the horse's rump to send it charging into the ealdorman's scattered men, then kicked Sigelf in the face as he tried to get up. I put my right boot on his skinny chest and pinned him to the ground. "I'm Uhtred," I said, but only loud enough for Sigelf himself to hear me. "You hear me, traitor? I'm Uhtred," and I saw his eyes widen before I rammed the sword hard down into his scrawny throat and his scream turned to a gurgle and the blood spilled wide onto the damp ground and he was twisting and shaking as he died.

"Horn!" I called to Oswi. "Now!"

The horn sounded. My men knew what to do. They turned back toward the marsh, retreating into the dark beyond the fires, and as they went a second horn sounded and I saw Osferth leading a shield wall from the trees. My banner of the wolf's head and Osferth's charred cross showed above the advancing wall. "Men of Cent!" Osferth shouted. "Men of Cent, your king is coming to save you! To me! To me! Form on me!"

Osferth was the son of a king, and all his ancient lineage was in his voice. In a night of cold and chaos and death, he sounded confident and certain. Men who had seen their ealdorman cut down, who had seen his blood splash color into the firelit dark, went toward Osferth and joined his shield wall because he promised safety. My men were retreating into the shadows, then going southward to join Osferth's right flank. I pulled off my helmet and tossed it to Oswi, then strode along the face of the growing shield wall. "Edward sent us to save you!" I shouted at the Centishmen. "The Danes betrayed you! The king is coming with all his army! Form the wall! Shields up!"

There was a gray edge to the eastern sky. The rain was still spitting, but dawn was close. I glanced north and saw horsemen. The Danes must have wondered why the sound of battle and the bray of horns had disturbed the night's ending, and some were riding down the road to see for themselves and what they saw was a growing shield wall. They saw my banner of the wolf's head, they saw Osferth's blackened cross, and they saw men lying amidst the wreckage of the fires. Sigelf's leaderless men were still in chaos, with no more idea than the Danes what was happening, but our shield wall offered safety and they were picking up their own shields, their helmets, and their weapons and running to join the ranks. Finan and Osferth were pushing men into position. A tall man, helmetless, but carrying a bare sword ran to me. "What's happening?"

"Who are you?"

"Wulferth," he said.

"And who is Wulferth?" I asked, sounding calm. He was a thegn, one of Sigelf's richer followers, who had brought forty-three men to East Anglia. "Your lord is dead," I said, "and the Danes will attack us very soon."

"Who are you?"

"Uhtred of Bebbanburg," I said, "and Edward is coming. We have to hold the Danes till the king reaches us." I plucked Wulferth's elbow and walked him toward the western marsh on the left of our defensive position. "Form your men here," I said, "and fight for your country, for Cent, for Wessex."

"For God!" Osferth shouted from close by.

"Even for God," I said.

"But . . ." Wulferth began, still confused by the night's events.

I looked him in the eye. "Who do you want to fight for? Wessex or the Danes?"

He hesitated, not because he was unsure of the answer, but because everything was changing and he was still trying to understand what was happening. He had expected to march south toward Lundene, and instead he was being asked to fight.

"Well?" I prompted him.

"Wessex, lord."

"Then fight well," I said, "and you're in charge of this flank. Form your men, tell them the king is coming."

I had seen no sign of Sigebriht, but as the weak gray daylight suffused the east I saw him approaching from the north. He had been with the Danes, doubtless sleeping in whatever warmth and comfort Huntandon had to offer, while now he was on horseback and behind him a man carried the standard of the bull's head. "Oswi!" I shouted. "Find me a horse! Finan! Six men, six horses! Wulferth!" I turned back on the thegn.

"Lord?"

"Find Sigelf's banner, have a man raise it next to mine."

There were plenty of Centish horses tethered in the woods behind our position. Oswi brought me one, ready saddled, and I hauled myself up and kicked the animal toward Sigebriht who had stopped some fifty or sixty paces away. He and his standard-bearer were with five other men, none of whom I knew. I did not want the men of Cent responding to that bull's head flag, but luckily the rain made it hang damp and forlorn.

I curbed the horse close to Sigebriht. "You want to make a name for yourself, boy?" I challenged him. "Kill me now."

He looked past me to where his father's troops were readying for battle. "Where's my father?" he asked.

"Dead," I said, and drew Serpent-Breath. "This killed him."

"Then I'm ealdorman," he said, and he took a deep breath and I knew he was going to shout at his father's men to demand their loyalty, but before he could speak I had kicked the borrowed horse forward and brought the blade up.

"Talk to me, boy," I said, holding Serpent-Breath close to his face, "not to them."

Finan had joined me and five more of my men were just paces away now.

Sigebriht was frightened, but forced himself to look brave. "You'll all die," he said.

"Probably," I agreed, "but we'll take you with us."

His horse backed away and I let it take him out of reach of my sword. I looked past him and saw contingents of Danes crossing the bridge. Why had they waited? If they had crossed the previous evening they could have joined Sigelf and been marching south by now, but something had held them back. Then I remembered those mysterious fires burning in the night, the three great blazes of burning halls or fiery villages. Had someone attacked the Danish rear? It was the only explanation for the Danish delay, but who? Yet the Danes were crossing the river now, hundreds of them, thousands, and streaming over the bridge with them were Æthelwold's men and Beortsig's Mercians, and I reckoned the enemy army outnumbered us by at least eight to one.

"I give you three choices, puppy," I spoke to Sigebriht. "You can join us and fight for your rightful king, or you can fight against me, you and me, right here, or you can run away to your Danish masters."

He looked at me, but found it difficult to hold my gaze. "I'll feed your carcass to the dogs," he said, trying to sound scornful.

I just stared at him and he finally turned away. He and his men rode back to the Danes and I watched him go, and only when he had vanished among the enemy's thickening ranks did I turn the horse and walk it back to our shield wall. "Men of Cent!" I curbed the horse in front of them. "Your ealdorman was a traitor to his country and to his god! The Danes promised to make him king, but when have the Danes ever kept a promise? They wanted you to fight for them, and when you had done their work they planned to take your wives and your daughters for their pleasure! They promised Æthelwold the throne of Wessex, but do any of you think he would keep the throne longer than a month? The Danes want Wessex! They want Cent! They want our fields, they want our women, they want our cattle, they want our children! And tonight they treacherously attacked you! Why? Because they decided they didn't need you! They have enough men without you so they decided to kill you!"

Much of what I had told them was true. I looked along the Centish ranks, along the shields and spears and axes and swords. I saw anxious faces, scared faces. "I am Uhtred of Bebbanburg," I shouted, "and you know who I am and who I have killed. You'll fight alongside me now, and all we need do is hold this treacherous enemy at bay until our king reaches us. He's coming!" I hoped that was true, because if it was not then this day would be my death-day. "He's close," I shouted, "and when he reaches us we will slaughter those Danes like wolves ravaging lambs. You!" I pointed at a priest. "Why are we fighting?"

"For the cross, lord," he said.

"Louder!"

"For the cross!"

"Osferth! Where's your banner?"

"I have it, lord!" Osferth shouted.

"Then let us see it!" I waited till Osferth's cross was at the front and center of our line. "That is our banner!" I shouted, pointing Serpent-Breath at the charred cross and hoping my own gods would forgive me. "Today you fight for your god, for your country, for your wives, and for your families, because if you lose," I paused again, "if you lose then all those things will be gone forever!"

And from behind me, from beside the houses close to the river, the thunder began. The Danes were clashing their spears and swords against their shields, making the war-thunder, the noise to weaken a man's heart, and it was time to dismount and take my place in the shield wall.

The shield wall.

It terrifies, there is no place more terrible than the shield wall. It is the place where we die and where we conquer and where we make our reputation. I touched Thor's hammer, prayed that Edward was coming, and readied to fight.

In the shield wall.

I knew the Danes would try to get behind us, but that would take time. They needed to either skirt the marshland or find a way across the swamp, and neither could be done in less than an hour, probably two. I had a messenger back down the road with orders to find Edward and urge haste on him, because his troops were the only ones who could block a Danish encirclement. And if the Danes did try to surround us, they would also want to pin me in place, which meant I could expect a frontal attack to keep me busy while part of their forces looked for a way to reach our rear.

And if Edward did not come?

Then this was where I would die, where Ælfadell's prophecy would come true, where some man would claim the boast that he had killed Uhtred.

The Danes advanced slowly. Men do not relish the shield wall. They do not rush to death's embrace. You look ahead and see the overlapping shields, the helmets, the glint of axes and spears and swords, and you know you must go into the reach of those blades, into the place of death, and it takes time to summon the courage, to heat the blood, to let the madness overtake caution. That is why men drink before battle. My own men had no ale or mead, though the Centish forces had enough and I could see the Danes passing skins down their line. They were still beating their weapons on their willow shields and the day was lightening to cast long shadows across the frost. I had seen horsemen go east and knew they were looking for a way around my flank, but I could not worry about those men for I did have enough troops to counter them. I had to hold the Danes in front till Edward came to kill those behind.

Priests were walking down our line. Men knelt to them and the priests blessed them and put pinches of mud on their tongues. "This is Saint Lucy's Day," one priest called to the shield-warriors, "and she will blind the enemy! She will protect us! Blessed Saint Lucy! Pray to Saint Lucy!"

The rain had stopped, though much of the winter sky was still shrouded by cloud beneath which the enemy banners were bright. Sigurd's flying raven and Cnut's shattered cross, Æthelwold's stag and Beortsig's boar, Haesten's skull and Eohric's weird beast. There were lesser jarls among the enemy ranks and they had their own symbols; wolves and axes and bulls and hawks. Their men shouted insults and beat their weapons on their shields, and slowly they came forward, a few steps at a time. The Saxons and East Anglians of the enemy army were being encouraged by their priests, while the Danes were calling on Thor or Odin. My men were mostly silent, though I suppose they made jokes to cover their fear. Hearts were beating faster, bladders emptying, muscles shaking. This was the shield wall.

"Remember!" the Centish priest shouted, "that Saint Lucy was so filled with the Holy Spirit that twenty men could not move her! They harnessed a team of oxen to her and still she could not be moved! That is how you must be when the pagans come! Immovable! Filled by the Spirit! Fight for Saint Lucy!"

The men who had gone eastward had vanished in a morning mist that seeped from the marshes. There were so many of the enemy, a horde, a killing horde, and they came closer still, a hundred paces, and horsemen galloped in front of their tight-knit shield wall and called encouragement. One of those horsemen slewed toward us. He wore bright mail, thick arm rings, and a glittering helmet, and his horse was a magnificent beast, newly groomed and oiled, its harness bright with silver. "You're going to die!" he shouted at us.

"If you want to fart," I shouted back, "go to your own side and stink them out."

"We'll rape your wives," the man called. He spoke in English. "We'll rape your daughters!"

I was happy enough that he should call such hopes, for they would only encourage my men to fight. "What was your mother?" a Centishman called back. "A sow?"

"If you lay your weapons down," the man shouted, "then we shall spare you!" He turned his horse and I recognized him. He was Oscytel, Eohric's commander, the brutal-looking warrior I had met on Lundene's wall.

"Oscytel!" I shouted.

"I hear a lamb bleating!" he called back.

"Get off your horse," I said, taking a step forward, "and fight me."

He rested his hands on his saddle's pommel and stared at me, then he glanced at the flooded ditch that had sheets of thin ice crusting its water. I knew that was why he had come, not just to insult, but to see what obstacle faced the Danish charge. He looked back to me and grinned. "I don't fight old men," he said.

That was strange. No one had ever called me old before. I remember laughing, but there was shock behind my laughter. Weeks before, talking with Æthelflaed, I had mocked her because she was staring at her face in a great silver platter. She was worried because she had lines about her eyes and she had responded to my mockery by thrusting the plate at me, and I had looked at my reflection and seen that my beard was gray. I remember staring at it as she laughed at me, and I did not feel old even though my wounded leg could be treacherously stiff. Was that how people saw me? As an old man? Yet I was forty-five years old that year, so yes, I was an old man. "This old man will slit you from the balls to the throat," I called to Oscytel.

"This day Uhtred dies!" he shouted at my men. "And you all die with him!" With that he circled his horse and spurred back towards the Danish shield wall. Those shields were eighty paces away now. Close enough to see men's faces, to see the snarls. I could see Jarl Sigurd, magnificent in mail and with a black bear's pelt humped from his shoulders. His helmet was crested with a raven's wing, black in the dawn's gray light. I could see Cnut, the man with the quick sword, his cloak white, his thin face pale, his banner the broken Christian cross. Sigebriht was beside Eohric, who in turn was flanked by Æthelwold, and with them were their fiercest, strongest warriors, the men who had to keep the kings and the jarls and lords alive. Warriors were touching crosses or hammers. They were shouting, but what they bellowed I could not tell because the world seemed silent in that moment. I was watching the enemy ahead, judging which one would come to kill me and how I would kill him first.

My banner was behind me and that banner would attract ambitious men. They wanted my skull as a drinking cup, my name as a trophy. They watched me as I watched them and they saw a man covered in mud, but a warlord with a wolf-crested helmet and arm rings of gold and with close-linked mail and a cloak of darkest blue hemmed with golden threads and a sword that was famous throughout Britain. Serpent-Breath was famous, but I sheathed her anyway, because a long blade is no help in the shield wall's embrace, and instead I drew Wasp-Sting, short and lethal. I kissed her blade then bellowed my challenge at the winter wind. "Come and kill me! Come and kill me!"

And they came.

The spears came first, launched by men in the third or fourth enemy ranks, and we took them on our shields, the blades thumping hard into the willow, and the Danes were screaming as they rushed us. They must have been warned about the ditch, but even so it trapped scores of men who tried to leap it and instead skidded on our bank, their feet flying out from under them as our long-hafted axes flashed down. When we practice the shield wall I put an axman next to a swordsman, and the axman's job is to hook his blade over the rim of the enemy's shield and haul it down so the sword can slide over the top and into the enemy's face, but now the axes crunched down through helmets and skulls and suddenly the world exploded in noise, in screams, in the butcher's sound of blades cleaving skulls, and the men behind the Danes' first rank were pushing through the ditch and their long spears were thumping into our shields. "Close up!" I bellowed. "Shields touching! Shields touching! Forward a pace!"

Our shields overlapped. We had spent hours practicing this. Our shields made a wall as we pushed forward to the ditch's edge where the steepness of the slick bank made the killing easy. A fallen man tried to stab his sword up under my shield, but I kicked him in the face and my iron-reinforced boot slammed into his nose and eyes and he slid back and I was thrusting Wasp-Sting forward, finding the gap between two enemy shields, ramming the stiff short blade through mail into flesh, shouting, always watching their eyes, seeing the ax come down and aware that Cerdic, behind me, caught it on his shield, though the force of the blow hammered his shield down onto my helmet and for a moment I was dazed and blinded, but still grinding Wasp-Sting forward. Rollo, beside me, had hooked a shield down and as my vision cleared I saw the gap and flicked Wasp-Sting into it, saw her tip take an eye, skewered it hard. A massive blow hit my shield, splintering a board.

Cnut was trying to reach me, bellowing at his men to make space, and that was foolish because it meant they lost their cohesion to let their lord come to the killing place. Cnut and his men were in a frenzy, desperate to break our wall, and their shields were not overlapping and the ditch trapped them and two of my men drove spears hard into the oncoming men. Cnut tripped on one and sprawled in the ditch and I saw Rypere's ax smash into his helmet, only a glancing blow, but hard enough to stun him because he did not get up. "They're dying!" I shouted. "Now kill all the bastards!"

Cnut was not dead, but his men were dragging him away and in his place came Sigurd Sigurdson, the puppy who had promised to kill me, and he screamed wild-eyed as he charged up the ditch, feet flailing for purchase, and I swung my damaged shield outward to give him a target, and like a fool he took it, lunging his sword Fire-Dragon hard at my belly, but the shield came back fast, deflecting Fire-Dragon between my body and Rollo, and I half turned as I drove Wasp-Sting up at his neck. He had forgotten his lessons, forgotten to protect himself with his shield, and the short blade went under his chin, up through his mouth, breaking teeth, piercing his tongue, shattering the small nasal bones and jarring into his skull so hard that I lifted him off the earth for a moment as his blood poured down my hand and inside my mail sleeve, and then I shook him off the blade and swept it backhanded at a Dane, who recoiled, fell, and I let another man kill him because Oscytel was coming, shouting that I was an old man, and the battle-joy was in me.

That joy. That madness. The gods must feel this way every moment of every day. It is as if the world slows. You see the attacker, you see him shouting, though you hear nothing, and you know what he will do, and all his movements are so slow and yours are so quick, and in that moment you can do no wrong and you will live forever and your name will be blazoned across the heavens in a glory of white fire because you are the god of battle.

And Oscytel came with his sword, and with him was a man who wanted to hook my shield down with an ax, but I tipped the top back toward me at the last moment and the ax skidded down the painted wood to strike the boss and Oscytel was slamming his sword two-handed at my throat, but the shield was still there and its iron rim caught his blade, trapping the tip, and I thrust the shield forward, unbalancing him, and drove Wasp-Sting under the lower edge, and all my old man's strength was in that wicked blow that comes from beneath the shield, and I felt the blade's tip scraping up a thighbone, ripping blood and flesh and muscle, and into his groin and I heard him then. I heard his scream filling the sky as I gouged his groin and spilled his blood into the ice-shattered ditch.

Eohric saw his champion fall and the sight stopped him at the ditch's far side. His men stopped with him. "Shields!" I shouted, and my men lined their shields. "You're a coward, Eohric," I called, "a fat coward, a pig spawned in shit, runt of a sow's litter, a weakling! Come and die, you fat bastard!"

He did not want to, but the Danes were winning. Not, perhaps, in the center of the line, where my banner flew, but off to our left the Danes had crossed the ditch and made a shield wall on our side of the obstacle and there they were thrusting Wulferth's men back. I had left Finan and thirty men as our reserve and they had gone to bolster that flank, but they were hard pressed, hugely outnumbered, and once the Danes came between that flank and the western marsh then they would curl my line in on itself and we would die. The Danes knew it and took confidence from it, and still more men came to kill me because my name was the name that the poets would give to their glory, and Eohric was thrust across the ditch with the rest of the men and they tripped on the dead, slipped in the mud, climbed over their own dead, and we screamed our war song as the axes fell and the spears stabbed and the swords cut. My shield was in scraps, hacked by blades. My head was bruised, I could feel blood on my left ear, but still we were fighting and killing, and Eohric was gritting his teeth and flailing with a huge sword at Cerdic, who had replaced the man on my left. "Hook him," I snarled at Cerdic, and he brought his ax up from beneath and the beard of the blade snagged in Eohric's mail and Cerdic hauled him forward and I hacked Wasp-Sting down on the back of his fat neck and he was screaming as he fell at our feet. His men tried to rescue him, and I saw him stare up at me in despair, and he clenched his teeth so hard that they shattered and we killed King Eohric of East Anglia in a ditch that stank of blood and shit. We stabbed him and slashed him, cut him and trampled him. We screamed like demons. Men were calling on Jesus, calling for their mothers, shrieking in pain, and a king died with a mouth full of broken teeth in a ditch turned red. East Anglians tried to haul Eohric away, but Cerdic kept hold of him and I hacked at his neck, and then I shouted to the East Anglians that their king was dead, that their king was killed, that we were winning.

Only we were not winning. We were indeed fighting like demons, we were giving the poets a tale to tell in the years to come, but the song would end with our deaths because our left flank gave way. They still fought, but they bent back, and the Danes streamed into the gap. The men who had ridden to take us in the rear had no need to come now, because we had been turned, and now we would form a shield wall that faced in every direction and that wall would shrink and shrink and we would go to our graves one by one.

I saw Æthelwold. He was on horseback now, riding behind some Danes, shouting them onward and with him was a standard-bearer who flew the dragon flag of Wessex. He knew he would become king if they won this battle and he had abandoned his white stag banner to adopt Alfred's flag instead. He had still not crossed the ditch and he was taking care not to be in the fighting, but instead exhorted the Danes forward to kill us.

Then I forgot Æthelwold because our left flank was pushed hard back and we had become a band of Saxons trapped by a horde of Danes. We made a rough circle, surrounded by shields and by the men we had killed. By our own dead too. And the Danes paused to make a new shield wall, to rescue their wounded, and to contemplate their victory.

"I killed that bastard Beortsig," Finan said as he joined me.

"Good, I hope it hurt."

"It sounded that way," he said. His sword was bloody, his grinning face smirched with blood. "It's not very healthy, is it?"

"Not really," I said. It had begun to rain again, just a small spitting rain. Our defensive circle was close to the eastern marsh. "What we could do," I said, "is tell the men to run into the marsh and go south. Some will get away."

"Not many," Finan said. We could see the Danes collecting the Centish horses. They were stripping our dead of their mail, their weapons, and whatever else they could find. A priest was in the center of our men, on his knees, praying. "They'll hunt us down like rats in the marsh," Finan said.

"So we'll fight them here," I said, and there was little other choice.

We had hurt them. Eohric was dead, Oscytel was slaughtered, Beortsig was a corpse, and Cnut was wounded, yet Æthelwold lived and Sigurd lived and Haesten lived. I could see them on horseback, pushing men into line, readying their troops to slaughter us.

"Sigurd!" I bellowed, and he turned to look for me. "I killed your runt of a son!"

"You'll die slowly," he shouted back.

I wanted to goad him into a wild attack and kill him in front of his men. "He squealed like a child when he died!" I shouted. "He squealed like a little coward! Like a puppy!"

Sigurd, his great plaits twisted about his neck, spat toward me. He hated me, he would kill me, but in his own time and in his own way.

"Keep your shields tight!" I shouted at my men. "Keep them tight and they can't break us! Show the bastards how Saxons fight!"

Of course they could break us, but you do not tell men about to die that they are about to die. They knew it. Some were shaking in fear, yet they stayed in line. "Fight beside me," I told Finan.

"We'll go together, lord."

"Swords in hand."

Rypere was dead. I had not seen him die, but I saw a Dane hauling the mail from his skinny body. "He was a good man," I said.

Osferth found us. He was usually so neat, so immaculately dressed, but his mail was torn and his cloak was shredded, and his eyes wild. His helmet had a great dent in its crown, yet he seemed unhurt. "Let me fight along with you, lord," he said.

"Forever," I told him. Osferth's cross was still aloft at the center of our circle, and a priest was calling that God and Saint Lucy would work a miracle, that we would win, that we would live, and I let him preach on because he was saying what men needed to hear.

Jarl Sigurd pushed into the Danish shield wall opposite me. He carried a massive war ax, wide-bladed, and on either side of him were spearmen. Their job was to hold me still while he hacked me to death. I had a new shield, one that showed the crossed swords of Ealdorman Sigelf. "Has anyone seen Sigebriht?" I asked.

"He's dead," Osferth said.

"You're sure?"

"I killed him, lord."

I laughed. We had killed so many of the enemy's leaders, though Sigurd and Æthelwold lived, and they had power enough to crush us and then defeat Edward's army and so put Æthelwold on Alfred's throne. "Do you remember what Beornnoth said?" I asked Finan.

"Should I, lord?"

"He wanted to know how the story ended," I said. "I'd like to know that too."

"Ours ends here," Finan said, and made the sign of the cross with the hilt of his sword.

And the Danes came again.

They came slowly. Men do not want to die at the moment of victory. They want to enjoy the triumph, to share the wealth that winning brings, and so they came steadily, keeping their shields tight-locked.

Someone in our ranks began to sing. It was a Christian song, perhaps a psalm, and most of the men took up the tune, which made me think of my eldest son, and what a bad father I had been, and I wondered if he would be proud of my death. The Danes were beating blades and spear-hafts against their shields. Most of those shields were broken, ax-split, splintered. Men were bloodied, blood of the foemen. Battle in the morning. I was tired and, looking up at the rain clouds, thought this was a bad place to die. But we do not choose our deaths. The Norns do that at the foot of Yggdrasil and I imagined one of those three Fates holding the shears above my thread. She was ready to cut, and all that mattered now was to keep tight hold of my sword so that the winged women would take me to Valhalla's feasting-hall.

I watched the Danes shouting at us. I did not hear them, not because I was out of earshot, but because the world seemed strangely silent again. A heron came out of the mist and flew overhead and I distinctly heard the heavy beat of its wings, but I did not hear the insults of my enemies. Plant your feet square, overlap the shield, watch the enemy's blade, be ready to counterstrike. There was pain on my right hip, which I only just noticed. Had I been wounded? I dared not look because the Danes were close and I was watching the two spear tips, knowing they would strike the right-hand side of my shield to force it back and let Sigurd come from my left. I met Sigurd's eyes and we stared at each other and then the spears came.

They hurled dozens of spears from their rear ranks, heavy spears arcing over their front ranks to crash hard into our shields. At that moment a man in the front rank must crouch to let the shield protect him, and the Danes charged as they saw us go down. "Up!" I shouted, my shield heavy with two spears. My men were screaming in rage, and the Danes beat into us, shrieking their war cries, hacking with axes, and we pushed back, the two lines locked, heaving. It was a pushing match, but we were only three ranks and the Danes were at least six, and they were driving us back. I tried to skewer Wasp-Sting forward, and her blade struck a shield. Sigurd was trying to reach me, screaming and shouting, but the flow of men forced him away from me. A Dane, openmouthed and with a beard riddled with blood, hacked an ax at Finan's shield and I tried to slide Wasp-Sting over my own shield into his face, but another blade deflected mine. We were being forced back, the enemy so close we could smell the ale on their breath. And then the next charge came.

It came from our left, from the south, horsemen crashing up the Roman road with spears leveled and a dragon banner flying. Horsemen from the small mist, horsemen who screamed their challenge as they spurred into the rearward ranks of the enemy. "Wessex!" they shouted, "Edward and Wessex!" I saw the close-packed Danish ranks judder and shift under the impact, and the second rank of the oncoming horsemen had swords that they hacked down at the enemy, and that enemy saw yet more horsemen coming, bright-mailed horsemen in the dawn, and the new flags showed crosses and saints and dragons and the Danes were breaking, running back to the protection of the ditch.

"Forward!" I shouted, and I felt the pressure of the Danish attack ease and I bellowed at my men to thrust into them, to kill the bastards, and we screamed like men released from death's valley as we charged them. Sigurd vanished, protected by his men. I hacked at the bloody-bearded Dane with Wasp-Sting, but the pressure of men swept him off to my right and the Danes ahead were breaking, horsemen among them, swords falling, spears striking, and Steapa was there, huge and angry, snarling at his enemy, using his sword like a butcher's cleaver, his stallion biting and kicking, wheeling and trampling. I guessed Steapa's force was small, maybe no more than four or five hundred men, but it had panicked the Danes by attacking their rear ranks, yet it would not be long before they recovered and came back to the assault.

"Get back!" Steapa roared at me, pointing his red sword south. "Go back now!"

"Fetch the wounded!" I shouted at my men. More horsemen came, helmets bright in the gray daylight, spear-blades like silver death, swords striking down at running Danes. Our men were carrying the wounded south, away from the enemy, and in front of us were the bodies of the dead and dying, and Steapa's horsemen were re-forming their ranks, all but one, who put spurs to his stallion and galloped across our front, and I saw him crouching low over the beast's black mane, and I recognized him and dropped Wasp-Sting to pick up a fallen spear. It was heavy, but I launched it hard, and it flew between the horse's legs and brought it down. I heard the man scream in fright as he thumped onto the wet grass and the horse was thrashing its legs as it tried to stand, and the rider's foot was caught in the stirrup. I drew Serpent-Breath, ran to him, and kicked the stirrup free. "Edward is king," I said to the man.

"Help me!" His horse was in the grasp of one of my men, and now he tried to stand, but I kicked him down. "Help me, Uhtred," he said.

"I have helped you all your life," I said, "all your miserable life, and now Edward is king."

"No," he said, "no!"

He was not denying his cousin's kingship, but the threat of my sword. I shuddered with anger as I drove Serpent-Breath down. I drove it at his breast and that great blade tore through his mail, forcing the shattered links down through his breastbone and ribs and right into his rotten heart, which exploded under the steel's thrust. He screamed still, and still I plunged that blade down, and the scream dribbled away to a gasp and I held Serpent-Breath there, watching his life leak away into the East Anglian soil.

So Æthelwold was dead, and Finan, who had rescued Wasp-Sting, plucked my arm. "Come, lord, come!" he said. The Danes were shouting again, and we ran, protected by the horsemen, and soon there were more horsemen in the mist and I knew Edward's army had come, but neither he nor the leaderless Danes wanted a fight. The Danes had the protection of the ditch now, they were in their shield wall, but they were not marching on Lundene.

So we marched there instead.

Edward wore his father's crown at the Christmas feast. The emeralds glinted in the firelight of the great Roman hall at the top of Lundene's hill. Lundene was safe.

A sword or ax had cut into my hip, though I had not realized it at the time. My mail coat was being mended by a smith, and the wound itself was healing. I remembered the fear, the blood, the screams.

"I was wrong," Edward told me.

"True, lord King," I said.

"We should have attacked them at Cracgelad," he said, then stared down the hall where his lords and thegns were dining. He looked like his father at that moment, though his face was stronger. "The priests said you couldn't be trusted."

"Maybe I can't," I said.

He smiled at that. "But the priests say that God's providence dictated the war. By waiting, they say, we killed all our enemies."

"Almost all our enemies," I corrected him, "and a king cannot wait on God's providence. A king must make decisions."

He took the reproof well. "*Mea culpa,*" he said quietly, then, "yet God was on our side."

"The ditch was on our side," I said, "and your sister won that war."

It had been Æthelflaed who delayed the Danes. If they had crossed the river during the night they would have been ready to attack earlier and they would surely have overwhelmed us long before Steapa's horsemen came to the rescue. Yet most of the Danes had stayed in Huntandon, held there by the threat to their rear. That threat had been the burning halls. Æthelflaed, ordered by her brother to ride to safety, had instead taken her Mercian troops north and set the fires that had frightened the Danes into thinking another army was behind them.

"I burned two halls," she said, "and one church."

She sat on my left, Edward on my right, while Father Coenwulf and the bishops had been pushed to the ends of the high table. "You burned a church?" Edward asked, shocked.

"It was an ugly church," she said, "but big, and it burned bright."

Burned bright. I touched her hand, which rested on the table. Almost all our enemies were dead, only Haesten, Cnut, and Sigurd remained alive, yet to kill one Dane is to resurrect a dozen. Their ships would keep coming across the sea, because the Danes would never rest until the emerald crown was theirs, or until we had crushed them utterly.

Yet for the moment we were safe. Edward was king, Lundene was ours, Wessex had survived, and the Danes were beaten.

Wyrd bið ful ārǣd.

Historical Note

The Anglo-Saxon Chronicles are our best source for the events of the period during which the Angles and Saxons dominated Britain, but there is no single chronicle. It seems probable that Alfred himself encouraged the creation of the original text, which offered a year-by-year summary of events beginning with Christ's birth, and that first manuscript was copied and distributed to monasteries that, in turn, kept updating their copies so that no two versions are alike. The entries can be maddeningly obscure and are not always reliable. Thus, for the year AD 793, the Chronicles record fiery dragons in the skies above Northumbria. In 902, the Chronicles record a battle at "the Holme," a place that has never been identified, though we know it was somewhere in East Anglia. A Danish army led by King Eohric and by the claimant to the throne of Wessex, Æthelwold, invaded Mercia, crossed the Thames at Cracgelad (Cricklade), harried Wessex, and then retreated. King Edward followed them into East Anglia and took his revenge by ravaging Eohric's land. Then comes the Chronicles' tantalizing account of the battle: "When he (Edward) meant to leave there, he had it announced to the army that they would all leave together. The Kentish stayed on there against his command and seven messages he had sent to them. The force came upon them there, and they fought." The entry then gives a list of the most notable casualties, among them Æthelwold, King Eohric, Ealdorman Sigelf, his son Sigebriht, and Beortsig. "On either hand," the Chronicles tell us, "much slaughter was made, and of the Danes there were more killed, though they had the battlefield." That suggests the Danes won the battle, but in winning, lost most of their leaders. (I am using a translation of the Chronicles by Anne Savage, published by Heinemann, London, 1983.)

What is most tantalizing in that brief account is the puzzling refusal of the Kentish forces to withdraw, and my solution, that Ealdorman Sigelf was trying to betray the West Saxon army, is pure invention. We neither know where the battle was fought, nor what really happened there, only that there was a battle and that Æthelwold, Edward's rival for the throne of Wessex, was killed. The Chronicles tell us about Æthelwold's rebellion in a long entry for the year 900 (though Alfred's death was in 899). "Alfred, son of Æthelwulf, passed away, six nights before All Saints Day. He was king over all the English, except for that part which was under Danish rule; and he held that kingdom for one and a half years less than thirty. Then his son Edward received the kingdom. Æthelwold, his father's brother's son, took over the manors at Wimbourne and at Christchurch, without the leave of the king and his counselors. Then the king rode with the army until he camped at Badbury Rings near Wimbourne, and Æthelwold occupied the manor with those men who were loyal to him, and had barricaded all the gates against them; he said that he would stay there, alive or dead. Then he stole away under the cover of night, and sought the force in Northumbria. The king commanded them to ride after, but he could not be overtaken. They captured the woman he had seized without the king's leave and against the bishop's command, because she was hallowed as a nun." But we are not told who the woman was, or why Æthelwold kidnapped her, or what became of her. Again my solution, that it was Æthelwold's cousin, Æthelflaed, is pure invention.

The Chronicles give us the bare bones of history, but without much detail or even explanations for what happened. Another mystery is the fate of the woman Edward might, or might not, have married; Ecgwynn. We know she gave him two children and that one of them, Æthelstan, would become immensely important to the creation of England, yet she vanishes from the record entirely and is replaced by Ealdorman Æthelhelm's daughter, Ælflæd. A much later account suggests that Edward and Ecgwynn's marriage was not considered valid, yet in truth we know very little of that tale, only that the motherless Æthelstan will, in time, become the first king of all England.

The Chronicles note that Alfred was "king over all the English," but then add the cautious and crucial caveat, "except for that part which was under Danish rule." In truth most of what would become England was under Danish rule; all of Northumbria, all East Anglia, and the northernmost counties of Mercia. Alfred undoubtedly wanted to be king of all the English, and by the time of his death he was by far the most notable and powerful leader among the Saxons, but his dream of uniting all the lands where English was spoken had not been realized, yet he was fortunate in having a son, a daughter, and a grandchild who were as committed to that dream as he was himself, and in time they would make it happen. That story is the story behind these tales of Uhtred; the story of England's creation. It has always puzzled me that we English are so incurious about our nation's genesis. In school it sometimes seems as if Britain's history begins in AD 1066, and all that went before is irrelevant, but the story of how England came to exist is a massive, exciting, and noble tale.

The father of England is Alfred. He might not have lived to see the land of the Angelcynn united, but he made that unification possible by preserving both the Saxon culture and the English language. He made Wessex into a stronghold that withstood assault after assault from the Danes, and which was strong enough, after his death, to spread northward until the Danish overlords were overcome and assimilated. There was an Uhtred involved in those years, and he is my direct ancestor, but the tales I tell of him are pure invention. The family held Bebbanburg (now Bamburgh Castle in Northumberland) from the earliest years of the Anglo-Saxon invasion of Britain almost until the Norman Conquest. When the rest of the north fell to Danish rule, Bebbanburg held out, an enclave of Angelcynn among the Vikings. Almost certainly that survival was due as much to collaboration with the Danes as to the immense natural strength of the family's fortress. I separated the Uhtred of this tale from Bebbanburg so he can be closer to the events that will create England, events that begin in the Saxon south and slowly move to the Angle north. I wanted him close to Alfred, a man he dislikes almost as much as he admires.

Alfred is, of course, the only British monarch to be called "the Great." There is no Nobel-like committee to award that honorific, which seems to spring out of history by consent of the historians, yet few people would argue with Alfred's right to the title. He was, by any measure, a most intelligent man, and he was also a good man. Uhtred might be inimical to a Christian society ruled by law, but the alternative was Danish rule and continuing chaos. Alfred imposed law, education, and religion on his people, and he also protected them from fearsome enemies. He made a viable state, no small achievement. Justin Pollard, in his wonderful biography *Alfred the Great* (John Murray, London, 2005), sums up Alfred's achievements thus: "Alfred wanted a kingdom where the people of each market town would want to defend their property and their king because their prosperity *was* the state's prosperity." He made a nation to which people felt they belonged because the law was fair, because aspiration was rewarded, and because government was not tyrannical. It is not a bad prescription.

He was buried in Winchester's Old Minster, but the body was later moved to the New Minster, where the tomb was sheathed in lead. William the Conqueror, wanting to dissuade his new English subjects from venerating their past, had the lead-encased coffin moved to Hyde Abbey just outside Winchester. That abbey, like all the other religious houses, was dissolved under Henry VIII, and became a private home and, later, a prison. In the late eighteenth century Alfred's tomb was discovered by the prisoners, who stripped it of lead and then threw away the bones. Justin Pollard surmises that the remains of the greatest Anglo-Saxon king are probably still in Winchester, scattered in the topsoil somewhere between a car park and a row of Victorian houses. His emerald-studded crown fared no better. It survived until the seventeenth century, when, so it is said, the wretched Puritans who ruled England after the Civil War prised out the stones and melted down the gold.

Winchester is still Alfred's town. Many of the property lines in the old city's heart are those laid out by his surveyors. The bones of many of his family lie in stone boxes in the cathedral that replaced his minster, and his statue stands in the town center, burly and warlike, though in truth he was sick all his life, and his first love was not martial glory, but religion, learning, and the law. He was indeed Alfred the Great, but in this tale of England's making his dream has not yet come true, so Uhtred must fight again.

About the Author

Bernard Cornwell is the author of the acclaimed *New York Times* bestsellers *Agincourt* and *The Fort*; the bestselling Saxon Tales, which include *The Last Kingdom, The Pale Horseman, Lords of the North, Sword Song, The Burning Land* and, most recently, *Death of Kings*; and the Richard Sharpe novels, among many others. He lives with his wife on Cape Cod.